ONCE UPON a Devastatingly Sweet KISS

#4 The Whickertons in Love

BY BREE WOLF

WOLF PUBLISHING

Once Upon a Devastatingly Sweet Kiss by Bree Wolf

Published by WOLF Publishing UG

Text by Bree Wolf
Cover Art by Victoria Cooper
Paperback ISBN: 978-3-98536-021-5
Hard Cover ISBN: 978-3-98536-022-2
Ebook ISBN: 978-3-98536-020-8

WOLF Publishing - This is us:

Two sisters, two personalities.. But only one big love!

Diving into a world of dreams..

...Romance, heartfelt emotions, lovable and witty characters, some humor, and some mystery! Because we want it all! Historical Romance at its best!

Visit our website to learn all about us, our authors and books!

Sign up to our mailing list to receive first hand information on new releases, freebies and promotions as well as exclusive giveaways and sneak-peeks!

WWW.WOLF-PUBLISHING.COM

ALSO BY BREE WOLF

The Whickertons in Love

The WHICKERTONS IN LOVE is a new series by USA Today bestselling author BREE WOLF set in Regency era England, portraying the at times turbulent ways the six Whickerton siblings search for love. If you enjoy wicked viscounts, brooding lords as well as head-strong ladies, fierce in their affections and daring in their search for their perfect match, then this new series is perfect for you!

#1 Once Upon a Devilishly Enchanting Kiss

#2 Once Upon a Temptingly Ruinous Kiss

#3 Once Upon an Irritatingly Magical Kiss

#4 Once Upon a Devastatingly Sweet Kiss

#5 Once Upon an Achingly Beautiful Kiss

More to follow!

Prequel to the series: Once Upon A Kiss Gone Horribly Wrong

ONCE UPON a *Devastatingly Sweet* KISS

PROLOGUE

London, Spring 1803 (or a variation thereof)

Bradley Jackson, Duke of Clements, glared across his late father's heavy mahogany desk, his dark gaze fixed upon Mr. Martin, his solicitor, as though the elderly, gray-haired man was more than a mere messenger. "And you are certain of this?" he growled, breathing in to calm the thundering pulse in his neck.

The frail-looking man seated across from him gave a quick nod. "I'm afraid so, your grace. Your mother's will is very specific."

Bradley breathed in again, silently counted to five, and then exhaled. "Why am I only informed of this now?"

An irritatingly indulgent look came to Mr. Martin's face. "I'm afraid your late mother wanted it like this. She made it quite clear that you were only to be informed of the stipulation a year before your thirtieth birthday."

Leaning his elbows onto the smooth wooden surface of his father's desk, Bradley steepled his fingers, still glaring at his solicitor. It was irrational; after all, the man had merely followed orders. It had not been his doing; and yet, he was the only one left to provide answers, the only one at whom Bradley could direct his anger.

The moment the thought crossed Bradley's mind, he felt something inside him roar with disapproval. No, he would not be angry. Anger would not serve him. Anger had never served anyone. It was a useless emotion, much like all the others; he would do well to keep a clear head and focus on the facts. "To be clear, Mr. Martin," Bradley willed himself to say in an even and collected voice, "my mother's will states that if I do not marry before my thirtieth birthday, I will lose Laurelwood Manor. Is that correct?"

Mr. Martin gave a quick nod. "Yes, precisely, your grace."

Bradley paused for a moment, trying to reach back in his mind and remember the woman who had been his mother. He only recalled bits and pieces, nothing that would explain why she had seen fit to add this stipulation to her will. "Is there anything else I ought to be aware of?"

"No, your grace," Mr. Martin replied, his eyes sweeping over the document in his hands. "That is the full extent of it." He looked up. "Would you like to see for yourself?"

Bradley shook his head. "That will not be necessary, Mr. Martin." Although somewhat hesitantly, his breath evened, and Bradley felt his mind think more clearly. "Are you aware of why my mother felt the need to include this stipulation?"

A warm smile came to the old man's face. "I'm afraid I am not, your grace. Your mother made this change to her will shortly before she passed. She was quite insistent upon this; however, she never explained her motivation...and I did not think it appropriate to ask."

Bradley nodded. He could understand the wisdom of keeping one's nose out of other people's affairs, even as their solicitor. "Very well then. I thank you for your counsel, Mr. Martin."

The frail old man gave a quick nod, then rose to his feet and took his leave. The moment the door closed behind him, Bradley sat back in his chair, willing his breath in and out at even intervals. He could feel the pulse in his neck still beat faster than he would have liked, betraying his emotional entanglement with this issue.

Laurelwood Manor.

The name conjured distant memories of a small manor house built with cobbled stones and overgrown with ivy. He remembered the smell of lilacs and roses, as well as the fresh scent of apples from the orchard nearby. Something tightened in his chest as the echo of a soft voice danced through his head, whispering in his ear in a way that sent a sudden ache through his body.

Bradley closed his eyes. It had been a long time since he had dared remember his mother. He had not allowed his thoughts to venture back to Laurelwood Manor in a long time. "Why?" he whispered, his quiet voice echoing through the stillness of the study.

Sighing, Bradley shook his head, knowing that he would never receive an answer. Why his mother had seen fit to include the stipulation of marriage in her will, in order for him to maintain ownership of Laurelwood Manor, was beyond him. Of course, he would marry one day. He was a duke, and it was a duke's duty to marry and continue his line. Why then had his mother done this?

One day.

Indeed, it could no longer be *one day*. Now, it had to be soon. Within the year...

...or he would lose Laurelwood Manor.

In truth, the small estate was an insignificant part of his vast holdings. It contributed very little, and he had not visited it in many, many years. Why then did the thought of losing it bother him? After all, it served no purpose.

Pushing to his feet, Bradley strode over to the window, hands linking behind his back as he looked out at the vast gardens of Clements Park, his ancestral home. Everything was immaculate, the lawns neatly trimmed and the hedges growing straight like walls without a single branch out of place. Flowers bloomed in specific, designated areas, their colors complementing the light stone façade of the house. Everything was in its place, carefully planned and maintained.

Everything was as Bradley wanted it.

Clements Park was different in every way from Laurelwood Manor. Indeed, it appeared the two estates belonged to different worlds. Why then did the thought of losing Laurelwood Manor bother Bradley? Yes, it felt like a heavy weight in his chest, and no matter how often he inhaled a deep, slow breath or straightened his shoulders and lifted his chin, it could not be dislodged.

"Marriage is inevitable," Bradley mumbled to himself as his gaze swept over Clements Park. Still, his eyes did not see its neatly trimmed rosebushes, but the wild ones of Laurelwood Manor growing in great abundance wherever they pleased. "Yes, this is nothing more than a simple reminder of my duty to the dukedom, to my family." He straightened his shoulders. "I am almost thirty years of age, and it is about time I choose a wife."

Inhaling a deep breath, Bradley returned to his desk and seated himself, reaching for a sheet of parchment. "Better make a list," he said to himself, thinking about what qualities his future duchess ought to possess. "Lady Easton will no doubt be of assistance." A widow now, Bradley's aunt, his late father's eldest sister, had successfully married off her five children, procuring them suitable and most advantageous matches. Yes, she would be the right one to turn to in this matter.

His quill almost flew over the parchment as Bradley wrote down how he imagined his future wife. Yes, they ought to share the same values, uphold family tradition and reputation at all cost. She ought to be aware of the dignity of her new position in society and conduct herself with the greatest elegance and grace at all times, her manners impeccable and her demeanor almost regal. He imagined a wife with a quiet disposition would suit him best. His aunt could make the necessary introductions.

A small smile came to Bradley's face as he looked down at his list. Indeed, he could not recall why he had been so...disconcerted. After all, marriage was a simple matter, was it not? It was like everything else in life, just another step upon the path he had been set upon since birth. One more task to accomplish, nothing more.

Indeed, he ought to have it taken care of by the end of the year. It was his duty to the dukedom, and it would secure Laurelwood Manor. Still, Bradley made it quite clear to himself that maintaining ownership of his mother's estate was not the reason he was doing this. No, it was simply a byproduct.

A bonus.

Utterly inconsequential.

Yes, indeed.

CHAPTER ONE
FREE TO CHOOSE

Pinewood Manor, Summer 1803
A few months later

Lifting her skirts a good bit above her ankles, Lady Harriet Beaumont, youngest daughter to the Earl of Whickerton, stood with her feet set apart upon the lawn, her gaze fixed on her little niece, her eyes slightly narrowed and watchful. "Do you truly think you can best me, Sam?" A challenging tone swung in her voice.

For someone who had only reached her fifth year, Samantha possessed a calm that surprised Harriet. Her sharp green eyes were fixed upon Harriet's face, and the moment Harriet moved, the little girl charged forward.

Only a few paces separated them, and before Harriet knew what was happening, they collided. Harriet's arms came around Sam, ensuring that the girl would not be harmed as they tumbled down into the grass, their skirts tangled around their legs.

Laughter flew from both their mouths, and Harriet was certain she heard other voices joining in from up on the terrace. "Do you yield?" she demanded, tickling Samantha.

The girl shrieked with joy, rolling sideways, and out of reach before she jumped to her feet. A wide grin came to her face, one full of triumph and daring. "You will not catch me again, Auntie Harry!" Then she dashed toward the small table Harriet had done her best to defend and snatched up the lemon tart with a bellow of victory.

Scrambling to her feet, Harriet feigned a look of defeat, waving an angry fist against the sky and cursing the gods. "I humbly admit that your skill far surpasses my own." She bowed low to her little niece, her gaze sweeping over her grass-stained skirts.

Applause erupted from the terrace, and Harriet and Samantha looked up at smiling faces. Harriet's sister Christina as well as her husband Thorne, Samantha's adoptive parents, stood waving, their eyes aglow as they beheld their child. Thorne then caught his little daughter as she came charging toward him. "Did you see that, Father? Did you? I won! I won the tart!"

He laughed, twirling her in a circle. "You certainly did." He grinned at his wife, Christina, and then at Harriet as she stepped onto the terrace, a bit out of breath. "Then enjoy your spoils of war."

"Are you not a bit old," Harriet's eldest sister Juliet remarked with a bit of a hesitant look upon her face, "for...these games?" A sweeping movement of her arm seemed to encompass not only today's tournament, but all those that had come before, as well as all those that would surely follow.

Harriet laughed, fighting to draw air down into her lungs. "One is never too old for fun," she told Juliet, knowing her eldest sister never once dared set even one toe out of line. "Wouldn't life be utterly dreadful without fun?" She lifted her brows challengingly.

Juliet swallowed, a knowing look coming to her face. "I have fun," she insisted; her voice, however, wavered as though she was uncertain whether she spoke the truth.

Indeed, the oldest and youngest Whickerton sisters were complete opposites. With her soft brown hair and gentle eyes, Juliet possessed not only the means, but it seemed also the determination to blend into the background, to be forever overlooked and hardly ever noticed. Harriet's fiery red curls stood in stark contrast, her need for adventure always daring her to cross that invisible line, not merely by a step, but by leaps and bounds.

"I do not doubt you," Harriet told her sister with a smile. "I acknowledge that not everyone has fun the same way." Her gaze swept over the extensive gardens of Pinewood Manor, her sister's and brother-in-law's home, little Samantha's home, and she sighed. "But I need...this." Her gaze met her sister's. "I need to feel my heart beat in my chest with such force that I fear it might split my ribcage in two. I need to feel the wind in my face, tugging upon my hair and my skirts. I need to run until my legs feel as though they are ready to fall off." She shrugged, heaving a deep breath. "It makes me feel alive." She took a step closer, her own dark green eyes seeking Juliet's pale ones. "Do you ever feel like that?"

A flicker of regret came to her sister's eyes, and yet she straightened, lifted her chin and smiled at Harriet. "I feel life in other ways," she whispered, her eyes darting past Harriet's shoulder to their sister's little family. "I enjoy taking care of others, to see them happy and at peace." Again, her eyes moved; this time to settle upon their sleeping grandmother, seated in a chair by the terrace doors.

Harriet watched her eldest sister carefully. "Do you? Truly?" For a long time now, Harriet had found herself wondering whether Juliet's diligent way of tending to her family was truly her heart's desire or simply something she considered her duty.

Juliet's eyes widened. "I love grandmother," she exclaimed as though Harriet truly doubted that. "I truly enjoy being her companion."

Harriet grasped her sister's hands. "I love her as well," she assured her in hushed tones, well aware that their grandmother had a tendency to fake sleep in order to overhear others' conversations. "Still, there are other things I want than to merely keep her company. You are allowed to want other things as well; you know that, don't you?"

"Of course, I do," Juliet assured her a bit too quickly; it made Harriet wonder if her sister ever truly dared to dream.

"Auntie Harriet! Auntie Harriet!" came Samantha's little voice a moment before the little girl came darting across the terrace. "Will you chase me again?"

Harriet laughed. "Of course, I will. As soon as we procure a new prize."

Laughing, Christina and Thorne came walking over. "I've never seen her like this," Harriet's new brother-in-law remarked as his daughter dashed away, no doubt rushing toward the kitchen in order to ask cook for another lemon tart.

Harriet shrugged, unable to keep the corners of her mouth from drawing upward into a wide smile. "What can I say? I bring out the best in people."

Christina rolled her eyes. "You do what you want. You've always done what you wanted."

Harriet met her sister's gaze. "Do you disapprove?"

Christina heaved a deep sigh. "I never have, not truly." A contemplative looking came to her face. "However, now that I am a mother, I cannot help but wonder what would be best for my child."

Juliet frowned, and before Harriet could say anything, she asked, "Are you saying you do not want her to choose freely? As Mother and Father have always allowed us to do? As they still do?"

Exchanging a look with her husband, Christina shook her head. "I am saying nothing of the kind. I simply cannot help but wonder how these choices will affect her life."

Harriet laughed. "Although I am not a mother, I suppose that is absolutely normal. Believe me, I cannot count the times I've seen a look of concern upon Mother's or Father's face when they learned of my newest...idea." She grinned. "Yet they never interfered. They asked and counseled, but they allowed me to make my own choices, my own mistakes." A deep sigh left her lips. "Honestly, some of the greatest times of my life have been the most horrible mistakes I've ever made."

Thorne chuckled. "Truly?"

Harriet nodded, exchanging knowing glances with her two sisters. "Do you remember that summer years ago when I climbed the tall oak tree on the southern edge of Whickerton Grove?" She looked from Juliet to Christina, seeing awareness come to their eyes. Then she turned back to her new brother-in-law. "On one of the tallest branches, there had been a bird's nest. One egg had fallen out, but as Fate would have it, it remained intact. It was like a miracle in itself."

"And so you got it into your head to return the egg to its nest?" Thorne asked, exchanging a look with his wife.

Harriet nodded. "Yes, and I did. I returned the egg to its nest, safe and sound."

Christina snorted. "Don't forget to mention the part where you fell from the tree and broke your arm."

Thorne's mouth dropped open. "You broke your arm and that is still a fond memory for you?"

"Well, without breaking my arm, it wouldn't have been one of my greatest mistakes, now would it?" Harriet demanded, before her thoughts once more drifted back to the days that followed the accident. "Still, the egg made it back home, and eventually, a baby bird hatched. I watched it grow and mature and eventually fly off." A deep sigh left her lips. "I cannot even describe how that made me feel. It was a wonderful, precious moment, and I don't regret it. Not for one second."

Indeed, life was not rational. It was not a straight path with specific steps one could count off on one hand. It turned and twisted, its path always obscured. Life meant mistakes. It meant trial and error. But it was only through these mistakes that one could truly grow.

Harriet did not mind mistakes. She did not fear making a fool of herself. She never worried about what others might think.

What she feared were regrets.

And so, Harriet spent her days giving in to her heart's desires. If she wanted to dance in the rain or slide down the banister in the great hall, nothing could stop her. And if she wanted to chase her niece through the gardens, she would.

"Auntie Harriet! Auntie Harriet!" With a new lemon tart in her hands, Sam jumped over the threshold of the terrace doors. "Let's go again!"

Harriet nodded, then offered her sisters and brother-in-law a polite smile and said, "Pardon me, but I must ready myself for battle."

Life was good, and it would always be good as long as Harriet remained true to herself. It was what she believed with every fiber of her being.

CHAPTER TWO

ORDER & CHAOS

After mounting his horse, Bradley directed the chestnut mare down the long, straight drive that led up to Clements Park. It lay flanked by tall trees on either side, the interval between them precise and to the point. A mild breeze stirred the leaves overhead, and Bradley frowned as it carried specks of bark and pollen through the air to land upon his immaculate jacket. Lifting a hand, he brushed the offending specks away, then turned his mount eastward.

The air was fresh, but warming, and Bradley was grateful for the shade near the forest's edge. It was a beautiful day, and Bradley could feel the tension in his shoulders slowly dissipate.

Over the past few days, Lady Easton had asked him all kinds of questions regarding his future duchess. His late father's eldest sister seemed quite diligent in the task he had bestowed upon her, the look upon her face often whispering of serious contemplation. She was not one to make lists—as Bradley preferred; however, following such a conversation between them, he often found her standing by the window, gazing outside as though looking at something in particular. Her gaze, however, appeared absent, directed inward, no doubt examining every answer he had given her.

Indeed, his aunt was taking this matter most seriously, and Bradley knew that by the time she was finished, she would present him with the perfect wife.

Bradley was grateful for her assistance. Nevertheless, their discussions always served to point out the change that was about to take place in his life. Bradley disliked change even if it followed the rules set down for all those in their social circle. He knew precisely what to do, how to choose a wife, how to conduct himself in her presence, and what to expect from her in return.

Whenever picturing his future life, Bradley still imagined himself sticking to the same routines that had shaped his life for the past decade. He would still rise early in the morning, have a bit of breakfast and then go about his day, tending to his estates and seeing to his duties. He would spend the Season in London and the rest of the year at Clements Park. He would converse with others of his standing about political matters and societal aspects. He would dance the occasional dance—no more than deemed necessary—and he would retire at a reasonable hour.

Slowing his mount, Bradley directed the chestnut mare down a well-trodden forest path. He liked the forest. He liked this path. He knew every tree and bush. Everything around him felt familiar, and he was relieved to see that in this place, at least, things did not change. Yes, the seasons came and went, but, even, they stuck to a specific schedule. This change was reliable. Bradley knew precisely what to expect, and he liked that.

But what of marriage?

As much as Bradley tried to remind himself that taking a wife would not in its essence change his life, he could still not help but wonder what it would be like to see her at breakfast, to converse with her over daily affairs. Would it feel odd to be seated next to one another in the carriage on the way to a ball? Would oppressive silence linger between them? Or would they be able to converse easily?

Bradley scoffed. Never in his life had he been able to converse easily with anyone. He was not a fool. Far from it. He knew well that he had a somewhat...off-putting personality. He liked things in order. He disliked anything surprising. Most people did not see the world as he did. Most people thought him a bore and sought to flee his presence at the earliest opportunity.

Bradley did not mind. With their shrill and chattering voices, spending time with other people more often than not brought on a headache. He did not like them any more than they liked him.

It was a mutual feeling, and yet...

A part of Bradley longed to find another who was like him, who saw the world as he did. Someone who could relate. Someone who would understand. Would his aunt be able to find him a wife who possessed that ability? Someone who disliked company as much as he did? Someone quiet and calm and proper?

The thought brought a smile to Bradley's face, for it was a very peaceful one.

Yes, peaceful.

That was what Bradley wanted.

What he needed.

A proper wife, who spoke little and enjoyed silence as much as he did. Where did one find such a creature?

Dressed in her emerald riding habit, Harriet quickly made her way downstairs. She felt the need to move in her bones and was eager to be off. It was a beautiful day. The sun shone brightly, and a mild breeze stirred the air.

"Off again?" came Grandma Edie's chuckling voice from the bottom of the large staircase. Although she leaned heavily upon her cane, her eyes twinkled lively, and something rather mischievous played over her face. Indeed, she seemed far too young to be a grandmother, and Harriet had always loved that she had an adventurous side.

Smiling, Harriet stepped off the last stair and gave her grandmother a quick peck on the cheek. "You know me too well."

"You always ride to the east," her grandmother remarked, the look in her eyes making Harriet wonder what she might be up to this time. After all, the Dowager Countess of Whickerton was known far and wide for her meddlesome tendencies and hidden agendas.

"Very observant of you, Grandma." Harriet did not volunteer more but waited for what else the old lady might say.

A knowing smile lit up Grandma Edie's face before she shook her head and chuckled. "If you dare," she finally said, something challenging sparking to life in her eyes, "I suggest you ride westward today."

Harriet frowned. "What is daring about that?"

Her grandmother shrugged, that odd look still on her face. "Well, I can see clear as day that you suspect something, that you believe me to have some kind of secret intention; therefore, any suggestion I am putting to you must be part of my plan to achieve my goal, must it not?" Her right brow arched upward.

Harriet grinned and crossed her arms over her chest. "And it doesn't?" Harriet challenged, wishing for once her grandmother would speak plainly. However, hoping for that was something Harriet had given up long ago.

Instead of answering her granddaughter, Grandma Edie merely looked at her and then said, "Do you dare?"

Harriet huffed out a deep breath, equally amused and annoyed with her grandmother. Never had she liked secrecy, and yet her grandmother's words whispered of excitement and adventure. What to do?

Trying her utmost to appear disinterested, Harriet shrugged, then let her arms hang loosely down her sides. "Honestly, Grandma, all I care for today is a long ride through the countryside." She gave her another peck on the cheek. "Perhaps tomorrow."

As Harriet stepped outside, she could hear her grandmother's amused chuckles follow her. Indeed, they both knew that Harriet was incapable of ignoring a challenge. It was her greatest flaw, one she wished she would conquer one of these days.

Finally seated atop Moon, Harriet gazed toward the far horizon in the east, remembering the far-reaching meadows, the soft slopes and seas of wildflowers. Day after day, she had chased the sky there, galloping along on Moon's back.

A deep sigh left her lips, and she felt her gaze tug westward. A silent curse flew from her lips, for she knew it had been her grandmother's words that now spurred her on. She simply could not resist the challenge. Why had her grandmother dared her to ride west? What was there? What did her grandmother know that she, Harriet, did not?

"There's only one way to find out," she murmured, patting her dapple-gray mare's neck. "Are you ready for a new adventure, Moon?"

As though answering her question, her mare tossed up her head and neighed.

A slow smile danced onto Harriet's face as her eyes swept over the far horizon in the west. Her eyes settled upon a large forest, a barrier between her and whatever lay on its other side. What would she find there?

CHAPTER THREE

STRANGERS IN THE WOODS

Bradley felt the little hairs on the back of his neck stand on end. A shiver of awareness danced down his spine, and he could not help but sweep his gaze over his surroundings.

Someone was nearby.

Few people ever dared enter the forest and proceed in this far. Never once had Bradley come across another soul on one of his explorations. He knew this area well. He knew the animals that called it their home. He recognized their tracks, their feeding grounds, their burrows and dens and nests. Everything his eyes fell upon spoke with familiarity. Everything was as it should be, as Bradley had expected to find it.

Yet that odd feeling remained. Was he imagining it?

Slowing his pace, Bradley reached out with his senses, listening intently to any sound that seemed out of place. Who could be hiding here in the forest? Was someone hunting?

That thought made him grit his teeth, for the land was his and he had not given permission to anyone to do so. More than anyone encroaching upon his land, Bradley disliked rule breakers, for their deeds were the very ones that rendered order and continuity inconsequential. Nothing held meaning if rules were not upheld.

Rules were the foundation of civilized life, and those who acted against them...

Bradley shook his head, unable to imagine why anyone would do so. Could it be that there were people in this world who liked disorder and anarchy? Even craved it?

He could not imagine such a creature.

A soft rustling sound echoed in Bradley's ears, and his head turned toward a wild-growing thicket, no doubt hiding someone from his view. But who? And why?

Steeling himself, Bradley turned his mare so that he faced the thicket. "Come out!" he commanded in his iciest tone, wondering if a pistol might be trained upon him at this very moment. Unfortunately, his own pistol lay safely locked away at Clements Park. "Whoever you are, I demand you show yourself immediately!"

For a moment, nothing happened. Nothing moved. In fact, the forest suddenly seemed stiller than it ever had been.

Then, the snap of a twig shot to Bradley's ears. His hands upon the reins tensed, and his mare's ears flattened as she pranced nervously.

Placing a calming hand upon the animal's neck, Bradley continued to stare straight ahead, waiting. When his eyes finally detected a fleeting movement through a small gap in the overgrown bush, he felt his heart give a slight jerk.

Twigs moved and shifted, and the sound of boots treading over dry twigs and leaves as well as the soft nicker of a horse drifted to his ears. He could make out the outline of someone carefully picking their way closer, flashes of red and emerald here and there visible through the tall-growing underbrush.

And then, the last branches parted, revealing a young woman leading a horse by the reins. Her hair was as bright and wild as dancing flames, matching the daring gleam in her watchful eyes. Her emerald riding habit was torn at the hem, dark green and brown stains covering it everywhere as though she had rolled down a hill. Yet she stood tall, her chin raised as though issuing a challenge.

Indeed, Bradley would have expected her to be too frightened to meet his eyes. He would have thought any woman encountering a stranger in the woods would be terrified out of her wits.

But not her.

Bradley had no clue who she was. What he was certain of, however, was that this woman...was trouble.

And he did not like trouble.

Not at all.

Harriet had to admit that her grandmother's counsel had been good. Whatever had prompted her to give it, Harriet still did not know. Nevertheless, she had spent the most wonderful afternoon carefully picking her way through a dense-growing forest, sneaking after a rabbit and watching it disappear in its burrow. Granted, her riding habit probably looked as though she had rolled through the mud. She doubted it could be salvaged, but it was a small price to pay for the joy she had found.

Harriet loved animals. They were honest and free and daring. They had to be, and she truly appreciated that about them. The rabbit had reminded Harriet of the injured one she had found not long ago near Whickerton Grove. She had nursed it back to health, and unable to part with it, she had even taken it back to London. However, the city was no place for a wild creature, and eventually, she had been forced to set it free. She had watched it disappear with a smile on her face and tears in her eyes.

"Are you well, Madam?"

With her sight now unobstructed, Harriet looked across the narrow forest path at the stranger atop his chestnut mount. He carried himself like a true aristocrat, a haughty expression in his dark eyes, his wide shoulders drawn back as though he stood in front of the Queen. Indeed, even after riding through the forest, Harriet spotted none of his attire out of place. Was there even a speck of dust or dirt upon his boots?

Harriet felt a sudden need to tease this man, to break through that polished exterior of his and see his feathers ruffled. "I am well; thank you, good sir." She stepped out onto the path, then she dusted off her skirts before her right hand reached up to run through her tangled hair. "Oh," she exclaimed with feigned surprise, "I must've lost my bonnet." Then she paused, allowed her jaw to drop a little and her eyes to open wide before she let an amused chuckle drift from her lips. "Come to think of it, I don't even remember putting one on."

The stranger continued to watch her as though she were an explosive about to go off. Disapproval marked his features, his lips thinning as his gaze swept over her, then past her. "Have you been in some sort of accident? Where is your companion? Your...chaperone?" The last word dripped with such ill-concealed disapproval and reproach that Harriet had to laugh.

Immediately, the stranger's gaze narrowed into slits. "Are you well?" he asked once more before he—undoubtedly, reluctantly—dismounted. Indeed, his body language clearly suggested that he did not want to follow his gentlemanly duty of seeing to her safety. For a second, the need to comfort and reassure him sparked in Harriet's veins, but she could not help but laugh again. Who was this odd creature?

The stranger took a step toward her, but then stopped, clearly concerned with the lack of supervision. "Are you well?" he repeated for the third time, his words slow as though he suspected she had suffered some kind of head injury and no longer possessed the ability to make sense of the words he spoke.

Harriet inhaled a deep breath, trying her best to chase away that lingering amusement. "I am well, yes. And, no, I did not suffer an accident nor lose my companion."

The stranger held her gaze, then turned his head from side to side, his eyes sweeping over their surroundings.

"I rode out by myself," Harriet clarified, for he clearly seemed to expect some sort of *companion* to step out from in-between the trees. "I find other people only get in the way." As much as Harriet enjoyed the company of others, she loved the peaceful solitude she found when out riding.

The stranger's lips thinned further, and for a moment, he seemed unable to form a coherent sentence, shock clear in his brown eyes.

Indeed, they were a dark shade of brown, like chocolate, with sparks of hazel in them. Harriet would have expected eyes like his to be soft and gentle, one look into them offering comfort and reassurance. The stranger's eyes, however, seemed hard and…lonely.

Harriet felt a sharp twist in her heart, not unlike the kind she often experienced when coming upon a wounded animal.

"You should return home," the stranger said in a tone that made it an order. "Immediately." Then he turned upon his heel and made to mount his horse.

"What is your name?" Harriet asked, releasing Moon's reins and stepping forward. "I'm Harriet."

The stranger turned to eye her with those hard eyes of his, the brown now almost black, as though their color could change to reflect his mood. He hesitated, then gave a quick nod. "Bradley Jackson, Duke of Clements."

Harriet felt her nose crinkle. "You don't look like a Bradley," she surmised, watching him most carefully as his expression darkened even further. Yes, disapproval was now rolling off him in waves, and Harriet wondered if this man had ever smiled.

Had ever known the meaning of joy.

She doubted it; but he would.

That, she vowed.

CHAPTER FOUR

A WICKED LADY

Shock reverberated in Bradley's bones as the unkempt hellion repeated his given name. The nerve of that woman to criticize him, of all people!

It was unthinkable! People might find his demeanor less than charming or his way of conversation sleep-inducing—all fair observations!—but to find fault with his name! He was a duke, after all. No one had ever dared—

"Jack!" the hellion—he would not call her by her given name; not if his life depended on it!—exclaimed with utter joy. "Yes, Jack suits you much better!"

Dumbfounded, Bradley stared at her, continued to stare at her, for he knew not what else to do. His body and mind seemed frozen, completely incapable of handling this utterly unexpected situation. Yes, the hellion had shocked him, Bradley was loath to admit. How had this happened? What on earth was she doing?

Judging from her manners—or lack thereof—Bradley would have expected her to be of a lower social standing; however, despite her frankness, her speech as well as the way she expressed herself spoke to a highborn lady. So did her riding habit. Despite the dirt staining it in various places, Bradley could see that the material was of the highest quality, as was the mare by her side, an animal of the finest stock.

For all intents and purposes, this woman ought not be scrambling through the underbrush of the forest, leaves tangled in her red hair and smudges of dirt upon her cheeks. No, she ought to be riding across the meadow near a stately manor, a companion by her side, before returning to the delicate pastimes of which ladies were fond.

Concerned for her well-being as much as for her reputation, Bradley knew that the most honorable thing to do was to send her back home immediately by making her understand the precarious situation she had put herself in. "Where do you reside?" Bradley inquired, hoping to dispose himself of her with the utmost expedience.

A thoughtful expression came to the hellion's face. She continued to watch him, waiting as though carefully weighing how to answer him. "I'm visiting my sister," she finally replied, her wide green eyes still observant, as though curious to see his reaction to such a simple statement. "She and her husband live at Pinewood Manor."

Bradley gave a brief nod. He had heard of the estate, of course, for it was only half an hour's ride from Clements Park. His steward had informed him that the place had been purchased by someone in trade not too long ago; however, Bradley had yet to meet this Mr. Sharpe. "I suggest you return immediately."

A slow smile came to the hellion's face. "I'd rather not," she had the nerve to reply.

Bradley blinked. "Pardon me?"

The hellion inhaled a deep breath, her arms stretching wide as though she were savoring the scents of the forest. "It is such a beautiful day that I cannot bring myself to leave it behind just yet." Looking at him, she stepped closer. "Do you live near here? Do you know this area? This forest?" Her eyes swept over their surroundings, a deeply enchanted look in her wide green eyes.

Bradley swallowed, completely thrown off guard by her unusual behavior. "Miss, I must urge you to halt your steps." He held out a hand, palm facing her, hoping that even if his words held no meaning for her, this simple gesture would.

To Bradley's relief, the hellion did pause, her feet drawing to a halt. Unfortunately, though, it was only to gawk at him with an expression that held an odd mixture of confusion and amusement. "You look deeply worried," she remarked, as though he had no reason to. "Is there something dangerous in these woods?"

Confused, Bradley shook his head. "Are you not concerned for your reputation?" Again, his gaze flew past her, wondering if her absence had been noted by her sister and brother-in-law, if perhaps they had sent someone out to find her. If she were found in his company, alone...

His gaze returned to her. Did she truly not care? Or was she a simpleton, unaware of the consequences of her actions?

"My reputation?" the hellion asked, chuckling. "Oh, Jack, you are such an endearing man." She gave a quick laugh. "No, I've never in my life been worried about my reputation." Her right eyebrow rose into an arch. "But you obviously are. Why?" Something devilish sparked in her eyes, and although Bradley was not well-versed in conversing with the fair sex, he could tell that she was teasing him.

Clearing his throat, Bradley drew back his shoulders and willed an icy look into his eyes. "I am certain your sister and brother-in-law would object to you being here, alone, conversing with me, without any kind of supervision." Momentarily, he wondered about her parents. Had they already passed? Or were they simply unaware of their daughter's escapades?

Unfortunately, his words forced neither concern nor regret into her green eyes. Instead, she still seemed amused—annoyingly so. "My sister has known me since the day I was born. Believe me, Jack, she knows me well." She inhaled a deep breath and drew back her shoulders a little. "And she does not mind."

"I must insist that you refrain from calling me Jack!" Bradley demanded in a voice that was far from composed, and he quickly reminded himself to remain calm. After all, emotions served no purpose.

"Why? It suits you. Do you disagree?"

Bradley shook his head at her. "You are to address me as *your grace*... if at all." He held her gaze and lifted his brows, hoping she would finally comprehend the underlying meaning of his words. "Pray tell, what is your name?"

"Harriet, but you may call me Harry if you like."

Bradley closed his eyes, willing himself to remain calm as he inhaled a slow, deep breath and silently counted to five. "I'm afraid that will not do. What is your surname so that I may address you appropriately?"

For a moment, the hellion paused, eyeing him most curiously. "Beaumont," she then said before adding, "however, if you truly wish to address me appropriately, call me Lady Harriet."

"Lady Harriet," Bradley mumbled as he watched her approach his mare, her hands reaching out to brush over his mount's nose. She stood much too close, and Bradley felt the need to step back when her gaze met his, flecks of amber dancing in her emerald eyes. "She's beautiful," Lady Harriet whispered, running her hands over his mare's neck, a warm smile curling up her lips "and kind. What is her name?"

Bradley swallowed, completely unaccustomed to conversing with a lady outside the ballroom, especially a lady like Lady Harriet, who behaved unlike any lady he had ever met. "Shine," he blurted out without thought, belatedly reminding himself that she needed to leave.

The sooner the better.

"Oh, that is a fitting name. Her eyes do shine like two stars, do they not?" Lady Harriet exclaimed before looking over her shoulder and giving a soft, melodic whistle. Instantly, her own mare came trotting over, nuzzling her hand. "And this is Moon."

Bradley had to admit the name suited the dapple-gray mare, her coloring reminding him of the moon's surface when it was full. He was about to say so when he called himself to reason. "That is of no importance. Pray tell, who is your father?" Indeed, he had not heard of another lord in the area, at least not within riding distance.

Something undetermined sparked in Lady Harriet's eyes. "The Earl of Whickerton," she answered him, once more watching him intently as a slow smile spread over her face. "Does that shock you?"

Of course, it did! After all, Bradley imagined that everyone in the *ton* had heard of the *Wicked Whickertons*...especially of late. The sisters were notorious for scandalous behavior, all of them a favorite with the gossips. What on earth had he gotten himself into?

Lady Harriet needed to leave.

Now!

CHAPTER FIVE

PUSHING THE BOUNDARIES

Harriet chuckled, amused to see Jack's face turn somewhat pale. "It looks like it does shock you," she remarked, intrigued by the way he continued to look at her. "Why? Are you worried about your reputation?"

For a moment, he remained quiet, his face almost immobile as his dark eyes continued to watch her, something indecisive in them. "Return home," he told her in a clipped tone, his hands tightening upon Shine's reins. "Now!"

Harriet smiled at him. "You have nothing to fear from me, Jack. I promise."

His face darkened. "Please stop calling me that!" Anger resonated in his voice, and yet Harry could tell that it bothered him. Why would it bother him to show emotion? He was indeed an odd creature but a most intriguing one.

"Do you truly prefer Bradley?"

This time, he rolled his eyes at her, unable to prevent it, before a look of contrition came to his face. He was no doubt disappointed with himself for allowing her to bait him into such a reaction. "You are to refer to me as *your grace*, and I will address you as Lady Harriet. That is how it's done. You should be aware of that."

"Oh, I am aware of that," Harriet replied, "however, I do not agree with it." She held his gaze, curious to see what he would do, to hear what he would say. Clearly, he disagreed with her; and yet she could not help but think that at least a part of him was as intrigued by her as she was by him.

His dark gaze lingered upon her face, and for a moment, Harriet felt like an odd specimen put under a microscope to be observed and studied by an eager scientist. "Am I to understand that...you always ride out by yourself?"

Harriet could see that the mere thought was inconceivable to him, and so she merely smiled, allowing him time to absorb something his mind had clearly never fathomed existed. How truly sad, she thought to herself.

His gaze left her face and traveled down over her riding habit, the stains of dirt and grass, down to the rip in her hem. "How...?" His gaze returned to her, his mouth opening and closing, his mind unable to form the question.

Harriet chuckled. "You see, there was a rabbit. And I like rabbits. A little while back, I saved one after it had been hit by a carriage and I nursed it back to health." Longing tugged at her heart at the mere thought of the cute, little creature. "I named him Sir Lancelot. My sisters thought it was a hilarious name for a rabbit, but I thought it suited him nicely." She exhaled. "When I saw this one today, I simply..." She shrugged, remembering the very moment she had seen its bushy little tail and those wide, deep eyes. "I simply had to follow it."

When Harriet returned her attention back to the man standing in front of her, she saw that his expression spoke of utter incredulity. Clearly, every word she had spoken had confused him, for he seemed to stare at her like a man who had just come upon a mythical creature and did not dare believe his eyes. Harriet had to admit she quite liked that thought. "You've never had a rabbit?"

For a brief moment, Harriet thought he would burst out into laughter; surprising though, he did not. A fact she found rather disappointing. "No," was all he said, that sense of disapproval once more in his voice.

"Do you often ride out in the forest?"

Jack's gaze darkened. "It is my forest."

"That does not answer my question," Harriet pointed out.

"Yes."

"Will you be riding out again tomorrow?"

His brows knitted together as he stared at her.

"I thought that perhaps we could ride together," Harriet suggested, fully expecting her words to shock him witless once again.

Not surprisingly, Jack's lips thinned. "Are you truly suggesting we ride out together?"

"Yes."

"With a chaperone?"

Harriet allowed a slow grin to spread over her face, then she softly shook her head. "I'd rather not."

"That is impossible!" Jack snapped, that mixture of disapproval and reproach back in his voice. "You'd be ruined! The implications—!" He clamped his lips shut. "You cannot ride out alone, and I urge you to reconsider."

"You ride out alone," Harriet pointed out, well-aware—how could she not be?—that society made a clear distinction between what women were allowed to do and what men were allowed to do.

Jack gawked at her, clearly thinking as society did. Unfortunately, he did not argue his point. Instead, he took a step back, something final coming to his eyes. "I suggest you return home." He pulled Shine closer and then mounted swiftly. "I cannot imagine your father approves—"

"My father would never stand in my way," Harriet interrupted, holding his gaze as he looked down upon her. "He knows me. He understands me." She stepped closer, her hand once more brushing Shine's nose. "My parents broke the rules and found happiness that way." She grinned at him. "I intend to do the same."

A muscle in his jaw twitched. She could see that something lay at the tip of his tongue. Still, he did not say a word, merely tipped his hat and then rode back along the path he had come.

Heaving a deep sigh, Harriet turned around when Moon brushed her head against her shoulder. "He is unlike anyone I've ever met,"

Harriet whispered to her mare, belatedly realizing that her words were false…or were they not?

Indeed, at first glance, Jack appeared like all the other snobbish, stuffed lords who believed themselves the kings of this world, put here to rule over women from their lofty thrones. At second glance, however, Harriet could not help but think that…

In truth, she could not quite put her finger on it, much less put that odd emotion into words. Had it been something in his eyes? That sadness? That loneliness she had glimpsed?

Something about Jack intrigued her, and she would not rest until she found out what that was…whether he liked it or not.

Of course, he would not like it. She had no trouble imagining his shock if he were to…say, *stumble* upon her yet again.

Harriet chuckled, feeling a familiar eagerness pulse beneath her skin. "Do you think he is the one," she whispered to Moon, "Grandma meant for me to meet?"

Of course, Grandma Edie was well-aware of her granddaughter's dislike for the haughty men of the *ton*; however, Harriet knew her grandmother enjoyed pushing boundaries as much as she did herself. Yes, she would not put it past the old lady to tease her by sending her to cross paths with the Duke of Clements.

Oh, but it had been fun!

CHAPTER SIX
SECRETS

"We should hold a ball here at Clements Park," Lady Easton suggested as they sat in the drawing room later that day, "in a few weeks' time." She took a sip from her tea, her gaze momentarily distant as she no doubt contemplated who to invite. "Do you agree?"

Bradley nodded. "Certainly. It appears to be an expedient way to settle this matter."

An approving smile came to her face. "Very well. Leave everything to me. I know we shall find your duchess before the year is out."

"Thank you," was all Bradley said, for his thoughts were inexplicably drawn back to earlier that afternoon, to the red-haired hellion he now knew to be Lady Harriet, one of Lord Whickerton's notorious daughters.

"Clements," Lady Easton addressed him, the tone in her voice suggesting that it was not the first time she had done so.

Had he been woolgathering? Bradley wondered, appalled with the idea itself. He was a duke. He did not woolgather or drift off or—

"Clements."

"Yes." Bradley's head snapped up, fully aware of the concerned look upon his aunt's face. "I apologize. There is a matter that..." His voice trailed off.

Lady Easton held up her hand. "There is no need. I do not doubt that there are countless matters that require your attention." She rose from the settee. "I'll leave you to them then."

Bradley barely heard the door click shut behind her before his thoughts strayed back to Lady Harriet. He could not help but wonder if he ought to speak to Lord Whickerton. The man could not truly approve of his daughter's escapades. However, doing so would reveal how the two of them had met that day...alone...in the forest...unsupervised. Bradley wondered if that would be wise. Would Lord Whickerton demand Bradley marry his daughter? After all, strictly speaking, he had compromised her...or would if he spoke of their encounter.

Still, what if Lady Harriet continued to conduct herself in this manner? He did not even dare imagine all the harm that might befall her. Was it not his responsibility to...do something?

Certainly, but what?

Bradley groaned. If only he had not ridden out today! If he had not, he would never have met her and would not be thinking of her again!

Correction: he would not be thinking of the risk she posed to herself yet again! Yes, that was it.

Indeed, she was a most unusual creature. Not a simpleton at all, but fully aware of the repercussions should her actions become known. However, she did not seem to...care. Was that possible? How could she not care? If her reputation were ruined, she would never make a suitable match or a match at all. Perhaps he ought to remind her of that... if he were to happen upon her again, that is.

Bradley rather doubted it. After all, no woman in her right mind would dare risk all Lady Harriet had yet again. Yes, he felt reasonably certain that he had misunderstood her. Of course, she did not ride out without a chaperone regularly. Today had merely been...an exception.

Yes, an exception, nothing more.

"Where are you going?" came Christina's voice as Harriet was about to pull herself into the saddle.

Pausing, Harriet turned to face her sister, Christina's blond curls dancing upon the soft breeze that blew past the stables. "What does it look like?" she countered with a shrug. "I'm going riding."

Coming to stand right in front of Harriet, Christina eyed her little sister with a most careful look. "And where to?"

Harriet frowned. "Why do you ask?"

Something contemplative rested in Christina's blue eyes before she shrugged. "Grandma Edie said something that made me think..." Her voice trailed off, but her brows rose meaningfully.

Harriet laughed, remembering the mischievous gleam she had seen in her grandmother's eyes when she had returned the day before. Clearly, the old lady had been dying to know what had happened during Harriet's ride, but she had not asked; and Harriet had not said a word. "What did she tell you?"

Christina shook her head. "Nothing. I cannot recall her exact words, but they made me think that..."

"That?" Harriet pressed with a chuckle.

Christina heaved a deep sigh. "That she was up to something. You know how she sometimes likes to meddle."

Harriet broke out laughing. "Sometimes, dear sister? Now, that is truly the greatest understatement I have ever heard."

A knowing smile came to Christina's face. "Yes, I know. I know. She's..." She shrugged. "There are no words. She is in a class all her own." She breathed in deeply, the look upon her face becoming more serious. "Still, she is rarely wrong." Her gaze flitted to Moon. "Where are you going?"

Harriet heaved a deep sigh, wondering what to tell her sister. While all the Whickertons disapproved of lying, they all equally seemed to agree that under certain circumstances withholding the truth was acceptable. Was this such a case? Harriet wondered, realizing that she did not want to speak to her sister of Jack.

Oddly enough, a part of her wanted to keep him a secret.

Hers, all alone.

At least, for now.

"I do not wish to tell you," Harriet told her sister honestly, holding up a hand when Christina looked ready to argue. "Not yet, at least. Trust me, Chris. Please."

Her sister fixed her with a pointed look, her chest rising and falling with each contemplative breath. "Very well," she finally said, then held up her forefinger in warning. "But don't make me regret it."

Harriet smiled at her.

"Be careful," Christina urged. "Or I shall tell Mother and Father." The corners of her mouth twitched.

Harriet laughed. "And do you think they would forbid me from going riding?"

Her sister rolled her eyes. "No," she finally admitted. "But they would no doubt counsel you better than I ever could."

Harriet hugged her sister. "You're being a wonderful mother to Sam," she told her, meeting Christina's blue eyes. "Don't doubt yourself."

"Do you truly think so?"

"I know so," Harriet assured her, then quickly pulled herself into the saddle, worried her sister would fire another question at her. "I'll see you later."

"Be careful!" Christina called after her as Harriet urged Moon into a trot.

"Always!"

"Yes, I've heard that before!"

Harriet laughed, then she loosened her hold on the reins and let Moon run as she wished.

Westward, of course.

Toward Jack.

Thank you, Grandma!

CHAPTER SEVEN

A SWEET MAN

Bradley could not help but think that he ought to have skipped his ride today. Yet he was a creature of habit, and he did not appreciate having to rearrange his schedule because…

His gaze flew over the meadow and toward the forest's edge, his heart beating faster than usual in his chest. Shine, too, seemed to move with more eagerness, as though she longed for something. She pranced on the spot, her ears flitting back and forth before she threw up her head and neighed.

"All is well," Bradley murmured, patting her neck reassuringly. "All is well."

Still, his mare did not calm, and so Bradley gave her free rein.

Within an instant, she shot forward, her long legs carrying them across the meadow. The wind whipped into his face, and Bradley squinted his eyes as he leaned forward in the saddle.

Truth be told, Bradley rarely allowed himself this kind of wild and completely unrestrained behavior. Nor did he have any wish for it. He preferred order and predictability.

And Lady Harriet represented neither.

Frowning, Jack sat up in his saddle, wondering why on earth he was thinking of her again. Indeed, she had continued to linger in his mind ever since meeting her the day before. No matter in which direction his thoughts traveled, inevitably they always returned to her. But why?

Drawing in a deep breath, Bradley flinched when another horse suddenly shot past him in a blur. He barely glimpsed red hair billowing in the wind before Lady Harriet's voice called, "Race you to the forest!"

Shock froze Bradley's limbs, and he almost toppled out of the saddle. His eyes widened and remained fixed upon Lady Harriet's fiery curls as they danced upon the wind, her mare's hoof beats echoing in his ears. His hands tightened on the reins, and he was about to halt his mount—After all, this was lunacy! Just like the woman herself! And she was not even riding sidesaddle!—when quite inexplicably...he did not.

Perhaps urged on by the other mare's thunderous steps, Shine quickened her own. Bradley could feel her flanks heaving, her legs moving with greater speed, and without thinking, he leaned forward, lowering himself to her neck.

Again, the wind whipped into his face, tugging upon his hair and stinging his skin. It was an odd sensation, and yet Bradley did not slow down. Every rational part of him urged him to cease racing across the meadow...but he did not.

Slowly, step by thunderous step, he caught up with Lady Harriet, now only a horse's length between them. She looked over her shoulder at him, her green eyes wide and her mouth curled into a smile unlike any Bradley had ever seen. She looked radiant, as though glowing from within with something he might, perhaps, in another life, have called...happiness.

"You can try all you might," Lady Harriet called to him over the soft howling of the wind, "but you will never catch me, Jack!"

Bradley gritted his teeth at her overly familiar address but still did not cease his efforts. He kept his gaze straight ahead, doing his best to ignore her, to not look at her, at those teasing green eyes that seemed to linger upon him for far too long. No, instead, he kept his eyes focused on the tree line ahead, calculating the distance they would still have to cover, the distance it would take to slow their mounts before the tree line would be upon them.

Closer and closer, they thundered toward the imposing forest that barred their way. Bradley felt a cold shiver dance down his spine, and despite his vow to the contrary, he jerked his head sideways to look at Lady Harriet. "We need to slow down!"

Laughing at him, she spurred her mare onward. "If you do, you will lose!"

Bradley cursed under his breath—something he never did. Come to think of it, he had done a lot of things he never did in the past twenty-four hours, and they were all linked to this infuriating woman riding up ahead. "It is not safe!" he called, not daring to rein in Shine, concerned that a growing distance might prevent Lady Harriet from hearing him. "You need to slow down! Now!"

The tree line was now dangerously close, and Bradley reluctantly pulled upon his reins, urging Shine to slow, his eyes fixed upon Lady Harriet. Was she mad? Silly question! Of course, the woman was mad! He had known so the first moment he had laid eyes on her. Never in his life had he encountered a creature with such disregard for her own safety, her own well-being!

In horror, he watched as her mare flew onward, fully expecting to watch disaster unfold when, all of a sudden, Lady Harriet sat up in her saddle. She pulled on the reins and guided her mare sideways until they were parallel with the forest line, giving her more room to slow her steps. Her face still glowed with excitement, laughter spilling from her lips as she patted the dapple-gray's neck. "Well done, Moon. Well done. Good girl."

Bradley knew he ought to simply turn around and leave, forget he had ever met her; but he did not.

He could not.

"Are you mad?" he demanded, urging Shine closer, his eyes searching her face for any sign of understanding. He found none.

Lady Harriet heaved a deep sigh, her eyes rising to meet his. "Yes, I suppose I am." She stretched her arms wide, breathing in deeply in a way that made Bradley think she was truly enjoying herself, savoring the moment. "Does this not make you feel alive? Was this not wonderful?"

Bradley knew he was probably gawking at her like a fool, yet he could not seem to help it. "Wonderful? It was reckless! You could have—"

"I knew what I was doing," Lady Harriet interrupted him, guiding her mare closer, something defiant blazing in her eyes. "I'm not a fool. I know you must think me to be one, but you're wrong. I know how to ride. I know myself, and I know Moon. I turned her sideways the moment I knew I needed to." She heaved out a deep breath, eyebrows rising in a challenging gesture as she held his gaze.

Bradley cleared his throat, unwilling to admit that she had seemed in control of the situation. Perhaps it had merely been his concern that had made him picture the worst. "You did," Bradley grudgingly admitted, the tension in his jaw growing to such an extent that pain radiated down his neck. "What are you doing here in the first place?"

Lady Harriet shrugged, the pulse in her neck still thundering from the wild ride. "I asked you to go riding today, did I not?"

Bradley gave her the most condescending look he could muster, an icy stare that had never once failed to intimidate those before him. "And I said no," he growled, feeling the pulse in his neck speed up once more. Why was it that merely speaking to this woman chased this odd energy through his veins as though he were running at a breakneck speed?

To Bradley's surprise and annoyance, a slow smile spread over Lady Harriet's face, no sign of intimidation appearing in her eyes. "Yet, Jack," he could not help but think that this time at least she had intentionally used this odd nickname in order to upset him, to bait him and tease him, "you are here." Her brows rose in triumph, daring him to contradict her. "Why?"

Bradley cleared his throat, very much aware that, yes, he could have chosen a different path, a different direction, a different time, ensuring that they would not happen upon one another. Instead, he had once more returned to the forest where they had first met. "I go riding every day."

Lady Harriet nodded slowly, undoubtedly aware of the defensive tone in his voice. She kicked her mare's flanks, pushing the animal closer until the two mounts stood side by side, her knee so close that it almost brushed against his. Her wide green eyes never left Bradley's, and he had to swallow around the lump that had suddenly formed in his throat as he waited for her to speak. "So do I," Lady Harriet replied, her voice almost a whisper, as though she was sharing something deeply intimate with him. "I cannot go a day without chasing the sky, can you? It is a feeling like no other." Her smile seemed to deepen as she looked at him. "I find I enjoy it even more with you by my side. Does that surprise you?"

Truthfully, if lightning had struck Bradley in that moment, he would have been less surprised. Indeed, no one had ever enjoyed his company nor had he ever wanted anyone to; and he did not now. "Again, you are without a chaperone," he chided, determined to lead this conversation back to safer terrain.

Lady Harriet chuckled. "As are you."

Bradley could feel his head spinning. "It is not the same," he snapped in reply, "and you know it."

"It should be," Lady Harriet replied with a shrug.

"That is not an answer!" Bradley could once again feel his pulse spike higher, despite his efforts to remain calm. Why on earth did he have to meet such an infuriating woman?

"It is my answer," the lady replied in that slightly amused, completely unconcerned way of hers.

Bradley stared at her in disbelief. He was at the end of his ropes, no longer knowing what to say or how to make her understand. "Do you truly not care? How can you not care about your own well-being? Your own future? Do you not even have the slightest inkling of what could happen to you out here by yourself?" He shook his head, feeling completely dumbfounded.

To his utter shock, Lady Harriet then reached out and placed her hand upon his lower arm, a gentle and soft weight that seemed to sear through his sleeve and leave an imprint upon his skin. "Oh, sweet Jack, you don't need to be concerned for me. I always have a blade tucked in my bodice when I go riding." She cocked an eyebrow at him, and a bit of a quizzical look came into her eyes. "Don't you? I mean, are you not armed?"

Bradley stared at her long and hard, unable to choose which outrageous piece of information to respond to first. One: She had called him

Jack...again. Two: no proper lady would refer to her *bodice* in a man's presence. Three: she truly had a blade tucked in said bodice? And four: no one had ever called him *sweet* before.

Nor had he ever wanted anyone to, and yet the word continued to echo in his mind, pulsing like a separate entity suddenly come to life. It felt warm and soothing, and it made him forget about all the other things she had said that had first given him affront. His gaze became distant, his mind suddenly sluggish, unable to catch a clear thought.

"Are you all right?" Lady Harriet inquired, and her hand upon his arm gave a little squeeze. "Jack? Are you all right? You look pale." She dipped her head to look into his downcast eyes, and a small smile played over her lips. "Have I shocked you too much for one day? If so, I apologize. It was never my intention. Please, sweet Jack, will you not look at me?"

Bradley blinked, and then his eyes found hers and he knew in that moment that he would never forget this feeling. As odd as it was, the feeling was shockingly unique. It had never assailed his chest before, tightening his muscles and sending this soothing warmth through him in waves.

She had called him *sweet.*

Again.

To his utter shame, Bradley could not deny that—whether or not he deserved it—he did like it. He ought not, but he did.

Oh, this did not bode well!

CHAPTER EIGHT
A WALK IN A MEADOW

Something had shocked him. Deeply. Harriet had seen it in the way his eyes almost glazed over, drawn away from the here and now to reflect upon something...something she had said? If only she knew what had stirred him so. Yes, she had wanted to shock him, to tease him, to draw a response from him that would allow them to continue their conversation.

Indeed, he was a most proper man, always concerned with society's rules, with right and wrong according to other people, with never stepping across that invisible line. And yet there was something deeply endearing, almost innocent about him. He did not reprimand her out of a misplaced sense of superiority or the notion that she was truly incapable of making her own choices. No, for reasons she could not understand, rules made Jack feel at ease. He clung to them as a drowning man would cling to a piece of driftwood.

Looking at him now, at his pale face and his wide eyes, Harriet understood that her words had somehow shaken the foundation of his world. But why did he need them? Why could he not feel safe without these rules?

Harriet sighed, feeling her heart go out to him. He was such a sweet man, his own heart safely tucked away and protected by a thick layer of stoic adherence to society's rules, afraid that if he did not...

What was it he feared? Harriet wondered, giving his arm another little squeeze, hoping to draw him back from this inner contemplation. "Jack?"

He cleared his throat. "Yes?"

Harriet smiled, surprised to feel such delight that he had responded to her name for him. "Are you all right?"

Again, he cleared his throat. "I'm fine." A slight frown came to his face as his eyes flitted over her in a way that made Harriet think it was almost involuntary. As if he could not help it.

"Come," Harriet said gently, giving his arm a slight tug. "We'll walk a bit."

Without arguing, Jack nodded and then slid out of the saddle. He patted Shine's neck, his hands gentle as he brushed along her nose and ruffled her mane. He tried to appear so cold and detached, as though no heart beat in his chest that Harriet had to smile when she saw his actions.

"Will she run off if you release her?" Harriet asked, securing Moon's reins so she would not step on them. Then she gave the mare a pat and let her graze freely.

Jack shrugged. "Honestly, I've never..." His voice trailed off as his gaze swept over the meadow, touched upon the two horses, then returned to her.

"You've never strolled through a meadow?" Harriet did not wish to laugh at him but a part of her had a truly hard time believing what he had said. What a sad life he had to lead! "I don't think she'll wander far. She likes you, and she feels safe in your presence."

Her words clearly bothered him, for he turned away, all but hiding from her as he shortened Shine's reins with a knot so they sat low upon her neck. Harriet could not fathom why. Never had she met anyone who disliked being cared for, being someone others felt at ease with.

Harry breathed in deeply and lifted her head to the sky, eyes closed to savor the warmth upon her skin. "Is it not a beautiful day?" She waited, but when no reply came, she opened her eyes and turned to look at Jack.

Deep frown lines creased his forehead as he stared at her. Once again, he had that look in his eyes that made him seem like a man who had spotted a mythical creature, despite knowing that they did not exist. When he realized she was looking back at him, he dropped his gaze and cleared his throat. "I should leave." Yet he remained where he was.

"Why?" Harriet inquired, stepping closer to better read his expression. "You want to be here. Can you not feel it?"

Again, that deeply unsettled look came to his eyes before he slowly shook his head, as though trying to rid himself of something he simply could not understand nor dare try to. "Please, tell me you understand what I'm saying. You understand what risk you're putting yourself in by being here with me, do you not?" He stared at her face as though afraid he might miss the very moment that she would respond to his request.

Harriet heaved a deep sigh, then sank down and settled herself in the tall grass. She looked up at Jack and patted the spot beside her, urging him to sit.

He tensed, and for a long moment, he remained immobile. When he finally did move, he stepped around her, careful to maintain a proper distance before seating himself rather awkwardly across from her.

Harriet wanted to laugh, but she was worried it would offend him and so she did not. "Yes," she finally answered his question. "I am aware of the rules you speak of. I know what is expected of me, and I know why you are so shocked. I know all of these things. I always have. I simply do not agree with them." She paused here, curious to hear what he would say.

His frown deepened. "It is not for you to agree or disagree with them. They are there to protect us, to give us something to hold on to, to guide us through life. There is always cause and consequence, and because of these rules, we can predict what will happen, what will follow our actions." His gaze held hers, and she could see in his eyes an almost desperate desire for her to understand, to acknowledge what he had said.

Harriet shook her head because she could not. "I cannot see the world the way you do. To me, these rules are nothing but restrictions. They rob me of my freedom to choose. Yes, actions have consequences. Out of one thing follows another; but I don't think it fair to any of us that these rules hobble us the way they do."

"Hobble us?" Confusion marked his features as he absentmindedly pulled out a blade of grass and began running it through his fingers.

"Yes," Harriet replied. "I want to go riding without a chaperone, but I'm not allowed to. If I do it, I'll have to...*suffer the consequences*," she said with a bit of dramatic flair. "Is that not what you're so worried about?"

As though he had all but forgotten about his earlier concerns, Jack shifted uncomfortably. He held her gaze and, after a moment, nodded his head. "I should leave," he said once more, proving her point.

"I don't want you to leave," Harriet said, straightforward, without holding back.

Jack paused in the process of rising to his feet, his eyes snapping back over to meet hers.

Harriet smiled. "Does that shock you? Indeed, it seems that it does. Why is that, sweet Jack? Can you truly not imagine that anyone would enjoy your company?" Holding his gaze, she leaned forward. "Truth be told, I've been looking forward to meeting you here today ever since we parted ways."

Harriet could not help but think that a part of him enjoyed hearing her words, enjoyed hearing that she cared, that despite their brief acquaintance he meant something to her. Yet the look in his eyes made it clear that it also made him uneasy. "That is of no consequence," Jack finally said in a gruff voice before pushing to his feet. He brushed off some stray blades of grass and then met her gaze once more. "You ought to return home."

"You keep saying that." Harriet rose to her feet, watching the wary expression upon his face as she took a step toward him.

"That's because it is true," he replied, retreating a step. "I cannot believe that your father truly would not mind if he knew we were here together...alone." He swallowed hard, clearly uncomfortable with the direction of their conversation.

"Although my parents do not agree with everything I do," Harriet told him, feeling a fresh wave of gratitude toward her parents wash over her, "they would never dream of taking my life's choices out of my hands." She gazed at him. "Never." She took another step toward him. "Did yours?"

CHAPTER NINE

SORROW & REGRET

At her question, Bradley flinched. He did not know why, but a sudden jolt went through him. He could not explain it, for he hardly remembered his parents. His mother had died before his tenth year, and although, his father had only passed away after Bradley had returned from his tour of the Continent, the two of them had barely seen each other following his mother's passing. Why then did the mere mention of his parents cause such an acute tightness in his chest?

"It is different for gentlemen," Bradley replied, pushing that constricting feeling aside and focusing his mind on the matter at hand. "Riding out on my own, I do not have to be concerned for my...reputation," he finished lamely, completely unaccustomed to speaking to a lady. Had he been though, it would probably have provided little assistance, for Lady Harriet was a lady unlike any he had ever encountered.

"Is that so?" she challenged him as he had known she would. "If we were found alone together, would you not be equally pressured into proposing marriage as I would be into accepting it?"

For a split-second, the notion of marrying Lady Harriet tied his tongue, and he found it impossible to force even a single word past his lips. "Perhaps," Bradley finally admitted after rediscovering his voice. "However, if I were to refuse, my reputation would recover. Yours would not."

Lady Harriet's eyes narrowed as he spoke, and she looked at him as though suspecting that he was not telling her all that was on his mind. "Even with my reputation in ruins, I could still ride out and enjoy myself." She shrugged. "I don't see the harm in doing what I do."

"But as a woman, you—" Bradley broke off when he realized that—perhaps for the first time in his life—he had spoken without thought, without knowing precisely what he wanted to say.

Clearly intrigued—as he had known the hellion would be!—Lady Harriet stepped closer, a teasing smile curling up her lips. "Oh, do go ahead. Teach me something about being a woman."

Bradley swallowed, not fool enough not to realize that this was a trap. No matter what he said, she would find a way to twist it against him. "All I'm trying to warn you about are the consequences of your actions. What if you had been thrown? What if you had suffered an accident? What if…?"

She cocked an eyebrow. "What if…?"

Bradley heaved a deep breath, feeling a hint of mortification warm his cheeks. "If you were to encounter someone…anything could happen to you."

"I met you," Lady Harriet pointed out. "So, forgive me for seeing no harm in this. Quite on the contrary."

Determinedly, Bradley ignored that wave of warmth that rolled over his heart at her words. "What if you had encountered someone… less honorable?" he said carefully, barely able to meet her eyes.

A grin teased her lips before a look of feigned apprehension fell over her face. "What do you suppose could have happened if I had met…a less honorable man?"

Bradley gritted his teeth. This was definitely not a topic to discuss with a lady, even a less than proper one like Lady Harriet.

That slow smile once more returned to her face as she stepped closer, leisure steps closing the distance between them. Her wide green eyes looked up into his as Bradley all but held his breath. "Sweet Jack, are you worried someone might take advantage of me?"

For a brief moment, Bradley felt as though his head were about to explode. "I insist you stop calling me that!" he hissed, hoping to distract her from the mortification that burned in his cheeks.

The smile upon Lady Harriet's face told him that he failed miserably. "Call you what?" she asked. "Jack? Or sweet?"

"Both," Bradley ground out. "It isn't proper."

"And should I not worry about *you* taking advantage of me?" Lady Harriet asked all of a sudden.

Bradley felt his eyes go wide in shock, briefly concerned that they might pop out of his head. "Of course not! I would never—! I—!" He clamped his lips shut, belatedly realizing that she was once again teasing him.

"I know, sweet Jack," the hellion assured him with a devilish smile. "But are you not worried that I," she suddenly moved closer, her hands coming to rest upon his chest as she lifted her face to hold his gaze, "might take advantage of you?" For a brief moment, her green eyes remained upon his before they suddenly grew closer as she pushed herself up onto her toes. Her hands slid to his shoulders, and before Bradley knew what was happening, he felt her lips brush a kiss onto his left cheek.

Time stopped.

Rooted to the spot, Bradley forgot to breathe. He still felt the soft pressure of her delicate hands upon his shoulders, of her body leaning against his, her heartbeat far calmer than his own. Her breath teased his skin, and he felt goosebumps break out all over his body at the feather-light touch of her lips.

And then, time resumed its normal pace, and he found himself looking down into Lady Harriet's smiling face. "You're almost too tall to kiss, Jack."

Stunned by what had just happened as well as that nonsensical statement, Bradley pulled away. "You need to go home," he growled, then stepped around her and strode over to where Shine stood grazing next to Lady Harriet's mare. "Now!" he added without bothering to look over his shoulder.

"I apologize if that was forward of me, Jack," he heard her say, "but—"

"Go home!" he growled once again, gathering Shine's reins and then working to undo the knot before swinging himself into the saddle. All the while, Bradley kept his gaze firmly fixed on anything but Lady Harriet, the grass beneath his boots, Shine's chestnut coat, the far horizon.

"Jack, wait! I—"

Bradley pulled his mare around, and his gaze collided with Lady Harriet's. "I apologize for my lack of judgement, my lady, in remaining here with you for as long as I have." He gave her a brief nod. "Farewell." Then he turned Shine around and kicked her flanks, relieved when she sprang forward without a moment of hesitation.

"Jack!" he heard Lady Harriet call after him once or twice before the wind as well as the distance, he was finally—finally!—putting between them carried her voice away.

On and on, Bradley rode, never once turning to look over his shoulder as his father's last words echoed in his head. *I knew I loved her the first time I kissed her. I knew it even then. If only I hadn't. If only I had never kissed her. Promise me you won't repeat my foolish mistakes. Promise me.*

And Bradley had promised his father. He had promised because he had known how his mother's death had devastated his father in every way.

From one day to the next, the kind-hearted, cheerful man Bradley had known all his life had been gone. Often had he wondered if his father would have rather followed his mother to the grave than continue on living a life that no longer held any meaning for him.

Bradley dimly remembered happier times when his parents had both been alive. He remembered picnics in the meadows surrounding Laurelwood Manor. He remembered evenings spent in front of its cozy fireplace, listening to his father's soothing voice as he had read to him and his mother. He remembered laughter and tears dried with a comforting hand.

Bradley did not remember those moments well. What he did remember well were the ones that had come after.

His father's sorrow.

His grief.

His anger.

And finally, his regret.

The realization had come in the year after his mother's passing when his father regretted having lost his heart to her all those years ago. He regretted having met her. Most importantly, he regretted ever having kissed her.

To his father, it had been that moment that had sealed his fate. It had been that moment when his heart had become hers.

That kiss.

That first kiss.

And after years of not being a father to Bradley, he had wrenched that promise from his son on his deathbed. Bradley knew it had been the one thought his father had clung to over the years. And Bradley had promised, had savored the moment because it had brought his father back into his life.

If only for a moment.

For a short, fleeting moment before his father had closed his eyes and finally—finally!—joined his wife in the grave.

That moment, that promise had been Bradley's only remaining connection to his father, to a past he now barely remembered. And he had clung to it, clung to it with all his might. He had promised, and he had kept that promise.

Until today.

CHAPTER TEN
FAMILY REUNION

On the ride back to Pinewood Manor, Harriet continued to see that shocked, and yet forlorn look on Jack's face. She could not be certain what specifically had shocked him in such a way that he had all but fled her presence. Could it have been that quick peck on his cheek?

He had run from her immediately afterward, so it was reasonable to assume that it lay at the root of his reaction. But why?

As Pinewood Manor came into view, Harriet saw with one glance that the rest of her family had arrived. Three carriages waited in the drive, and countless footmen scrambled to unload trunks and chests. She spotted her parents embracing Christina, who welcomed them graciously to her new home.

"Off by herself," their sister Louisa remarked as Harriet pulled Moon to a halt. "What a familiar sight!" A wide grin stretched across her face.

Harriet returned it, then jumped out of the saddle, tossing the reins to a stable boy who came running over. "Not unlike another sister I know. What was her name again? I believe it begins with an 'L'."

A feigned frown came to Louisa's face as she turned quizzical eyes to their other sister, Leonora. Although Leonora's disposition was quite opposite to Louisa's and Harriet's, she, too, had done a fair bit of sneaking off when first becoming acquainted with her future husband. Perhaps secrecy was in their blood!

Embracing her sister, Harriet smiled at her brother-in-law Phineas, a thick-headed daredevil with a good heart. "She has not yet ripped your head off?" She grinned at her sister. "Miracles do happen after all."

While Phineas laughed, Louisa rolled her eyes at Harriet and then at her husband. "You have to admit she is not wrong," Phineas interjected before Louisa could say what no doubt was at the tip of her tongue. "You've threatened to do so more than..." His gaze drifted off in thought, and for a second, Harriet thought he might start counting off the instances upon his fingers. He would need a lot more fingers to get close to the actual number!

Chuckling, Harriet embraced her only brother Troy—eldest of the Whickerton siblings—and then Leonora. "You're smiling again," she whispered to her, knowing the hardship her sister had suffered recently. "And I suppose we have your husband to thank for that."

Leonora blushed very becomingly, her eyes wandering to her husband Drake, a man best described in three words: tall, dark and scowling. Still, beneath that hard exterior beat a very kind and devoted heart.

"Hello Harriet," Drake greeted her with one of his tentative smiles. "Have you accumulated any more animals since last we saw each other?"

"Not yet," she told him with a grin, then added quietly in her mind, *Perhaps one. But he walks on two legs and speaks in full sentences.*

"Are you serious?" Leonora asked with a bit of a disbelieving look upon her face. "After you gave that talking parrot to Christina as a parting gift, I thought for certain you would *stumble* upon another creature in need within a week or two."

"I resent that," Harriet told her sister with a look of deepest, although feigned, outrage. "I don't stumble. I—"

"Harry!" Their father's quiet voice instantly made her turn, a wide smile coming to her face as she saw her parents striding toward her.

"Oh, I've missed you, darling girl." He embraced her, and she leaned her head against his shoulder.

"I missed you, too, Father." She smiled up at him, then turned to hug her mother. "The both of you. What are you doing here now? I thought you would not arrive until mid-summer." She looked from one parent to the other, her mother's pale blue eyes glowing with utter joy as they swept over her children. "Oh, what can I say," her mother breathed out a sigh. "We couldn't wait. *I* couldn't wait to see all my children under the same roof once more."

Her father laughed, a deep, warm sound, then grasped Harriet's chin and looked deep into her eyes. "Why? Are we inconveniencing you?" His gaze narrowed, but the smile upon his lips remained. "I can all but see the cogs in your head turning. You're up to something. You've got that same look upon your face my mother always gets when she pretends to be innocent."

Harriet laughed. Indeed, there were worse compliments than being compared to their shrewd grandmother. "Am I not allowed my secrets?" she challenged good-naturedly.

Her father's lips twisted into something almost painful. "You are," he admitted begrudgingly. "But they make me very uncomfortable." He heaved a deep sigh. "Please, promise me to be careful."

Harriet held her father's gaze, touched by his concern and restraint. "I promise, Father."

He nodded, then turned to his wife. "Let's step inside then and meet that granddaughter of ours I've heard so much about." Indeed, Harriet could feel excitement humming in the air, for her family had yet to meet little Samantha.

As a babe, Samantha's true mother had placed her upon Thorne's doorstep and then vanished, never to be seen again. Thorne had raised her all these years, had become her father and been utterly relieved to see his new wife and daughter bonding over the past few weeks. Although Harriet had to admit that Christina seemed to be a natural at mothering the little girl, it felt odd to see her slightly elder sister acting so mature, so grown-up. Yes, becoming a mother truly had changed Christina.

They spent the afternoon most delightfully as a family, sitting together, exchanging stories and simply enjoying being all together once more after weeks apart. Although wide-eyed and a little fearful in the beginning, Samantha soon warmed to her new family, clearly cherishing all the attention each one of them lavished upon her. She smiled and giggled, danced across the drawing room, doing little pirouettes, and then proudly presented Biscuit.

"He can talk," Sam told everyone with pride in her eyes as they glided over her new feathered friend. The parrot, in turn, continued to sit rather sleepily on the armrest of a chair, gazing at the assembled family as though he were used to being gawked at by large groups. "He often repeats words." She turned to the red-feathered parrot. "You're a good boy, Biscuit."

"*Biscuit! Biscuit!*" The parrot squawked. "*Good boy! Good boy*!"

Everybody laughed and clapped, suddenly delighted with the same bird they had claimed was nothing more than a nuisance not too long ago.

Harriet sighed, wondering if perhaps it had a bit more to do with Samantha than the bird. Whatever the reason, she did not mind, but she was relieved that Biscuit had found a wonderful home and that Samantha was so delighted with him.

That night, Harriet lay awake for far too long, her thoughts returning to earlier that day, reliving the moment Jack had turned and fled. A part of her felt impatient, a desperate need to know, to understand pulsing in her veins. What had happened? How had she offended him?

Long before she finally fell asleep, Harriet knew that the very next day she would return to the meadow, hoping to see Jack again, hoping to clear up whatever misunderstanding stood between them. Even though she knew it was futile, Harriet's thoughts continued to linger, to circle, unable to focus on anything else but her need to understand what had happened. She barely spoke after seating herself at the breakfast table the next morning, and before long, her observant family noticed, casting curious glances in her direction.

"Are you well?" Christina finally asked, leaning closer. Still, Harriet knew well that the rest of their family was listening closely.

Harriet shrugged. "Why ever would you think I am not?"

Christina scoffed, and Harriet detected a few eye rolls and suppressed grins coming to the others' faces. "Truthfully, I cannot recall a day with you saying as little as you have this morning. It is worrisome." She looked up, her eyes looking around the table, waiting for agreeable nods before returning to look at Harriet. "Very worrisome."

Harriet shrugged. "It is nothing," she told her sister as well as the rest of her family, still reluctant to reveal her secret, especially now, especially when she felt so uncertain. "I simply have a lot on my mind. That is all." Unfortunately, it seemed her words did not convince her family because they continued to look at her with quizzical expressions on their faces, their brows slightly drawn down in concern. "I believe I shall go for an early ride," Harriet declared after shooting to her feet, unable to bear their interest and concern a moment longer.

Before anyone could object or offer to accompany her, Harriet rushed from the breakfast parlor. She quickly changed and then headed down to the stables, where Moon waited for her eagerly. "Are you in the mood for a run, girl?" Harriet whispered, scratching her mare behind the ears. "I am as well."

Waving away the stable boy that rushed over, offering his assistance, Harriet saddled Moon herself. As always, she cherished doing things that were not expected of her, that she was not even supposed to do. It felt good. It made her feel strong, as though she were swimming against the tide and continued to do so, never once daring to tire for fear of being swept away.

The moment Harriet raced Moon across the meadow, she felt her heart grow lighter. A wide smile came to her face, and she briefly closed her eyes as the wind washed over her, tugging upon her hair. The sun shone warmly upon her back, and all around her, the world seemed to glow, the different shades of vibrant green, a beautiful contrast to the soft blue glow of the sky, here and there interspersed with snow-white clouds.

Harriet's heart soared...and then plummeted when Moon swept around the outer border of the forest and headed down into the meadow where she had met Jack the day before.

Only now, it lay deserted.

"He might still come," Harriet reassured herself as her eyes swept over the endless sea of tall grass stalks, gently swaying in the breeze. "I am early. He might still come."

And so, Harriet lingered in the meadow, alternating between riding back and forth between the forest's edge and allowing Moon to graze freely while Harriet herself wandered around rather aimlessly, picking a flower here and there before tossing it aside.

Again and again, her eyes searched the sky in the direction from whence Jack had come the day before. Was he merely late? Or would he not come at all?

Jack had struck her as a creature of habit. Had he not said as much? Harriet could not recall; however, she was fairly certain that Jack was the kind of person who knew exactly what he would do every day of the week. If not today, would he come tomorrow?

Harriet heaved a deep sigh, annoyed with herself for allowing this to bother her so much. Why did it? After all, he was no one to her. They had barely even met, spoken to one another upon no more than two occasions. Why was it that his absence bothered her so?

Eventually, Harriet gave up and turned Moon towards home, towards Pinewood Manor. Perhaps a race through the gardens with Samantha would take her mind off things.

Unfortunately, the next three days brought no sign of Jack. Harriet did not know how many hours she lingered in the meadow, eyes again and again turning toward the horizon, her heart clenching in her chest as she waited and hoped. Slowly, anger found its way into her heart that he would cast her aside so easily. Had she truly offended him so deeply? That he would stay away without even a word?

Harriet heaved a deep sigh, reminding herself that he owed her nothing. She clearly was no one to him, no one of importance at least. He had found her bothersome, had he not?

Feeling deeply distraught, Harriet was brushing down Moon upon returning to Pinewood Manor when the soft thump of Grandma Edie's walking cane drifted to her ears. She looked up and found the old woman hobbling toward her, eyes slightly narrowed in contemplation.

Harriet heaved a deep sigh, well aware that her chances of keeping anything from her grandmother were slim to none. "What are you doing out here? It's a rather far walk from the house, wouldn't you say?"

A knowing grin came to her grandmother's face when she stopped outside Moon's stall. "I wish to speak with you, and I do not wish to be overheard."

Harriet patted Moon's neck and stepped from the stall. "What is it, Grandmother?"

Her grandmother's pale eyes watched her intently before she spoke. "You've met the Duke of Clements?"

Despite her own suspicions, Harriet gave a brief start at her grandmother's blunt words. "So, he *was* the reason you sent me westward?"

Grandma Edie nodded.

"Why?" Harriet asked, wondering why her grandmother had wanted them to meet. Was she playing matchmaker again? Indeed, Harriet was almost certain that three of her older sisters had only recently found husbands and been married thanks to their grandmother's covert meddling!

A saddened expression came to Grandma Edie's eyes. "Although he does not mingle much, I've seen him at the occasional ball, and whenever I did, he seemed...lost." Her pale eyes met Harriet's, something imploring in them. "Are you not one to help lost souls?" A teasing grin came to her lips. "I thought perhaps you could help him."

Harriet heaved a deep sigh. "He does not want my help." With her shoulders slumped, she leaned back against the stall. "He does not even want my company."

Her grandmother chuckled. "I never knew you were one to give up easily." Her brows rose in challenge.

Harriet grinned. "I have no intention of giving up, however..." Her words trailed off as she remembered Jack riding off the last day she had seen him.

"However?" her grandmother prompted, something resembling mischievous delight sparkling in her eyes.

Harriet straightened, feeling a new sense of determination sweep through her. "You're right," she mumbled as she pictured Jack's forlorn-looking face. "I should not give up. If he refuses to come to me," she turned to look at her grandmother, "then perhaps I should go to him."

"That's my girl," Grandma Edie beamed, tapping her cane onto the cobbled stones of the stable floor. "If I'm not mistaken, Clements Park is only half an hour away. I'm certain you can find it."

Harriet hugged her grandmother. "Thank you." She stood back. "You know Father would roll his eyes at you if he knew you were *advising* me to sneak off, don't you?"

Grandma Edie chuckled. "My son has been rolling his eyes at me all his life, and I'm still here." She grinned. "Do what you deem right. That's precisely what I've been doing for as long as I can remember."

Laughing, Harriet hugged her grandmother again. "Thank you. Tomorrow, I shall heed your words and see what Jack says." Harriet could easily imagine his face draining of all remaining blood the moment he caught sight of her, undoubtedly believing her unchaperoned appearance upon his property a grave mistake.

Harriet could not disagree more; still, she had to chuckle. He truly was a sweet man!

"Jack?" her grandmother inquired with raised eyebrows and a teasing smile curling up her lips.

Harriet smiled. "Yes, Jack."

CHAPTER ELEVEN
TO LIE OR NOT TO LIE

Staring at a sheet of parchment that might as well have been blank for all it told him, Bradley sighed, then closed his eyes and rested his head upon his hands. Why was it he suddenly could not seem to concentrate? Why was it that his thoughts all too often seemed to stray to a red-haired hellion?

A red-haired hellion he had not seen in four days.

Lifting his head, Bradley drew in a deep breath, his eyes sweeping over the familiar sight of his study: tall shelves, his great-grandfather's desk upon which rested the same silver ink pot at least three generations of Jacksons had used before him—

Jack.

Bradley cursed under his breath. Why was it so blasted hard to concentrate these days? He could not possibly...be...missing... her...could he?

Bradley shook his head, everything within him flinching away from the thought. It was preposterous! He barely knew her. Perhaps he was simply lacking in company; although, admittedly, it had never bothered him before. Quite on the contrary, Bradley had always cherished solitude.

A knock upon his door made Bradley almost jump out of his skin.

This had to stop! "Yes," he bellowed, more at himself than at his butler.

A deep frown line showed upon the man's face as he entered. "Begging your pardon, your grace, but there is a...lady here who insists on seeing you."

Bradley's heart stilled in his chest, for he did not miss that small, but significant, pause before his butler spoke the word *lady* as though Arnold was not quite certain the term applied.

"A lady?" Bradley inquired, trying his best to remain calm. "Did she...give a name?" Oh, he did not doubt that the hellion would be foolish enough to do so! What on earth was she doing here? Did she truly have no care for her reputation? Bradley doubted very much that she had come in company of a chaperone.

Arnold cleared his throat, his gaze briefly dropping to the polished hardwood floor. "The...lady said her name was Harry." A bit of a questioning look came to Arnold's face before he took a step backward. "Am I to...?"

"Where is she at present?"

"In the gardens," Arnold said instantly, no doubt relieved to have this uncomfortable conversation come to an end. "She refused to wait in the hall."

"Of course, she did," Bradley mumbled under his breath as he rushed from his study without another word to his befuddled-looking butler. He hastened along the corridor at a pace he could not recall ever having seen reason to use and then out onto the terrace, his eyes sweeping over Clements Park's extensive gardens. Where on earth was she? He could not call out...for many reasons, and he did not feel inclined to search for her all afternoon.

"Jack!" came Lady Harriet's voice from somewhere near the maze. Of course, the hellion wouldn't mind calling out!

Bradley gritted his teeth and turned toward her, barely catching a glimpse of fiery red hair before she disappeared into the maze. Was this a game?

Naturally, Bradley felt no inclination to humor her, to play her game, to give in; however, at present, what choice did he have? He had to remove her from Clements Park before anyone found out that she was here.

Alone.

Without a chaperone.

Lady Harriet might be willing to risk her reputation, her future, but Bradley was not. If she would not see reason, then he would be forced to make this decision for her.

Large strides carried him down a small grassy slope and toward the maze. He occasionally glanced left and right over his shoulder, concerned about how many of his staff had taken note of her arrival and were at present occupied with spreading said information near and far. Why people gossiped was something that had always been beyond Bradley's comprehension. It served no purpose. Quite on the contrary, more often than not, gossip was the very thing that destroyed someone's life.

The sun shone brightly overhead as Bradley entered the maze, his gaze sweeping left and right before he hurried onward, following the path he had seen Lady Harriet take. But where was she? Had she truly walked deeper into the maze, expecting him to follow?

He scoffed. Of course she had! For a reason Bradley could not name, he already knew her quite well, even despite their brief acquaintance. Perhaps it was simply her straightforward character, the honest expression of her thoughts, her disinclination to hide anything.

Indeed, Bradley found her utterly frustrating; yet the honesty in every word she spoke meant he need not doubt her character or question her motives. He liked that. He liked that very much.

Stopping in his tracks, Bradley found himself surrounded by thick leafy hedges, growing higher than his own tall height. He could not see above them nor around them, and knowing how far the maze stretched, he sighed deeply and finally relented. "Lady Harriet!" he called as loudly as he dared, which truthfully was not all that loud.

Still, the hellion immediately materialized from only a few steps away, a wide grin upon her face and an odd sparkle in her eyes as she looked at him. "You called, your grace?" She batted her eyelashes at him, something wickedly amusing dancing across her face before she stepped toward him. "Oh, Jack, this place is wonderful!" Her eyes were wide with awe as they swept over the hedges, and yet her feet continued to dance toward him.

To Bradley, she seemed like a wood sprite or a water nymph or some kind of spirit of the forest. Deep here in the maze, her pale skin glowed in the shaded light, making her seem almost ethereal. Her eyes shone in the deepest shade of green he had ever seen, reminding him of the rolling hills of Ireland. That hair of hers, that fiery, flame-like color wild and untamed, but also soft and smooth, seemed to possess a life of its own as it curled around her head.

Bradley swallowed, then cleared his throat, recalling why he was here. "Are you mad?" he heard himself say, anger hardening his voice. He had not meant to be so blunt, but it seemed Lady Harriet's presence addled his mind. Why else did it seem so impossible for him to convince her to stay away?

Lady Harriet's eyes settled upon his, and he saw a bit of that wondrous glow drain from her face. "Mad?" she asked, and her eyes narrowed as she watched him. "Why would you think that?"

Bradley scoffed. "I thought that was obvious." He looked around them, then shrugged his shoulders. "You're here, are you not? Alone! Again!" He shook his head at her.

Harriet frowned. "Are you truly surprised, Jack? Did I not make it abundantly clear that this is exactly the way I always conduct myself?"

"I suppose I had hoped you were merely jesting." Bradley inhaled a deep breath, overwhelmed by the situation at hand. If she would not take his advice, what was he to do? "Why are you here?"

A soft smile came to her face, and he saw some of that wondrous glow return. "To see you, sweet Jack. Do you truly have to ask?"

Bradley knew he should object to her informal address. He should reprimand her for such improper conduct. He should demand she leave.

Immediately.

Oddly enough, though, Bradley did none of these things. He simply stood and stared at her, her voice, her words echoing in his mind. Indeed, no one had ever sought his company the way she did, and it made him feel...wanted?

Warm and strangely content.

Bradley remembered a dim echo of such a feeling. He had known it before but not since his mother had passed away.

"Are you all right?" Blinking, Bradley found Lady Harriet suddenly standing in front of him, her hands coming to rest upon his chest as her deep green eyes looked up into his. "You look pale." She held his gaze for a moment longer before the bridge of her nose crinkled in thought. "Are you shocked because I am here? Or are you shocked because I am here to see you?"

Bradley swallowed, fighting the impulse to move her away, to put a greater distance between them. He knew he ought to, but, somehow, he did not wish to. "Why...do you wish to see me?" It made no sense, and the world ought to, ought it not?

The corners of her mouth twitched. "I missed you."

Staring at her, Bradley shook his head. "You barely know me."

Lady Harriet shrugged. "Everything I already know about you only makes me want to know you better." Again, her lips twitched, and a deeply enchanting smile came to her face. "You're sweet, Jack, and kind and honest. You think of others before you think of yourself, and you're willing to go to great lengths to protect someone you don't even know," her brows rose in a bit of a mocking gesture, "because you think it the right thing to do." A soft chuckle drifted from her lips. "Is that not so?"

People had called Bradley many things, especially behind his back when they thought he could not hear. No one, however, had ever described him the way Lady Harriet had just now. Was this truly how she saw him? "There is no need to speak falsely simply to—" He broke off when he felt her fingers curl into his lapels and saw her brows draw down into a frown, her eyes sparkling with anger.

"I do not lie." Something almost wounded rested in Lady Harriet's eyes as they looked deep into his, holding on until Bradley finally nodded.

"I apologize, my lady. I did not mean to offend you." He watched her closely, fascinated by the deep emotions he saw.

Exhaling the breath she had been holding, Lady Harriet finally relaxed her hands. They released his lapels and came to lie upon his chest once more. "I know you did not," Lady Harriet whispered, all anger suddenly evaporated into thin air. "Are you...Are you not the least bit happy to see me?"

Bradley knew that this was his chance to rid himself of her, to ensure that she would not return. All he had to do...was lie. He abhorred lying, and yet this lie would serve a greater purpose, would ensure her safety and the protection of her reputation. Was a lie for the right reasons truly still a lie? As bad as one uttered for selfish purposes?

Whatever the answer, the shocking truth was that Bradley could not bring himself to lie because she was right. A part of him buried under demands of etiquette *was* happy to see her.

Dear heavens, how had this happened? She was wrong for him in every way, and yet...he liked her.

In a matter of days...

...he had come to care for the hellion.

CHAPTER TWELVE

A HEART'S DESIRE

Harriet wanted to hug him. There was something so endearingly confused, lost even in his eyes, that Harriet felt the need to comfort him. He had not known, had he? He truly had not known that he cared for her.

Neither had she. At least not until she had seen him, that angry scowl upon his face, as he had hurried down the lawn toward her, obviously determined to remove her from his property as swiftly as possible.

Yes, Harriet had known then that the reason he had stayed away from the meadow these past few days had been that dreadful sense of honor ingrained in him. He had wanted to protect her...even if only from herself.

A part of Harriet felt the need to rebel against such treatment, such patronization. Still, another, quite unfamiliar part of Harriet felt delight at his concern and his willingness to sacrifice in order to see her safe.

"I...am," Jack finally said in an unsteady voice, his words leaving his lips so slowly, as though he was not quite certain he wished to speak them. That look of confusion remained upon his face as his brown eyes narrowed, looking down into her face as though trying to make sense of something.

"But you don't want to be, do you?" Harriet asked, hoping to lighten the mood.

Instead, a deeply contrite look came to Jack's face. "No, I do not." A muscle in his jaw tensed, and he took a step backward.

Harriet's hands fell from his chest, her arms once more hanging limply at her sides. "Why?" It was a single word, a simple question, and yet Harriet could not help the feeling that she had never dreaded an answer more.

The truth was that she wanted him to like her, to care for her, to want to see her. It was the way she felt about him, and the thought that he might not feel the same bothered her more that she liked to admit.

For a long moment, Jack did not say a word, the look in his eyes distant as though he was deeply lost in thought. Then he cleared his throat. "You should return home. Now."

"I will not leave until you answer me," Harriet insisted, unwilling to leave this question hanging in the air between them.

His jaw hardened. "You should not have come." His eyes narrowed, looking at her pointedly. "Does your family know that you are here?" He scoffed. "Of course, they do not. What—?"

"Yes, they do!" The words flew from her lips before Harriet even realized that what she was protesting against was the idea of him thinking low of her. It nettled her!

His brows quirked upward, disbelief in the way he fixed her with an unflinching look. "Truly?"

Crossing her arms over her chest, Harriet held his gaze, refusing to answer. Yes, strictly speaking, her family did not know. The only one who knew was Grandma Edie, who, of course, was family as well... simply not all the family she had.

Jack shook his head. "And they do not object?" His head continued shaking from side to side. "You might not be in any rush to marry, but surely your parents must know that if your...transgressions became known, there would never be a chance for a suitable match. I find it hard to believe that they do not care."

Harriet heaved a deep breath. "Jack, perhaps I have not made myself clear before. I will not marry! Not now! Not ever!" She held his gaze, feeling no small sense of frustration rising within her at that dumbfounded look upon his face. He did not understand her. She might as well have spoken to him in an unfamiliar language for all the sense she had made. Harriet knew that. What she did not know was how to make him understand.

Why was it that women were expected to have no aspirations beyond marriage, while men were allowed to strive for more?

Long moments passed, in which Jack continued to eye her warily. She thought he would speak a couple of times as his mouth opened and closed, thoughts all but written upon his face. He remained quiet, though, considering her, watching her.

Then he straightened, that look in his eyes still as confused as before. "What about...children? Have you considered this?" He swallowed, a look of unease passing over his features. "I've heard women yearn to be mothers." His brows rose in question.

Harriet could not help the smile that came to her face, knowing that the words about to leave her mouth would no doubt shock him witless. "One can have children without being married, don't you know that, sweet Jack?"

As expected, Jack instantly paled, a slight widening of his eyes all that spoke to his surprise at hearing her speak so bluntly or with such knowledge. Harriet wondered which one it was. Perhaps both? "How do *you* know that?"

Harriet laughed at seeing her suspicions confirmed. "Not from personal experience, if that is what you think," she replied with a chuckle. "But I possess eyes and ears as well as a functioning brain. Just like you."

Jack gawked at her, the expression upon his face quite hilarious if it weren't for the hammering pulse in his neck. "You cannot be serious!"

Harriet frowned, refusing to take this seriously. Why did everything in life have to be so serious? "About what?"

"About...About wishing to," he began stuttering, his pale face suddenly darkening with mortification, "to...to bear a child out of wedlock."

Harriet heaved a deep sigh. As much as she adored Jack, his narrow-mindedness was quite tiring. "I never said such a thing."

"You did just now!" he snapped with insistence and outrage alike.

"I merely pointed out that it was a possibility, not that it was my plan." Harriet held his gaze, watching the meaning of her words sink in.

For a moment, Jack seemed relieved before his features hardened again. "Then why are we discussing this?"

"Because you keep bringing it up!" Harriet snapped back, hands on her hips.

A bird trilled in the distance as the two of them stared at one another. Harriet wished she knew his thoughts, for the look upon his face had all but turned blank. Her own emotions were darting back and forth between amusement and annoyance.

"You need to leave," Jack blurted out once more before he spun around on his heel and made to return the way he had come.

"Not before you answer me!" Harriet insisted, digging in her heels —at least metaphorically.

He paused and reluctantly looked over his shoulder at her. "Answer you?"

Harriet nodded. "You admitted you were happy to see me, but you did not tell me why you don't like that you are." She swallowed, surprised to find a lump had settled in her throat. Inhaling deeply, Harriet stepped toward him. "Am I such an awful creature, Jack?" she asked, once again surprised to hear a tremor in her voice. "Am I so horrible that you cannot bear the thought that I might hold a place in your heart?"

At her last words, Harriet watched Jack's blanch in a way that seemed to rock him back on his heels. Yet his eyes no longer saw her but had turned to something or someone long ago.

Harriet could see it upon his face. She could tell from the way his hands balled into fists and the pulse in his neck seemed to pause for the briefest of moments. But who?

"I'm sorry," Harriet whispered as she tried to meet his eyes. "I did not mean to..." Her voice trailed off, for she did not know what her words had done to him.

Jack cleared his throat. "It is nothing." The look in his eyes softened. "You should leave."

Harriet heaved a heavy sigh. "I will," she relented, "but only if you promise to meet me tomorrow morning in our meadow."

"Our meadow?" Jack echoed her words, that look of confusion back upon his face. Only this time, Harriet thought to see a hint of incredulity as well.

"Yes, our meadow."

He regarded her cautiously. "If I meet you, you will leave?" His brows rose questioningly.

Harriet nodded.

"Why?"

Slowly, Harriet reached out until the tips of her fingers brushed against the sleeve of his jacket. She watched his eyes follow the movement, his shoulders unmoving as though he had forgotten to draw breath. "Because I wish to see you again, sweet Jack."

He swallowed. "And so you resort to blackmail?" His voice was hard, but Harriet thought to hear a whisper of delight linger there as well.

Smiling at him, she shrugged. "A girl has to do what she must."

That endearing frown came to his face once more before he sighed. "Very well. Tomorrow."

Harriet nodded, feeling like a general who had snatched victory from the jaws of defeat. "Tomorrow."

CHAPTER THIRTEEN

THE WORLD TURNS

Returning to Pinewood Manor, Harriet knew that something was going on the moment she stepped into the hall. Everything looked as it always did, and yet everything felt not quite as usual. Harriet could not put her finger on it, but she felt it like a shiver trailing down her spine.

A murmur seemed to hang in the air, whispers echoing along the corridors only to fall silent the moment she approached.

Changing out of her riding habit, Harriet went in search of her family, surprised to find them huddled in the drawing room, their faces tense with apprehension.

"We cannot know for certain if she is who she claims to be," her brother Troy cautioned, his right forefinger raised in warning as his gaze moved from Thorne to their father and back. "You cannot truly mean to trust her word?"

Thorne shook his head. "Of course not. I will send someone to investigate her story; however, until we know more, she and her son will remain here."

Harriet frowned. "What happened?" she asked, looking from her brother to the rest of her family. All of them looked somewhat ill at ease; only Grandma Edie sat leisurely in an armchair, eyes half-closed as though drifting off to sleep.

Christina drew in a deep breath, exchanged a meaningful look with her husband and then stepped toward Harriet, taking her hand. "A woman showed up earlier today," Christina told her quietly as the rest of their family resumed their discussion, "claiming to be Samantha's mother."

Harriet felt her jaw drop. "What?" She looked around the room but could not spot the little girl. "Who is she? What is she doing here now? After all these years?"

Christina's face seemed pale and strained, a slight tremble in her hands as they held Harriet's.

"You're worried," Harriet remarked, pulling her sister aside. "Do you not believe her? What does she want?"

Christina heaved a deep sigh. "I don't know." She shrugged her shoulders helplessly. "She said she lost her husband shortly before Samantha was born, and as she had another sickly child, she could not keep her."

"Another sickly child?"

"Owen." Christina nodded, and Harriet could see compassion soften her sister's tense features. "He is perhaps two years older than Sam." The look in her eyes darkened. "He...He cannot walk." She exhaled. "Oh, Harry, but it is not even that, but the way he lashes out at every kind word spoken to him as though..."

"As though he always expects the worst because that is what he knows," Harriet finished for her sister, finally understanding that look of anguish in Christina's eyes.

"Yes."

"Where are they? The boy and his mother?"

Again, Christina looked to her husband, and Thorne paused in his explanation to smile at her. "They are upstairs," Christina replied as her gaze moved back to her sister. "We agreed they could stay...for now."

"Does Sam know?"

Her sister's eyes widened. "No, not until we know her story is true."

Harriet nodded. "That is wise. And Sam? Where is she?"

"With Mrs. Huxley."

Harriet did not like the rotund and overly stern governess, but at least the woman would keep Samantha safely away from the newcomers until the family could swarm around her again.

Wicked or not, the Whickertons were fiercely protective of their own...and Samantha was now one of them.

Heaving a deep sigh, Harriet hoped with all her heart that this would end well. She could no longer imagine a life without Samantha and knew her family felt the same. The girl belonged with them now.

But what if this woman truly was Samantha's mother? What then?

Never in his life had Bradley felt torn about anything. Every step he took down the corridor, then out the door and toward the stables, even as he led Shine out into the sunlight, seemed to be weighted with lead. There was a whisper in his head, urging him to turn back, to rethink this and change his mind. He ought not ride off and meet a young lady without someone suitable to chaperone.

It was not right.

It was not proper.

Quite frankly, it was wrong.

Yet, oddly enough, his feet kept moving, and before Bradley knew what was happening, he sat atop Shine, all but charging down the drive. He felt something humming in his limbs, an eagerness that sped his pulse and made him impatient. Never had Bradley experienced such a sensation. Yes, perhaps he remembered a dull echo of it from his childhood, but it was nothing more than that: a vague memory. Nothing to hold on to. Nothing to pinpoint.

The moment the meadow came into view, Bradley reined in Shine, his eyes widening as they searched his surroundings. It took only a second or two for them to land upon a young woman standing in the clearing, her flame-like hair billowing in the wind as she gathered a bouquet of wildflowers in her hand, her dapple-gray mare grazing patiently nearby.

Bradley felt himself breathe in deeply, his chest rising and falling with the weight of this moment. It was such a peaceful and soothing scene, and it called to him.

Approaching quietly, Bradley waited for when she would notice his presence. A part of him felt as though he ought to alert her to it, that it was not right to watch her the way he did. Only his lips would not move, nor would his tongue form any words. And so, he continued on, allowing Shine to pick her own path across the meadow, his eyes glued to the most infuriating, and yet utterly bewitching woman he had ever known.

Indeed, Lady Harriet was a far cry from the woman Bradley thought he would marry one day. She was nothing like a woman of the peerage ought to be. She was wrong for him in every way.

Still...

The moment she looked up and their eyes met, Bradley thought he would slide straight out of the saddle. An enormous smile transformed her face, made it glow in a way that made him ache, her eyes wide and shining, beckoning him closer. "Jack!" she called, waving the bouquet of wildflowers over her head.

Never had anyone felt such joy at seeing him, and Bradley had a hard time believing that it was truly because of him. That he was the reason for the happiness that shone upon her lovely features. For a moment, he felt tempted to turn and look over his shoulder, certain that she could not possibly mean him!

"Good morning, Lady Harriet," Bradley greeted her before he slipped out of the saddle, granting Shine the same freedom Lady Harriet had given to Moon. "I hope you are well."

An amused chuckle left her lips. "Oh, Jack, must you always be so formal?" She strode toward him, that delighted smile still upon her face. "Will you not call me Harry or at least Harriet?"

"I cannot," Bradley replied instantly. "It wouldn't be proper." Yet the thought of calling her...Harry...

Bradley almost smiled as she rolled her eyes at him. "I will not give up, you know?" She stepped toward him, the bouquet of wildflowers raised like a warning finger pointed at him. "One day. Mark my words. One day, you shall call me Harry." She stopped only a step in front of him, her light green eyes looking up into his, the corners of her mouth curled up in challenge. "One day."

Inclining his head to her, Bradley held her gaze, completely mesmerized. "I would have expected nothing less from you, my lady." Where on earth had this sudden fascination come from? It was most inconvenient; after all, she would never be his bride. He could not have her; he did not *wish* to have her. She was not the kind of woman he was meant to marry. He wanted a level-headed, well-behaved and not at all sarcastic wife. Yes, he wished for a quiet life, and finding himself married to a hellion like Lady Harriet would no doubt be hell on earth.

The moment the thought crossed Bradley's mind, he had to admit at least to himself, that suddenly hell no longer seemed like such a terrible place to find oneself in.

"Will you walk with me, Jack?"

Nodding, Bradley fell into step beside her, feeling a slight frown descend upon his forehead at the way she bowed her head, her own thoughts clearly drifting elsewhere. Had something happened? Indeed, he now saw small signs of unease, a lingering tension in her shoulders as well as a tightness in her jaw. Something had happened!

"Are you all right?" Bradley finally asked after they had walked beside one another without a word spoken for over a minute at least. "You seem...concerned."

Lady Harriet paused in her steps, then turned to look at him with wide eyes before a slow smile curled up the corners of her mouth. "You know me too well, Jack. I like that."

Bradley almost flinched at her words. Did he? How could he possibly know her after such a brief acquaintance? But...yes...he liked it as well.

Heaven help him, but he liked *her*.

CHAPTER FOURTEEN
TO FEEL AGAIN

Harriet enjoyed the way Jack was looking at her. It was neither a stare nor a fleeting glance. It did not speak of reluctance, suggesting he only inquired out of obligation. No, his brown eyes were warm as they looked down into hers, and she saw in them the deep need to help, to understand. She saw his concern, concern for her, for her well-being, and she knew that despite his best efforts to the contrary, he truly cared for her.

Heaving a deep breath, Harriet told Jack about Mrs. Miller and her son, about the threat to her family, the threat that they might lose Samantha. "I only met her a few weeks ago, and yet," she sighed and looked up at him, "she is my little niece. I do not want to lose her. I don't know what will happen, and a part of me does not truly believe that we *will* lose her, but..." She shook her head, unable to put into words what had robbed her of sleep the night before.

Jack nodded, understanding in his gaze despite her inability to explain herself properly. "There is no certainty," he finally said. "Whether you like it or not, you cannot know what will happen."

"No, I cannot." She took a few steps and then turned around to look at him. "Perhaps I am being unfair, but a part of me cannot help but think that Mrs. Miller is not telling us the truth. I've seen her with her son. She is a most devoted mother. It took only five minutes to realize that."

Earlier that morning, Harriet had watched little Samantha try her utmost to lure Owen out of his shell. The boy had a continuous scowl upon his face, eyeing the world around him with disdain and rejection. His mother had been by his side, never straying far, constantly attuned to any need he might have, which was not a surprise considering that he could not walk, could not help himself.

"If that is the case," Jack began, his eyes searching hers as he took a step forward, "then what is your concern? If she is a devoted mother to her son, would it then not also be safe to assume that she would treat Samantha the same way?"

Harriet frowned, recalling the moment. "But she does not. Yes, she has not seen the girl in years, not since she gave her up shortly after birth. But would that not be all the more reason to be curious, to seek a connection?" She shook her head. "She's polite and kind to her, but she volunteers nothing of herself. She does not seek closeness. She treats Samantha...like a stranger's child." Again, she shook her head. "Not like her own."

For a long moment, Jack remained quiet, his gaze suddenly distant, as though her words had made him recall something he had not thought of in a long time. "You don't know what happened," he finally said, his words barely a whisper, his gaze still not directed at her. "Loving one's child does not come easily to everyone. Sometimes, even our best intentions are not enough. We might wish for something, but that does not change the fact that it is outside our reach." He swallowed, then blinked, and his gaze once more found hers...but only for a second before he turned away abruptly, his gaze straying to the far horizon.

"Jack?" Harriet whispered carefully, well aware of the tension that lingered in his shoulders. She saw the way he held his hands linked behind his back as though needing the movement to square his shoulders, to remain formidable and not give into emotions that had once threatened to tear him apart. She could all but feel his pain, could see it on his face even from where she stood, even considering the way he held himself away from her. His face turned toward something safer than her inquisitive eyes. He clearly wished for her to leave him alone, but would that ultimately serve him? Or would it simply assure that he would forever remain alone in this?

Whatever *this* was?

Slowly, Harriet stepped around him. The bouquet of wildflowers slipped from her fingers as her eyes searched his face.

It remained stoic, immobile, no emotion visible as he stared straight ahead. Everything within him remained rigid, a rock able to face the tides of time.

"Jack?" Harriet whispered as she came to stand in front of him, her eyes looking up into his face. Only his own never moved to look into hers but continued to stare over her head at the far horizon.

As much as Harriet longed to know what occupied his thoughts, she could tell from the steely expression in his eyes that he would not share them with her. She had known long before today that Jack was not used to sharing with another what he felt in his heart. She wondered if he had ever done so, if there had ever been a time when there had been someone in his life, someone who had cared. What about his parents? His mother? His father?

Harriet burned to ask but realized it was not what he needed. He could not speak to her about it. Not now. Perhaps one day, but that day had not yet come. Still, what he needed was...comfort, compassion... someone who cared.

If not with words, then...

Praying that he would not flee from her once more, Harriet slowly closed the remaining distance between them. She reached out, her hands sliding around him, underneath his arms, still linked behind his back. Her head came to rest against his shoulder, and she could feel his heartbeat against her own. She leaned into him and held him tightly, hoping that it would be enough, that he would know that she cared.

Bradley had not expected this. It had been a long time since he had felt that heavy weight upon his chest, like a boulder attached to his feet dragging him down, holding him underwater as he fought to breathe.

Yes, it had been a long time. So long that Bradley had expected himself to be able to handle it now.

Yet, in that moment, he once again felt like that little boy he had once been, from one day to the next, left alone by everyone he had held dear.

Suddenly, his world had darkened, plunged into a black void. Everything had been hard and cold, and he remembered shivering uncontrollably.

Day after day.

Week after week.

Month after month.

Year after y—

The moment Bradley felt Lady Harriet's hands upon him, he found his breath lodge in his throat. He had not even noticed her approach, so lost had he been in his own past.

And then, from one moment to the next, his entire being seemed to zone in on her. He felt her drift closer, her arms coming around him, embracing him, holding him to her. Her head rested against his shoulder, her wild curls tickling the skin of his neck. He could feel the steady beat of her heart against his own, a calming presence to counteract his own wild emotions. Where had these emotions come from after all this time? He had thought them all but lost, a rational mind that could not be influenced by his heart's desires the only thing left. He thought he had silenced his emotions, never expecting to feel them again.

Bradley felt that old shiver sneak up his spine once more, and his muscles tensed of their own accord, readying themselves for battle. Only now there was her.

Her warmth.

Her embrace.

Her steady heartbeat.

Bradley wanted to reach out to her. He wanted to lean in and hold her. He wanted to keep her where she was until the end of time.

But he could not.

His body was trained to remain stoic, to not give in. Long years had taught him that he was alone in this world and that he could rely on no one but himself.

Lady Harriet was here now. But would she still be tomorrow?

Yet the moment she pulled away, her arms loosening their hold on him, something inside Bradley snapped.

All of a sudden, he could not bear the thought of being apart from her, of losing that warmth, that closeness. His hands released their vice-like grip on one another, and then his arms moved to embrace her before she could slip away. He pulled her back against him, hearing a slight gasp leave her lips as his arms tightened around her almost possessively.

Bradley knew he ought not embrace her, but he could not help himself. And so, he held her, resting his chin on the top of her head and breathing in that wild, untamed scent of her that reminded him of the flowers growing all around them.

And Lady Harriet let him.

Without a moment's hesitation, she leaned back into his embrace, her arms slipping around his middle once more, hugging him back. "I'm here," she whispered, and he could feel her warm breath upon his left hand as it lay upon her shoulder, holding her to him. "I'm here with you, Jack."

Jack. Her name for him from the start. It was inappropriate and scandalous...and Bradley loved it. He was not supposed to, but he did.

For so long, all he had concerned himself with had been those many expectations put on him from the world around him. He had only ever thought of what he was *expected to do*, of what he was *supposed to do*, of what he *ought to do*.

And then *she* had come...and upended his world.

Inhaling a deep breath, Bradley loosened his hold on her. His chin slid from the top of her head, and he looked down at her, his eyes finding hers. "A fortnight ago," he mumbled under his breath, amazed to see golden flecks flicker in the deep green of her eyes, "I did not even know you existed, and now..."

The smile that came to her face nearly brought him to his knees. Bradley could not recall ever having felt this vulnerable; at least not since he had been a boy.

Her left hand reached out to cup his cheek, a feather-light touch that he felt to the very core of his bones. "I'm your friend, Jack. Of course, I'm here."

Bradley swallowed, unable to fight that bitter taste of abandonment he could not seem to shake. "For how long?" he all but growled, his teeth gritted together painfully.

Instead of taking affront at his words or tone of voice, Lady Harriet half-smiled and half-rolled her eyes at him. "Oh, Jack," she chided, then moved her hand to grasp his chin the moment his eyes strayed from hers. "For always," she told him, "if you let me."

Staring down at her, Bradley wanted to believe her. More than that, he needed to believe her. It was an almost desperate need that suddenly pulsed to life in his heart, a need he no longer had the strength to quell, to stamp into dust, to eviscerate without mercy.

He knew he ought not speak. He knew he ought not say these words, but he could not help it. They flew from his lips with nothing holding them back, fighting their way out into the world. "Marry me."

Oh, dear goodness, what had he done?

CHAPTER FIFTEEN

TWO WORDS

"Marry me."

Those two little words shocked Harriet more than anything she had ever experienced in her life. Jack, too, looked thunderstruck. Clearly, he had not meant to say them. It had been...the magic of the moment. Nothing more. He had needed comfort, and she had answered his call.

"Jack, I—"

Abruptly, his arms released her, his eyes suddenly unable to meet hers. "I apologize, my lady." He took a step back, away from her, and then another. "I ought not have..." His voice trailed off, and she saw his jaw grit together tightly.

"I understand," Harriet hastened to say, relieved when he dared look at her once more, a slight frown upon his face. "I am your friend, and I understand."

He swallowed, then nodded. "Thank you." The corners of his lips curled into a grotesque resemblance of a smile, forced and painful. "Good day." He spun around on his heel and began marching toward Shine.

"Will you meet me here again tomorrow?" Harriet asked, hastening after him. She had the terrifying feeling that if she did not wring a promise from him now, she might never see him again. "Please!" She reached out and grasped his arm, holding him back.

Reluctantly, Jack turned to face her, his expression strangely sunken. "Very well," he said without argument, stunning Harriet, for she had expected push-back, questions, a reprimand even.

"Good. Thank you."

His gaze moved to her hand upon his arm, and Harriet instantly released him. She hated the sudden distance between them but did not know what to do about it. Perhaps all Jack needed was a little time.

After giving her a quick nod, Jack mounted Shine. "Go home," he told her imploringly before pulling on the reins and turning Shine toward Clements Park.

Harriet smiled as she watched him ride away because even when he felt deeply unsettled, he still thought of her, always concerned for her well-being. Harriet had to admit that she rather liked that.

Surprised to find her hands trembling as she pulled herself into Moon's saddle, Harriet headed home, Jack's words echoing in her head. For once, she did not feel the need to contradict him, to oppose him, to rebel against an instruction.

It was an utterly foreign sensation!

Later that afternoon, Harriet found Samantha and Owen seated on the terrace. The boy's mother was, as always, at his side, and the whole Whickerton clan had gathered nearby, sipping tea or playing chess; but each one of them was eyeing the other three curiously. While Mrs. Miller looked up from time to time, an uncomfortable look upon her pale face, Samantha seemed utterly oblivious. She prattled on happily, as she always did, doing her best to draw a reluctant Owen into a conversation.

"Any news yet?" Harriet asked and found a clear answer in multiple heads being shaken no. Of course, after only one day, what news could there have possibly been?

Harriet knew they would have to be patient, patient and vigilant. Indeed, Mrs. Miller had little interest in Samantha; however, Harriet could not help but notice that Samantha's interest was clearly directed at Owen and not his—and potentially her—mother. Perhaps all the little girl needed was other children to play with.

"Walk with me," came Grandma Edie's voice a moment before the old woman slipped her arm through Harriet's, giving it a gentle tug. "Come." Her pale eyes swept over Harriet's face.

With one last glance at the scene on the terrace, Harriet allowed her grandmother to lead her down into the garden. They shuffled along slowly, the old lady's walk somewhat unsteady as she leaned heavily upon her walking cane as well as Harriet's arm. The sun shone warmly onto their backs, and they turned toward a small grove where a bench rested in the shade of a cluster of oak trees.

"Feel free to pace, my dear," Grandma Edie said with a chuckle. "I, however, am in need of a bit of rest." Releasing Harriet's arm, she let herself drop onto the bench with an audible sigh. "Ah, this is much better."

Harriet looked down at her grandmother. "Why do you think I need to pace?"

Grandma Edie shrugged, then leaned back, another sigh drifting from her lips before her watchful eyes once more came to rest upon Harriet. "There is a tension in you, is there not? One that wasn't there this morning." She cocked her head sideways, the contemplative look in her eyes intensifying. "Does it have anything to do with the duke?"

Despite every conviction to the contrary, Harriet felt a sudden jolt go through her, an echo of her grandmother's words, and it was only in that moment that she realized that, yes, there was an odd hum beneath her skin. It continued to linger, making her shift from one foot to the other and then back again. Sometimes it even felt like a slight chill, and she found her arms rise to wrap around herself in order to fend it off. What was it? Where had it come from?

A warm chuckle drew Harriet's attention back to her grandmother. "I must say I have never seen you thus confused, dearest Harriet." A satisfied sigh left her lips. "However, it does suit you. Will you tell me what happened?"

Harriet huffed out a deep breath. "Do I have a choice?"

Grandma Edie grinned. "Of course, you have a choice."

"You mean the choice between telling you myself and letting you find out through snooping?" Harriet inquired, doing her best to put a firm note into her voice and failing miserably. For a reason she had never been able to identify, it seemed utterly impossible to be angry with her grandmother.

For all of them.

Grandma Edie laughed. "If you insist it is not something for me to know, then I will respect that. However, I must admit I'm quite eager to learn the reason for that slight tremble you cannot seem to shake." Her eyes narrowed and once more traveled over Harriet's face. "I assume the duke is not as cold as his reputation would lead one to believe, is that not so?"

Knowing that it would be a futile attempt to keep anything from her grandmother, Harriet heaved a deep sigh and then seated herself on the other end of the bench. "He is not cold at all," she told her grandmother, surprised by that feeling of relief that instantly swept through her heart. Yes, perhaps it was wise to speak to someone. Someone who would understand. "He tries to be, but he is not. Far from it." She remembered the many moments when it had appeared he was doing his utmost to rebuff her. "It upsets him that despite his best efforts to the contrary, his heart is not made of stone. I think he would prefer that."

A knowing look came to her grandmother's face. "He has loved and lost in the past, has he not?"

Harriet nodded. "Of course, I cannot be certain, for he is not one to share the details of his life. However, I do believe you're right even though I do not know who it was or what happened." Harriet remembered well the way he always seemed to force a certain distance between them, not only for propriety's sake, but…to protect himself? And yet there had been that one moment this morning when he had not backed away, but turned toward her.

Harriet felt her breath shudder past her lips as she recalled the feel of his arms around her, the way her head had rested against his chest, the feel of his heartbeat beneath her palm. She had meant to comfort him, but in return she had also been given a moment that had made her feel.

Feel something she had never experienced. A sigh had drifted from her lips, one that had spoken of contentment and peace of mind. In that moment, she had felt as though she had finally found the very place where she belonged. But how could it be? How could her place be at anyone's side?

"There is more, is there not?" Grandma Edie observed shrewdly, a delighted smile coming to her face. "He unsettled you." Her gaze narrowed a bit more. "Pray tell, how did he do that?"

Closing her eyes, Harriet felt her teeth sink into her lower lip as she bowed her head in defeat. There would be no point in denying it, in pretending that it had not happened because she knew come nightfall she would once again find herself unable to leave the day behind and drift off to sleep. "He asked me to marry him," Harriet finally said, surprised to feel her heart quicken at the memory.

Surprise widened Grandma Edie's eyes, a look one rarely saw upon her face. After all, the woman had the uncanny ability to know those around her better than they knew themselves. She was always the first one to notice sudden changes or hear whispers of things that had occurred. Indeed, Harriet could not recall ever seeing such a deep sense of surprise upon her grandmother's face.

"Did he now?" Grandma Edie mumbled, lights dancing in her eyes as her fingers tapped upon her walking stick. "My, my, my, that I had not expected."

Frowning at her grandmother, Harriet shook her head. "Why did you send me to him in the first place? What did you expect to happen? We both know you've been playing matchmaker for my sisters. Don't try to deny it! You're the reason they are now all married. Well, except for Jules." She met her grandmother's eyes. "Do not tell me this is not exactly what you had hoped for? You want me to...marry him, do you not? Even knowing who I am?"

With a somewhat indulgent smile upon her face, Grandma Edie reached out and patted Harriet's hand. "All I want, dear, is for you to be happy. Whether or not you marry is ultimately inconsequential so long as you find happiness in your choice."

Harriet eyed her grandmother carefully. "Do you truly mean that?"

"Have I ever pressured you to get married? If so, please tell me now, for I am wholly unaware of it."

"Then why did you send me to meet him?" Harriet pressed, certain that despite her words, her grandmother had some kind of hidden agenda. The woman always did. It was in her nature.

Again, her grandmother gently patted her hand. "Quite frankly, my dear, I did it more for him than for you." She heaved a deep sigh, a look of sadness coming to her eyes. "As I told you, I first noticed him roughly a year ago at a ball. He stood out because..." She shrugged. "I cannot quite say. His manners were impeccable. He smiled at appropriate moments, spoke to those around him, showed interest and behaved as any gentleman is expected to. Yet, everything he did seemed...forced." Leaning against the backrest of the bench, Grandma Edie turned her gaze toward the house, half hidden behind a tall hedge. "And so, I continued to watch him whenever I could, whenever he would attend an event. I never once saw a moment of honest joy, and it made me wonder." Her gaze returned to meet Harriet's. "And then when I heard that Pinewood Manor bordered on Clements Park, I thought who better to shock him out of that stupor than you, my dear." Grinning, she once more reached out and patted Harriet's hand. "It seems you were quite successful."

Harriet laughed. "You might be right about that, Grandmother. I cannot even count the many times he stared at me in utter shock. Everything I say and do makes him look at me in complete disbelief." The smile faded from her face, and she felt regret well up in her heart. "I don't know what happened, but for some reason he is terrified of allowing anyone close, of admitting that his heart longs for something. He does what is expected of him and nothing more."

"And yet he asked you to marry him," Grandma Edie pointed out with a chuckle.

Harriet shrugged. "Why would he not? He is a duke, and he is expected to marry, is he not?"

Grandma Edie nodded. "But you?"

Unable not to take her grandmother's words as an affront, Harriet scoffed. "Why ever not me? Aside from the obvious reason that I never wish to marry."

Her grandmother chuckled. "While I am quite fond of you, my dear, even you must admit that you do not qualify as a proper lady, the kind he no doubt believes he ought to marry." Her brows rose in a daring challenge. "I am certain your duke has a very precise idea of the bride he wishes to see stand beside him at the altar, and I doubt that the qualities he deems necessary coincide with the ones you possess."

Harriet could not help but stare at her grandmother. "Are you saying I am not good enough for him?"

Grandma Edie chuckled. "I am saying nothing of the kind, Harry. All I am saying is that you are not the kind of woman he no doubt intends to marry, and yet...he proposed to you." One brow rose in question. "However, did you manage that?"

"I don't know," Harriet whispered as that odd tremor once more danced over her skin. "I comforted him, and he..." She shook her head, trying to clear her thoughts. "Perhaps it was simply the weakness of the moment, nothing more."

"Then why do you seem so upset?"

Harriet frowned. "I am not upset."

Again, that knowing grin came to her grandmother's face. "Could it be perhaps that his words unsettled you so because some part of you is tempted to accept him?"

Thunderstruck, Harriet gawked at her grandmother.

CHAPTER SIXTEEN

THE DAY AFTER

"Invitations have been sent out, Clements," his aunt told him over breakfast the following day.

Bradley frowned. "Invitations?"

Deep frown lines appeared upon Lady Easton's forehead. "To the ball. Here at Clements Park. What else have we been talking about these past few weeks?" She eyed him with a look of concern. "Are you well?"

"I apologize." Recalling his aunt's purpose here at Clements Park, Bradley did his best to look...well—lest she felt justified in her concern for him. "Of course, I recall what we discussed. I was merely... distracted by other matters." The memory of Lady Harriet wrapped in his arms resurfaced in that moment, and Bradley determinedly pushed it away. "I am most grateful to you, Lady Easton, for all you've done, for all your assistance in this matter."

A smile came to his aunt's face. "I am happy to lend a hand, Clements. Your father would've wanted you to find the same happiness he did with your mother."

Bradley felt every muscle in his body tense, as though she had just slapped him across the face. "Of course," he barely gritted out. "If you will excuse me," he pushed to his feet, "there are certain matters I need to attend to."

Lady Easton graciously inclined her head. "Certainly."

Without a moment of hesitation, Bradley strode from the room, well aware that he was, for all intents and purposes, running away. Although he knew better than anyone that his parents had shared a love match, Bradley could not bear to have his aunt look at him thus and speak in a way as though his father truly would have wanted him to find the same. Indeed, the man had warned him not to be foolish enough to enter into such a marriage. It had been the last thought upon his mind before he had passed on, the last advice he had ever provided.

Instead of returning to his study, Bradley rushed outside and toward the stables. He knew he could not concentrate. He needed to clear his head, and perhaps a ride across the country would do him well.

Unbidden, his thoughts strayed to Lady Harriet once again, remembering his promise to her. Yet it was still early in the day, and he doubted she would already be waiting for him. Perhaps it would be wise to take the long route through the forest. It would give him plenty of time to settle that raging pulse of his. After all, he could not face her like this. She would see instantly that something had unsettled him. Indeed, the hellion had the infuriating ability to look at him...and know.

Guiding Shine towards the north, Bradley entered the forest, his mind too preoccupied to notice his surroundings. It was not until he came upon a well-trodden path that he took note of the faint scent of burning wood. Instantly, Bradley reined in Shine, every fiber of his being alert as he tried to locate where the smell was coming from. He dismounted and then carefully trod ahead, leaving the path and finding his way through the thicket. Branches were broken off here and there, heavy footprints in the soft soil guiding his way until he eventually came upon a small campsite.

The fire had been doused a while back, but the faint scent of burning wood still lingered. Bradley frowned, wondering who could have been here. Occasionally, hunters entered the forest even without asking his permission first; however, looking around, Bradley doubted that whoever had been here had come to hunt. Indeed, a hunter was stealthy and knew how to find his way through the forest.

Whoever this was did not.

Following the trail away from the campsite, Bradley finally lost it when he came upon a small stream. He knew it ran eastward toward Pinewood Manor, a thought that instantly jarred him awake, reminding him of his promise to meet Lady Harriet in the meadow.

Vowing to search for further tracks later in the day, Bradley mounted Shine and turned her away from the stream. They returned to the path and then followed it back out of the forest.

The moment the trees fell away, Bradley's gaze swept over the countless wildflowers swaying in the soft breeze. They stretched like a carpet ahead of him, a wide range of colors sparkling in the summer sun. It was a beautiful sight, made even more beautiful by the arrival of a fiery-haired hellion.

Bradley knew he ought not think of her thus. After all, he now knew her name. Still, somehow he felt as though the term suited her, and a part of him doubted she would take affront. He could easily imagine her laughing about it, delighted by his choice of words.

After a moment of hesitation, Bradley urged Shine onward, his gaze fixed upon Lady Harriet as she dismounted. It was as though an invisible force drew him closer, while at the same time, he could not deny that a part of him was apprehensive. Indeed, what good could come from associating with her further?

The simple and soul-crushing answer was: nothing.

Marry me.

Those two words echoed in his mind, and yet Bradley still could not believe he had spoken them out loud, had thought of them to begin with. What on earth had possessed him to do so? She was not the kind of woman he ought to marry, and he had risked the future of the dukedom by proposing to her. Fortunately, unlike him, Lady Harriet had held on to her senses, making it quite clear that a union between them was more than simply ill-advised.

She had refused him, and Bradley was glad for it; at least, he told himself he ought to be.

The moment Lady Harriet beheld him and her eyes lit up like two stars in the night sky, Bradley knew that he was lying to himself. He was not glad, not even a little. Instead, he felt regret, a realization that almost made him turn Shine around and head back to Clements Park.

Yes, there was no good reason why they should continue meeting here.

None!

"Jack," Lady Harriet called in an eager voice, and yet Bradley could not help but think that something almost hesitant rested in her green eyes. A certain measure of awkwardness now existed between them. Had it been his proposal that had put it there? Would they never again be able to converse the way they had before?

Bradley almost chuckled when he realized that as much as her direct manner had shocked him in the beginning, he had truly come to cherish it and would regret having lost it.

"How are you, Lady Harriet?" Bradley inquired as he dismounted, patting Shine on the neck. "How is your family?" Part of him still could not believe that her parents condoned their daughter's behavior, accepted that she came out here every day to meet a stranger with no kind of protection.

Lady Harriet heaved a deep sigh, and he could see the strain upon her face that had not been there before. "It is unclear yet what will happen. I admit, I am a bit concerned, but there has never been anything we as a family could not manage." She lifted her chin, and a determined look came to her green eyes. "I believe that all will end well."

To Bradley's ears, it sounded more like wishful thinking than honest belief. "I pray you will see your hopes realized."

And there they stood, perhaps three arms' lengths separating them, each carefully, somewhat hesitantly looking at the other, and...waited.

Bradley did not know how to continue, and it seemed neither did she. Something had changed since the day before. The ease with which she had always addressed him seemed to have disappeared, the direct way she usually looked at him had changed to fleeting glances that no longer lingered on him. Did she, too, feel unsettled by what had happened?

Bradley cleared his throat. "I apologize for—" The words left his lips before he could think them through, forcing him to break off mid-sentence when he realized that there was no way he could say the rest out loud.

Still, Lady Harriet nodded. "Shall we simply pretend that it never happened?" she suggested, taking a bold step toward him. "I wish for it more than anything in the world."

Bradley swallowed hard, torn between relief and regret. He could not help but feel a certain measure of resentment that she would dismiss his offer with such ease; nevertheless, deep affection swung in her voice as she spoke. Was it truly possible that despite her refusal, she still cared for him?

"I would like that very much," Bradley finally said, delighting in the small smile that came to her face.

"Good," Lady Harriet exclaimed, a deep breath rushing from her lungs as she stepped toward him. "Let us speak of other matters, then. Tell me of your family."

Bradley found himself tense, hoping she did not notice. "You first."

Lady Harriet chuckled. "Well," she began, stepping up to him and grasping his arm, pulling him along so he fell into step beside her. "I am the youngest of six. Troy is the eldest. Then there are Jules, Lou, Leo and Chris...and me, of course."

Bradley frowned.

"What is it? You look confused. Was I speaking too fast? Shall I give their names again?"

Bradley shook his head. "No, I simply thought..."

Stopping in her tracks, Lady Harriet turned and looked at him. "You thought what?"

Clearing his throat, Bradley forced himself to hold her gaze. "The way people spoke of..."

"The wicked Whickertons?" Lady Harriet supplied with a grin.

Bradley nodded. "Well, I thought you had sisters, at least one or two."

Lady Harriet laughed as though he had just told the greatest joke the world had ever known. Tears glistened in her eyes and her hand upon his arm tightened, holding on in a way that made him want to step closer.

"What is so humorous?"

Fighting to draw in a deep breath, Lady Harriet did her best to calm herself. "Troy is the only brother," she finally explained. "We are five sisters in total."

"But..."

Lady Harriet shook her head at him. "Have you never heard of nicknames, sweet Jack? My sisters' names are Juliet, Louisa, Leonora, Christina, and as you well know, I am Harriet."

Somewhat stumped, Bradley mumbled, "Jules, Lou, Leo, Chris..." His gaze met hers. "Harry."

Lady Harriet nodded. "Yes, that is us. Do you have any siblings?"

Bradley cleared his throat. "No." He wished they could leave it at that, but knowing Lady Harriet, Bradley was certain she would make further inquiries into his life. "Have you encountered anyone on your ride over here?" he asked, as much to change the topic as to learn more about whoever currently made his way through the forest between Clements Park and Pinewood Manor.

Lady Harriet gave him a look that said loud and clear that she knew he was trying to change the subject. Still, she answered him. "I have not. Why?"

"I came across a small campsite and tracks leading off toward Pinewood Manor. I don't know who it is, but I doubt it is someone looking to hunt."

A frown appeared upon her forehead. "How could you possibly know?"

"Those who hunt know how to move through the forest unseen. Whoever this was left tracks easy enough to follow." He paused and, without realizing it, reached to grasp her hands. "I would ask you not to ride out alone any longer, at least not until I know who this is."

Her lips thinned, and he could see that she wanted nothing more but to argue her point. Still, she held herself back, her eyes looking into his in a way that made his hands clasp hers harder. He could feel her smooth skin against his, here and there slightly roughened where

Moon's reins had chafed along her fingers. Of course, a woman like Harriet refused to wear gloves when riding.

Opening her mouth to speak, Lady Harriet paused before a single word had left her lips. Her gaze fell from his and came to linger upon their linked hands. A slow smile spread over her face before she looked up at him once more. "Are you concerned for me, sweet Jack?"

Bradley wished she would not address him in such a familiar way, but he knew to argue with her would change nothing. "I am concerned for your safety, my lady." Perhaps it would be wise to lead by example and to simply continue to address her in the way he ought to.

In answer, Lady Harriet's brows drew down in disapproval, and the sight of it almost made Bradley smile. An utterly unfamiliar sensation!

"Did I not tell you that I know how to take care of myself?" she finally said, her brows rising once more in challenge. "Did you not believe me when I said that I never ride out unarmed?"

Bradley frowned.

"I meant what I said."

Searching her face, Bradley did not know how to respond.

"Do you want me to prove it to you?" Lady Harriet demanded, and her hands tensed upon his, a hint of indignation coming to her eyes. "I am quite capable of defending myself."

Bradley could see that she truly believed that she could, and so, he was uncertain how to best broach the subject of what dangers might lie in wait, dangers she could not possibly imagine. "I do not mean to suggest otherwise; however—"

In all honesty, Bradley could not say what precisely happened in the next moment. He remembered standing upright and speaking to her before suddenly finding himself flat on his back in the grass. She had moved with such swiftness that he could barely recall anything at all. All he remembered was that from one second to the next, his legs were knocked out from under him, and he crashed to the hard ground, having the air knocked from his lungs.

Stunned beyond comprehension, Bradley blinked his eyes to focus and then felt something cold and sharp pressed against his throat.

Instantly, he stilled, his eyes fixed upon Lady Harriet's face as it hovered above him. What had just happened?

CHAPTER SEVENTEEN

A MOMENT OF CHANGE

Harry knew she ought to have held herself back. She ought to have counted to ten in her head until her pulse had calmed and then discussed this matter rationally. However, her impulsive nature had once more gotten the better of her. Why was it that she could not seem to restrain herself whenever a challenge was presented to her? And everything Jack said or did seemed to present a challenge.

Yes, she thought him sweet for being so concerned for her while at the same time experiencing moments of outrage that he thought her so incapable of taking care of herself.

Well, now, here they were. Him flat on his back in the grass, and her half kneeling upon his chest, her blade pressed to his throat. Despite her weight, she could feel his chest rise and fall with each breath, as though she were as light as a feather. His brown eyes were wide as he stared up at her, his brows drawn down in confusion as he searched her face, no small measure of shock visible upon his features.

"Do you believe me now?" Harriet demanded, leaning closer until her head hovered right above his, their eyes connecting in a way they had not before. "Do you believe me now?"

For a long moment, Jack simply looked up at her, his features almost frozen, as though he truly knew not what to say. His breathing seemed to calm, becoming slower and deeper, and all the while, he held her gaze.

Bit by bit, Harriet felt the triumphant smile slide off her face as a quite unfamiliar feeling settled in her chest. It felt warm and tempting, completely different from the joy of winning, of catching another off guard. She could not quite say what it was, but it took everything she thought she knew and turned it upside down.

The hand that remained curled around the hilt of her dagger slowly moved, sliding the blade back into a hidden place in her bodice with practiced ease. Harriet, though, paid the dagger little heed for her gaze remained locked upon Jack's, her other hand braced against his shoulder as she continued to hover above him.

A part of her urged her to retreat, to rise to her feet and allow him to regain his own...

...but she did not.

In all honesty, Harriet had to admit that she rather enjoyed being so close to him. What had begun as a challenge, a struggle of wills, had turned into something deeply emotional. Harriet could see the same effect of this lingering moment in Jack's eyes, for despite the absence of the blade, he had yet to move.

He could have easily gotten up, but he had not. He remained flat on his back with her half sitting upon his chest, their faces so close that she felt his breath against her skin.

"This is not proper," Jack suddenly grumbled, that somewhat offended look back upon his face. Still, he did not move, nor did he ask her to do so.

"Nothing I do is proper," Harriet chuckled, wondering what he would do if she were to lean a little closer...

The muscles in his neck tensed, and a warning came to his dark gaze. "You've made your point, my lady." He breathed in a slow breath before his gaze darted to her lips for the briefest of seconds. "You should..."

Harriet grinned. "I should what?" Her hand slid higher onto his shoulder, and she felt his pulse hammer against the tips of her fingers.

His throat worked, and she could see him grit his teeth. She gave a quick start when she suddenly felt his hands closing around her upper arms. "You should get to your feet, my lady." His voice was rough, hard with determination. "Now."

Harriet heaved a deep sigh, disappointed that he would rob them both of something that promised to be quite pleasurable. Never had she experienced such a strong desire to kiss someone. Although Harriet had shared the occasional kiss with a suitor now and then, it had been more for explorative purposes than the desire to feel the other's lips against her own. "Are you certain?"

His hands upon her arms tensed, and she felt a slight pressure, urging her away. "I am."

Reluctantly, Harriet slid off him and then pushed to her feet. "Very well. If you insist," she added, grinning before holding out a hand to help him up.

For a moment, Jack looked from her face to her proffered hand and then back into her eyes. Then he reached out his own and slid it into her hand.

Leaning back, Harriet pulled him to his feet. "Do you believe me now?" she asked, watching him straighten his attire. "That I can defend myself, that is? If I was not mistaken, it was you in danger of being taken advantage of, not me." She grinned at him, hoping to lighten the mood.

Unfortunately, that hard look upon his face remained, his eyes suddenly guarded, as though he no longer trusted her. Had he ever? The thought that he might not trust her bothered Harriet, and she stepped toward him, her eyes trying to look into his. "Jack, I'm sorry if I...offended you. I did not mean to..." Honestly, she could not quite say what she had meant to do. She had once again acted on instinct alone, tripping him to prove her point and then...

Looking up into his eyes, Harriet could not deny that she still felt the same urge to move closer, to lean in and...

Jack drew in a sharp breath. Then he took a step backward as though he had read her mind. "I will escort you home." He turned away, large strides carrying him toward Shine.

For a moment, Harriet stood there rather dumbfounded, staring after him. "What?" The word flew from her lips when this abrupt change in their conversation suddenly sank in. "No!" She marched after him. "I'm not going home. I—" She could not even finish that sentence, knew not what to say, what remained unresolved between them. All she knew was that she could not leave him like this. If she did...she feared she might not see him again.

There was something odd in his eyes. Something she could not make sense of. Somehow, after what had happened, he barely allowed himself to look at her.

"I shall see you home," he insisted in a stern voice, nodding his head toward Moon, demanding she mount her mare as well. "I cannot in good conscience let you ride off alone, not with someone lingering in the woods." He pulled himself into the saddle.

Staring up at him, Harriet crossed her arms over her chest, hating the sudden distance between them. It sent a chill down her limbs and made something rather terrifying grow in her heart. "I will not leave!" she insisted, raising her chin stubbornly. "We are not done here. Go ahead, ride on, but I will not follow you."

Pulling on Shine's reins, Jack whirled around, his brown eyes hard and unyielding. "You will do as I say. You will mount your horse and you will go home." He stared at her hard, and she could see that he meant what he said.

A part of Harriet was tempted to challenge him again, to see what he would do should she oppose him. But what if he then turned from her for good?

Although, at first, Harriet had simply enjoyed his company, their conversation, the way they were constantly at odds with one another, now, Jack meant more to her than that, than a mere diversion. She had come to care for him. The thought that he might ride off and not return brought tears to her eyes.

Stunned beyond belief, Harriet stared at him. She had not expected this. She had seen others...fall in love. Her sisters even. Yet, somehow, she had always thought herself...immune?

Was that a foolish thought?

"Why?" Harriet asked, her voice suddenly far from strong. "Why now?"

The hands that held Shine's reins were balled into fists. "Because it is not safe for you out here," he growled in a voice that was quite unlike him. He had been offended or upset before, but he had never been angry.

Not truly. Why was he now?

"Am I not safe here with you?" Harriet asked, despite her own strong aversion to rely on another, to admit that there was something she could not do herself. Was there truly someone dangerous out there? Or was Jack merely being a condescending ass, like all the other gentlemen who believed women could not take a single step without tripping over their own feet?

Jack's lips thinned but the burning look in his eyes remained. He did not answer her question, but merely flung out an arm and pointed at Moon. "On your horse! Now!"

Swallowing a heated reply, Harriet bowed her head and reached for Moon's reins. A part of her still wanted to fight this out here and now, while another urged her to be patient. Never had she seen Jack like this before, and perhaps he simply needed some time to calm down.

Side by side, without looking at one another, they rode back across the meadow toward Pinewood Manor. Harriet frantically searched her mind for something to say, willing to resort to any measure to break this tense silence between them.

But nothing came to mind, and before long, Pinewood Manor came into view.

"Wait!" Harriet called, reining Moon in. "Let me go alone from here."

Jack turned Shine around and came toward her. "Why?" he demanded, dark suspicions in his eyes.

Of course, he was correct. After all, she had sort of told a lie or at least a half-truth. No one except Grandma Edie knew about him, and Harriet wanted to keep it that way. She wanted him all to herself, for she was enjoying their secret meetings far too much. But would there be any more after today?

Harriet heaved a deep sigh. "My sister's home is within view. You cannot truly believe anything will happen to me on this short ride down the slope." She urged Moon closer, wishing she could reach out and take his hand. The look in his eyes discouraged her though. "You can watch me from here if it'll make you feel better."

Eventually, Jack nodded in acquiescence.

Harriet sighed deeply. "Until tomorrow," she told him, then kicked Moon's flanks and urged her mare down the slope. Far too late, she heard Jack mumble something that sounded like *goodbye*.

Had she misunderstood him? Or was he truly—?

Anger began to burn in Harriet's veins at his callous dismissal. She was about to pull Moon around and confront him...

...when she realized it would only seal her fate. No, they both needed some time apart to calm down before they spoke to each other next. Right now, every word seemed to be weighed down by something Harriet could not quite grasp.

Still, the next two days passed in agony. In every waking hour, she thought of Jack, of that hard look upon his face, of that one whispered word before she had left his side. At night, she tossed and turned, and then when she finally slipped off into slumber, she dreamed of him, of the moment before he had pushed her off him. She had seen something in his eyes.

Temptation, perhaps?

Longing?

On the third day, Harriet once again saddled Moon, wanting nothing more than to find out what had made him push her aside so callously. If she knew how she had offended him, she could apologize and they would be done with it.

Unfortunately, Jack never came to the meadow. Harriet paced along the forest's edge for hours as she had on the two days prior, picking one bouquet of wildflowers after another before hurling them away with a growl of frustration.

The next day, Harriet did not feel like herself. She felt drained and exhausted, her limbs heavy and her mind strangely foggy. Worst of all, her heart ached.

"You look rather glum, my dear," Grandma Edie remarked as she stepped up to the balustrade Harriet was resting her hands upon, her eyes directed out into the garden. "What happened?"

Harriet heaved a deep sigh. With her family still discussing the matter of Mrs. Miller's sudden reappearance in Samantha's life—Thorne had only just informed them all that she had lied about certain details—Harriet had hoped no one would pay much attention to her own dispirited mood. Of course, though, she ought to have known that her grandmother would not be so easily discouraged.

Standing a good deal off to the side, Harriet let her gaze sweep over the lush garden of Pinewood Manor, her family's voices sounding distant, as though they were only an echo from far away. Still, a part of her wished she could simply join them and forget what had happened.

A few days ago, that had seemed like a simple feat. But now? What had happened? What had happened to her?

Out of the corner of her eye, Harriet saw her grandmother's weathered hand settle beside her own, the other wrapped around her cane. "Will you not tell me?"

"What if I don't?" Harriet snapped, instantly regretting the harsh tone in her voice, grateful that no one else had taken notice. She sighed. "Will you then torture me for information? Or have me followed by one of your spies?"

Her grandmother chuckled. "I have my ways." Then she placed a gentle hand upon Harriet's shoulder. "Did you quarrel?"

Harriet swallowed. "I...am not sure what happened." She cleared her throat. "But he doesn't want to see me any longer. He is avoiding me." A sharp pain shot through her heart at the admission, and Harriet could feel tears gather in the corners of her eyes.

A warm smile came to her grandmother's face. "And you let him?" she asked, her brows rising in question before an undoubtedly wicked chuckle fell from her lips.

Despite the tears that blurred her eyes, Harriet laughed, and suddenly the tight knot inside her chest loosened. "I should not, should I?" she mumbled, embracing her grandmother, wondering about her own state of mind. She ought to have been more daring! She was, was she not? Usually, she was. What had happened to her? Why on earth had she waited these past few days, hoping for Jack to change his mind instead of seeking him out? After all, she had before. Indeed, she had not been herself! "Thank you."

"Go and find him." Reaching out a gnarled hand, Grandma Edie brushed the tears from Harriet's eyes. "He might be waiting for you."

Harriet's heart skipped a beat...and then another when she spotted Christina rushing up the slope toward the terrace. Her sister had left not long ago in the company of her husband, determined to confront Mrs. Miller and finally learn the truth. They had followed the children, who had gone down toward the forest's edge with Samantha's governess as well as Mrs. Miller; Owen in a Bath chair as he could not walk himself.

"Help!" Christina called as she came rushing toward them, her face flushed and her eyes wide as she stumbled along. "Help! We need help!"

Harriet's heart tensed painfully, and she felt her own feet carrying her toward her sister without another thought, barely aware that she was not the only one to answer Christina's desperate call. What on earth had happened?

CHAPTER EIGHTEEN
HER DARKEST HOUR

Once again, Bradley sat behind his late father's massive desk, his eyes trained upon the page in one of his many ledgers, his mind unable to absorb the information upon it. He stared at the letters, willing his mind to focus, to concentrate...but it was no use.

Days had passed since he had last seen Lady Harriet, since he had bid her farewell, determined to keep his distance, to stay away. Yet even without her nearby, his thoughts continued to return to their meadow and to her. Why was that?

With a growl of frustration, Bradley dropped the ledger onto the desk and then shoved to his feet. He felt restless, his legs beginning to pace as he pulled back his arms and leaned his hands behind his back. Never had he been one to pace, his mind, his body so restless that he did not know what to do with himself. Never had he felt like this.

Never.

Stepping up to the window, Bradley focused his gaze outside. He made his eyes take in the lush garden, the straight hedges forming the intricate design of the maze. He made himself look and notice each and every color of the many blossoms as he slowly breathed in and out.

In and out.

Slowly, the tumult in his head seemed to calm. Yet his thoughts lingered where they had before. Perhaps all he needed was more time, more distance. Perhaps he ought to leave Clements Park and go elsewhere.

Anywhere.

Anywhere far from here.

Anywhere far from her.

Still, no matter how far he might run, Bradley suspected that, at least, in his thoughts she would follow. As much as he tried, he could not seem to shake the moments they had shared. They lingered upon his mind, her soft weight upon his chest, her brilliant green eyes looking down at him. More than once, she had completely turned his world upside down, shocked him, surprised him. At first, Bradley had been far from pleased. He still clung to every routine and the predictable nature of his life; still, part of him had slowly come to cherish the way Lady Harriet always threw him off balance.

Bradley remembered well how Lady Harriet had knocked his legs out from under him to prove her point, how he had found himself lying in the tall grass, completely dumbfounded by how swiftly she had moved. She was incredible with that zest for life, that humming energy that seemed to carry her from day to day. She seemed to pulse with life itself, always eager for more.

Never had Bradley known anyone like her.

Marry me.

Those two words still echoed in his mind. He still wondered why he had spoken them, but knew deep down that perhaps not all the desires he thought to have laid to rest were irrevocably gone. Perhaps he had said those two words...because he had truly meant them?

Closing his eyes, Bradley huffed out a deep breath, reminding himself that even if he had, even if he truly wanted her, Lady Harriet was perhaps the only woman in England who did not wish for an advantageous match...or a match at all. At first, he had not believed her. After all, all women wanted to be wives, did they not? It was the way of the world.

But not Lady Harriet's world. She made her own, determined not to bow to anyone else's rules. No, even if he meant it, she would not marry him, would she?

Yet she kept seeking him out. She had called herself his friend, had she not? Bradley could not shake the memory of her soft weight on his chest, those green eyes looking down into his as she had moved closer. For the first time in his life, he had felt tempted to break the promise he had made his father. When his hands had curled around her arms, he had wanted to pull her closer, not move her away.

He had wanted—

Bradley paused, a frown coming to his face, as hurried footsteps echoed closer from outside in the corridor. Dimly, he heard Albert's voice, a hint of agitation in it. What was going on? Bradley stepped away from the window when the door suddenly flew open and not only Albert burst into the room.

"Jack." As though his thoughts had conjured her, Lady Harriet stood only a few paces away, her wild curls entangled as though she had chased the wind itself. Her chest rose and fell with rapid breaths, her eyes wide as they sought his. She seemed more than merely agitated but...frightened?

Unable not to, Bradley stepped toward her, barely noticing his butler fidgeting uncomfortably at the rim of his vision. "It's all right, Albert. You may leave us." Quiet footsteps retreated, and the door closed.

Lady Harriet swallowed, and he noticed her hands trembling as she came toward him. "Jack, I need your help."

All thoughts of distance instantly evaporated. And yet it was not the tremble in her voice nor the fear in her eyes that made him see how shaken she was, but that she had come to him for help.

Perhaps a fortnight had passed since Bradley had first laid eyes upon her; still, a part of him felt as though he knew her well. In all their time together, she had always made a point of doing as she wished, on her own, almost desperate to prove that she did not need to rely on anyone. She wanted to be independent and self-sufficient, cringing away from even the mere thought of relying on another.

If she was here now to ask for his help, something devastating had to have happened.

"Are you hurt?" Bradley asked, allowing his gaze to sweep over her. "What happened? What are you doing here?" He could feel small stirrings of anger that she had once again gone against his wishes and come to Clements Park on her own.

Drawing a deep breath into her lungs, Lady Harriet moved toward him. As always, there was no hesitation in the way she moved. Within the blink of an eye, she stood before him, her hands coming to rest upon his chest as though they belonged there. Green eyes looked up into his, and he could feel her breath against his skin. "I'm fine, Jack. But I need your help. Something awful has happened."

Although every instinct told Bradley to step away, he felt his hands move toward her and settle upon her shoulders, offering comfort. "Anything," he heard himself say, the look in her eyes like a heavy weight upon his chest.

In a sigh of relief, air rushed from her lungs, and she momentarily closed her eyes. "Thank you," she whispered. "Thank you."

Those whispered words did something to Bradley he did not even dare analyze. He was well aware he was going against everything he had set out for his own life. There were rules about how to act, how to behave, how to react and treat others, how to handle situations. There were rules and procedures about everything, but right now, here, in this moment, Bradley could not remember a single one of them.

And then words flew from Lady Harriet's lips, rushed and tripping over one another as she did her best to explain what had brought her to Clements Park in such a state. "Mrs. Huxley, Sam's governess, and Owen were struck down. The boy's still unconscious, but Mrs. Huxley said that there was a man. He took Mrs. Miller and Sam. That is all she knows, all she said before she blacked out again." Her hands curled into his lapels as she spoke, the muscles in her body strung tight like a bowstring. "We don't know where they could've gone. We don't know where the man could have taken them. We don't know this area." She heaved a deep sigh. "But you do. Will you help us?"

Reminding himself that nothing good ever came from losing one's head, Bradley gave an affirmative nod. "Come with me." Without thinking twice about what he was doing, he reached for her hand and pulled her along. They hurried out of his study and down the corridor, across the foyer, and out a side door. Large strides carried them to the stables, and he spotted Moon prancing nervously, her reins held tightly by a stable boy.

"I've come across more and more tracks in the past few days," Bradley told her as he stepped into the dim light of the stables. Barely aware that he was still holding her hand, he tugged her along toward Shine's stall. "Perhaps whoever is lingering in these woods is the very man who took your niece." Reaching for Shine's bridle and saddle, Bradley stepped into the stall.

"Do you know where he is?" Lady Harriet asked as she took the bridle from his hands and swiftly pulled it over Shine's head. The mare nuzzled closer, rubbing her head against Lady Harriet's arm.

"I cannot be certain," Bradley told her, not wishing to raise hopes that would only be dashed. "However, there is a small hut deep in the woods, and from what I can tell, the tracks are leading toward it. I had planned to seek it out in the next day or two to see who it could be." Indeed, he did not like strangers lingering in his woods. "It is not much, and I doubt anyone would linger there for too long."

"Then we need to hurry," Lady Harriet exclaimed as Bradley pulled the saddle girth tight. "Thank you, Jack."

Bradley turned to look at her, only now noticing the way she was looking back at him. He could not quite say what lay in her gaze, but only a heartbeat passed before she suddenly stepped toward him. Reaching up on her tiptoes, her arms came around his shoulders and she hugged him tightly. "Thank you, Jack."

As he had the other day in the meadow, Bradley felt torn between reestablishing the necessary distance and holding her as tightly as he could. However, this time, his hesitation lasted only a second. His arms closed around her, returning her embrace in a way he had never thought possible. He had never thought he could enjoy another's closeness in such a way. Oddly enough, he realized he felt a lot more at ease with her close by than with her far away. How had this happened?

Unwilling to dwell on that question and everything it entailed, Bradley finally released her and stepped back. "We need to leave. Go and get Moon."

Lady Harriet nodded, and then she dashed out of the stables.

Bradley led Shine out of the stall, gently patting her neck and murmuring words of reassurance as the mare flicked her ears in a slightly agitated manner.

And then they were off, galloping down the long drive leading away from Clements Park and toward Pinewood Manor. Both mares seemed to be aware of the urgency that rested in their riders' bones, their long legs eating up the ground as though it meant nothing.

Although Bradley tried to keep his gaze fixed on the horizon and where they needed to go, he could not keep from glancing at Lady Harriet every so often. Deepest concern had replaced that carefree and lighthearted manner that always seemed to linger about her. Never had he seen her like this before. Always had she seemed unconcerned with the world around her, never worrying, never thinking too deeply about anything that could happen or might happen.

And then she turned her head, and her eyes met his. A small smile tugged on the corners of her mouth, and Bradley knew he had been the one to put it there. She breathed in deeply as the wind tossed about her wild mane, and he could not help but think that the look of fear in her eyes had lessened. Once again, she moved with purpose and confidence, as though she felt certain that no matter the obstacles in their way, everything would turn out all right.

Bradley frowned. Where had that reassurance come from when only moments ago she had seemed so vulnerable? How had she so suddenly reclaimed the strength he had always seen in her?

And then Pinewood Manor appeared in front of them, and Bradley refocused his thoughts, reminding himself that she had come to him for help.

And he would provide it.

He would not let her down.

Never.

CHAPTER NINETEEN
MINE ALONE

It was already well into the afternoon when they finally returned to Pinewood Manor. Harriet's heart was beating furiously, and yet she could not help but notice that the tight grip of fear that had lingered there before, had held it in its clutches was now gone. Of course, she was still anxious, but she no longer doubted that everything would turn out all right. She felt like herself again, unburdened by fears of the future. She once again felt capable, her mind clear and her heart a source of strength. How had this happened?

Her gaze moved to Jack.

His jaw was set in determination, something calculating in his gaze. She could all but sense his thoughts as he contemplated the situation she had forced on him. It had to be a big adjustment for him to dive headfirst into something unknown, and yet he had not hesitated. She had come to him for help, and he had offered it.

He was here with her.

Harriet could not help but smile.

Drawing Moon to a halt outside the front stoop, Harriet jumped to the ground and then rushed up the few steps and all but burst through the front door. She was not surprised to find her family standing in the foyer, looking ready to get moving, to do something, anything.

If only they knew what.

"Have you learned anything new?" Harriet asked, looking from Christina to Thorne to her father and the rest of her siblings. Behind her, she could hear Jack's measured footsteps, and she breathed in deeply, knowing the moment had come to reveal her secret.

"We have not," her father replied as he stepped toward her, a slight frown drawing down his brows as his gaze moved from her to Jack. "May I ask where you have been?"

Harriet offered her father a smile, hoping it would reassure him, for she could see the slight tension that lingered upon his face. "I went to fetch someone who can help." Then she looked over her shoulder and offered the same reassuring smile to the man who had come to mean more to her than she ever would have thought. "Jack."

Stepping forward, Jack held himself rigid, his shoulders drawn back and a rather ducal expression upon his face, as though he were entering a ballroom and facing his peers. Harry could only imagine how he felt in this moment, coming face to face with her family so unexpectedly. No doubt, he saw the curiosity in their eyes as they watched him, questions lingering in their gazes that Harriet ought to have answered a while back.

Yet she had not. She had wanted to keep him all to herself.

"May I ask your name, sir?" her father asked, a cautious tone in his voice as he addressed Jack.

Harriet flinched as Jack's eyes snapped to her, confusion in them before a hint of anger blazed to life. His jaw moved, his teeth grinding together almost imperceptibly before that old look of reproach once more came to his face. Of course, her father's question had made Jack realize that she had not been completely honest with him. He had expected her family to know who he was, to know his name as well as the fact that they had been meeting countless times over the past few weeks.

Clearing his throat, Jack turned his attention to her father. "I apologize; however, I was under the impression that your daughter had informed you of our acquaintance." His dark gaze moved back to Harriet, and she could feel a shiver dance down her spine. She rather liked the way he glared at her, for it spoke of deep emotions, emotions he all too often held in check.

Giving him a wicked grin, she said, "A girl has to have her secrets."

Jack's gaze darkened even further, and Harriet could not help but wonder what he would have done had they not been standing in the foyer of Pinewood Manor surrounded by her family. As they were, Jack turned his attention from her rather dismissively and once more addressed her father. "I am Bradley Jackson, Duke of Clements. My ancestral home is less than half an hour's ride from here."

Harriet could see that most of her siblings as well as her parents were familiar with Jack's title. They had heard of the reclusive Duke of Clements, for even though he attended events upon occasion, he never seemed quite *present*, as her grandmother had phrased it. Of course, the *ton* mumbled as it always did, whispering about why he always kept to himself and never quite interacted with others.

"I do not wish to be rude," Thorne said into the sudden stillness, anguish in his eyes, speaking loud and clear of his concern for his missing daughter. "However, there is a most dire situation that requires our attention." His gaze moved from Harriet's father to Jack. "Is there any way you can help us locate my daughter?"

Meeting Thorne's gaze, Jack nodded. "I believe I can." In a few quick words, Jack explained about the odd tracks he had come across in the past few days, leading to a rundown hut deep in the forest.

With every word he spoke, the expression on everyone's faces had brightened, hope now mingling with fear. "Can you lead us there?" Thorne inquired, squeezing Christina's hand as they eagerly waited for Jack's response.

He gave a quick nod. "Of course."

"Thank you," Christina said to Jack, gratitude shining in her blue eyes. Then she turned to look at their family. "Who will join us?"

As one, the Whickertons stepped forward as Harriet had known they would. She smiled and then turned to Jack, ushering him outside ahead of the others. "I'm sorry," she whispered as the two of them moved down the steps toward their horses.

Jack's jaw seemed tight. "For what?" he all but growled. "For lying to me? Or to them?"

Harriet huffed out a deep breath. "I did not lie. I merely...stretched the truth."

Jack stepped toward her, a look of utter incredulity in his eyes. "You stretched the truth?" His lips pressed into a thin line. "Either you lied or you did not, there is no in-between." His eyes closed briefly, and he shook his head, a look of self-reproach coming to his face. "I should've known. I should've known no father would allow his daughter to..." His voice trailed off, and his dark gaze once more looked down into hers. "If I were your father, I would..." His jaw ground together. "If he knew what we..." A myriad of thoughts seemed to swirl in his gaze, emotions tugging him in various directions.

Harriet could not help but smile at seeing that endearing fluster. "My father might not delight in my secret adventures, but neither would he forbid me from embarking upon them. Yes, he is concerned for me, but he trusts me. He trusts my judgement, sweet Jack." She placed her hands upon his heaving chest. "And I trust you. I have from the start. Can you fault me for it?"

Jack stilled under her touch, the muscles in his jaw still tight as he looked down at her, his gaze moving back and forth between her eyes and her hands where they lay upon his chest. "You still lied."

"My grandmother knows," Harriet replied with a chuckle at his stubborn insistence. "She has known from the start."

"If you told her," Jack asked, before his gaze swept up to the door where voices were drawing closer, "then why did you not tell the rest of your family?"

Knowing that the doors would be flung open in a matter of seconds, Harriet moved quickly. She grasped Jack by the lapels and tugged him closer so their noses almost touched. She saw his eyes widening and felt his breath shudder past his lips. "I wanted you all to myself, sweet Jack," Harriet whispered, loving the way his dark brown eyes saw only her as though nothing and no one existed but them. "I found you, and I claimed you as mine. Mine alone. And I'm not sorry for it."

And then the doors did open and out poured her family. Harriet instantly released Jack and stepped back. Still, her heart jumped in her chest as she saw the look upon his face. He barely got his features back under control before her father stepped toward him. "I thank you for your assistance, Clements." Her father's questioning gaze moved to Harriet, and she smiled at him. "You make friends wherever you go, do you not, Harry?"

"Don't look so surprised," she told her father with a laugh. "I am a most delightful creature, in case you have forgotten."

Her father merely chuckled and then headed toward the stables with the others. Horses were quickly saddled, and before long, they were rounding the manor towards the meadow and the forest beyond.

While Jack rode at the front, guiding the way, Harriet rode in the middle with her sisters. She caught their curious glances, but only smiled in reply, still determined not to give away too much. As they entered the forest, they slowed, and occasionally she caught Jack looking back at her, the look in his eyes different, reminding her of the moment they had stood close when she had looked up at him and told him he was hers.

And she had meant it. Odd as it was, she still did. What did that mean? And what was she to do now?

CHAPTER TWENTY

A STRANGER IN THE FOREST

Bradley struggled to focus his thoughts, for they continued to stray to the most infuriating woman he had ever met. Still, whenever their eyes met, the only thing he felt was an echo of the moment she had pulled him to her, holding on as though never wishing to let go.

Mine alone.

Those two words echoed in his mind, and he knew he would not forget them until the end of his days. But what did they mean? Bradley could not deny that every time she stepped within reach, he wanted her closer still. He ought not to, but it was the truth. Bradley had never been one to lie to himself. Lies complicated everything, and yet the truth was far from simple.

Forcing his gaze from Lady Harriet, Bradley willed himself to focus on the tracks they were following. He knew where the hut was located but felt reassured whenever his gaze fell upon a footprint or a broken branch that led in that very direction. Around him, the Whickertons were quiet, their eyes focused and determined. Tension lingered in the air, and Bradley watched them with a mixture of stunned surprise and unexpected awe.

Never had he known a family like theirs. After his parents had died, he had been alone, distant relatives all that remained. He saw his aunt and cousins a couple of times a year. Their conversations, however, always lingered upon the mundane, never truly going deeper. They were his family, and yet he did not know them...and they did not know him.

With the Whickertons, it was different. Whatever the gossips might be currently whispering behind their backs, Bradley easily saw that this was a family that stood together...every day. Although three of the six siblings were already married, they were all here. Not because of the current emergency, but simply because they wanted to be together. Bradley could see it in their eyes, in the way they looked at one another.

And it reminded him of his own childhood. Before his mother had passed away. Before his father had cut himself off from everyone. Before he had been alone.

A long time ago, life had been good. For years now, Bradley had not dared think of those precious first few years. But now, those memories seemed to come back to him more and more, no matter his attempts at keeping them at bay. He could almost see his mother's lovely smile, that warm glow that had made him feel safe and treasured. It was a distant memory, but it was there.

He had thought it forgotten, but it seemed he had been wrong.

Again, his gaze drifted to Lady Harriet, and he could not deny the tightness that came to his chest when their eyes met yet again.

Mine alone.

Bradley could not help but wonder what she would say if he claimed her in return.

I will not marry! Not now! Not ever!

Those had been her words, and Bradley did not doubt that she had meant them. But if she truly did not wish for marriage, why—?

"The sun is setting," Mr. Sharpe exclaimed with a worried look as his gaze swept outward. Indeed, the light was fading, the dense foliage of the trees overhead blocking most of its remnants.

Soon, it would be dark.

Willing his thoughts back on track, Bradley led them onward, well aware that time was of the essence. In the dark, he could not follow any tracks. He would still find his way to the hut, but if whoever had taken the girl had moved on, he would be unaware of it.

Eventually, when Bradley had trouble seeing his hand before his eyes, he pulled Shine to a halt, then jumped off. "From here, we will have to continue on foot." He moved quickly through the underbrush and gathered a few thicker branches, tied bits of dried grass around them, and then struck a spark to light each torch. Once aflame, he handed the torches to the surrounding men.

Nearby, he heard Lady Harriet chuckle. "Of course, he wouldn't think to hand me one."

In the dark, Bradley could not help but smile. Again, a most unfamiliar sensation!

Bradley knew he rarely smiled; *rarely* being an absolute understatement. However, he had never realized how odd that truly was before meeting Lady Harriet.

On foot, they continued onward, staying close together as they made their way through the forest. A small path guided their way through the thicket of the forest until eventually a faint light appeared in the dark up ahead. It was a good distance down the path, and Bradley knew it came from the rundown hut they had been searching for.

His body tensed, knowing what the light meant. Someone was there. Hopefully, the girl. However, if she was, it also meant she was not alone.

Bradley knew very little of what was going on here. He could not say with certainty why someone had taken the child. For ransom? Or was there another motive? Was the woman the girl's mother? Last he had spoken with Harriet, she had not been certain yet. Was she now? What awaited them up there?

At Jack's suggestion, they silently split up and approached the hut from various sides. Of course, Lady Harriet and her sisters refused to remain behind. Although Bradley had suspected as much, it still came as a bit of a surprise. While Lady Harriet might be the most daring of the sisters, she was not the only one to do as she pleased.

Stepping off the path to the left, Bradley turned when he felt someone's arm brush against his. "I'm coming with you," he heard Lady

Harriet's voice as she slipped her hand through the crook of his arm. "I hope you don't mind." A teasing note rang in her voice, and yet he thought he detected a hint of apprehension.

"Perhaps you should go with your father or –"

"I'm coming with you," she interrupted him, and even in the dim light from the torch in his hand he could feel her eyes looking into his, her lips pressed into a determined line.

Bradley nodded. "Very well," he mumbled, knowing that there was nothing he could say to deter her. With his gaze fixed on the faint light from the hut, he did his utmost to ignore the way Lady Harriet clung to his arm. He felt her warmth, her presence, even the beat of her heart, if that was possible. He felt *her*, so close, and yet not close enough.

Clearing his throat, Bradley gritted his teeth, willing his thoughts not to stray but to focus on the muffled voices drifting to his ears from afar. They were growing louder with each step they took before a shriek suddenly ripped through the stillness of the night.

On his arm, Harriet tensed, and her hands gripped his arm tighter. "That didn't sound like Sam," she whispered, looking up into his face, her eyes wide.

Bradley nodded, his focus still trained on the hut and the noises coming from it. It sounded as though things were being moved inside, not with care, but with anger instead. Out of the corner of his eye, he could see the other torches moving through the dark forest, all closing in on the small hut.

"Where is she?" a hard voice bellowed from inside the small structure. "What did you do?"

"Nothing," came a female voice, fear constricting her words. "I do not know where she is. I was asleep like you."

Bradley looked down at Lady Harriet, a question in his eyes. Was that the woman who claimed to be Samantha's mother?

Lady Harriet nodded, then flinched when they heard the sound of more objects being tossed about only a few paces ahead of them. They bounced off the walls of the hut, a clattering sound echoing through the silence lingering upon the forest.

"I will go after her!" the male voice bellowed. "If I cannot find her,

I will—!" The man's voice abruptly broke off the moment he pulled open the door and his gaze no doubt fell upon the flickering torches moving toward him in the dark.

Bradley could barely see the man from where they stood on the left side of the hut. Now that they had been discovered, he urged Lady Harriet closer to the hut, quiet footsteps bringing them around. What were they to do? Where was the child? How committed were the Whickertons to saving the woman? Did she *need* saving?

Rather abruptly, Bradley's thoughts came to a halt when the man pulled a knife and jerked the woman in front of him, pressing the blade to her throat. In that moment, Bradley experienced an odd flashback to that afternoon in the meadow when Lady Harriet had knocked him into the grass. He pressed his eyes closed, willing his thoughts to refocus.

Angry voices were flung back and forth, the man demanding they leave, while Mr. Sharpe insisted on seeing his daughter returned to him. Back and forth, the shouts echoed, neither one giving ground. Anger swept higher, and Bradley wondered if there was any chance of this ending well. Still, the girl was nowhere to be seen.

"I cannot see Sam anywhere," Lady Harriet whispered beside him, echoing his own thoughts. She squinted her eyes, a furrow appearing between her brows. "Perhaps she slipped away." Her eyes rose to meet his, and Bradley could see that she longed to hear him agree with her assessment; he gave a quick nod. "Perhaps that was why the man got so angry."

Lady Harriet flinched as a choking sound drifted from the woman's lips. Their heads whipped back around, and Bradley gritted his teeth as he saw the blade dig deeper into the woman's throat. "Oh, no, we have to help her," Lady Harriet mumbled, her hands slowly slipping from his arm as though she planned to rush toward her and...? "Whoever she is, Owen needs her. We cannot allow that man to—" Her voice broke off, and Bradley felt a moment of utter shock when he spied the blade of her own little dagger gleam in the orange light of his torch.

Knowing that she would hate him for this, Bradley still did as he saw fit. "Give me this," he snapped under his breath, quickly twisting the dagger out of her hand before replacing it with the torch he carried.

As expected, her eyes snapped to his, and her jaw hardened in affront. Her lips parted, and he knew beyond the shadow of a doubt what she would say.

Without thinking, Bradley's arm came around her waist and pulled her against him before she could utter a single sound. Her eyes widened as the distance between them shrank. "Stay here!" Bradley growled quietly, willing himself to ignore her soft breath as it fanned over his lips. "Do not move from this spot! Is that understood?"

Lady Harriet stilled, but her jaw worked as she gritted her teeth, no doubt fighting the urge to say her piece. Then she gave a quick nod.

Exhaling the breath he had been holding, Bradley released her, then stepped away from the torch in her hand and into the shadows of the forest. He could see the other torches nearby as well as the dim outlines of those standing around them. He took another step and then another, Lady Harriet's dagger still in his hand. "If you harm her or the child," Bradley called out, hoping the man would come to his senses if he realized he was surrounded, "you will not leave this forest alive." His heart was pounding in his chest as he gripped the dagger more tightly. "I suggest you choose wisely."

In the next instant, a shot rang out, shattering the stillness of the night.

CHAPTER TWENTY-ONE
LIGHTS IN THE DARK

Harriet flinched, and she dropped the torch as her heart threatened to beat out of her chest. "Jack." His name fell from her lips without thought, fear filling every fiber of her being.

A moment later, Jack was right in front of her, his dark gaze trained upon her face as his hands flew over her shoulders and down her arms. "Are you all right? Are you hurt?" His voice was strained, urgent and... laced with fear; the same fear that coursed through her own limbs as well.

"I'm fine," she assured him, sinking into his arms with a relieved sigh. "You?" She felt him nod, his chin brushing over the top of her head.

And then, Harriet sensed movement around them, feet rushing out of the dark forest and toward the hut. Her head swiveled around, and she stared at Samantha's kidnapper, illuminated by the soft glow from inside the small cabin. His eyes were wide with shock, and blood gushed from a bullet hole in his neck. He still clung to Mrs. Miller, his blade digging deeper into her throat as his legs slowly gave out.

In the next moment, however, Thorne darted up the last few steps, his hands reaching for the blade and twisting it out of the man's hand while Drake pulled Mrs. Miller aside. Had one of them fired the shot? Most likely, Drake.

Within moments, everything was over, and Harriet once more sank into Jack's arms. She could hear the rest of her family rushing over, asking questions, their anxious voices drifting through the night. Still, Harriet remained where she was.

Only for a moment longer.

One more moment.

Jack's arms still held her tightly, and she could feel the rapid beat of his heart. "Are you certain you're all right?" he whispered near her ear, his warm breath tickling her skin.

Harriet looked up, barely able to make out the look in his eyes. "I'm fine," she repeated, her hands still clinging to his arms. "I...I like it when you hold me." It was a simple statement, and yet it meant so much more.

Harriet knew it, and it frightened her. It terrified her. She had not known how deeply she had come to care for Jack. It made her vulnerable. It made her want things...she should not want.

Things she never thought she would *ever* want. If only she could see his face and know if—

Footsteps echoed over from the hut, and Harriet felt Jack ease her out of his embrace. Still, he kept a hand on the small of her back as they drew closer.

Drake stepped forward, his gaze moving over them all as they stood waiting. Everyone bore a tense expression, even Phineas. "The girl slipped out the back," Drake informed them. "Let's fan out and find her."

Murmurs echoed in Harriet's ears, and she saw her brother, father, Drake, Leonora and Phineas return to the shadows, the only light coming from the torches in their hands. A moment later, Thorne and Christina joined them, their arms linked as they began searching for their little girl. "We should move to the back of the cabin!" came Thorne's voice from up ahead. "For she slipped out the back window."

Harriet watched Jack bend down to pick up their torch, then he stepped toward her, his dark gaze holding hers, and offered her his arm.

Smiling, Harriet once more snuggled close, her thoughts drifting back and forth between the man at her side and her little niece out there somewhere. Where had Samantha gone? How had she slipped out unseen? Harriet could not deny that she was proud of the girl. Even so young, she was resourceful and brave, saving herself instead of waiting to be rescued. The thought brought a smile to Harriet's face.

Still, where was she now?

On they walked, carefully picking their way around trees and bushes, brambles pulling on her skirts and roots threatening to trip them. Her family's voices calling Samantha's name echoed to her ears, and she spied the light of their torches like fireflies dancing between the tall-growing trees.

"Do you think we'll find her?" Jack asked carefully, and she could feel his arm tense beneath her hand.

Harriet exhaled a sharp breath. "Yes!" she said with conviction, then looked up at him, his face softly illuminated by the soft glow of the flickering flame. "She is strong and brave. She got away, and she is out there waiting for us to find her." Harriet lifted her chin. "And we will."

Jack's gaze remained upon hers for a long moment before he finally nodded. He did not say a word, but Harriet could not help but feel as though her words had touched him in a deep way.

"What of your parents, sweet Jack?" Harriet asked into the darkness as they stepped over a large tree root. She needed something to focus her thoughts, to keep them straying to thoughts she would rather not dwell upon. "You never speak of them."

Again, his arm beneath her hand tensed, and he remained quiet for a long enough moment to make it meaningful. "My mother died when I was young, and my father followed her to the grave a few years ago." That was all he said; yet Harriet felt certain that his choice of words was telling. After all, he could simply have said that his father had passed on a few years past, could he not?

Instead, Jack had chosen the words, *followed her to the grave*.

Without a doubt, Harriet knew that there was pain there. Not simply the pain over losing a loved one, but something else as well.

"They loved each other very much, did they not?" Harriet asked on a hunch.

Jack stopped in his tracks, and his gaze lowered to meet hers. "I do not speak of them." Then he continued onward.

"Why?"

He exhaled a deep breath, and Harriet could tell that he wanted nothing more but for her to drop the subject. "There is no point."

"Of course, there is. They were your parents." She pulled on his arm, and he turned to look at her. "You loved them very much."

A muscle in his jaw moved, but he turned away without a word. His steps quickened as he strode forward, and Harriet had to rush to keep up with him as he pulled her along.

The trees grew farther apart, and it became easier to pick their way around them. In the far distance, they could spot other shadows moving, heading in the same direction. Then a clearing opened up to them, a small lake glistening peacefully in the moonlight from above.

Harriet abruptly pulled to a halt as her gaze fell on Thorne and Christina, kneeling below a tall, gnarled oak tree on the opposite side of the small lake. Their arms were wrapped around little Samantha while a swarm of fireflies danced above their heads. "It's like in her story," Harriet whispered as tears filled her eyes.

"Her story?" She could hear the frown in Jack's voice.

Looking up at Jack, Harriet smiled, utter relief chasing itself through her veins. "Chris is a wonderful storyteller. I cannot remember how many nights I fell asleep listening to her voice." Her gaze moved back to the soft glow of the fireflies across the lake. "In one story, a girl gets lost in the woods and is led home by fairies."

"Fairies?" Jack asked beside her, one brow quirking upward.

Harriet elbowed him playfully. "They look like fairies, don't you think? They're beautiful. Perhaps Sam saw them and followed their light." She searched Jack's gaze. "Did your mother ever tell you stories?"

Instantly, his jaw clenched, and his gaze moved from hers. "Perhaps we should alert the others. Let them know that—"

"They're already here," Harriet interrupted him as her gaze swept over her father and Troy stepping out into the clearing, closely followed by other shadows.

"Then we should return," Jack insisted. "It will be a long way back to Pinewood Manor."

As he tried to turn away, Harriet held on to him, urging him to turn back to her. "Why can you not speak of them?"

His gaze was hard when it met hers. "I simply choose not to."

"But why?"

His jaw tightened, and Harriet could see that her questions were pushing him in a direction he had adamantly avoided for years. What had happened in his family?

"Tell me, sweet Jack."

"Do not call me that," he growled out, holding himself away from her.

Ignoring his protest, Harriet stepped in front of him. As it had been a while since he had last protested against her intimate form of address, this moment here now was quite telling. A blind man could see that anger had seized him, that he was quickly losing control of emotions he never allowed himself to feel. "I want to help you," she whispered, reaching up to touch his face.

"I do not need your help," he grumbled, snatching her wrist before her fingers could brush against his skin.

In the shimmering glow of the moon, they looked into each other's eyes, unspoken words hanging between them. "Thank you," Harriet finally said, not wanting to push Jack beyond what he could bear tonight, but, eventually, she would do it for his own good. "Thank you for helping, for everything you did tonight. We would never have found Sam without you."

His gaze dropped from hers, but the muscles in his jaw seemed to relax ever so slightly. "Of course." Slowly, he lifted his gaze to hers. "Always." Then his gaze darted past her to where Christina and Thorne were holding Samantha in their arms. "Your sister...your family does not mind..." His eyes settled back on hers, his brows rising meaningfully. "Perhaps I should not ask this," he mumbled before moving to turn away.

Harriet reached out to hold him back, her eyes seeking his. "Sam is ours in every way that matters. We will always stand with her. Always."

At her words, something in Jack's gaze shifted. Where before there had been confusion and incredulity, she now saw an almost desperate longing mingling with deepest regret.

Harriet's heart twisted painfully at the sight, and without thought, she stepped forward and wrapped her arms around him, her head coming to rest against his shoulder as though it belonged there.

And Jack did not push her away. Instead, he held her, wrapped her in his embrace in a way that did not speak of reluctance. His chin came to rest upon the top of her head once more, his heartbeat thudding below her ear. "I've never met anyone like you," he whispered into the night. "Where did you come from?" His voice was distant, as though he had not meant to speak out loud the thoughts that lingered in his head.

"My grandmother sent me to you," Harriet whispered, snuggling deeper into his embrace.

Oh, if only this did not feel so right!

CHAPTER TWENTY-TWO

A GRANDMOTHER'S COUNSEL

By the time Pinewood Manor appeared like a hulking beast in the dark, exhaustion lingered in all their bones. Bradley could see the little girl sleeping soundly in her father's arms as they rode the last stretch toward the house. Light streamed out of a few windows, and the door flew open as they pulled to a halt in the yard. Three women poured out into the night, their faces taut as they rushed toward them.

Bradley heard whispered words pass back and forth as the girl was welcomed home with warm embraces and joyful tears. It was a sight that pulled on long forgotten memories deep inside, and he quickly dismounted, then turned toward Lady Harriet.

Not surprisingly, though, she had no need for his assistance, her feet hitting the hard ground only a moment after his. "Will you stay the night?" she asked, stepping toward him. "It is late, and we're all exhausted."

Bradley shook his head. "I cannot."

"Why?"

Of course, she would ask this. The hellion always knew what to ask, where to poke to make it hurt, how to make him uncomfortable.

Fortunately, he was saved from having to think of a reply by the sudden appearance of Lord Whickerton by their side.

"Harry, dear, will you give us a moment?" her father asked, his calm gaze moving from Bradley to his daughter.

Lady Harriet's eyes narrowed slightly. "What secrets do you intend to keep from me?" she asked with a teasing chuckle. "He is mine, you know? You cannot have him."

Despite the humor in her voice, Bradley almost keeled over at her words, shocked beyond comprehension as his mind desperately searched for ways to explain Lady Harriet's inappropriate and highly scandalous words.

To Bradley's relief and surprise, though, Lord Whickerton merely chuckled, the murderous glare Bradley had expected to see in the man's eyes strangely absent. "Go. Now," he said to his daughter, giving her hand an affectionate squeeze before she finally relented and strode away.

Straightening his shoulders, Bradley met Lord Whickerton's gaze, completely at a loss for words.

"My daughter seems quite taken with you," Lord Whickerton remarked as he watched his daughter disappear into the house with the others. A sigh left his lips, and he turned back to look at Bradley. "I thank you for your help tonight," he paused for a moment, "and I am glad to see that my daughter has found such a devoted friend."

Bradley tensed at hearing Lord Whickerton's words. For one, he was uncertain whether the man truly meant them. Was Whickerton fishing for information about the true nature of Bradley's relationship with his daughter? Was he suspicious? Was there a well-concealed reproach in his words that Bradley had conducted himself in a way not befitting a gentleman? And two, Bradley could not deny that the term *devoted friend* bothered him. Indeed, he well remembered that Lady Harriet had called herself his friend before as well. Oddly, it had not bothered him at the time; however, it seemed something had changed...because it did now.

"If you like," Lord Whickerton continued, a watchful expression upon his face, visible even in the dim light of the early morning hours, "we can have a guestroom readied for you. There is no need for you to return to Clements Park tonight." He chuckled. "Or rather this morning."

Bradley's gaze moved to the house, to the door through which Lady Harriet had disappeared. He knew her to be inside there somewhere, and he could not deny that there was an odd tug urging him forward, closer, back to her side.

Clearing his throat, Bradley straightened. "That is very kind of you, Whickerton. However, Clements Park is not far. I shall be home shortly."

Lord Whickerton inclined his head. "As you wish."

The other man was about to turn away when Bradley suddenly heard himself speak, "I apologize for—" Abruptly, his voice broke off, for he did not know how to put into words what he wanted to say.

Lord Whickerton chuckled. "There is no need." He heaved a deep sigh, and his gaze briefly moved toward the house. "My daughter has always been a wild spirit. She does as she pleases, and it would be wrong of me to stop her. We all need to find happiness in our own way," his gaze moved back to meet Bradley's, "because if we allow others to dictate our choices, we shall never find it."

Although Bradley had often heard Lady Harriet speak of her parents and the choices they granted her, he was still surprised to hear those words from Lord Whickerton himself. "Still, I ought to have made certain that you were aware of our acquaintance."

Grinning, Lord Whickerton shook his head. "Harry led you to believe that we knew, did she not?"

Bradley heaved a deep sigh, uncertain how to reply, for he did not wish to cause trouble for her.

Lord Whickerton chuckled. "Yes, I thought as much."

"I assure you that nothing untoward happened between us," Bradley blurted out, unsure where the words had come from, unsure if they were even true. After all, there had been moments...

Lord Whickerton's gaze narrowed, although not in anger or suspicion, but in contemplation. "I can see that you care for her," he said quietly, "and so I shall say this to you: From a very young age, my daughter has declared that she intends to remain unwed. One might consider this a fanciful outburst of a young mind; however, my daughter has always been rather steadfast in her opinions. I do not think it likely she will change her mind."

Bradley stared at Lord Whickerton, belatedly realizing that Harriet's father was trying to warn *him*, urging him to be cautious with his own heart because ultimately Lady Harriet would not accept him. "And you approve?" Bradley heard himself ask, fascinated to find himself face to face with a man whose utmost goal it was to see his daughter happy rather than see her advantageously matched.

"As I said, she's free to make our own choices as we all should be." He heaved a deep sigh. "I may not always agree with her, and from time to time, I may counsel her, even urge her to reconsider, but in the end, she will have to make her own choice...and live with its consequences." The sound of shuffling feet drifted to their ears, and Lord Whickerton glanced over his shoulder. Bradley saw an indulgent smile come to the man's face before he turned back to look at him. "May I introduce you to my mother, the dowager countess."

Bradley peered into the dim light, able to make out the faint outlines of an elderly woman, leaning heavily upon a cane. Slowly, she stepped toward them; her gaze trained upon his, curiosity written all over her face as she smiled at him. "My, my, the Duke of Clements." She chuckled and looked at her son.

"Am I right to assume that you had something to do with this, Mother?"

"This?" the dowager countess asked innocently; yet, even in the dim light drifting into the yard, Bradley could see a wicked gleam in her eyes, a gleam he had seen far too often blaze to life in Lady Harriet's green eyes.

Lord Whickerton laughed, his gaze moving back to Bradley. "Consider yourself warned." Then he took a few steps back. "I bid you a good night." Another few steps later, he vanished into the house.

Bradley could not help but feel that he had stumbled from one interrogation into another. Although he had expected Lord Whickerton to make more specific inquiries into Bradley's connection to his daughter, the man had still done his best to make out Bradley's character. Of course, he was concerned for his daughter's well-being. Even if he allowed her to make her own choices, he could not help but be a parent and worry. It was simply part of life, was it not?

But why was the dowager countess here? Why had she stepped out into the night and come to speak to him? And what had Lord Whickerton meant by, *Am I right to assume that you had something to do with this?*

"I've heard it whispered," the dowager countess remarked, "that you are looking for a bride." Her brows rose almost imperceptibly.

Bradley cleared his throat. "I am," he replied truthfully, sensing that there was no point in denying the truth.

The dowager countess nodded, only mild interest upon her face. "And may I ask, have you already found a suitable lady?"

Bradley regarded her thoughtfully and then spoke with equal frankness. "Are you suggesting that I make Lady Harriet my duchess?" Indeed, speaking those words sent an odd shiver down his spine.

The dowager countess chuckled. "Do you truly deny that you're tempted to do just that?"

Bradley swallowed, suddenly disconcerted by that knowing look in the dowager's eyes.

"My granddaughter told me you already asked her to marry you. Or did I misunderstand?"

Exhaling a slow breath, Bradley shifted from one foot onto the other. "You did not," he finally admitted, feeling more and more uncomfortable discussing this matter with Lady Harriet's grandmother. After the day he had blurted out his proposal—if one could call it that! —they had never spoken of it again. She had never truly refused him, and he had not asked her to.

With both hands resting upon the cane, the dowager countess leaned forward, her eyes slightly squinted as though to see him better. "She might need a little persuasion."

Bradley almost rocked back on his heels at the dowager's words. After the way Lord Whickerton had just spoken to him, he was utterly surprised to hear Lady Harriet's grandmother suggest such a thing. "I assume you know that Lady Harriet is determined not to marry. Ever."

The dowager countess chuckled. "Of course, I am aware, and I see you are as well." She hobbled a step closer, those seeing eyes of hers were deeply unsettling as she peered up at him. "What will you do now?"

Bradley frowned. "Do now?" He shook his head. "There's nothing to..." He gritted his teeth, reminding himself to remain calm, something that seemed exceedingly difficult as of late. "Lady Harriet and I have become...friends of sorts, and—"

"Friends?" the dowager chuckled. "Indeed, that is a very good foundation."

"Foundation?"

"For marriage, would you not agree?"

Bradley could not help but wonder if the dowager countess suffered from memory lapses. After all, was that not an occasional side effect of advanced age? "Lady Harriet does not wish to be married," he reminded her carefully.

"I am aware of that," the dowager replied, as though she had just read his thoughts. "I know my granddaughter to be a stubborn young lady, and I cannot help but wonder about the reasons for her insistence."

"You disapprove?"

"Not in its entirety," the dowager replied with a shrug. "Harry's not wrong to seek her own life, to demand her own choices. She has been wise to discourage every suitor who has ever dared approach her." Bradley felt his teeth grit together painfully at the thought of Lady Harriet receiving proposals of marriage from other gentlemen. "However, she would be equally wrong to refuse the one man who would be her perfect match in every way." Her brows rose meaningfully, and for a heartbeat or two, Bradley merely stared back at her, shocked almost witless by the underlying meaning of those few words. "Good night, Lord Clements." And with a last smile, the dowager countess hobbled back into the house.

As eventful and unusual as this entire day had been, Bradley knew it was this moment that would stay with him.

Her perfect match in every way.

CHAPTER TWENTY-THREE

AN IMPROPER WOMAN

After sleeping until noon, Harriet felt a new eagerness to start her day. Although the events of the previous night had been tumultuous, her heart beat strong and in a way that made her smile, a smile which she could all but feel in the tips of her toes.

Joining her family in the parlor for a late breakfast, Harry was relieved to see them all in good spirits. Yes, the strain of the previous night still lingered, but everything had turned out all right. Samantha prattled on happily as she sat on Christina's lap, every few minutes snuggling closer as though she needed reassurance. Still, Harriet saw a familiar spark in the little girl's eyes and knew that she would recover swiftly. Samantha was a little fighter, and with a family like theirs, always eager to tease and distract, she would no doubt find her way back quickly.

"Where are you going?" Louisa inquired as Harriet pushed to her feet.

With her mouth still full with the last bite of her breakfast, Harriet chewed quickly, then swallowed, well-aware that all eyes had turned to her. "It's such a beautiful day. I thought I'd go for a ride."

Hugging her new daughter close, Christina grinned at Harriet over the top of Samantha's head. "To meet the duke?"

Chuckles erupted around the table as they all waited for her to answer, ill-concealed curiosity in their eyes.

Harriet could not deny the hint of warmth that swept up into her cheeks; still, she willed it back down as she held her ground, meeting her family's inquisitive eyes with a stubborn set of her jaw. "Perhaps. Perhaps not. What is it to you?"

Phineas, Louisa's husband, grinned wickedly. "Perhaps we should have a talk with him, find out what his intentions are." His brows rose mockingly. "After all, a delicate flower like yourself—"

Swiftly, Harriet reached for an apple from the fruit basket on the side table behind her and flung it at her brother-in-law.

To her utter regret, Phineas caught it with ease. "How did you know I was in the mood for an apple?" Again, his brows rose mockingly before he took a bite out of the fruit in his hand and chewed noisily.

Louisa rolled her eyes at her husband. "Ignore him," she told Harriet, giving Phineas a slap on the shoulder. "Go and have fun!" she grinned, then she lifted a finger in warning. "But not too much fun, mind you."

Everyone chuckled, and Harriet decided it was best for her to simply take her leave. With the echo of her family's voices following her, Harriet hurried out of the breakfast parlor, quickly changed into yet another riding habit—thank goodness, she had possessed the foresight to order so many of them!—and then hurried down to the stables to saddle Moon.

The sun shone brightly as Harriet urged Moon faster across the wide expanse of meadow in front of them. The mare eagerly complied, clearly enjoying stretching her legs as much as Harriet did.

Unfortunately, circling around the forest between Pinewood Manor and Clements Park, Harriet found their meadow deserted.

Jack had not come.

Although Harriet was disappointed, she could not say that she was truly surprised. A lot had happened the day before, and she remembered how upset he had been with her for keeping their acquaintance a secret from her family. Was he still upset?

Whatever the reason, this time, Harriet would not stand back and wait. Instead, she turned Moon towards Clements Park, determined to receive answers today. On top of that, she could not deny that she longed to see him. Only a few hours had passed since they had bid each other farewell, and yet...

As Moon trotted down the drive toward Clements Park, Harriet's gaze swept over the ducal estate. Indeed, it looked like Jack in all its facets, speaking to his desire for order and predictability. Every hedge looked neatly trimmed, and she supposed that every blade of grass on the vast lawns was precisely the same height. Flowers blossomed according to color, blues and violets to the east and reds and pinks to the west.

Harriet chuckled, wondering how Jack would react once he learned of her presence here. Would he be happy to see her? Or would he be upset that she had once again come here without a chaperone? Or perhaps a little of both?

Giving her mare a pat on the neck, Harriet tossed the reins to a stable boy, then rushed up the stairs to the front door. It opened swiftly, and a butler with a most formal bow welcomed her to Clements Park. Harriet remembered him from her previous visits, and she had no trouble discerning the slight disapproval that came to his eyes upon finding her unaccompanied.

All her life, Harriet had found joy in the many ways people reacted to her rather unsuitable behavior. She loved seeing their eyes widened in shock and their jaws drop. It proved to her that she was truly free to act as she pleased, as she saw fit. "Is his grace at home?"

After a moment of hesitation, the butler nodded.

"In his study, I presume?" Harriet inquired without waiting for a reply.

The man's lips thinned further before he gave a brief nod. "If you will wait in the drawing room, I—"

"There is no need," Harriet told him cheerfully before rushing past him, across the hall and down the corridor toward Jack's study. After all, she had been there less than twenty-four hours ago when she had come to seek his help.

Hastened steps carried her onward, her eyes fixed upon the door, her hand reaching for the handle without breaking stride. Harriet threw the door open, and she sailed across the threshold, her eyes finding Jack without a moment's hesitation.

With his back to her, he stood by the window, arms linked behind his back. However, upon her entrance, he turned around, the slight frown of confusion quickly vanishing from his face, replaced by the familiar disapproval she had come to expect. "Lady Harriet?" His jaw hardened, and his shoulders drew back in determination. "I must insist you leave this instant. Even if your father does not object to you coming here, I cannot in good conscience—" His voice broke off the moment she all but flung herself into his arms.

Harriet had not known she would do so. She had not planned it. She had not come here intending to sink into his embrace. Indeed, she was as surprised as he was.

Perhaps even more.

And yet she did not regret it.

Bradley felt rooted to the spot, his breath lodged in his throat as Lady Harriet's arms snaked around him. Every measure of outrage over her insistence to visit him unchaperoned vanished in the blink of an eye as he felt her head come to rest against his shoulder, a soft sigh leaving her lips.

His own arms were still clasped behind his back as he found himself at present unable to move at all. He simply stood there, not quite certain he was awake. Was she truly here?

"You're not good at this," Lady Harriet remarked with a hint of reproach, her heartbeat almost calm compared to his own.

"Pardon me?"

Without releasing him, she lifted her chin, her wide green eyes looking up into his. "This is a hug, sweet Jack. Are you not familiar with the concept?"

Still utterly thunderstruck, Bradley stared down at her, once again wondering if all this was merely a dream. Certainly, no woman in her right mind would ever—

"When was the last time you hugged someone?" Lady Harriet inquired as her left hand brushed upward over his chest.

Bradley inhaled a sharp breath as his thoughts drifted back to a moment in their meadow. "Aside from you, I…I do not recall. I…"

Her hand stilled, and she pulled back a little to better look at him. "You don't recall?" A frown pulled upon her brows. "You mean when I hugged you the other day, that was…?" She drew in a slow breath. "Oh."

After finally releasing the tight grip of his hands, Bradley moved them to her upper arms, determined to dislodge her hold on him. This was most improper! Had he not mere hours ago promised her father that nothing untoward had happened between them?

Unfortunately, Lady Harriet had no intention of releasing him. "Then I'll teach you," she said with a teasing chuckle. All but ignoring his attempts to put distance between them, she allowed her hand to continue its upward travel until her fingers gently grasped his chin. "Are you paying attention?"

Again, any words Bradley ought to have uttered in that moment remained stuck in his throat as he looked down at her, her wide green eyes holding him immobile.

"A hug is simple," she told him with a smile, and he felt her right arm tighten around him. "In fact, you did it quite nicely the other day. Do you recall?"

In frightening detail, was the answer. Wisely, though, Bradley refrained from saying so out loud. Instead, he simply gave in, knowing day would turn to night before Lady Harriet would let him off the hook.

His arms slowly came around her, pulling her closer as he kept his gaze fixed on something on the opposite wall of his study. Still, he could not block out the feel of her as she sank into his embrace without restraint. He felt her warmth and smelled wildflowers in her hair, realizing that she had first gone to their meadow before coming to Clements Park. The realization made him hold on to her even tighter, and he closed his eyes when he heard a contented sigh drift from her lips as she snuggled closer. "I was wrong. You *are* good at this."

"Why are you here?" Bradley whispered, his voice sounding hoarse to his own ears.

For a moment, Lady Harriet did not reply, and Bradley wondered if he had indeed spoken out loud. "I missed you," she said then, without preamble, and he felt her left hand curl into his lapel.

A shuddering breath escaped Bradley's lips. "We...We only bid each other farewell a few hours ago. How can you...?" He could not say more. He did not dare.

"I'm sorry if this shocks you," she whispered softly. "I did not plan to come here, but when I didn't find you in our meadow, I knew I had to." He felt her shoulders rise and fall in a soft shrug. "I wanted to see you." She raised her head slightly and smiled up at him. "Neither did I intend to rush into your arms the way I did." She chuckled, her emerald eyes sparkling in the soft light shining in from the gardens. "But then...I couldn't help myself."

Bradley did not know what to do or say. All he could do was hold her, his eyes unable to move from hers.

"Will you promise to meet me there tomorrow?" Lady Harriet asked, such heart-felt longing in her eyes that Bradley knew he could not refuse her anything.

He nodded, and the look upon her face brightened, shining like the sun itself. "Will you take a walk in the gardens with me?" she inquired, a slight curl coming to her lips. "Or will you insist I return home?"

Bradley heaved a deep sigh, torn between the unexpected desire to keep her in his arms a while longer and the knowledge that honor demanded far more than for him to merely release her. "If you promise not to return here without a chaperone."

"Very well," Lady Harriet finally relented. "Unless it's an emergency."

Deep down, Bradley suspected that Lady Harriet would have no qualms turning anything into an emergency if need be. What was even more shocking, however, was that if he were honest with himself he would not mind.

CHAPTER TWENTY-FOUR
AN UNEXPECTED REVELATION

"How is the girl?" Jack asked as they strolled through the maze, tall-growing hedges hiding them from sight. "Samantha, is it?"

Harriet nodded. "She is well. A little fearful, which is understandable, but well."

Once again, Jack had linked his arms behind his back. "And the woman?" His brows drew together as her name eluded him. Harriet was not even sure she had ever mentioned it to him. "Were you able to determine if she is the girl's mother?"

Harriet heaved a deep sigh, remembering the many revelations of the past day. "She is not."

Jack's jaw hardened. "Then why did she pretend to be?"

"Although I do not approve of what she did," Harriet told him with a stern look, "I understand why she did it. She was out of options, all alone in the world and responsible for a sick, little boy. She did what she did for him."

Jack's eyes searched her face. "You would not lay blame at her feet for what happened? What about the man who took them? Were you able to determine who he was?"

Harry decided not to go into too much detail. "Let's just say he was an acquaintance of hers, who learned that she was here. He saw a chance to enrich himself, and so he took it. He kidnapped Samantha and Mrs. Miller against their will and threatened her son's life if she were to go against him."

Jack inhaled a deep breath, and a contemplative look came to his eyes. He stood still for another moment and then continued onward, slow steps carrying him toward a small pond in the center of the maze. It was perfectly circular, framed by smooth rocks draped around it like a frame. A fountain sat in its center, and curved stone benches stood on all four sides.

Harriet slowly trailed after him, wondering what was currently going through his head. When he sat down on a bench, she moved to sit beside him. His gaze was still distant, and she reached out her hands to place them on top of his.

Jack blinked, and his gaze rose to meet hers.

"Tell me of your mother," Harriet whispered, and the hands beneath hers jerked. "When did she die?"

Jack's face immediately hardened, and Harriet could see that he was most reluctant to speak of it, that probably he never had before. Still, she remained where she was, her gaze fixed upon his, urging him to confide in her. She half expected him to push to his feet and try to escape her.

But he did not. He stayed, and then after a while, his eyes slowly closed. "I was eight," he whispered. "I do not know what ailed her, but I remember her coughing a lot. No one told me anything, and I did not ask."

Harry closed her hands tightly around his. "She knew she would die."

Jack nodded. "I did not know it then, but I know it now." He lifted his head and met her eyes. "My grandfather left her a small estate, Laurelwood Manor. She loved it there. She always called it her own little paradise." His eyes narrowed, and he shook his head ever so slightly, as though the memory had only just now come to him. "It was our home. We never lived here." His gaze rose and swept over their surroundings, over Clements Park. "I haven't been there since the day she died."

"Why not?"

Jack shrugged. "My father closed up the house and moved us here. Over the years, I never much thought about it, but then..." He inhaled a deep breath. "My solicitor informed me recently that apparently there is a stipulation in my mother's will. She left Laurelwood Manor to me, but only under the condition that I marry before my thirtieth year, which means," he swallowed, "that I will need to marry within the next six months." He scoffed, shaking his head. "I've been...wrecking my mind, trying to figure out why she did that."

Harriet moved closer until her knee touched his. "Perhaps she simply wanted to assure herself that you would have a family of your own." She squeezed his hand. "And your father?"

Jack's lips thinned. "I barely saw him after she died. He sent me off to school, and that was it. He no longer saw me. No longer was he the father I remembered."

Thinking of her own parents, Harriet wondered what such a loss would do to either of them. Always had she thought of them as two halves of a whole. What would it feel like to lose that other half for good? "Her death broke him," she whispered, "and it broke you as well."

Jack's shoulders slumped, and he hung his head. He looked so forlorn, so lonely, so very, very lonely.

Draping an arm over his shoulders, Harriet pulled him close. "Is there no one left for you? No family at all?"

"I have aunts and uncles as well as a handful of cousins," Jack finally said as he lifted his head, awkwardly shrugging out of her embrace. "In fact, my aunt is here now at Clements Park. I asked her to assist me in choosing a wife." His gaze held hers, tension marking his features.

At his words, Harriet felt herself still. Whatever she had expected him to say, that revelation surprised her, stunned her. She swallowed hard and then inhaled a deep breath. "And has she been...successful?"

His eyes continued to hold hers. "There will be a ball here at Clements Park soon...for that purpose. If I wish to retain Laurelwood Manor, I will need to make a choice soon."

Harriet nodded. "I see." She released his hands and sat back, suddenly unsure what to say...or how to feel about this information.

"Then I wish you the best of luck," she told him a moment later, willing a smile onto her face because that was what one did, was it not?

Jack nodded, the look upon his face as stoic as before. "Thank you."

Pushing to her feet, Harriet busied herself brushing nonexistent leaves off her skirts. "Then I shall see you tomorrow?"

Again, Jack nodded. "Tomorrow."

Harriet willed the corners of her mouth into a smile before she turned around and hurried back the way they had come. Deep down, she knew she was not merely leaving.

Deep down, she knew she was running away.

CHAPTER TWENTY-FIVE

A RACE ACROSS A MEADOW

Bradley did not know what to expect when he urged Shine toward their meadow the next day. He knew he could not break his promise nor did he wish to; still, part of him dreaded seeing her. Something had changed between them the day before. He was uncertain if it had been his revelation about his parents or about his upcoming nuptials. Something had unsettled her, bothered her even. But what was it? After all, had she not always said that she did not wish to marry? If that had been the truth, then why should the thought of him marrying another bother her?

As always, Lady Harriet awaited him in the meadow, dressed in another dark green riding habit, her left hand clutching a bouquet of wildflowers while the other continued to add to it. The moment she heard his approach, her head rose and that....smile came to her face.

It was a smile like no other. Bradley knew it well, and yet every time he saw it, it threw him off guard. It was warm and sweet and held nothing back. It was for him alone, and it led him to believe that she had longed to see him just as much, unable to quiet her thoughts or the rapid beating of her heart. Never—not since his mother had passed away—had anyone reacted to him quite like this...with such candid joy.

Quite on the contrary, people fled his presence as quickly as possible. He was not well-versed in upholding a conversation, nor did he possess the ability to pretend interest when he felt none. Never had it truly bothered Bradley before. Being alone had always meant peace and solitude. Those had been cherished moments that allowed him to be alone with his thoughts, unbothered by the world around him. Now, whenever she was not nearby...something was missing.

Something essential.

What would it feel like when their time together ended? When *she* would return to London to events and dancing and...other suitors? When *he* would marry a woman that would make a fine duchess, but...?

Would being alone then suddenly make him feel...lonely?

After Bradley dismounted and gave Shine free rein, they walked across the meadow side by side, slow steps carrying them onward, their eyes directed not at each other but at something indistinguishable in the far distance. Bradley could sense that she was lost in thought as well, the previous day lingering, all that had been said as well as all that remained unspoken.

Abruptly, Lady Harriet exhaled an exasperated breath. Then she spun around to face him, annoyance clearly visible upon her face. "This feels odd, don't you agree?"

Bradley almost smiled. "I do not disagree."

The corners of her mouth twitched. "Then what are we going to do about this?" She settled her hands upon her hips. "Frankly, I do not care for it. I want...I want back what we had before. I'm uncertain how we lost it," her eyes searched his face, "but today feels different."

Bradley nodded. "What do you suggest?"

With her gaze slightly narrowed in thought, Lady Harriet put the tip of her right forefinger against the corner of her lips. "Let's see," she mused. "How about a race?" Her green eyes lit up with challenge. "From here to the tree line. The winner gets to...ask any question he or she chooses, agreed?" She stepped back and held out her hand to him.

Deep down, Bradley sensed that this would not go well. In his experience—especially his experience with Lady Harriet—questions led to places he did not wish to go. Why was she proposing this? Did it mean that she already had a question in mind she wished to ask? If that were the case, though, why did she not simply do so?

"Well?" Lady Harriet prompted. "Do you forfeit?" A sly grin came to her face.

Bradley inhaled a deep breath and then slid his hand into hers. "Agreed."

"On the count of three." She stepped back, hands curling into the fabric of her skirts, lifting them up a bit, giving her legs room to move. "One. Two. Three!" And she dashed away.

Delaying only a second, Bradley rushed after her, knowing that if he did not try, if he did not do his best, she would no doubt berate him for it later. She was not the kind of woman who would want him to let her win.

Long strides carried Bradley closer until they were running side by side. Lady Harriet grinned at him, then doubled her efforts. Still, he was slowly pulling ahead, suddenly wondering what on earth he was doing! He was a duke! And he was running across a meadow like a little boy! The thought almost made him trip, but he kept his legs under him and chased ahead, his gaze now fixed upon the tree line.

Only a few more strides and Bradley reached it, pulling up short before entering the forest. His breath came fast, and he turned around a second before Lady Harriet came rushing straight at him. He barely had time to lift up his arms to catch her, because, for whatever reason, she did not think it necessary to slow down. He caught her around the waist, his arms lifting her off the ground as he turned and spun her in a circle. Her hands dug into his arms, and he could see a wide smile upon her face the moment before laughter spilled forth.

By the time he set her back down on the ground, they were both panting for breath. Bradley saw a wide smile upon her face, joy dancing in those brilliant green eyes. "That was fun, was it not?" Lady Harriet demanded with a chuckle. "I think it was precisely what you needed. That frown has disappeared from your face. Did you notice?"

As though to prove her wrong, Bradley felt himself frown. Still, he was surprised to detect a slight strain in the muscles of his cheeks, as though he had used them more than he usually did. Had he been smiling as well? It felt as though he had. "Was that why you proposed a race?" he inquired, searching Lady Harriet's face. "To make me...?"

Grinning, she nodded. "To make you smile, yes. You looked so serious, and you did not say a word."

"Neither did you," Bradley defended himself.

Lady Harriet rolled her eyes at him. "Because I was trying to figure out what was wrong. I even contemplated asking you outright, but then I thought…" She broke off, her eyes slightly narrowed as she once more searched his face.

"You thought what?"

She huffed out a deep breath. "You know that you rarely volunteer information, do you not? If I were to ask you now, would you answer me?" Her brows rose in challenge.

Inhaling a deep breath, Bradley straightened his attire. "I suppose that depends on the question." He regarded her thoughtfully. "Do you have a particular one in mind?"

A slow smile curled up the corners of her mouth. "You were the one to win," she pointed out. "Therefore, you are the one who gets to ask the question." Heaving a deep sigh, she slipped her arm through his and then pulled him out of the forest's shade and back out into the meadow. "You know, you remind me a bit of my brother." She glanced up at him as they walked. "You would not know it by looking at him today, but years ago—I remember it only vaguely because I was too young at the time—he used to be a very lighthearted person." She shook her head, a slight frown upon her face as though she were trying her best to reach a memory that continued to slip away from her. "I do not remember it in great detail, but I remember noticing that from one day to the next he seemed to change."

Bradley wondered why that would remind her of him. After all, he had always been the person he was today, had he not?

Lady Harriet stopped, then turned to look at him. "I believe that someone broke his heart," she whispered, her green eyes holding onto his, "and now he's afraid…afraid to have it happen again."

A question lingered in her gaze, and Bradley swallowed hard. "You think someone broke my heart?" he asked reluctantly. "Frankly, I do not recall ever having been in love." Bradley knew well that if anyone else had asked, he would not under any circumstances have replied in the way he just had. Still, despite his natural tendency to keep himself apart from people, there was another part of him that continued to urge him in the opposite direction whenever Lady Harriet was near.

Something about her made him want to be a different person.

"Your parents," she whispered, her eyes still holding onto his as she closed the distance between them, and her hand settled upon his chest like an anchor keeping him in place. "They broke your heart. Your mother when she died, and your father when he pushed you away... when you needed him most."

Bradley stared down at her, his gaze briefly lingering upon the tear that had collected in her right eye. It lingered there for a moment, then slowly snaked its way down her cheek. Bradley traced the tear with his gaze, utterly fascinated by the slow movement. Then, without thought, he reached out and brushed it from her cheek with the pad of his thumb.

"I believe," Lady Harriet whispered softly, "that once upon a time you were a different person and that, at least, a part of you still longs to reclaim that part of yourself." She reached out and cupped a hand to his cheek. "Every once in a while, it shines through. It did just now. Do you not wish to rediscover it? Do you truly intend to hide from that part of you for the rest of your life?"

A part of Bradley wanted to pull away, to hide from her inquisitive gaze. She saw far too much, and it unsettled him more than anything ever had. Yet he knew that her relentless nature would never allow him to pull away. Even if he were to leave, she would simply follow him, ignoring the promise she had made him only the day before because...

...yes, to her it would seem like an emergency, would it not?

An emergency of the heart.

"May I ask my question now?" Bradley inquired out of the blue, his voice oddly strained.

Lady Harriet paused. "Of course. What do you wish to know?"

Bradley gritted his teeth, urging himself to reconsider, knowing that her answer might ruin everything that had happened these past few weeks, everything Bradley felt for her. Yet he knew he would never be able to shake the thought of what could have been if he did not ask. "Are there no circumstances under which you would consider marriage?"

Her eyes narrowed ever so slightly, and Bradley had his answer. He swallowed hard and took a step back, his hands grasping her arms to remove hers from his face. "I see."

As he made to walk away, Lady Harriet reached out and stopped him with a hand upon his arm. "Why are you asking me this? Why now?"

He looked into her eyes. "Because it is what I wish to know. You said I could ask any question I chose." He gave a quick nod. "I chose that one."

Lady Harriet's lips thinned as she watched him carefully. "Then I wish to ask a question of my own." Her brows rose, urging him not to refuse her

After a long moment, Bradley finally inclined his head in acquiescence. He knew it was foolish, for the look in her eyes told him loud and clear that whatever she was about to ask...would lead them onto dangerous terrain.

Inhaling a deep breath, Lady Harriet stepped closer, her green eyes lingering upon his. "The day I tripped you," she said, and Bradley could feel his heart twist in painful foreboding, "did you want to kiss me?"

Indeed, he had been right.

This was most dangerous terrain.

CHAPTER TWENTY-SIX

EMBRACING THE PAST

Harriet was tempted to reach out and hold on to him, for he had that look in his eyes that told her loud and clear that he wished to run away. Her question unsettled him as much as his had unsettled her. If nothing else, she sought to even the ground between them. "Will you not answer me?" she dared him.

It seemed they had both discovered a question to put to the other that held no simple answer. A part of Harriet could not help but think that it should be simple between them. Obviously, they felt something for one another. It was a fact she did not wish to deny. Still, they were very different people with very different expectations of life. There was no simple answer, no simple path. But would it truly be wise to pretend that there was nothing between them and part ways without speaking their minds?

Harriet knew she was not such a person. Even if she were to lose him, even if she would have to give him up to remain true to herself, she would still rather know the truth than hide from it. "Did you want to kiss me that day?" she asked, taking a step closer, making it crystal clear that she would not back down.

Jack's jaw tightened, his teeth grinding together as he stared at her, something fiery in his eyes that she had rarely seen before. Yes, he felt deeply. He was not the cold man he was pretending to be. There was another side to him, one he kept locked away, afraid of where it might lead him.

A small eternity passed and Harriet was about to press him for an answer, yet again, when one single word fell from his lips. "Yes."

Rather unexpectedly, his answer sent a shiver down her back, and she inhaled a shuddering breath. "Then why didn't you?"

For a moment, Harriet thought he would walk away, but he only shifted on his feet, looking torn about what to say. His gaze kept returning to hers, his lips parting before pressing shut once more.

"Why, Jack?"

Anger sparked in his eyes, and for a second, Harriet thought he might try to hide behind it. Then, however, he paused as though a new thought had suddenly occurred to him. His gaze narrowed, and he took a step toward her, his eyes searching her face. "Did you?"

"Did I what?" Harriet demanded, wanting him to say the words even though she knew exactly what he wanted to know.

Jack swallowed. "That day, did you want to kiss me?"

Only too well did Harriet remember how she had felt that day. She remembered the urge to move closer, to reach for him and feel him. She remembered her disappointment when he had pushed her away. "Yes."

His frown deepened as though he did not believe her, and yet she noticed a slight tremble grip his tall frame. "And the day before that," he continued, "why did you kiss me then? Was it merely–?"

Confused, Harriet shook her head. "When did I kiss you?"

Not saying a word, Jack held her gaze as he touched the tips of his fingers to his cheek.

Understanding dawned, and Harriet briefly closed her eyes. "That was not a kiss. That was a peck on the cheek."

"It was still a kiss," Jack insisted with a growl. Indeed, the direction of their conversation seemed to bring out deep emotions for him. Always had he seemed so in control, detached even. Now, it was different.

Very different.

"It was not a true kiss. Surely you know that," Harriet said gently, remembering that she only had meant to shock him that day.

Something sparked in his eyes. "How would...you...know that?"

Harriet chuckled. "Well, I've been kissed once or twice. Do not for a second believe you're the only one with experience in that regard. I've done my fair share of experiments, as my sister Leo would say."

Jack's face darkened, and Harriet found the air yanked from her lungs when she suddenly realized that...he was jealous. Indeed, the thought of her kissing another infuriated him. It was a fact that both pleased and upset her. "Don't look at me like that," she chided. "Surely, you are not one of those men who go around kissing half the world; but insist that women remain unkissed until marriage. From a mathematical standpoint alone, that makes no sense. Who are men ever supposed to kiss if all women are supposed to remain the epitome of chaste?" She lifted her brows in a daring challenge; she had had quite enough of men like that and she never for a second would have believed that Jack was one of th—

"I've never kissed a woman," he suddenly blurted out.

For the first time in her life, Harriet found herself shocked witless. Her mind ground to a halt, and every thought felt suspended as though in midair as she stared at Jack. "W-Why ever not?" she croaked after a short eternity. "Not once?"

His gaze fell from hers, and he cleared his throat. "It causes emotional entanglements that are ill-advised."

Harriet had never heard anything more ludicrous in her life; and she could not deny that it sounded like something he had been telling himself for a long time, hoping that one day he would come to believe it. "A kiss does not cause emotional entanglements," she insisted, stepping closer and daring him to look her in the eyes. "In fact, the moment you truly desire to kiss another, your emotions are already entangled."

His jaw seemed to tense to the point of breaking as he stood before her. She wondered if he was even aware that his hands had balled into fists and that the pulse in his neck was beating so rapidly it seemed to want to jump from his body.

"Who told you that?" Harriet inquired, wondering how he had come to that ludicrous conclusion.

Confusion flickered in his eyes.

"If you have truly never kissed anyone, how do you know a kiss leads to *emotional entanglements*?" Her gaze narrowed as she regarded him. "Who was hurt because...?" Her voice trailed off. Her gaze, however, remained locked upon his.

Some of the anger fell from Jack and was instantly replaced by a look of deep sorrow. "My father," he finally gritted out as exhaustion swept across his features.

"Your father?" Shaking her head in confusion, Harriet sought his gaze. "But I thought... Didn't you say that...?" Had she misunderstood him? Truthfully, she could not quite recall the words he had used to describe his parents' marriage.

Jack's shoulders slumped. "After...my mother passed, my father became a stranger to me. Years passed, and we hardly spoke, hardly saw each other. When he got ill, he did not send for me." He swallowed hard, regret in those dark brown eyes of his. "But then—I suppose he sensed the end was near—he had me called to his bedside. I thought perhaps..." He shrugged, a helpless look on his face that made Harriet think of the little boy he had once been.

"You thought he had finally realized how wrong he had been all those years...to push you away," Harriet finished for him. She moved closer, looking up into his eyes. "You wanted him to say that he was sorry, that he loved you."

Gritting his teeth, Jack nodded. "Instead, he seemed angrier than I had ever seen him. He raved on and on about the biggest mistake of his life. He told me not to be a fool. He made me promise..."

Without thinking, Harriet stepped forward and wrapped her arms around him. His body was rigid, his heart pounding under her ear. "He was not himself," she whispered, running her hands up and down his back as he stood in her embrace like a stone column. "He was lost."

For a long time, all Harriet heard was the thundering beat of Jack's heart and the harsh breaths leaving his lungs. His muscles were tense and hard, his body unyielding as she clung to him. "Hug me, Jack," she finally urged him, wondering if he even knew that she held him. "Put your arms around me and hold on."

Waiting patiently, Harriet wondered if he had even heard her. Then, however, she felt him shift ever so slightly. His arms rose and then came around her. At first, she barely felt his embrace, but when she tightened her own hold on him, his, too, grew more pronounced. A deep sigh shuddered past his lips, and then he pulled her against him, his chin coming to rest upon her shoulder. "Don't let go," he whispered then, his voice hoarse.

"I won't," Harriet assured him, meaning it with every fiber of her being. "I won't."

CHAPTER TWENTY-SEVEN

TO KNOW ONESELF

Bradley was dimly aware that his aunt was speaking to him; however, the words that came out of her mouth might as well have been in a foreign language. Every once in a while, he would remind himself to pay attention, to meet her gaze and appear interested, to nod along. Yet he could not.

Try as he might, he could not will his thoughts to linger upon the approaching ball. He did not care about the guest list or the menu or the music or…

All he could think about was—

"Clements, are you even listening?" Lady Easton's voice held a tinge of exasperation as she regarded him with a stern look that reminded Bradley of his old governess.

Apologizing, Bradley assured her that the only reason his thoughts continued to drift away was that he had a lot on his mind, which was true. However, he refrained from specifying what that something was, allowing his aunt to believe that he was referring to matters of the estate. Not quite a lie but definitely an omission!

"Do not worry, Clements," his aunt said, smiling indulgently. "Every young lady attending the first ball at Clements Park in years will dream of becoming your duchess." She patted his arm. "Leave all the details to me, and we shall have you married before the new Season begins." Then she walked away, her footsteps echoing on the polished marble floors.

Bradley stared after her, hearing her words echo in his mind. He could feel every fiber of his being revolting against the idea of making any young lady his duchess. It did not matter who they were, how perfectly they might suit him, or how diligently they would fulfill their role as the new Duchess of Clements. None of that mattered, and it was in that moment that Bradley realized he had made his choice long ago.

Whether or not she was right for him, Bradley knew he wanted no one but Lady Harriet.

A disbelieving laugh flew from his lips as he raked a hand through his hair, shaking his head at the surprising notion. Yet why was he even surprised? Had he not blurted out *Marry me* weeks ago? Had she not been the only thing on his mind since he had first laid eyes on her?

Stilling, Bradley stepped up to the window and allowed his gaze to sweep over the grounds. A new calm settled over him, for he finally knew what he wanted. The only problem was that Lady Harriet did not seek marriage. Quite the opposite. She was possibly the only woman in all of England who would refuse him. Yet she was also the only woman in all of England...who cared for him.

And she did, did she not?

Indeed, she had called herself his friend more than once. She had *claimed him as hers*. Yet had she said so in jest? How serious had she been about the words that had fallen from her lips?

By now, Bradley knew that Lady Harriet was an exuberant young woman. She was high-spirited and impulsive. She loved adventure and going against convention. She was daring and bold and utterly dauntless. Never would he have thought such a woman to be his perfect match, and yet he had never met a woman he felt so comfortable with. Despite their differences, she understood him; more than that, she cared to understand him. He mattered to her, which was perhaps the greatest surprise of Bradley's life.

Was there any chance that she would change her mind about marriage? Was there some way to convince her to accept him?

Bradley had to know. Somehow, he had to find out because he wanted her.

Again, a feeling of joy swept through his being at the realization. It had been so long since he had wanted anything. He had never allowed himself to want. Losing his parents had made certain of that, and the promise he had given to his father on his deathbed had been the final nail.

Bradley had always known he would remain alone. Certainly, he was to marry, but marriage did not necessarily mean closeness. He had always assumed that he and his duchess would simply live side by side, perhaps even on separate estates. He had never truly expected love or a family. Children were born to continue the line, not to love.

As that thought swept through his mind, Bradley frowned because memories long since buried surged to the forefront of his mind. He had not thought of them in years, had thought them all but forgotten, but it seemed they were still there. Lately, the memories had returned to him again and again, reminding him of the early years of his childhood when he *had* been loved. Once, he had been part of a family that had been more than obligation and lineage.

Once.

Don't be a fool! His father's strangled voice echoed in his head, and Bradley knew that his desire to marry Lady Harriet went against everything his father had wanted him to be. Everything his father had wanted him to avoid. Yet even without a kiss, he had come to care for her.

Deeply.

And while it might be true that he would lose her someday, she was still here now. If he turned away and chose another bride, he only would lose her that much sooner. It was ludicrous, was it not? How had he ever deemed his father's words wise advice? He had to have been a fool to make such a promise to an angry, bitter man, consumed by the grief for a wife he had lost more than a decade earlier.

Yes, perhaps the man his father had become would be disappointed with Bradley's decision; however, Bradley knew that the man his father had once been would be proud.

As the clock in the hall chimed, Bradley spun around, realizing how long he had stood here, lost in his own thoughts. But no more! He had spent too much of his life not even bothering to ask what it was he wanted. And he was finally done with that!

Shine pranced eagerly as he guided her away from Clements Park and once again toward their meadow. Perhaps she could feel his emotional state of mind, or perhaps she too enjoyed their outings, getting away from the confinements of life and galloping toward the horizon. It felt utterly freeing!

Today, Bradley was the first one to arrive, and for a moment, he feared that perhaps Lady Harriet would not come, that something had prevented her or that he had been utterly mistaken and she had changed her mind. And then a happy neigh drifted to his ears, and he turned to see Lady Harriet upon Moon's back, the mare's dapple-gray coat glistening in the bright sunlight, a stark contrast to the fiery curls upon Lady Harriet's head.

Bradley felt a nervous chill chasing itself up and down his arms, yet he could not ignore the somersault his heart did the moment Lady Harriet jumped out of the saddle and came striding toward him. Her smile made him feel weak in the knees, and the way her green eyes looked into his gave him hope. "Am I right?" she asked, a tinge of confusion in her voice before her gaze narrowed. "You seem different today."

Bradley swallowed, on edge about her ability to read him so well, but equally glad for it. "You've said from the first," Bradley began without preamble, "that you would never marry." He held her gaze and took a step toward her. "Why?"

For the first time that Bradley could remember, it was Lady Harriet's turn to look...taken aback, if not shocked. She swallowed, and the smile slid off her face. He wasn't certain if it was his question or rather the abruptness with which he had asked it.

"And I don't want to hear anything about the unfairness of the world," Bradley interrupted before she could utter a single word. Indeed, the look in her eyes told him loud and clear that he was not the only one influenced by his past. "What happened that made you look at marriage in such a harsh light? It could not have been your parents, for they share a marriage like no other, is that not true?" Holding her gaze, Bradley waited.

For a long time, Lady Harriet remained quiet, appearing strangely guarded as her eyes looked into his. She seemed on the fence about what to say, and for a moment, Bradley feared she would deny any knowledge of an event that had shaped her life so profoundly.

"It was my aunt," Lady Harriet replied on the heels of a long sigh. Her shoulders slumped, and suddenly, she appeared vulnerable.

Without thinking, Bradley reached out and took her hand, pulling her closer. "What happened? Will you not tell me?"

Again, her green eyes looked up into his before a warm smile teased up the corners of her mouth. "Of course, I will."

Bradley smiled.

CHAPTER TWENTY-EIGHT

WANT & WANTING

Harriet could not say what it was, but one thing was certain: something was different about Jack today. He seemed bolder. His eyes held hers in such a daring way that she blinked at him, wondering if perhaps her eyesight was strangely impaired. His voice, too, was firmer, ringing with purpose. What had happened? Why was he suddenly asking her such a question?

"I think I was twelve," Harriet began, realizing that she had never spoken to anyone of that day, "when my Aunt Francine showed up at Whickerton Grove in the middle of the night."

A slight frown came to Jack's face, and yet he said nothing, waiting patiently for her to continue.

Harriet inhaled a deep breath as she once again heard Aunt Francine's agitated voice in her head. "She had run away from her husband," Jack's eyes widened ever so slightly, "and she was begging my mother to help her escape to France." Harriet paused, curious what Jack would say. Would he be shocked? Appalled? Would he judge her aunt harshly without asking for further explanations?

"Why?" Jack inquired, and that one word made all the difference for Harriet.

Harriet smiled up at him, then slipped her arm through his and drew him along. For a moment, they walked quietly side by side as Harriet tried her best to think of a way to explain all that had happened that night and before. "My aunt was a painter. She loved what she did, and she was remarkably good at it. Yet once married, she was expected to abandon the person she had been to become…a wife." Harriet stopped and looked up at him. "I remember the despair in her voice, the disillusionment. Truth be told, I never saw her face. My sister Christina and I, we were standing outside the door of the drawing room, listening." She shook her head at the memory. "But for a long time, I kept reliving the moment in my dreams. It haunted me, and in those dreams, I finally saw her face. She'd always been such a vivacious woman. I remember, even when I was little, that I wanted to be like her. I never wanted to paint, but…there was something about her that made me look at her in awe. She always stood tall and proud, and even in her darkest hour, she refused to bow her head."

Again, Harriet looked up at Jack, surprised that he remained quiet. Generally, men had very strong opinions and rarely refrained from forcing them on others. "Lately, I've come to realize that what my aunt fought for that night was not her right to paint." She chuckled at the thought, then lifted her gaze to Jack's. "No, she fought for her right to choose, to be her own person. She fought for her right to stand by her husband's side as an equal, not behind him. And even though he loved her, he did not understand, leaving her no choice but to leave everything behind."

For a long time, Jack simply looked at her, the expression upon his face revealing nothing of what he felt or thought. Harriet began to feel frustrated, close to demanding a reply or reaction of any kind, when Jack suddenly nodded. "I see."

"You see?" Harriet demanded, wishing he would say something, anything that would tell her he…he was different. Oh, how she wanted him to be different! But was that not what her aunt had once thought of her husband? Had they not married because they had been in love? And yet, what had that love brought her?

"What do you want me to say?" Jack inquired, a thoughtful look in his eyes. "Do you want me to say that your aunt's husband was wrong? That he should never have demanded she stop painting?"

"Yes!" Harriet exclaimed, feeling her pulse thud wildly in her neck. "Of course!"

A slow smile curled up the corners of Jack's mouth, one that made Harriet strangely furious. "What are you afraid of?" he asked, eyeing her curiously. "What makes you so fearful of marriage?"

Harriet's teeth ground together. "I am not afraid. I merely know what I want and what I don't want, and I've chosen accordingly. Is that not what everyone does?" Her voice was harsh, and she could not help but think that Jack was baiting her.

"And what *do* you want?"

Harriet's mouth dropped open, and for a second, she could not think of a single thing to say. "I don't want to be robbed of my freedom. I don't want a husband who tries to rule my life. I don't—"

Jack took a sudden step toward her, the softness in his gaze suddenly gone, replaced by something sharp. "Can you not think of a single thing you *want*? Only of all that you do *not* want?" He inhaled a slow breath before his hands reached out and settled upon her waist, pulling her to him.

A startled gasp slipped from Harriet's lips. "What are you doing?" Her hands settled upon his chest as she looked up into his eyes, completely confused by this odd behavior of his.

His head lowered to hers. "You said I was yours," Jack whispered then as his eyes drilled into hers. "Why did you say that? Is it only friendship you want from me? Or...?" His brows rose meaningfully.

Harriet felt her heart almost beat out of her chest. Never had she been so tempted to sink into another's arms or so terrified. "We were speaking of my aunt," she insisted. "Then why would you—?"

"We were speaking of want and wanting," Jack whispered in a voice that sent goosebumps over Harriet's skin. "You said you wanted to kiss me. Friends don't kiss, do they?"

"I..." Overwhelmed, Harriet did not know what to say, for in that moment she felt as though every certainty had been taken from her.

Jack's jaw tensed, and the look in his eyes intensified. "I want you to be my wife," he said in a voice that left no doubt as to his sincerity. "I want you at my side. Always." He lowered his head until the tip of his nose almost touched hers. "I want you standing by my side as an equal, not behind me."

Harriet feared her knees would buckle at any moment. Men had spoken to her of marriage before, and not once had she been affected by it, let alone in such a profound way. "I told you I would not marry," Harriet gritted out, not because she meant those words, but because she knew she needed to say them.

The look upon Jack's face tensed. "Because you do not want me?"

Warning bells went off in Harriet's head. She could feel her heart softening toward him. She could feel longing grow in every fiber of her being, urging her to give in, to accept him, to throw caution to the wind and simply live in the moment. But she knew she must not! "A woman is not safe in marriage," she hissed, allowing her anger to grow, certain that it was the only thing to hold these overwhelming emotions at bay. "A wife is only an accessory. She is not her own person. Everything she is becomes her husband's upon marriage." She shook her head, then pushed his hands away, stepping out of his embrace. "The words you speak sound wonderful, but they do not reflect the truth. How can I be your equal when the law essentially makes me your slave? My aunt had to flee the country to be free, to be safe from her husband. And even today, should her husband ever learn of her whereabouts..." A shudder gripped her at the thought. "No, I will not marry."

CHAPTER TWENTY-NINE

AT THE MERCY OF ANOTHER

Never had Bradley seen fear in Lady Harriet's eyes. Until today, he would not have believed it possible. And yet here she stood before him, her jaw set in determination, her eyes wide as she shook her head while the pulse in her neck beat so fast that she seemed in danger of passing out.

Bradley could not deny that her vehemence hurt him. Yet he understood. After all, he, too, had clung to a life he thought safe for far too long. While Lady Harriet feared to lose herself, he had always feared to have his heart broken yet again, knowing he might not be strong enough to survive it a second time. So, it was better not to love at all, was it not?

Bradley had always thought so. Now, he thought differently. What frightened him more than having his heart broken was to lose Lady Harriet from his life.

"I am not saying you're wrong," Bradley began carefully, willing himself to remain where he was. For one look at her told him that she was close to bolting. She, too, suddenly wanted something she feared, and he knew that she would do her utmost to run from it. "But you must admit that the same holds true for a daughter, does it not? Yet you trust your father to grant you your freedoms, to not stand in your way, to respect your opinions. Why then can you not trust me?"

Again, Bradley could see the urge to give in light up her eyes before she pressed her lips shut, conquering that emotion with steely resolve. "I had no choice in becoming a daughter, and my father has proven himself to me again and again."

"Then give me the same chance," Bradley asked. "Let me prove myself to you."

Her eyes closed, and once again Bradley thought she wanted to say yes. "I cannot," Lady Harriet finally said. "There is no way. I cannot marry you and then have the marriage annulled the moment you prove untrue. There is only either or. There is no safe way to be certain of your word."

Bradley felt her words like a stab to the chest. "Is that truly how you see me? Do you think so lowly of me? Do you truly believe I would be untrue to you?"

A scoff fell from Lady Harriet's lips. "My aunt believed her husband, a husband she loved, a husband who loved her, and yet... How did it end?" She shook her head. "No, as much as you mean what you say right now, the day might come when things change. I cannot risk that." She heaved a deep sigh. "I'm sorry. I..." She licked her lips, and her gaze fell from his in an unusual show of vulnerability. "Part of me wishes I could," she whispered, not daring to meet his eyes. "Believe me, ever since our paths crossed, I wished every once in a while that I had not witnessed the night my aunt had come to my parents for help." She lifted her chin, and her eyes returned to his. "But I did. I cannot change that, and I cannot change who I am and how I feel. I'm sorry." Then she abruptly spun around and hastened toward Moon, quickly pulling herself into the saddle. Her eyes returned to his one last time before she urged her mare into a gallop. Soon, they had both disappeared from sight.

Bradley remained in the meadow until dusk finally fell over the world. His heart was torn between resignation and an all-consuming sense of determination not to give up. Yes, he could take her reply as her final word and accept her refusal. He could return home and aid his aunt in the preparations for the ball, and then...he could choose a bride.

A bride that was not Lady Harriet.

Or he could do none of the above. He could tell himself that the reason she had spoken so to him was out of fear to be at another's mercy. Of course, Bradley could understand how she felt, at least from a rational point of view. Yet he reminded himself that, at least, as an adult, he had never experienced it himself. What would it feel like to have one's choices taken out of one's own hands? To always be at the whim of another, even if it was someone caring and kind?

Before meeting Lady Harriet, Bradley had had no wish to marry. Of course, he had felt obligated to. However, deep down, he had known that it was his own choice. No one had the power to force his hand. And once married, Bradley would still have the option to choose. If he were not to acknowledge her opinions or wishes, his wife would have no say in his life. That was the truth of it.

So, yes, Lady Harriet had good reason to refuse to be a wife. But was he simply to give up? What were his options? He could not change the law. He could certainly try, yes, but Bradley knew that change was slow and would certainly not come into effect during his own lifetime. So, the only option he had was to somehow change her mind.

But how?

CHAPTER THIRTY

A RARE SMILE

This time, it was Harriet who stayed away from the meadow, uncertain if she wanted to see Jack, uncertain if it would be wise. Yes she wanted to be near him, but she also feared what might happen if she gave into that longing. More than once, she found her feet moving toward the stables, her hand reaching for Moon's bridle only to pause in midair and then withdraw.

A part of Harriet wished she could speak to her grandmother. Grandma Edie always had a way of simplifying things, seeing the essence of something that appeared utterly complicated to others. Unfortunately, Harriet's family had taken their leave a few days ago and returned to Whickerton Grove.

Only Harriet remained, insisting that she had wanted to spend more time with her new niece. Of course, Samantha had been delighted. Only the rest of her family had not believed a word she had said. Harriet had seen it in their eyes. They had all taken note of her fondness for the duke as they continued to refer to him. And she was fond of him, was she not?

Harriet heaved a deep sigh. Indeed, that was the problem. If only she did not feel for him the way she did! If only he did not insist on marrying her! Was there any way to change his mind, to take marriage off the table and remain friends? Perhaps...more than friends even?

Harriet sighed at the memory of him holding her close. At first, he had always been so careful to maintain an appropriate distance between them. However, after the night they had gone after Sam, something had changed. He still did not wish for her to risk her reputation, but when they found themselves alone in their meadow, it was as though the rest of the world did not exist. He allowed her close, even reached for her himself. Whenever she thought of the day he had clung to her after his revelation about his father and the deathbed promise he had made, Harriet found herself short of breath. Her arms itched to hold him once more, and his voice echoed in her head, *Don't let go*.

Harriet did not wish to. Only he wanted marriage, and she did not.

"Here, you are," Christina exclaimed as she walked into the stables. "Sam has been looking for you everywhere."

With an arm wrapped around Moon's neck, Harriet turned to look over her shoulder at her sister. "I'm sorry. I suppose...I was lost in thought."

Walking down the aisle between the stalls, Christina came to stand outside Moon's box. "Are you all right?" she asked, her blue eyes watchful as she regarded her sister.

"Why would you ask that?" Harriet asked, turning away to brush her hand along her mare's back.

A small chuckle escaped Christina's lips. "These past few weeks, you've always taken Moon out day after day. And now, it's been... What?...five days since you've gone to meet the duke?"

Harriet wheeled around, staring at her sister.

Christina laughed. "Please, I may not be as observant as Grandma Edie, but I'm not a fool, either. Nor am I blind." Her face sobered. "What happened?"

Harriet inhaled a slow breath, then shook her head. "It's nothing," she finally said, cringing slightly at the thought of lying to her sister. Yet she could not even begin to explain what stood between her and Jack. With Christina now happily married as well, would her sister even understand? "In fact, I was getting ready to ride out right now."

"You were?"

Pushing past her sister, Harriet fetched Moon's bridle and saddle, glad to have something to occupy herself. "Moon seemed to have been fatigued these last few days, so I thought I'd give her a break."

Harriet could feel her sister's eyes on her. Of course, if Moon needed a break, she could have always saddled one of the other horses in her brother-in-law's stable. It was an excuse, nothing more, and they both knew it. Fortunately, though, Christina did not press the matter.

Although doubts still clung to Harriet's mind, she felt a deep sense of relief as she pulled herself into Moon's saddle and then urged her out of the stables. The sun felt warm upon her skin, and she reveled in the way the wind tugged upon her curls. She spurred Moon onward, wondering if Jack would be in their meadow. Had he come these past few days only to find her absent? Or had he not returned after finding her absent that first day?

A part of Harriet wondered if he had been tempted to seek her out at Pinewood Manor. Yet she was glad he had not. Whatever was between them was nothing she wished to discuss out in the open. And with a family as nosy as hers, a visit from him would have given them far too much to talk about.

Rounding the forest's edge, Harriet felt her heart skid to a halt when her gaze fell upon Jack, seated in the tall grass, his gaze fixed upon the far horizon. As proper and upstanding—literally—as he often liked to appear, the sight of him settled upon the ground, with his knees pulled up and his hands twirling a blade of grass between his fingers, pleased Harriet more than she could say. "He's here," she breathed, disbelief swirling in her chest. "He's truly here."

Indeed, a dark part of her had feared that the way she had refused him might have destroyed everything between them. Any other man would have been furious with her, would have felt dishonored by the way she had treated him. A marriage refusal was something not easily forgotten, something that would forever alter the relationship between two people. Had Jack truly not taken affront? Did he somehow understand?

There was only one way to find out.

Urging Moon down into the meadow, Harriet almost slid out of the saddle the moment Jack's head swiveled around and his gaze fell on her. The effect was frightening, and Harriet could not help but wonder at what point his mere presence had come to unbalance her in such a profound way. She could not recall. Had it happened without her notice?

Rising to his feet, Jack stepped toward her, his hand running along Moon's neck. His gaze, though, never veered from Harriet's. "It's been five days," was all he said.

Harriet inhaled a deep breath before she reminded herself that she was still seated atop her mare. Swinging one leg over, she slid out of the saddle, grateful to avert her eyes for at least one brief moment. Then, however, she was forced to turn and face him, her heart all but banging against her ribcage. "It has," was all she could murmur. Where on earth had this odd flutter in her belly come from? Had she eaten something that did not agree with her?

Barely able to hold Jack's gaze, Harriet did not know where to begin. Never had she been uncertain of herself. Never had she felt unhinged in the presence of another, and every fiber of her being hated this odd quiver that made her feel weak.

Gritting her teeth, Harriet huffed out a deep breath, willing her eyes to settle more firmly upon Jack's. "It feels as though we are strangers once more, does it not?"

A corner of his mouth twitched, and Harriet wondered if perhaps for the first time he was the one more at ease. "Does it?"

Harriet frowned. "You don't agree," she realized, slowly shaking her head from side to side. "You seem...different today. Again. Why?"

Jack shrugged, then took a step closer. "I've had some time to think," he replied with a calm that felt deeply unnerving to her.

"And?" Harriet was uncertain if she wished to hear the answer.

"And I know what I want."

Harriet could not say what it was precisely, but there was something in his brown eyes that made her stomach flit yet again. "Do I dare ask?"

And then Jack suddenly stood right in front of her, his hands settling upon her waist as though they belonged there. "I want to kiss you."

A gasp left Harriet's lips, and an old instinct urged her to retreat. Unfortunately, Moon still stood behind her, now lazily grazing, completely unaware of the tension in the air. "Why?" was all Harriet managed under the circumstances.

Indeed, had she not been the one to raise the issue only a few days ago? Daring him to admit that he had in fact wanted to kiss her? Then, the thought had excited her, temptation pulsing in her veins. Why then was she suddenly so apprehensive?

"Because," Jack murmured, a sharp edge to his voice, as his head lowered toward hers, "I *want* to kiss you."

Harriet swallowed. "That's not a reason."

Again, one corner of his mouth twitched. Had it done so before? Or was that new? "It is not? And here I thought it was the best reason one could have."

"I was right," Harriet murmured as her eyes searched his face. "Something *is* different about you."

"Do you mind?"

Harriet shook her head. "Tell me what happened."

Jack exhaled a slow breath, its warmth teasing her skin. "My father warned me of loss," he whispered, a new glow in his eyes that made Harriet want to be closer, "but it is too late now. You were right. A kiss is not the cause of *emotional entanglements*," despite warning bells going off in her head, Harriet could not help but love the slight eye roll that accompanied those two words, "but the consequence." His gaze briefly strayed to her lips. "Loss is now inevitable; the only uncertainty is its precise moment in time."

Harriet swallowed hard at those words, her eyes wide as she stared at him.

"I'd rather not have it be today or tomorrow." Jack's hands moved to the small of her back and tightened. "Preferably some time in the distant future."

Apprehension settled in Harriet's chest. "What are you saying?"

Marry me! Unbidden, those two words echoed in her head, quickly followed by her grandmother's knowing voice, *could it be perhaps that his words unsettled you so because some part of you is tempted to accept him?*

Jack's hand slid into her hair as he inched closer, his gaze once more darting to her lips. "Don't be afraid," he murmured, something teasing in his brown eyes. "I won't bite."

Harriet chuckled as her gaze once more swept over his face in awe. "You can be funny when you want to be. I did not know that."

Jack grinned. "Neither did I."

"And I'm not afraid!"

A rather indulgent smile came to his face. "Of course, not."

"Do you believe me?" Harriet hastened to say the moment he leaned in, her heart thundering in her chest most disconcertingly.

Jack regarded her carefully, that teasing spark still in his eyes. "Does it matter?"

"Of course, it does. I—"

"You're stalling."

"Perhaps."

"Why?"

"Because..." Harriet swallowed hard, then inhaled a deep breath and threw caution to the wind. Never had she been one to shy away from anything, and she would not start now. "Because I'm afraid," she admitted sheepishly.

Oddly enough, the tightness in her chest lessened the moment those words left her lips. "How can I not be? What I feel for you makes me question everything I thought I knew, everything I thought I wanted."

"What you feel for me," Jack echoed her words, the need to press her for more visible in his eyes. Still, he did not press but leaned in. "Do you want me to release you?" he whispered against her lips.

Harriet knew she ought to say *yes*. She ought to send him away. She ought to make it unmistakably clear that she would not marry him.

Not ever.

"No." Her arms rose to wrap around his shoulders, and she lifted her face to his. "Kiss me, Jack."

Harriet felt him smile against her lips, and a part of her wished she could have seen it, for he rarely smiled. But he did now.

Here.

With her.

CHAPTER THIRTY-ONE

THE WEIGHT OF LOSS

Bradley barely recognized himself as he stood among a sea of wildflowers, a fiery-haired hellion in his arms and a longing in his heart that threatened to bring him to his knees. He could not remember ever having felt more at peace.

And then his lips touched hers, and he cursed and blessed his father for his ill-conceived advice. He could not help the anger he felt at the thought of years wasted because a bitter, old man could not bring himself to forgive his wife for leaving him. Bradley wondered if he would be here in this moment with Lady Harriet if his father had not wrangled that deathbed promise from him.

That thought, though, quickly fled his mind as Lady Harriet's fingers curled into his hair and she pushed herself onto her toes to be closer. Her lips felt soft and willing under his own, and Bradley marveled at the sensations that shot through him. He could not imagine a kiss with another woman would make him feel this way. The way he felt kissing Harriet.

Bradley could feel her smile against his lips, undoubtedly as surprised as he was himself about this unexpected turn of events. He was surprised but, definitely, pleased. The tips of her fingers brushed against his skin, sending shivers down his spine, and her response to his—granted!—inexperienced kiss whispered of eagerness and passion.

There were likely a dozen reasons why he should not be kissing her, but one very good one why he should.

And he did...

...and continued to do so...

...until Moon suddenly shifted, perhaps to move on to a tastier spot of grass, upending their balance in the process.

Lady Harriet's hands grasped his shoulders as they stumbled, her eyes wide, but a smile upon her face that had the power to make him forget everything. "Careful or we'll—!"

With a thud, they landed on the ground, his arms still wrapped around her.

"Fall," Lady Harriet finished with a grin. "Are you all right?"

Bradley nodded. "You?" He pushed himself back up onto his feet, pulling her along.

Brushing grass from her skirts, Lady Harriet nodded. "I'm fine. No harm done." Then her eyes met his, and Bradley could have sworn that the air around them hummed with energy. "So," she grinned at him, "I claimed your first kiss."

To his utter mortification, Bradley could feel himself blush. "You did, yes."

Her smile deepened as she stepped forward and touched a hand to his heated cheek. "Oh, sweet Jack, I do love to see you so flustered."

"Do you now, my lady?" Bradley challenged. "Perhaps—"

"Would you stop that?" Lady Harriet snapped, her eyes widening in annoyance.

"Stop what?"

Her eyes narrowed as she regarded him curiously. "You're still doing it, aren't you?"

"Doing what?" Bradley inquired, completely at a loss.

Lady Harriet held his gaze for a moment longer, then huffed out a breath and asked, "You still think of me as *Lady Harriet*, do you not?"

Bradley frowned. "That is who you are, is it not?"

Stepping forward, she grasped his hands, her eyes locked upon his. "I might be to all those foolish peacocks in London, but to you, I'm

Harry." She rolled her eyes. "Or at the very least, Harriet. No *lady*, do you hear me? Not even in your thoughts!"

Bradley heard himself chuckle and marveled at the odd sound. He could not recall having done it often...or at all. "If you insist...my lady."

The look upon *Harriet*'s face told him she wanted to box his ears... or worse.

Bradley lifted his hands in surrender. "Very well...Harry."

A deep breath lifted her shoulders, and she smiled at him approvingly. "Thank you."

And there they stood, in a sea of wildflowers, their eyes locked and their thoughts lingering on the moment they had just shared. But how to continue?

"Why did you come here today?" Bradley asked. "Why today?"

Harriet heaved a deep sigh. "I don't know. I wanted to see you, but I didn't know if it was wise."

Bradley nodded. "We want different things."

"We do," Harriet agreed before a grin split her face. "Except for that *one* thing. We both want that."

Bradley laughed. "With good reason."

"Very good reason."

He swallowed. "Where do we go from here?"

A long sigh left her lips, and Bradley could see that the ease that had existed between them before was slowly slipping away. Only moments ago, they had allowed themselves to exist in a bubble outside of time and space, ignoring what was and what would be. Still, in the end, they would be forced to face reality. "I do not know," Harriet replied as her eyes drifted from his and she bowed her head as though in defeat.

Bradley felt his insides twist painfully. While it was unmistakable that Harriet truly cared for him, it was also unmistakable that she had not changed her mind about marriage. "Is there nothing I can say?"

For a long moment, Bradley feared she might not even look up at him. Her eyes closed, and her shoulders rose and fell with one deep breath after another as though she was trying to calm her own pounding heart. Then she finally lifted her chin and met his gaze, the look in her green eyes whispering of sorrow and regret but equally of determination. "I will not lie to you, Jack. I want you in my life. I want to see you every day. I want to hug you and kiss you." She bit her lower lip as a wide grin stretched the corners of her mouth. "I want to be your friend, your confidante and your lover."

Bradley drew in a sharp breath at her open words. Indeed, never in his life had he met anyone like Lady Harriet—scratch that, Harry! She was his complete opposite, and yet perhaps it was their differences that made them feel so at ease with one another. His caution and her impulsiveness seemed to find some odd balance in one another, and Bradley could not imagine ever being without it again. Yet the look in her eyes told him she was not finished.

Harry grasped his hands, her green eyes soft and yet sorrowful. "I cannot be your wife. I *will* not be your wife." Slowly, she shook her head from side to side. "I cannot risk everything I am. I wish you could understand what it feels like to be at such a disadvantage as a woman." She swallowed hard, and he felt her hands squeeze his. "I know you must marry," she said abruptly, "to ensure your mother's estate remains yours. I will not stand in your way, but perhaps," she heaved a deep sigh, "we can pretend at least until the ball, until you have to make a choice."

Dumbfounded, Bradley stared at her, unable to believe his ears. "What are you suggesting?" he asked, pulling his hands out of hers more quickly than he had intended to.

Harriet's jaw clenched as she held his gaze, her own hardening. "I am suggesting all I can," she replied, something steely coming to her voice. "Either we part ways now or when you choose your future bride. As much as I wish it, there is no alternative." Again, her head moved slowly from side to side as she retraced her steps, one, then two, making it unmistakably clear that, no, she would not change her mind.

No more than he would change his. "I have already chosen my bride," Bradley growled, gritting his teeth against that sudden surge of anger that swelled in his veins. He knew very well from whence it had come, for he could sense a deep, dark pit of powerlessness that threatened to hollow out his insides.

"It cannot be me," Harriet insisted, retreating another step.

Bradley ran a hand over his face, his thumb and forefinger pinching the bridge of his nose as he thought about what to say, his mind searching for anything that might change the outcome of this discussion.

Unfortunately, there was nothing.

Only a few steps separated them, and yet it seemed like an insurmountable gap had opened up between them.

And not a bridge in sight. Was this truly it? Bradley wondered. Were those his only two choices? Bid her farewell today or in a few weeks from now?

It could not be. It simply could not. "What if...?" Bradley closed his eyes, pinching them shut as he tried to remember those childhood days at Laurelwood Manor. He caught a faint glimpse of his mother's smile and heard a dim echo of his father's voice. Yet more would not come, his memories buried deep, all but inaccessible to him. What he remembered was his father's warning, the last words the man had ever spoken to him. Only now, there was something else as well.

His mother...

...and the stipulation in her will.

For months now, Bradley had wondered why his mother had done so, why she would force him into marriage. Even from beyond the grave. Indeed, it had been Harriet who had suggested that his mother had done so in order to ensure he would never be alone but have a family in his life. If that was true, then Bradley knew that his mother would not object to him giving up Laurelwood Manor, if doing so would secure his happiness.

No, she would urge him to do so, would she not? Always had she put him first. Bradley remembered little, but he remembered that.

Inhaling one last deep breath, Bradley opened his eyes and looked at the woman he loved. How it had happened he did not know nor care. But it was the truth, and he knew he would do everything within his power to keep her in his life. "Then we will not marry if that is what it takes."

Harriet's features paled as she stared at him. He could see his words slowly sinking in, their meaning becoming clear as her eyes slowly widened. "You cannot mean that," she whispered, her head once again shaking from side to side as she retreated another step.

"I do," Bradley replied without hesitation, his voice sharp and without the slightest whisper of doubt. He stepped toward her, his legs crossing the distance between them even as she tried to retreat yet again. His hands reached for hers, pulling her back. "I mean every word. I want you in my life. Preferably as a wife, yes. However, if that is not possible," he looked deep into her wide, unblinking eyes, "I'll take everything you're willing to offer." His hands tightened on hers. "I want you. No matter what, I want you."

Tears misted in her eyes, and he could feel her hands responding to the pressure of his. "You would do that?" she asked in a whisper. "For me?"

A dark chuckle left Bradley's lips. "No, not for you," he said honestly, "for me." He tugged her toward him, his hands coming around her waist as he lowered his head to look deep into her eyes. "Can you not tell? I'm being selfish right here, right now. I want what I want, and I'm willing to do anything to get it." His voice was hard, a far cry from the romantic notes it probably ought to possess considering the words he spoke and the woman he was saying them to.

For a long moment, Bradley could see nothing but shock upon Harriet's features. Locked in his embrace, she held herself still, unmoving, as though time had stopped. Her eyes were wide and her mouth slightly open as though she was on the brink of saying something, but knew not what it was.

"I would never hurt you," Bradley murmured softly as he saw fresh tears collecting in her eyes. "Never. I swear it."

Her eyes closed, and a lone tear rolled down her left cheek. "I know," Harriet whispered then, meeting his eyes once more. "I want to believe you, and I do. Believe me, my heart urges me to accept you, to accept what you are offering, but I know it would not be right."

When Bradley made to object, she pressed a finger to his lips, cutting him off. "I cannot ask you to give up who you are so that I may remain the person I am. You do not truly want what you're offering, and it would be wrong of me to accept it. It would be selfish and not in the selfless way you are being selfish." She chuckled, and fresh tears rolled down her cheeks. "I would never ask you to be someone you're not, but neither can I become someone I am not. We are walking down two very different paths, and I'm afraid while they might cross now and then, they will never lead us in the same direction. It is a sad truth we will have to accept."

Bradley felt as though a heavy boulder was crushing his chest, for he could barely draw in a breath as he watched Harriet step away. Her wide eyes held his, and he could tell from the look in her eyes that she was bidding him farewell. "This cannot be it."

Harriet wiped the tears from her eyes. "I wish it didn't have to be." She retreated another step and then another until she bumped into Moon, grazing lazily behind her. "But I don't see another option. Neither one of us should give up who we are because if we did so, eventually the day would come that regret would find us. It is the way of the world, the way of life. It might seem worthwhile in the moment, but it is not. Foremost, we must be loyal to ourselves, for happiness cannot be found without it." She reached for Moon's reins. "Please understand, Jack. This is the hardest thing I have ever done, and I'm doing it for the both of us. I'm sorry." Then she turned, pulled up the reins and made to pull herself into the saddle. However, with one foot in the stirrup, she paused.

Still staring at her in disbelief, Bradley felt an agonizingly slow moment tick by as the wildflowers continued to sway around him in the soft summer breeze that suddenly felt cold and chilling. He watched her left foot slide out of the stirrup and fall back to the ground as her body slumped forward and she rested her forehead against the saddle. He could see her shoulders rise and fall with each deep breath, and then Bradley suddenly found her spinning around, her face tear-streaked, but her wide green eyes determined and her jaw set.

Without a word, Harriet rushed toward him, all but flinging herself forward and into his arms. Bradley caught her without thought, lowering his head to hers, the same desperate need pulsing in his veins that he had seen in her blazing eyes.

Their second kiss was far from gentle, fueled by their impending separation. They sank into each other, their hands clawing to get closer. Bradley forced his thoughts to remain in the here and now, his senses attuned to the feel of her in his arms, the touch of her lips, the sensation of her heartbeat against his. He did his utmost to ignore the moment that loomed upon the horizon.

The moment that would see the end of them. Only weeks had passed since they had first met, and now, the mere thought of life without her felt like the worst kind of torture. Perhaps his father had been right after all. Was this what loss felt like? Loss that could not be avoided? No matter how hard one fought or how much one was willing to sacrifice?

Pulling back, Harriet sank down onto her feet, her right hand cupping his face as she looked up at him with teary eyes. "Goodbye, sweet Jack. I shall never forget you." She pressed another quick kiss to his lips before darting out of his embrace.

Quick strides carried her to Moon, and she swung herself into the saddle with a swiftness that startled the mare. Her eyes found his once more, now dark with loss and regret, before she urged Moon around and sent her galloping down the meadow.

Bradley stared after them, his chest feeling hollowed out in the place where his heart had been. "This can't be it," he mumbled over and over again, unable to believe what had just happened.

Yet it had, had it not?

She was gone.

For good.

CHAPTER THIRTY-TWO

A WELCOME DISTRACTION

Harriet hardly knew how she found her way home, relieved to place her trust in Moon and have the mare carry her back to Pinewood Manor with no need for directions from her. She barely managed to dry her tears before reaching the stables, for once handing over her trusted friend to a stable boy before sneaking into the house through a side entrance. She could not imagine meeting Christina or Samantha, their curious eyes no doubt seeing with one glance that something was very, very wrong.

The moment the door closed behind her and she found herself in her bedchamber, Harriet felt fresh tears collect in her eyes, the need to cry almost overwhelming. She gritted her teeth against the impulse, feeling anger rise within her over her own weakness. Why was it that he affected her so? Had they not only met but a few weeks ago?

A growl rose from her throat as she stalked across her chamber, her feet carrying her toward the window and then back toward the door. Again and again, she spun around, unable to keep still, dimly aware that movement seemed to be the only thing keeping the tears at bay. What on earth was she to do now?

The mere thought of Jack almost brought her to her knees, and Harriet wondered how she was supposed to get through the day and the one after that. Was this what it felt like to have one's heart broken? Indeed, it was most awful, unlike anything Harriet had ever experienced. How did people survive it?

A violent tremble seized her, and she wrapped her arms around herself to keep still, to fight it down, but it would not relent. Her feet continued to move as Harriet continued to force her mind elsewhere, anywhere.

And then her gaze fell upon a letter that had been placed upon her vanity in her absence.

Harry lunged toward it like a hunter going after its prey. Her mind and heart instantly zeroed in on it, desperate for any kind of distraction, hoping for at least a momentary relief from this soul-crushing agony she had not seen coming.

Turning the letter in her hands, Harriet was surprised to see nothing more but her own name as well as her sister's address. There was no seal, no mention of who had sent it.

Quickly, Harriet tore it open, her eyes eagerly searching the parchment as her trembling fingers unfolded it. Her gaze flew over the handwriting, her mind recognizing it as familiar, before her eyes dropped to the bottom of the parchment. "Sarah?" Confusion swept through Harriet. "Why are you writing to me? And not to Christina?"

Indeed, since childhood, Miss Sarah Mortensen had been Christina's best friend. Once, her family had lived next door to their townhouse in London; however, since Lord Hartmore, Sarah's father, had amassed significant gambling debts, the family had been forced to sell the townhouse. In consequence of these financial issues, Sarah's parents had repeatedly tried to see their daughter married over the course of the last year or two...to men of fortune, of course.

My dearest Harry,

I can only assume that you are surprised to receive this letter, but I fear you're the only one I can turn to. I do not wish to burden Christina with this, for she will no doubt blame herself for my misfortune. Of course, nothing could be further from the truth. I wish her all the happiness in the world in her marriage, and I'm happy to hear that she and Mr. Sharpe care for one another so deeply.

Indeed, Mr. Sharpe—Thorne!—had been one of the suitors Sarah's parents had tried to force upon her. Christina had been outraged to learn that her dearest friend had been on the brink of betrothal to a man not of their societal circle, fortune or no. She had been afraid of what such a marriage might do to Sarah, who was a most delicate creature. And so, Christina had gone to great lengths to protect her friend...and in the process had found herself accidentally compromised by none other than Mr. Sharpe himself.

A happy accident because despite her sister's initial animosity toward him, Harriet knew Christina had come to love her new husband with all her heart. It had taken time, but Thorne had been most determined to win his new bride's affections.

And he had.

Harry, I hate to burden you with this, but I am at my wit's end. Last night, I overheard a conversation between my parents, and from what was said, I can only conclude that they are planning to see me betrothed to Lord Gillingham.

Harriet almost reeled back from the shock of it. Her eyes went wide as she stared at his name on the page. "How dare they!" Outrage burned in her veins, and her hands clenched on the parchment, crumpling it at the sides.

Not long ago, it had been revealed that Lord Gillingham had been the one to attack Harriet's sister Leonora at a masquerade ball. For over a year, her sister had been in the dark about who the man had been that had forced his attentions on her. She had become fearful of men in general, and it had taken an exceptional man like Drake to help her through her fears and restore her trust in herself and men in general. Still, to this day, Leonora met the world with more caution, more doubt. Harriet could see it in her sister's eyes. The memory of what happened to her still lingered; although, Leonora had taken a stand, openly accusing Lord Gillingham of his crime.

Leonora had allowed herself to be ruined, to warn others, and now—

Harriet's eyes returned to the parchment, her mind desperate for more information. How could Sarah's parents consider such a man for their daughter's husband? Were they mad?

I know what you must think, Harry. Believe me, I'm thinking it as well. Yet I know how desperate my parents are. You and your family know better than anyone how dire the situation is for us. Debtors keep knocking on our door, and we were forced to retreat to the house party at Atwell Park, praying that our whereabouts will not be discovered too quickly. I am uncertain if my parents asked Lord Gillingham to meet us here, if their plans extended that far, or if, perhaps, they have merely taken advantage of the situation.

"I would not put it past them," Harriet growled under her breath. Unlike her own parents, Lord and Lady Hartmore had never shown particular affection toward their own children. To them, they were a means to an end. Already they had married off their eldest daughter to an earl in possession of a large fortune and with the desire for a young wife.

I do not know what to do. I am deeply sorry to place this burden upon your shoulders, dearest Harry, but I feel I must tell someone. I know there is no solution to my dilemma, but I feel it already soothes my heart to pour it out to you and know that you understand how I feel.

Please, say nothing to Christina. I do not want her worrying about me. Perhaps nothing will come of it. However, I must admit even I know it to be wishful thinking.

After poor Leo revealed Lord Gillingham's true character to the world, I've heard it whispered that the man is finding it most difficult to procure himself a wife, and therefore, it seems with his current lack of choice, any sort of wife will do. Even I. My parents are delighted at the prospect. Though his reputation is tarnished, he is titled, wealthy and influential.

"And vicious, vile and violent," Harriet added through clenched teeth, her hands shaking with the effort to stay calm and not do something unwise.

Perhaps all is not as bad as it sounds. I know I have a tendency to see things at their worst. Perhaps marriage to him will be nothing more than another minor inconvenience. After all, it is my duty to abide by my parents' wishes, and I do not believe they would arrange a marriage for me that would see me harmed.

If only Harriet could reach out and slap her! Sarah had always been a rather doe-eyed young woman, all but terrified of the world. Perhaps with parents like hers, that was no surprise. Yet, Sarah possessed the ability to shut her eyes to the truth and sugarcoat everything until it frightened her less.

Please don't worry about me, dearest Harry. I shall be fine. I already feel better having confided in you. But if you have a moment, please write back. I do long to hear from you.

Your devoted friend,

Sarah

Unable not to, Harriet crumpled the parchment into a tight little ball and flung it across the room with a grunt of outrage. No, simply writing back would not do! If Sarah's parents truly forced her to marry

Lord Gillingham, her life would be ruined and Christina would never forgive herself for not preventing it.

Harriet gritted her teeth as she began pacing. If only her grandmother was still at Pinewood Manor! The woman always found a solution, even to the most unsolvable problems. Unfortunately, she and Juliet had gone to visit a friend of hers. Harriet could not quite recall where, but there was no time to make careful inquiries. No, time was of the essence. Something needed to be done now!

Unexpectedly, the thought of Jack crossed Harriet's mind and her heart instantly cringed in pain at the memory of what she had lost. "Not now," she gritted out as fresh tears shot to her eyes. "I'll not think about him now." Indeed, it was by far better and more productive to focus her attention on helping Sarah.

It was precisely the distraction Harriet needed!

Desperately.

Brushing the tears from her eyes, Harriet called her maid and instructed her to pack her things. Then, when she was sufficiently certain not to break out in tears again, Harriet went to inform her sister that she would return home on the morrow—after all, her sister was the last person who ought to know the truth. And so, while Christina was surprised by Harriet's sudden wish to depart, she did not argue and they spent a companionable evening together.

When Harriet finally returned to her chamber, she found sleep eluded her. Her mind continued to take her back to the meadow and to Jack, and she would find her body alternately curling around her pillow in agony and then her fists pummeling it in anger. Eventually, Harriet rose from the bed and sat down to pen a few lines to Jack in farewell. Perhaps if she did so, her mind could let go of the last shreds of hope that still seemed to linger.

Foolish hope. It would come to nothing. It never did.

Never.

CHAPTER THIRTY-THREE

A BEAUTIFUL DREAM

More than ever before, Bradley stuck to each and every one of his routines. Especially now, they served him, for he did not need to think about the next step to take. His body was so familiar with everything that followed after he had completed one task that his mind could remain blessedly absent. His feet carried him from one place to another, and his hands moved, picking up papers and setting them aside. He spoke to his steward and then later to his aunt, and all the while, his mind remained absent, lingering upon the one moment that had changed everything.

The moment Harriet had left, had bid him farewell...for good.

Bradley knew that if he were to ride out today and seek out their meadow, he would not find her there. The thought alone brought deepest agony to his heart, and he felt his hands clench together tightly until pain shot up his arms. He stood by the window in his study as he had countless times before, and yet he could not recall ever having felt this wretched. Was this supposed to be his life from now on? Was he simply to accept her decision and allow her to leave his life as quickly as she had entered it? Or was there anything at all that could be done?

Anything?

A knock sounded on the door to his study, and Bradley flinched. His first impulse was to berate Harriet for coming to Clements Park unchaperoned once again before he realized it could not possibly be her. Instead, it was Lady Easton who entered, a parchment in her hand, which proved to be the guest list for the upcoming ball. "I am quite pleased to say that the first ball at Clements Park in many years is being very well received." A warm smile shone upon her face as she looked at him. "Many young ladies will be present here that night, giving you ample opportunity to choose your duchess."

Bradley cleared his throat. His duchess? He had already found his duchess; only she did not want him. No, that was not entirely true. It was not him she did not want, was it? What she did not want was marriage! But did that distinction truly make a difference?

"Clements, did you even hear a word I said?" Blinking, Bradley realized his aunt was frowning at him. "I must say, over the course of the past few weeks, you have...frequently seemed rather...absent. Is something on your mind?"

Bradley almost laughed. Indeed, his mind had never been more preoccupied than it had been these past few weeks. Harriet had had such an all-consuming pull on him that he had thought of little else but her. At first, he had not even been aware of it, but now he knew. Would it ever lessen? If he truly let her go now and did his best to do his duty, would he eventually find himself free of her? Or would the years pass and this yearning in his chest would remain? Grow even? Would he end like his father, bitter and alone and praying for death?

Once again, a sharp knock echoed in Bradley's ears, and he turned to see Albert step into the room, a letter on a silver platter held out to him. "This just arrived for you, your grace."

Bradley sighed, then reached to take the letter. "Thank you, Albert." After offering a quick nod, his butler retreated instantly, closing the door behind him. Bradley's aunt, however, remained, her questioning eyes still fixed upon him. Bradley was relieved to drop his gaze to the letter in his hands...only to find his heart still the moment his eyes fell upon the words written there.

Never had Bradley seen Lady Harriet's handwriting, and yet he knew that this letter was from her. It was a feeling deep inside, one he could not explain nor dare try to. Never had he put much stock in *feelings* or *intuitions*, but life had changed, had it not? *He* had changed. He was no longer the man he had been a few weeks ago, and he no longer wanted what he had wanted then. No, now he wanted her.

And no matter what, he would not simply walk away nor allow her to walk away from him.

Tearing open the letter, Bradley unfolded it with trembling fingers, his gaze eager for the words written upon the parchment. Indeed, this was unusual. He would not have expected her to write him a letter. Why had she done so?

My sweet Jack,

Bradley could have groaned at her once infuriating, but now endearing nickname for him.

I feel the need to apologize for the way I left you the day before. Still, I cannot regret my decision, for I know it to be right, but I feel awful for leaving you. I admit I am torn and wish that the world could be a different place, a place where we both could have what we long for.

That being said, I believe it will do us both good to spend time apart from one another. It will help us let go of this beautiful dream we both harbored without truly realizing it. I did as well, and I want you to know it.

Bradley closed his eyes as he savored the words upon the parchment. They proved beyond any doubt that, yes, he had not imagined her affections. He had had his doubts when she had been able to simply walk away, but now he no longer did.

"Clements?" came his aunt's voice, a tinge of concern in it as she took a step toward him. "Are you all right? Who wrote to you? I hope it is not bad news."

Bradley looked up at her. "It is not, my lady." He was about to turn his gaze back to the parchment when he paused, his gaze lingering upon his aunt's face. She had known him ever since the day he had been born, and yet they did not truly know one another, did they? They did not share in each other's lives. Not truly. Bradley could not help but resent the fact that she continued to address him as *Clements*. It was a title far removed from who he was, just as far removed as she was from knowing the real him.

My sweet Jack. Harriet's words echoed in his mind, and he remembered the way her family spoke to one another, addressed one another, truly aware who the others were. Perhaps there were those who would frown upon such an informal way of address, but Bradley realized he would much prefer it.

He had changed in more ways than he had realized, and he did not wish to go back.

I received a letter from a friend in need. Some people might consider it a sign. In the end, whether it is does not matter. What matters is that it will take me away from Pinewood Manor.

Bradley's insides contracted painfully as his fingers tightened upon the parchment. She was leaving? When? Where to?

This will be good for the both of us. Believe me. You shall find yourself busy with preparations for the ball whereas I shall find ample distraction at Atwood Park, I have no doubt.

Perhaps one day in the not so distant future, we shall meet again. Then, with the necessary distance between us, we might find that a friendship is possible. I sincerely hope it will be. I shall miss you, my sweet Jack, and I wish you all the happiness in the world.

Love,

Harry

Dread spread through Bradley's body, reaching every fiber of his being; yet his gaze once more darted across the parchment, his eyes searching for two words in particular.

Atwood Park.

Frowning, he wondered if Harry had listed the estate she was to travel to on purpose. Why did she want him to know? Was there a part of her that wished he would follow? Bradley could not imagine not seeing her every day. He already began feeling restless as the time of their usual meeting approached, knowing it would not happen today. He could not go days, weeks, months or even years without seeing her. It was an impossible thought!

Without hesitation, Bradley reached for the bellpull. Only moments later, Albert reappeared in his study. "Is there anything I can do for you, your grace?"

"Have my things packed immediately," Bradley instructed the man, moving around his desk and penning a few words for his steward. "I will travel to Atwood Park today."

"As you wish, your grace," Albert nodded, then quickly hurried away.

"Atwood Park?" Lady Easton inquired, something shrill coming to her voice. "What is going on? You cannot leave now. The ball is less than a month away."

Bradley paused, inhaled a deep breath, and met her eyes. "I apologize, my lady. However, this is a matter of the utmost importance." He could not help but wonder if she would understand if he were to explain himself. Yet the sad truth was that they were not close enough for him to know, let alone do so. "I will do my utmost to return in time for the ball. You have my word."

Her jaw dropped, and her eyes widened. "You will do your utmost?" She spun around as he rushed toward the door, eager footsteps carrying him away. "You cannot be serious! Clements!" She called after him a few more times, but Bradley kept on walking.

Indeed, it felt good to have made a decision, and he would see it through.

CHAPTER THIRTY-FOUR

LESSER OF TWO EVILS

Utter joy stood on Lady Atwood's face when she welcomed Harriet into her home. Indeed, the Whickertons had received an invitation to this year's house party because of their rather scandalous reputation. The Atwoods had made it a habit of inviting those the gossips whispered about most. Therefore, it was no surprise that not only Lord Hartmore and his family as well as Lord Gillingham had been invited. Lord Hartmore's gambling debts and his family's desperate situation were widely known as was Lord Gillingham's recent set down by none other than Lady Pemberton, Harriet's sister.

"I admit I am quite surprised to see you here, my dear," Lady Atwood exclaimed, clasping her hands together. "And alone no less." Harriet could all but see the cogs in Lady Atwood's mind turning, no doubt contemplating what potential scandal this suggested. "However, I am most delighted. I hope you had a pleasant journey."

Lady Harriet offered her a polite smile. "It was quite uneventful." She allowed a bit of a grin to show upon her face.

As expected, Lady Atwood's features brightened considerably. "Oh, my dear, you will find nothing uneventful here. Quite on the contrary." She turned and waved to a footman. "Escort Lady Harriet to the blue room." A deeply satisfied sigh left her lips. "You will be most comfortable there."

Harriet nodded gratefully. "May I ask? Are Lord Hartmore and his family settled nearby? I am most eager to speak with Miss Mortensen, for she is a dear friend of mine, as you might know."

After Lady Atwood assured her that Miss Mortensen occupied a chamber only two doors down from Harriet's, she took her leave, assuring her hostess that she would be delighted to partake in the occasional parlor game later that day.

Quick steps carried Harriet up the stairs. She greeted the occasional acquaintance on the way, but did not allow herself to be drawn into a conversation. As soon as she reached the door to her chamber, Harriet instructed the footman to place her things inside and have a maid sent to unpack. Then she hurried to Sarah's chamber and knocked.

For a moment, Harriet wondered if perhaps Sarah was otherwise engaged, taking part in some game or walking the grounds or...being cornered by Lord Gillingham. But then the door opened, revealing a rather pale-faced Sarah, whose eyes opened wide the moment she beheld the one standing outside her door. "Harry?" she gasped, her jaw dropping. "Heavens, what are you doing here?"

"Inside," Harriet replied, then pushed past her friend and kicked the door closed with her boot. Undoubtedly, Sarah's parents would object to seeing the two of them together; after all, whenever one of their matchmaking schemes for their daughter had failed, it had been the Whickertons' doing.

And it would be again, Harriet swore silently.

As her gaze swept over Sarah, the anger in Harriet's heart grew.

While Sarah had always been a pale, rather fearful, young woman, the tension that now seemed to linger even in the smallest movement spoke bounds to the terror that lived in her heart. Even her usually warm blond hair seemed dull, as though it no longer possessed the energy to shine. Sarah continued to wring her hands, her blue eyes flitting nervously around the room as though she was expecting an attack at any moment.

Always had Harriet thought of Sarah as *delicate*, but this was beyond anything she had ever seen. "You look awful," Harriet commented, shaking her head at her friend.

A small chuckle escaped Sarah. "Direct as always, dear friend." A barely audible sob left her lips as her eyes looked at Harriet, as though she feared her friend might be nothing more than a mirage. "You're truly here," she mumbled, disbelief in her voice.

"Of course, I am. How could I not after—?"

Suddenly, Sarah flung herself into Harriet's arms, crushing her with a strength Harriet would not have expected. "It is so good to see you, Harry. It is so good to see a friendly face." She pulled back and wiped at the tears streaming down her face. "I missed you all so much. Is Christina all right? Is she happy? Did she receive my letter?"

Harriet nodded with a smile. "She is. Incredibly so, I assure you." She squeezed Sarah's hands. "And, yes, she received your letter. She knows your father is the reason you did not attend her wedding. Do not worry. She is not upset with you."

Sarah exhaled a slow breath, relief marking her features. "That is good," she mumbled. "That is good."

Harriet watched Sarah carefully, her hands coming to rest upon her friend's shoulders. "Now, tell me everything that's happened with... Gillingham." She all but growled the last word.

An abrupt shiver shook Sarah's delicate frame, and Harriet could see that her friend was far more afraid than she had let on. "Nothing has been agreed upon yet," Sarah finally said after a few deep breaths, her hands still trembling, but her features were marked by forced composure. "My father assures me that Lord Gillingham is an honorable man and that," she drew another lungful of air into her body, "beggars cannot be choosers." Sadness stood in her wide blue eyes.

Gritting her teeth against the anger that burned ever brighter inside her, Harriet stared at her friend. Sometimes she had trouble making sense of Sarah's personality. For all Sarah's determination to see only the good in people, to explain away any fault or flaw in their behavior or character, she appeared constantly afraid, sensing doom lingering around every corner. How had she become the young woman she was today? What had it been like for her to grow up with parents who saw only themselves and cared very little—if at all—for their own children? Harriet could not imagine having no one to turn to in a time of need. She knew beyond the shadow of a doubt that a single word from her would be enough to call all the Whickertons to her side.

It was a reassuring thought. Warm and comforting, and it gave her strength far beyond anything she otherwise would have had.

Harriet saw no such strength in Sarah. "I shall only ask you this once," she fixed her friend with the most severe look, "so consider your answer carefully."

Sarah stilled, her eyes wide and even more so as she looked at Harriet.

"Do you want to marry Lord Gillingham?"

The shudder that shook Sarah was answer enough, yet Harriet waited. She needed Sarah to make this decision. To speak the answer loud and clear and not have it taken from her.

Sarah swallowed hard, then she slowly shook her head from side to side, an apologetic look coming to her wide blue eyes. "I do not," she whispered in a voice that could be barely heard, as though she feared that speaking any louder might bring some sort of doom down upon her. "I know I should not say so, but I do not wish to marry him. The mere thought turns my stomach. I cannot stop thinking about what he did to poor Leo." Tears stood in her eyes, and she looked like Misery herself.

Harriet gave an acknowledging nod, struggling to maintain control of her emotions. She knew she was impulsive and hotheaded; and while her raging emotions had served her far more times than she could count, Harriet knew that here, now was not the time nor place. This moment called for levelheadedness, for patience and careful consideration. "As much as I hate to say this," Harriet began calmly, carefully maintaining an even tone, "the only way to keep you permanently safe from your parents' scheming is to see you married...or perhaps for you to leave the country altogether." For a split second, her thoughts strayed to Aunt Francine in France, and she wondered if perhaps she was being selfish by not truly considering sending Sarah far away.

Her friend's eyes, however, widened in a look of horror at the mere thought of leaving everything behind. "I cannot!" She shook her head frantically, her hands reaching out to grasp Harriet's arms. "I cannot leave. Please understand! I cannot leave!" Clearly, the thought terrified her.

"Very well," Harriet relented, never truly having believed it to be an option. "Marriage it is then. Only marriage to whom?" Her brows rose questioningly as she looked at Sarah. "Is there a particular gentleman you would consider?" More or less, anyone would be better than Gillingham.

For a brief second, Sarah closed her eyes and inhaled a deep breath. "If this were only about what I wanted, I suppose I would've married a while ago." A sad smile came to her face. "Even if there were such a gentleman, he would not want me. No one does, not even Lord Gillingham. The only reason he is now considering me as his wife is because he has no other option." She bowed her head. "It is very kind of you to want to help me, but there is no way." She released her tight grip on Harriet's arms and took a step back. "Perhaps you should not have come. I'm sorry I alarmed you with my letter but—"

"Don't you dare give up!" Harriet insisted in a harsh voice that made Sarah's head snap up. "I understand that you feel disheartened, but there is always a solution. Always. All we have to do is find it." As she spoke those words, Harriet could not help but hear a mild echo of her grandmother's voice in her head. It gave her strength and allowed her to believe that this was truly something that could be made possible. "Since we have little time—who knows how quickly your father and Gillingham might reach an agreement!—we need to move quickly. Here. At this house party." Again, she stepped towards Sarah and placed her hands upon her friend's shoulders. "Is there a gentleman here you would consider? A gentleman you may have spoken to, who seems kind and might simply need a little persuasion?"

Sarah hesitated, and Harriet did not miss a spark of something light up her eyes. It had only been for a moment, but it had been there.

"Who is it?" Harriet pressed, her hands upon Sarah's shoulders tightening. "Tell me now or I will find out some other way." She cast her friend an encouraging smile.

A chuckle fell from Sarah's lips, and a bit of the strain that lingered upon her face fell away. "It is...It is Lord Burnham."

Harriet frowned, for she remembered the rather dull but incredibly self-centered young Lord. "Why would you hesitate to speak to me of him?"

Sarah's teeth dug into her lower lip in an expression of contrition. "I remember you fancied him once, did you not? At least—"

"Fancied him?" Harriet blurted out. "I may have spoken with him upon occasion and danced with him once or twice, but that has been the extent of our acquaintance." Indeed, *spoken to* was a bit of a stretch, for the man himself spoke rather continuously, forcing those around him to merely listen. "I cannot say that I've ever harbored tender feelings towards him."

Sarah frowned. "Are you certain?"

Not wishing to speak ill of Lord Burnham now that Sarah obviously had taken a liking to the man, Harriet merely nodded. "Put your mind at ease, dear friend. We have only ever been acquaintances. Nothing more."

The expression upon Sarah's face relaxed, and a small smile appeared.

"Do you like him?" Harriet asked in a tone she hoped did not betray her own dislike for the man. "What about him appeals to you?"

Sarah shrugged. "I cannot say. He speaks kindly to me whenever our paths cross." She paused for a moment. "I like his smile. He seems kind." Sarah finished lamely.

Harriet saw that her friend did not in fact harbor deep feelings for Lord Burnham; however, compared to Lord Gillingham, he was the lesser of two evils.

Harriet could have groaned. She hated this with every fiber of her being. Marriage should not be the lesser of two evils. If marriage could not be avoided, then at least it should be for the right reasons, the very reasons that had led her parents and her siblings into matrimony. But what else could be done? How else were they to keep Sarah safe from Gillingham?

"Do you know where your parents are at present?" Harriet asked, glancing over her shoulder and out the window where the sun shone brightly upon the green lawns of Atwood Park. "Do you think we should risk sneaking outside for a bit?"

Sarah smiled at her. "I think I should like that. I stayed in my chamber because I did not wish to happen upon Lord Gillingham." She slipped her arm through Harriet's. "But with you by my side, dear friend, I shall like to step outdoors."

After Sarah had secured her bonnet upon her head and reached for a parasol, the two women slipped out of her chamber and proceeded down the corridor a few steps to Harriet's room. There, Harriet quickly changed out of her travel-worn clothes before they hurried down the stairs, carefully keeping their eyes and ears open, always worried the wrong pair of eyes might fall upon them. Fortunately, they made it outdoors without a hitch and were soon strolling through the gardens.

Various shades of green blazed everywhere, wild and lively, interspersed with radiant colors of blue, purple, red, and yellow. The sun felt warm upon Harriet's skin, for she had not bothered with a parasol herself. A mild breeze stirred her curls, and she knew if she were to close her eyes, she would find herself swept away to *their* meadow.

Jack's and hers.

"There he is."

For a brief second, Harriet's heart stilled, hope surging through her entire being as her thoughts instantly pictured the man she longed to see. Yet she knew it could not be.

Tearing herself away from her wayward thoughts, Harriet blinked. "Who?" Her gaze turned to Sarah and then followed the soft nod of her head as her friend did her utmost to appear aloof.

"Lord Burnham," Sarah mumbled in answer to Harriet's question.

A quick glance over her shoulder confirmed Sarah's words. Indeed, it was Lord Burnham who stood off to the side near the fountain, presently engaged in conversation with several gentlemen. Still, in that brief moment when she had dared look over her shoulder, Harriet had seen him look in their direction as well, his face lighting up as he beheld Sarah.

Perhaps this could work after all, Harriet thought. After all, simply because *she* found Lord Burnham mind-numbingly annoying, did not mean that Sarah had to feel about him the same way.

"Perhaps we should venture closer," Harriet suggested with a smile at Sarah. "Any good courtship begins with conversation, does it not?"

Another tremble danced down Sarah's arms before she straightened her shoulders and lifted her chin. "I suppose you're right." Yet she did not move until Harriet took a step forward, all but pulling her along.

"Lady Harriet, I had heard you had arrived," said a familiar but loathsome voice.

Harriet could not help but flinch at the sound of it, yet she clamped her lips shut to not let a startled gasp escape her lips at finding Lord Gillingham so close behind her. Sarah, on the other hand, reacted like a terrified little lamb, finding herself face to face with a wolf.

Inhaling a deep breath, Harriet turned around to face the vile man, clasping Sarah's trembling arm within hers. "Lord Gillingham," she addressed him with an icy voice and a look full of disdain, "how unfortunate to find you in attendance here as well."

The man's friendly façade vanished instantly, and a sneer came to his face that was most unbecoming. It revealed the hard twist of his lips, and the soullessness of his eyes. How anyone could consider him charming was beyond Harriet. Had the mask he had worn whenever stepping out into society truly been that immaculate? Was it only now that the mask had come off possible to see the real him? Would he have otherwise been able to fool her still?

Indeed, the thought was unnerving.

Lord Gillingham's cold eyes moved to Sarah, and the corners of his mouth rose in delight as he found her trembling before him. "I see you have met my...future bride." His brows rose in challenge, and Harriet could see that he was enjoying this moment, no doubt well aware how deeply she loathed the thought of a union between him and her friend.

Harriet's fingers itched to reach for the concealed dagger in her bodice. "That has yet to be determined," she told him as calmly as she could. "Nothing is certain until the 'I do's' have been spoken." She allowed a small, mocking grin to show upon her face. "Surely, you are aware of that, are you not, my lord?"

At her reference to his own failed attempts at seeking a union, at even bullying Leonora into marriage, Lord Gillingham's face turned a dark shade of red. Rage blazed in his eyes, and he took a threatening step toward her.

Yet Harriet held her ground, refusing to back down. Instead, she lifted her chin another fraction and held his gaze.

Lord Gillingham's lips thinned even further, and out of the corner of her eyes, Harriet could see his hands balling into fists at his sides. She could not help but wonder if she ought to tempt him to lash out at her. Would it do any good?

Before Harriet could decide, a shadow fell over her face. Her eyes darted to the left for only a second, but it was enough.

Her heart skipped a beat, and she could feel that familiar flutter in her belly soar to new heights. "Jack."

CHAPTER THIRTY-FIVE

MORE QUESTIONS THAN ANSWERS

Bradley could not be certain how much of a head start Harriet had; however, he was determined to reach Atwood Park as soon as possible. Every fiber of his being longed to see her, not necessarily in order to change her mind, but simply to gaze upon her, to speak with her, to be near her.

Only a day had passed since they had parted, and yet he already craved her presence as though they had not seen each other in months.

By the time Atwood Park came into view, Bradley felt like a bundle of nerves. His fingers were drumming impatiently upon his knees, and he kept jerking his head from side to side, hoping the change in direction would reveal that which he longed to see.

Perhaps one day in the not so distant future, we shall meet again.

Harriet's words kept echoing in his head, taunting him, tormenting him. Was that truly what she wanted? Would it be so simple for her to walk away from what had developed between them? Was it possible that he felt more strongly for her than she did for him? Had he perhaps misunderstood?

Bradley doubted it, or perhaps he was merely hoping that it was not so. Still, there was only one way to find out. Not everything had been said yet. He wanted a chance to once more address this issue that stood between them, that kept them apart despite the way he felt for her.

The way they felt for each other.

At the thought of how everything had changed in only such a short time, Bradley could not help but laugh, a severe sense of disbelief coursing through his veins. Indeed, Harriet had been something he had not seen coming. Only a few weeks ago, he would have had anyone committed who dared suggest he would fall head over heels in love with such a hellion, willing to give up anything to keep her in his life. Was this how his father had felt about his mother? Indeed, meeting Harriet had helped Bradley understand his father better than he had ever hoped to achieve.

Alighting from the carriage, Bradley found himself kindly received by Lady Atwood. Although he had not been invited, she was kind enough to extend an invitation, having a spare guest chamber readied with the utmost speed. "You are too kind, Lady Atwood," Bradley thanked her with a formal bow. "I have heard such good things about your hospitality. Do tell, who else is present here? I wonder if any of my acquaintances have found their way here as well."

Before long, Bradley had confirmed that Harriet was indeed at Atwood Park. Another few delicately phrased questions told him Harriet had been put up in the blue room, but was currently strolling the gardens with Miss Mortensen. It seemed Lady Atwood was always well-informed when it came to her guests.

"I assume after your long journey you long for a bit of rest," Lady Atwood suggested as she slipped her arm through the crook of his, drawing him towards the large staircase leading to the upper floor.

"You are too kind, my lady," Bradley replied as he stopped in his tracks. "However, I admit I do long to stretch my legs after being crammed up in the carriage for so long." He stepped back, disengaging his arm from hers. "I do not wish to detain you, for I am certain you have many other matters to see to with a house full of guests. I shall be perfectly fine, my lady."

A somewhat disappointed look came to Lady Atwood's face, for she no doubt longed to extract more information from him; however, she did not press the matter and soon hurried away, no doubt in search of a more entertaining companion.

Without delay, Bradley crossed the foyer and stepped into the adjacent drawing room. His gaze swept over many ladies and gentlemen he had heard gossips whisper about before. He gave a quick, courteous nod, but then he quickly stepped outside before anyone could address him. Long strides carried him down into the garden, his eyes constantly sweeping left and right. His heart beat wildly in anticipation, only to still every time he peered around a bush or hedge to find the spot behind it empty or taken by a person he had not come to see.

And then his eyes found her...

...and it was as though the world stopped turning. *Emotional entanglements*, he heard his father's voice echo in the back of his head. Only now, it made him smile...something he seemed to be doing with alarming frequency since meeting Harriet.

And then he frowned as a chill of dread suddenly stole over his skin.

Near a row of rose bushes, Harriet stood tall and fierce, her chin lifted and her eyes blazing, while the young woman upon her arm—presumably Miss Mortensen—looked about ready to faint. Only a few paces in front of the two women, Bradley spotted a young lord he was not acquainted with. However, it appeared Harriet and her friend were.

Even from quite a few paces away, Bradley could see that this man was not a friend. Indeed, the way he stood in front of the two women revealed him as a threat. His gaze narrowed and his hands balled into fists. While Miss Mortensen trembled with nerves, this stranger seemed to tremble with barely contained rage.

Without another thought, Bradley hastened toward them, his pulse quickening as he wondered what was going on.

Despite his own agitation, Bradley could not deny that every step he took toward Harriet made him feel more alive, eager and joyful. And then he reached her side, and nothing else mattered any longer.

For a moment, she seemed completely unaware of his presence. Then, however, her gaze darted to his, and the moment she saw him, Bradley could have sworn lightning had struck the ground somewhere nearby. "Jack." It was no more than a breathless whisper, and yet he had longed to hear her nickname for him fall from her lips once again.

Bradley would have smiled had it not been for the tense situation they found themselves in. "Lady Harriet," he greeted her with a formal bow. "How good to see you here. Are you well?" His gaze widened meaningfully as it held hers, urging her to trust in him should she need assistance in handling this *gentleman*...whoever he was.

"I am well," Harriet replied with a slight stammer, the look in her eyes revealing all too clearly that she could not quite believe he was truly here. "Thank you." Then she cleared her throat, glanced at her friend, and said, "I'm sorry. May I introduce Miss Sarah Mortensen? Sarah, this is J-Bradley Jackson, Duke of Clements."

The young woman bowed her head, a polite smile coming to her face as her pale blue eyes met Bradley's, then instantly retreated to look at Harriet. "It is a pleasure to make your acquaintance, your grace."

Bradley offered her a polite nod before turning his attention to the gentleman, who had observed their interaction with restrained curiosity. "May I ask who you are, sir?" Bradley could not help but despise this man with every fiber of his being, and he did not even know why.

Before the man could answer, Harriet said, "Lord Gillingham was just about to leave." Her tone was icy, and it sent a chill down Bradley's back. What had happened between them, for clearly something had? Although Harriet was one to fly into a fancy quickly, she was not one to hold a grudge. Bradley was certain of it. For Lord Gillingham to have earned her hatred, something truly heinous had to have happened. Bradley's stomach turned, considering what that might have been.

An evil grin claimed Lord Gillingham's face, his icy gaze trained upon Harriet. "I must admit I am quite enjoying your company, *my lady*." Mockery lay in his words. "Perhaps with time you will come to enjoy mine as well." He paused, and something sinister came to his eyes. "The way your sister did. How is dear Leonora these days?"

"Don't you dare say her name!" Harriet hissed menacingly, her body tense like that of a wildcat about to lunge itself at its prey. Her left hand was balled into a fist while her right hand lay flat upon her belly, moving toward—

Bradley almost flinched as Harriet's voice echoed in his mind. *Oh, sweet Jack, you don't need to be concerned for me. I always have a blade tucked in my bodice when I go riding.* Could it be that she was carrying a dagger even now? Oh, but she wouldn't dare—

Of course she would! It was Harriet, for heaven's sake!

"I suggest," Bradley said to Lord Gillingham, a warning look in his eyes, "that you take your leave, my lord."

Lord Gillingham chuckled, dark amusement in his eyes. "I assure you there is no need for you to protect her." His gaze moved back to Harriet, something vile in the way he looked at her. "I swear I mean her no harm." His words were dripping with insincerity.

Oddly amused, Bradley chuckled. "Oh, you misunderstand, my lord. I am not saying this to protect her." Lord Gillingham frowned at him. "I'm saying this to protect you." Holding the man's gaze, Bradley took a step closer. "*I* am not armed, but *she*…is." He indicated Harriet with a nod of his head. "Leave. Now."

Although clearly reluctant, Lord Gillingham finally stepped away as Bradley made it unmistakably clear that it was the only option. Still, he continued to watch the man stalk away, anger still radiating off him in waves. He needed to find out what had happened between that man and Harriet because such hatred could turn into something dangerous.

"Jack, what are you doing here?" came Harriet's rather impatient-sounding voice from behind him.

Bradley turned around to face her, fighting the urge to pull her into his arms. "I received your letter," he said, perhaps a bit too pointedly, for her eyes widened with understanding.

"I only meant to…" She clamped her lips shut, then drew in a deep breath. "I did not write it to ask you here. I didn't mean for you to follow me."

Bradley could not deny that he loved to see her flustered. "Then you shouldn't have—"

Sudden footsteps drew closer, accompanied by mumbled words, and Bradley turned around to find an elderly couple hastening toward them, their faces bearing frowns of disapproval, their eyes darting back and forth between Harriet and Miss Mortensen.

The young woman seemed to pale even further at the sight of whom Bradley presumed were her parents.

Instantly, Harriet stepped forward, a bright smile upon her face that did not reflect the inner turmoil Bradley was sure she felt. "Lord and Lady Hartmore, how wonderful to meet you here. May I introduce you to the Duke of Clements?"

Pleasantries were exchanged before Lord and Lady Hartmore quickly ushered their daughter inside. They did not seem to want for her to associate with Harriet. Yet another question that remained unanswered.

But not for long, Bradley vowed. It seemed there was a lot about Harriet he did not know but he intended to.

With a heavy sigh, Harriet looked after her friend as she followed her parents into the house. Then she spun on her heel, cast him a quick, somewhat exasperated look, and then she hurried past him. She rounded the corner of the nearest hedge and disappeared from sight.

Bradley instantly went in pursuit of her.

CHAPTER THIRTY-SIX

STOLEN KISSES

Harriet could sense Jack behind her, his light footfall upon the lawn almost inaudible. Yet it was as though she could feel his heartbeat now that he was close once more. Oh, how she had missed him! And yet it had barely been a day, had it not?

You're running away, a voice that sounded suspiciously like Grandma Edie's whispered in the back of her head. *Why are you running away from him?*

Oh, Harriet knew precisely why she was running away. She might not like to say it out loud, but she was no fool. She was running away because she was afraid of what she might do should he catch up to her. The instant she had seen him, she had been tempted to throw herself into his arms. What if she did so now? What if...? What if she allowed herself to be persuaded? She knew what *he* wanted, and she was afraid that if she allowed him close, she might give in. And what then?

"Harriet, stop!" Jack called after her, the sound of his voice much closer than she would have expected, would have liked. "Will you stop and talk to me?" Exasperation rang in his voice.

Instead of doing as he asked, Harriet hastened toward the end of the hedge, then turned around the corner and moved onward, deeper into the maze of Atwood Park, which—if gossips could be believed—had witnessed many secret embraces and stolen kisses. After all, Lord and Lady Atwood were very fond of scandals, openly helping them along.

Only belatedly, it occurred to Harriet that perhaps it would have been wise to run off toward a more *crowded* area. Alone with Jack, she could not be certain of what she would do.

And then his hand closed over her arm, cutting off her escape, and Harriet did not know whether she ought to complain or rejoice. "Will you look at me?" Jack asked, his voice harsh as he pulled her around toward him, exasperation in his eyes as they searched her face.

A deep breath shuddered past Harriet's lips as she found his dark brown eyes looking down into hers. His hand felt warm upon her arm, and before she knew it, his other arm snaked around her waist, pulling her closer, as they stared into each other's eyes.

"You should not have come," Harriet snapped as she felt her resolve slip away. Yet she could not bring herself to turn from his gaze.

"You should not have left," Jack countered in the same manner, his hold on her unyielding—as she had hoped and feared it would be.

"I had to," Harriet insisted. "You know I did." As she felt herself sway toward him, her breath coming faster than it ever had and her knees slowly turning to water, she lifted her hands and placed her palms upon his chest in an admittedly useless attempt to keep him away.

"I know no such thing!" Jack snapped, ignoring her futile attempt to push him back. "I was prepared to give you a few days to calm down, but," he heaved a deep sigh, his head slowly shaking from side to side in disappointment, "I never thought you would run off like that. Why did you not tell me?"

"I did!"

Jack scoffed. "You sent a letter. Why did you not come to me?"

Harriet could not deny that she liked this new side of Jack. Suddenly, he seemed to know precisely what he wanted...and what he wanted was her. Never had Harriet expected it to feel so intoxicating to be wanted by another in such a way. It made her skin hum with awareness and her belly do little somersaults, weakening her knees and stealing her breath. She barely remembered why they were there or what they were speaking of, in danger of losing herself in this moment that had found her so unexpectedly.

"Harry!" came Jack's demanding voice. "Why did you not come to me? Why did you not simply speak to me? You could've explained why—"

Harriet scoffed, reminding herself why she was trying so hard to keep him at bay. "Did you not always complain when I came to Clements Park without a chaperone? Now, you want—"

"Do not pretend that is why you ran away instead of speaking to me face to face!"

"Still, you shouldn't have come!" Harriet insisted stubbornly.

"I had no choice," Jack gritted out with equal vehemence. They stood head to head, neither one of them willing to back down.

"Of course, you did."

"Not that I saw." Jack exhaled a slow breath through his nose as he regarded her most carefully. Then his gaze narrowed ever so slowly, something sparking in his eyes that sent a shiver down Harriet's back. "Why does it bother you so that I'm here?"

Harriet swallowed hard, feeling suddenly immensely vulnerable. "Because I don't want you here."

"Why?"

"Because...Because I already bid you farewell," she insisted, once more leaning away from him; although, every fiber of her being wanted nothing more than to get closer, "and there is no use in doing it again."

A muscle in Jack's jaw twitched. "I don't want to bid you farewell." His hands slid more firmly onto her back.

Harriet drew in a shaky breath. "And that's...why you...should not have...come."

A slow grin curled up the corners of Jack's mouth as he watched her flustered reply. "To make it easier for you?"

"Yes!" Harriet snapped, her hands moving to push him away. "Yes!" She gave him a tentative shove that convinced neither him nor her that she was speaking the truth.

Still grinning, Jack lowered his head to hers. "Are you tempted, little hellion?"

Harriet stilled and stared up at him. Never had he called her that, and yet she could not help but think that, at least, in his mind he had referred to her in this way before. Harriet found it utterly endearing, which was most inconvenient given her present situation. "Oh, sweet Jack," she heard herself whisper, awe thickening her voice as she gazed up at him, "you're not as sweet as I thought, are you?"

His grin broadened. "And you are not as adamant as you like to believe." He gave her a pointed look.

Harriet felt her jaw tense, for she knew his words to be true. Yet she did not want them to be. "You're the worst sort of man!" Again, she gave him a shove, and again, he held onto her. "I should never have listened to my grandmother. I should never have gone west that day." Staring up at him, she shook her head. "I was perfectly fine before I met you, and now—"

"I was perfectly fine before I met you," Jack interrupted her, the same stunned disbelief in his gaze that Harriet felt pulsing in her own veins. "Life was simple before I met you. I knew precisely what my next step would be. I knew how to conduct myself. I knew what was expected of me. I was...content with my life." His jaw hardened, and she saw him grit his teeth as though in anger. "And then you came along and changed everything."

His words sounded like a reproach, yet Harriet knew them to be the greatest compliment she had ever received. After all, her own reproach had been meant the same way.

"I wish I could say I'm sorry," she whispered as something deep inside her suddenly hummed to life, shoving aside every argument she had brought forth to convince herself to leave his side. It was as though they had never been apart, and Harriet felt her hand snake upward and onto his shoulders. "Yet I would be lying if I did so." She smiled at him and saw his eyes light up in the most endearing way.

Before Harriet had a chance to convince herself otherwise, she pushed herself up onto her toes and pulled Jack down into a kiss. Dimly, she was aware of warning bells going off in her head, urging her to turn back, to reconsider, but Harriet ignored them.

Oh, how Lady Atwood would love this!

Indeed, Harriet could not deny the shiver of excitement that coursed through her at the thought that she and Jack were contributing to the house party's somewhat scandalous reputation. Yet the warmth that swept through her had nothing to do with secret embraces or stolen kisses and everything with the man holding her in his arms.

In fact, that was the problem as far as Harriet was concerned.

From the first, Jack had been different, unlike anyone she had ever met. He had challenged her in utterly foreign ways and continued to do so to this very day. Although she had gotten to know him well during their time together, he still surprised her, and she loved that about him.

The knuckles of his right hand gently grazed the line of her jaw before he trailed his fingers into her hair. The contact was minuscule, and yet Harriet felt it all the way to her toes.

"I love the way you kiss me," Harriet whispered against his lips before giving the bottom one a slight nip.

Jack chuckled. "I have no complaints, either," he whispered huskily. Then he kissed her again, his arms wrapped around her in a way that made Harriet forget the rest of the world.

If only it did not exist! If only they could make their own reality!

All of a sudden, Jack stilled, then he lifted his head, his brown eyes searching hers.

"What is it?" Harriet whispered, surprised by the serious expression that slowly stole onto his face.

Loosening his hold on her, Jack cleared his throat. "Lord Gillingham," he suddenly said, "how do you know him?"

Too stunned to react for a moment or two, Harriet simply stared up at him. Then she broke out laughing because right here and now she did not want to feel anger—and those were her only choices.

Jack's forehead furrowed. "What is so amusing?" Something tense rested in his voice as he tried to step back.

Harriet, however, held on. "Nothing ever happened between him and me." She scoffed. "Far from it." A hint of relief came to Jack's face, but before he could ask yet another question, Harriet once more pulled him down into a kiss.

Oh, she would not allow Lord Gillingham to ruin this for her! Not in a million years! Hell would freeze over before...

Her thoughts trailed off as Jack returned her kiss with the same eagerness that had prompted her own. His lips were soft but moved with urgency as he held her cradled in his arms. He was tall and strong, and Harriet half-expected to feel utterly vulnerable in his arms; yet he had never treated her with anything less than overwhelming tenderness.

"I could do this all day," Harriet murmured, twirling her fingers in his hair.

Jack pinched her chin. "Someone could come by." He nipped her lower lip as she had done to him before. "What then?"

Harriet pulled back and looked up at him. "I will never be forced into marriage," she told him with the utmost sincerity, needing him to understand beyond the shadow of a doubt. "Not by anyone."

Inhaling deeply, Jack nodded. "I know." Then he placed a tender kiss upon her lips and stepped back, his arms falling away. "Perhaps we should speak of something else then."

Harriet was surprised to see Jack retreat thus, but she saw the hurt in his eyes and knew that his own heart ached as much as hers. If only there were another way! If only they could be together without either one of them being forced to give up something vital!

The world, though, was not a perfect place. Far from it.

CHAPTER THIRTY-SEVEN
THE DEVIL INCARNATE

"How do you know Lord Gillingham?" Bradley asked, partly because he truly felt the need to know and partly because he needed something to distract himself from the memory of how she had just felt in his arms.

With her wild curls in even greater disarray, Harriet only stood an arm's length away, the scent of wildflowers lingering upon her skin as though they were far from Atwood Park and back in their meadow. Her green eyes were wide and so expressive, whispering of temptation, that Jack forced himself to look away, if only briefly.

"He is the worst sort of man I've ever had the misfortune of knowing."

At Harriet's words, Bradley's head snapped back up. He felt his insides tense, something deeply protective roaring to life. "What did he do to you?" He closed the short distance between them and grasped her chin, his eyes searching her face as she looked up at him.

Her shoulders rose and fell with a slow breath, and he could see deep sorrow hiding behind the anger that sparked to life in her eyes. "Not me," she finally said, and Bradley exhaled the breath he had been holding. "My sister."

Bradley frowned as he held her gaze, uncertain if he wanted to know more. The look in her eyes was painful to bear, and he realized that as sheltered a life as Harriet might have lived, she was far more acquainted with the harsh realities of this world than he would have liked.

"It happened a little more than a year ago," Harriet said quietly as she took a step back, a distant look coming to her eyes as her thoughts touched upon those memories. "Louisa and Leonora snuck out of the house one night to attend a masquerade. Once there, they got separated and… Gillingham came upon Leonora in a deserted corridor." Her lips pressed together into an angry snarl. "He attacked her, and she barely got away. As it was a masquerade, she did not know who it had been." Shaking her head, Harriet looked into Jack's eyes. "Can you imagine walking into a ballroom, not knowing which of the *gentlemen* asking for a dance or offering to fetch you a refreshment had been the one to attack you? She was never the same after that."

Bradley swallowed hard, not knowing what to say. Whatever he had expected, the story Harriet had just told him surpassed everything he might have imagined. "But today she is…I mean, she's married, is she not?" He tried to recall which of her sisters had been *Leonora*. Had it been the blond-haired Lady Barrington? No, he was fairly certain that it was the dark-haired Lady Pemberton.

Harry nodded. "Yes, her husband was the one who helped her overcome what had been done to her." A fleeting smile passed over her face. "She's happy again today because he helped her find the strength to face Gillingham and put him in his place as much as she could." Brushing a stray curl behind her ear, Harriet heaved a deep breath. "And now, he's on the brink of marrying a dear friend of mine." Her gaze held his, and she slowly shook her head. "I cannot allow that to happen. I cannot."

Confused, Bradley stepped closer. "What do you mean? Are you talking about that young lady…what was her name?…Miss Mortensen?" He frowned, remembering the pale-faced young woman who had stood like a stone column at Harriet's side. "Why would she marry him if—?"

A low growl left Harriet's lips. "Because it is not her choice!" She spun on her heel and walked a few paces away before whirling around again and heading back toward him. "Her father gambled away their fortune. They were forced to sell their London townhouse and who knows what else. They are in dire circumstances and need her to make an advantageous match. Unfortunately, all of London is aware of their situation. As lovely and kind as Sarah is, no one wants her."

Seeing the picture, Bradley nodded. "Only Gillingham."

Harriet huffed out an exasperated breath. "When Leonora accused him publicly, she ruined herself, but his reputation suffered as well. He has had some trouble procuring himself a wife." She all but spat those words. "The sad truth is that both Lord Gillingham as well as Sarah's parents are desperate to make a match and are both equally unable to do so. Therefore, it seems they have both agreed to look past the other's deficiencies and merely look to the brighter side of a union between them. While Sarah's parents will see their financial issues resolved, Lord Gillingham will have himself a society wife and a chance to continue his line."

Bradley could see Harriet's agitation and the way her shoulders rose and fell, the way her hands gestured rather wildly in front of her, the pulse in her neck hammering incessantly. "She asked you for help? Miss Mortensen?"

Harriet shook her head. "She did not. Sarah is a very *dutiful* daughter. She understands her place and would never go against her parents' wishes. She merely wrote to me to confide in me, to have someone to talk to. She never expected me to come." Harriet ran her hands over her face, pinching the bridge of her nose. "Knowing the kind of man he is, knowing what he did to Leonora, I cannot simply stand by and allow this to happen."

Bradley could see that she wanted him to understand, that she needed him to understand. Yet he could not help but think that Miss Mortensen's situation was rather hopeless. "What do you intend to do?"

Harriet's lips pressed into a thin line, and he could see that whatever she was about to say went against her better judgment. "The only way to truly see her safe from her parents' matchmaking schemes is to have her married." She scoffed darkly. "Is that not ironic?" She closed her eyes and inhaled a deep breath. "If we can find a gentleman willing to marry her," her eyes opened, and she looked at him, "then..."

Feeling her gaze, Bradley tensed, not wanting to believe what he thought she might be suggesting. "No!" Abruptly, he stepped toward her, his gaze fixed upon hers. "Do you hear me? No! I will not marry her."

Bradley held her gaze, and to his utter relief, she did not argue. Instead, she smiled. "I do not want you to. I do not want you to marry anyone, truth be told."

"Good," was all Bradley said, knowing that here and now was not the time nor place to press her for more. Yet a sense of hope settled in his chest, knowing that the thought of him tied to another upset her just as much as the possibility that she might be lost to him upset him.

Harriet explained they had set their sights on Lord Burnham. Still, she seemed most reluctant, clearly bothered by the idea of seeing Miss Mortensen tied to a man her friend did not want in order to protect her from one she feared.

"Unfortunately, it is the only way," Harriet said, resignation weighing heavily upon her, "and I will do for her what I can."

"What about Gillingham?"

Harriet frowned. "What about him? He's a nuisance. He's a blackguard. He's the devil incarnate. He—"

"He blames you and your family for his loss in social standing," Bradley warned, remembering the deep hatred he had seen upon the man's face as he had looked at Harriet. "You don't know what he might do, what he might feel persuaded to do." He reached out and gently took her hand. "Please, Harry, be careful. Do not go anywhere alone. Always surround yourself with others. Please."

Although Harriet's gaze softened and Bradley could see that his concern touched her, she lifted her chin in a defiant gesture. "I do not fear him, and I will not allow him to dictate my whereabouts. I know how to protect myself and—"

"I'm aware of that," Bradley interrupted before his gaze moved lower to where her hand once more lay upon her belly. Where exactly she had stashed her dagger, he could not be certain of; however, he did not doubt that it was there. "Nevertheless, I urge you to be careful, Harry. You don't know what he might do."

Inhaling a slow breath, Harriet nodded. "Very well. I shall be careful, but I will not allow that man anywhere near my friend." Her lips pressed into a determined line, and Bradley knew it was useless to argue. She had made up her mind, and he knew that Harriet, like all Whickertons, was fiercely protective.

CHAPTER THIRTY-EIGHT

IF ONLY

Midnight struck, and Harriet silently slipped from her bed. She pulled on a robe and slippers, then quietly stepped up to her door and opened it. No sounds could be heard, and she peeked out into the darkened corridor. For a moment, she waited, slowly breathing in and out as she listened.

Fortunately, it seemed the entire house lay sleeping, and so she pushed the door open a little farther and stepped out into the corridor. Only a few steps carried her to Sarah's door, and she lifted her hand to knock.

Two quick raps, then a pause, followed by four quick raps. It was a secret signal from their childhood, one they had used countless times, although not in recent years. Harriet prayed that Sarah remembered, that she was even still awake to hear. What if—?

The door to her friend's chamber opened a crack, and Harriet caught a faint glimpse of Sarah peeking out into the corridor. "Let me in," she whispered, looking left and right over her shoulder. Fortunately, everything remained quiet, and the corridor deserted.

With wide eyes, Sarah opened her door to allow Harriet inside, then quickly closed it after her. "What are you doing here?"

"We need to talk."

Sarah's shoulders slumped. "My parents are still angry with your family for everything that happened. They do not want me to talk to you."

Harriet sighed. "I gathered as much. However, this is not the moment to be the dutiful daughter. If you do not wish to marry Gillingham, then we need to do something." Her brows rose in question.

Sarah worried her lower lip, clearly undecided. "What do you suggest?" she finally said, wringing her hands.

Harriet smiled. "We proceed as planned. I promise I shall stay away from you to placate your parents; however, in order for you to gain Lord Burnham's affections, I shall do my very best to lead the two of you to each other. Keep an eye out for me and follow my signal, understood?"

Sarah nodded, though her eyes whispered of doubt. "Do you truly think he can be tempted into proposing?"

Harriet sighed. "I don't know, but we have to try." She squeezed Sarah's hands. "Do not worry too much. I shall be at your side at all times." Then she turned back to the door.

"Wait," Sarah whispered, placing her hand on Harriet's shoulder. "How did you come to be acquainted with the Duke of Clements? I admit I was quite surprised to see you address each other in such an... informal way." Her wide blue eyes searched Harriet's face. "I think I heard you call him *Jack*."

Meeting Sarah's eyes, Harriet sighed, uncertain whether or not she liked the reminder of Jack. "His estate borders Pinewood Manor, and one day, we happened upon one another while out riding. It is nothing more." Never in her life had Harriet heard a greater lie.

A slight frown came to Sarah's face as she watched Harriet. "Nothing more?" she echoed, doubt in her voice. "I find that hard to believe."

Again, Harriet turned away and toward the door. "It is late. You should go back to bed. We shall—"

"You care for him," Sarah almost gasped, her voice no more than an awed whisper. Harriet spun around, staring at her friend. Even in the dark, Sarah's blue eyes seemed to shine with excitement as she looked at Harriet. "Why will you not tell me?"

Harriet cleared her throat, very much disliking the turn this conversation was taking. "Because there's nothing to tell. I care for him, yes. But we want different things. Nothing can ever happen between us."

Again, Sarah eyed her with a strangely shrewd expression. "The way you speak leads me to believe that something already *has* happened between the two of you. Or am I wrong?"

For a moment, Harriet did not know what to say. Whenever Sarah's mind was not paralyzed by fear of the future, she was very perceptive in her observations. "Perhaps," Harriet finally admitted, surprised by the sudden surge of joy that jolted through her heart.

A joyous smile came to Sarah's face. "Oh, that is wonderful. I am so happy for you." She paused, her eyes searching Harriet's face. "You refused him, did you not?"

Harriet closed her eyes. "I will not marry." She looked at her friend, annoyed that everybody seemed to simply expect her to change her mind because her heart happened to have fallen...

"Would it truly be so awful," Sarah asked kindly, "to marry a man who cares for you? To marry a man you care for as well?" Yearning rested in Sarah's voice, and Harry knew that what she had found with Jack was something Sarah had been dreaming of all her life. Now, however, she had resigned herself to her fate, certain that love was something she would simply have to make do without.

"I don't know if it would be awful," Harriet replied, not knowing what else to say. "That is precisely the point. I don't know what will happen down the line. What if something changes? What if later I come to regret having married him?" She cast Sarah a small smile, then once more turned to the door. "Good night."

Stepping out into the darkened corridor, Harriet was about to close the door when she heard Sarah's whispered voice once more. "What if you come to regret not marrying him?"

Harriet paused, caught off guard for a moment. Then, however, she quickly closed the door and hurried back to her own chamber. Still, Sarah's question echoed in her ears, taunting her, daring her once again to change her mind, to allow herself to be persuaded. The most frightening thing of all was that there was a part of Harriet that longed to be persuaded.

To give in.

As expected, sleep would not come that night, a night that Harriet spent tossing and turning, Sarah's words ever present upon her mind. The moment she closed her eyes, Harriet saw Jack, his warm, brown eyes looking into her own. She once more felt his arms come around her and hold her tightly, safe and secure. If only it could forever remain so!

If only!

Over the next few days, Bradley continued to watch Harriet as she did her utmost to engage Miss Mortensen and Lord Burnham in conversation. They played parlor games or went outside into the garden, sat down to a card game, or strolled across the fields. Miss Mortensen clearly did her best to appear lively and interested; however, Bradley could not help but see the effort it took her to uphold this mask. Clearly, she did not wish to marry Lord Burnham either but preferred him to a man like Gillingham.

Slowly, with each day that passed, Bradley understood more and more why Harriet was so adamantly set against marriage. He felt only an echo of the hopelessness and despair he so often glimpsed in Miss Mortensen's expression, but it was already enough to rile him to anger. To feel helpless and at the complete mercy of another was a feeling he did not care for. He had once experienced it as a child; however, now as an adult, he cherished his freedom to choose. Certainly, even he felt certain pressures to oblige societal rules; however, if he chose not to, his life would continue on much the same.

The same could not be said for Miss Mortensen...or any other woman finding herself in such circumstances.

What could he do? Bradley wondered. Was there any way for him to grant Harriet the same rights, the same sense of security in life that men claimed for themselves every day without giving it a single thought?

"How is it going?" Bradley asked Harriet one night as they stood upon the terrace, gazing out at the slowly setting sun. "Do you think your efforts will bear fruit?"

Harriet heaved a deep sigh that did not whisper of triumph. "I don't know. He speaks kindly to her and seems to delight in her presence; however, Sarah said that he has yet to state his intentions." She shrugged. "Perhaps he simply needs some time."

Bradley nodded, wondering if perhaps Lord Burnham had quite another reason. It had not escaped Bradley—much to his displeasure—that Lord Burnham's eyes seemed to light up whenever he beheld not Miss Mortensen, but Harriet. Perhaps it was only Harriet's modesty that made her overlook that fact.

"Perhaps at the dance tomorrow night," Harriet whispered hopefully, "he will proclaim his affections for her." She looked at Bradley, clearly hoping for him to agree. "What do you think?" The right corner of her mouth curved upward into a lopsided smile. "I've seen you watching them."

Bradley chuckled. "You're mistaken."

"But I've seen you," she insisted, turning to face him more fully, her green eyes openly accusing.

Bradley turned toward her as well. "I have not been watching them," he told her earnestly, then continued when she was about to object. "I've been watching you."

Her jaw dropped a fraction before a smile came to her face. "Is that so?"

"It is. Do you mind?"

"I know I should," Harriet replied sternly. "However, that has always been my problem with you. That is why I do not want you near. How much longer do you intend to stay?" She lifted her chin in challenge. Yet while her words willed him away, the look in her eyes did the opposite.

Bradley held her gaze. "How much longer do you intend to pretend that you can simply walk away from this?" After a quick glance through the window at those sitting in the parlor, Bradley took a careful step toward her. "From us?"

The look upon Harriet's face fell. Clearly, she did not wish to consider the severity of the situation. Still, she could not deny that her heart, too, was in peril if, indeed, she decided to walk away. "I think I should return inside," she said instead of answering his question. "There's not much time left until the end of the house party. If he does not propose until then..." She heaved a deep sigh. "Good night, Jack."

"Good night, Harry," Bradley replied, remaining outdoors as he watched her slip back inside and hurry to Miss Mortensen's side. Perhaps he ought to have told her that her efforts were doomed. Yet he had not had the heart to do so.

What would she do once the end of the house party came with no proposal in sight? Bradley dreaded the moment because he knew it would break Harriet's heart...or make her do something quite drastic.

CHAPTER THIRTY-NINE

DESPITE BEST EFFORTS

Despite her best efforts, Harriet could not stop thinking that Lord Burnham was not at all smitten with Sarah. Yes, he smiled at her and spoke kindly to her and offered to fetch her a glass of lemonade. However, the look in his eyes only ever truly warmed and shone with something deeper when those dreaded eyes of his settled upon her, Harriet.

It was utterly frustrating! Perhaps they ought to have settled on another gentleman instead. Now, they had wasted all these days upon Lord Burnham with nothing to show for them. Harriet had hated this plan from the beginning, and now, she hated it even more when it became clear that it would not work. What was she to do?

More than once during the past sennight, her gaze had fallen upon Lord Gillingham, for he, too, seemed to be watching them, clearly amused by their futile efforts. It was as though she could read his thoughts whenever he looked at her, thoughts that stated clearly that no matter what she might do, she could not protect Sarah from him.

Always was he nearby, simply watching or speaking to Lord Hartmore, suggesting that their negotiations regarding a union were coming to fruition. He even had the nerve to approach Sarah again and again, whispering words that Harriet could see set her on edge, that widened her eyes and sent her pulse into an uproar.

Whereas Lord and Lady Hartmore did not dare snub Harriet openly, they did their utmost to find paltry excuses here and there to separate the two friends from one another. One sunny afternoon as they stood upon the terrace, Lord Hartmore nodded toward his daughter, urging her to join them as they stood speaking to none other but Lord Gillingham.

Harriet all but felt the icy shiver that made Sarah's limbs tremble. She saw her cheeks pale as Sarah found Lord Gillingham look at her in that way of his. It was as though he were a hunter and she the prey and there was nothing she could do to escape him.

Still, Sarah did her best to appear calm and collected. She swallowed hard and then cast a weak smile at Harriet. "Pardon me, but my father summons me."

Harriet almost cursed loudly. "I shall accompany you," she said instead, forcing her own emotions back under control. She would not give Lord Gillingham the satisfaction of seeing her defeated by one of these little games he liked to play.

Sarah paused. "Do you think that wise?" she asked, though it was clear that she longed to have Harriet accompany her. "You know what he will say."

"I do," Harriet agreed, "but I will not let him think even for a second that I am bowing my head in defeat." She slipped her arm through Sarah's. "Let's go."

As they approached, Harriet saw Lord Hartmore's face darken. His lips thinned in disapproval, yet he refrained from making any comment as they came to stand with them.

Lord Gillingham grinned that evil grin of his that always seemed to say, *I know you dislike me, but I do not care. I can still force your hand.* "My dear Miss Mortensen, you look radiant today."

Harriet felt Sarah's arm tighten upon hers as she tried her best to smile at Lord Gillingham, fully aware of her parents' watchful eyes. "You're too kind, my lord."

Lord Gillingham's smile continued to linger as his eyes slowly darted to Harriet, no doubt watching for a reaction that would please him immensely.

Gritting her teeth against the urge to scratch his eyes out, Harriet plastered a similarly polite but equally false smile upon her face. Their eyes met, and she could feel his challenge like a tug as though he tried to pull her in one direction, demanding she respond in the way he preferred. Harriet, though, stood her ground, smiling sweetly and not allowing him to bait her. Something not easily accomplished!

Clearly displeased, Lord Gillingham's eyes narrowed. Then he shifted on his feet, his attention returning to Sarah. "What pastimes do you enjoy, Miss Mortensen?" He gave Harriet a sideways glance before continuing on, not waiting for Sarah to reply to his question. "While picnics and balls are all good and well, I must admit to my fondness for...masquerades." The corners of his mouth curled into a devilish sneer.

Harriet inhaled a slow, steadying breath as his words reminded her of what he had done to her sister. Beside her, Sarah, too, tensed, not ignorant to Lord Gillingham's reference. "I...I...," Sarah stammered, not knowing where to look, and her eyes moved back and forth between Lord Gillingham and Harriet.

"Perhaps once we are wed," Lord Gillingham continued with a pointed look at Harriet, "you will join me upon one such occasion. I assure you masquerades can be great fun."

As Harriet was far too furious to reply and Sarah appeared incapable of forming a clear thought at the moment, Lord Hartmore stepped forward, a chuckle leaving his lips. "That sounds like a marvelous idea. I am certain my daughter shall enjoy accompanying you...as your wife."

Sarah looked ready to faint!

"Oh, I see Lady Atwood over there," Harriet exclaimed with a glance over Lord Hartmore's shoulder. "If you will excuse us, she promised to show Sarah and me the magnificent mare she purchased recently." She offered them a polite nod, then all but dragged Sarah away, across the terrace and down into the garden, toward Lady Atwood before anyone had the chance to object.

Least of all, Lord Gillingham.

"Oh, we're doomed," Sarah mumbled, her breath suddenly coming fast as her control upon her nerves slipped away. "I will have to marry him, won't I?" She turned wide, fearful eyes to Harriet.

Harriet gritted her teeth, wishing she could reassure her. However, at this moment, she was not certain at all. Although she spotted Lord Burnham looking at them from where he stood with a group of gentlemen near the fountain, he did not show the slightest inclination of seeking them out. Clearly, his interest had been of a passing nature.

Seeking out Lady Atwood, Harriet asked her to show them the stables, doing her utmost to uphold pretenses, lest Sarah's parents became even more of a nuisance than they already were. Still, Harriet's mind remained otherwise occupied, considering each and every gentleman present at the house party. Was there perhaps a better option? A better match for Sarah?

The unfortunate answer was that there was not. All those in attendance were already married or betrothed or less than likely to make an offer to Sarah.

Over the next few days, Harriet could not help but feel utterly defeated. It was an altogether unfamiliar sensation, for she had never seen herself confronted with a problem she could not solve. Perhaps she truly ought to write to Grandma Edie and ask for her help. Perhaps the old lady could think of something, some kind of solution that eluded Harriet.

"Are you all right?" came Jack's voice from behind her.

Standing outside her door, Harriet turned around, feeling her heart do that little dance it often did the moment he drew near. "I'm well," she assured him, but a heavy sigh left her lips. "I'm merely...exhausted. I think I will turn in early tonight."

Slowly, Jack drew closer, his brown eyes lingering upon her face. "It is not going well, is it?"

She allowed herself a small smile. "Have you been watching us again? Watching me?"

Coming to stand an arm's length in front of her, Jack nodded, an answering smile coming to his own face. "Always." He reached out a hand and brushed a stray curl from her forehead, tugging it gently behind her ear. The tips of his fingers grazed her skin, then trailed along the line of her jaw before he playfully pinched her chin. "Is there anything I can do?"

Harriet shrugged. "If you could conjure a good and honest man who would care for Sarah and treat her as his equal, I would be much obliged." She offered him a weak smile, knowing that even the best intentions sometimes were not enough.

Jack chuckled, then his eyes became serious. "I know of one such man," he said then, his voice calm but emotional. "His heart, however, has already been stolen by another." The look in his eyes made Harriet want to throw herself into his arms and turn and run from him at the same time.

"It is these times we live in, is it not?" she tried her best to say it lightly. "You turn away for one moment, your attention elsewhere, and find yourself robbed of something you never thought needed protection."

Jack nodded knowingly. He seemed to be on the brink of saying more but then thought better of it. His shoulders drew back, and he glanced down the corridor as distant voices echoed in their ears. Still, no one appeared.

"Will you attend tonight's dance?" Jack inquired, and Harriet could see that he truly wanted her to. If only she did not have all these worries upon her mind! "We've never danced together, you and I." His brows rose teasingly. "Do you dare?"

Harriet chuckled, amazed that he could make her smile, laugh even in a moment like this. "I would not miss it for the world."

For a long moment, Jack held her gaze, something indecisive in his own. Then, suddenly, he reached out and tugged her into his arms. His head swooped down, and before Harriet knew what was happening, his lips claimed hers in a swift kiss.

Harriet barely had time to enjoy herself, to lean into him and respond when he released her. "I'll see you tonight then," Jack whispered, his warm breath teasing her skin. "Harry."

"Tonight," Harriet replied breathlessly, watching him walk away with equal parts relief and regret in her heart. Never had she encountered a greater challenge or a greater threat...or a greater promise. If only she knew what to do about it!

Stepping inside her chamber, Harriet slipped out of her shoes and lay down on the bed. Yet somehow, her early exhaustion had vanished. She no longer felt dead tired, unable to keep her eyes open. Instead, she felt invigorated...but confused. Her mind continued to spin, her thoughts torn between Jack and Sarah as her emotions danced from joy to apprehension to excitement to defeat. Never had Harriet been so unsure of herself in every way. What was it she wanted? What was it she was supposed to do?

All of a sudden, nothing made sense any longer. Nothing seemed clear any longer. "I need help," Harriet whispered to herself as she lay on her back, staring up at the ceiling. "Tomorrow morning, I shall write to Grandma Edie and ask her to come. She will find a way. Some way to fix all of this."

Try as she might, Harriet could not bring herself to slip into a quick nap. Yes, it would have been wise considering tonight's dance, but her eyes simply would not close. And so, by the time the sun slowly began its descent, Harriet found herself still wide awake and, on top of everything, feeling rather impatient. She rose to her feet and paced the length of her room a couple of times before turning to her wardrobe. Within a matter of moments, she had chosen an emerald green gown, one her father had said made her eyes shine. Would Jack agree, she wondered.

With a smile, Harriet placed it upon her bed, running her fingertips over the soft silk. Still, it was too early to ring for her maid and change. "Perhaps a quick stroll through the garden," Harriet muttered to herself, the need to move growing more pronounced. Always had she been a physically active person, riding out every day or simply strolling through the country on foot. However, over the last week or two, she had done little else but stand in drawing rooms and sit down to card games.

Reaching for her cloak, Harriet slipped out of her room and quickly headed downstairs. The sky shone in vivid colors as she set foot onto the terrace, breathing in deeply the soft evening air. It already felt cooler than during the day but still as fragrant as before.

Quick steps carried her down into the garden, and Harriet could feel her limbs relax with the movement, her muscles enjoying the brisk pace. Her eyes swept over the soft tinges of violet and orange, mingling with the darkening blue stretching across the horizon. Indeed, it looked like a painting, a masterpiece that held the power to sooth rattled nerves and calm aching hearts. It was beautiful, breathtaking, and Harriet could not help but smile, feeling her worries drift away.

At least for the moment.

Stepping into the maze where she had kissed Jack that first day at Atwood Park, Harriet paused when she suddenly thought to hear footsteps nearby. Had he followed her again? The thought instantly made her smile, and she proceeded onward, wondering why he had come... and what he might do.

Feeling like a silly debutante, Harriet tried her best to wipe that wide grin off her face. However, her thoughts remained with Jack and stayed despite her best intentions.

Closing her eyes, Harriet drew to a halt and waited. Slowly, the footsteps drew closer. In fact, they seemed somewhat hesitant, as though Jack was trying his best to approach without her realizing it. Was he here to frighten her? Had he not been the one to warn her not to go anywhere alone? Was he eager to prove his point?

All of a sudden, a cold shiver slowly snaked down Harriet's back and she made to spin around. However, in that moment, arms seized her from behind, pinning down her own and wrapping her in a tight embrace. She felt a hard chest against her back and opened her mouth to scream, for instinct told her that...this was not Jack.

Instantly, a hand clamped down over her mouth, cutting off her voice. She struggled against the tight grip that held her, and a shudder crawled over her skin at feeling her attacker's warm breath on the side of her neck. "Sneaking out at night," Lord Gillingham sneered, glee in his voice as he held her ever tighter, his mouth only a hair's breadth from her ear. "My, my, my, Lady Harriet, from you, I would have expected more...especially knowing what happened to your poor sister."

Fear and shock froze Harriet's limbs as she stared at the far horizon, Lord Gillingham's arms wrapped painfully around her. How had this happened? What did he want from her? Was this how Leonora had felt the night of the masquerade?

For a moment, Harriet felt her limbs grow weak, her body ready to admit defeat.

Ready to surrender.

No! Something screamed out deep inside her. *No!* She would not allow him to triumph over her. She would not!

Balling her hands into fists, Harriet inhaled a slow breath through her nose, then slowly lowered her chin to her chest. She waited for a heartbeat or two, and then she jerked her head abruptly backwards, feeling it collide with Gillingham's face.

A howl of pain escaped him, and instantly, his arms fell away.

Freed at last, Harriet immediately dashed away, her legs carrying her as fast as they could while her right hand tried to reach for the dagger hidden in her bodice. Her eyes flew over her surroundings, now growing ever darker, but nothing looked familiar. Everything seemed to be the same leafy hedge, now wrapped in shadows. Which was the way out?

Harriet could not recall.

And then a hand clamped down upon her shoulder, and she crashed to the ground. The dagger she had only just reached fell from her hand as Gillingham spun her around, his hands pushing her down against the hard ground. "How dare you?" he snarled into her face, blood dripping from his nose onto her neck as he fumbled with something in his pocket.

Harriet tried her best to push him away, to dislodge his hold on her, but a moment later, she felt his hand press a piece of cloth onto her mouth and nose.

Panic welled up, and she clawed at his hands and arms...as her eyelids grew heavy with sudden fatigue. Her mind felt heavy and languid, her vision blurring before her eyes finally closed.

Then every one of her senses went dark...and she lost all hold on reality.

CHAPTER FORTY

DESERVED PAYBACK

Harriet had never struck Bradley as one to arrive fashionably late. Yet the dance had begun and there had been no sign of her. He had spent an hour strolling through the ballroom, then inspecting the nearby parlors and drawing rooms. In his search, he had stumbled upon a couple or two who had sneaked away from the festivities to find a deserted room that would grant them privacy. But Harriet remained absent. Where on earth was she?

After another half an hour, Bradley sought her out. He rushed up the stairs to the upper floor and knocked on the door to her chamber. No answer came, and after a moment of hesitation, he simply opened the door and stepped inside.

The room was dark and deserted, but upon her bed he found an emerald gown, its soft fabric glistening in the silvery glow of the moon. It would look stunning on her. Why was she not wearing it?

Bradley could not help the sense of foreboding that came over him. Although Harriet had left Pinewood Manor without seeking him out in person, she *had* sent him a letter. She had not simply left. Even if she had changed her mind about the dance, about being here at Atwood Park, she would have said something. She would not simply have left. Bradley was certain of it.

On top of everything, her belongings were still here. But where was she?

Fear chased itself through his veins, slowly infesting every part of his body, as Bradley hurried back to the ballroom. Yet even now, she was nowhere to be seen.

His gaze moved from guest to guest, from face to face. All seemed to be enjoying themselves, laughing and chatting, dancing and drinking. He spotted Lord Gillingham in the corner with Lord Hartmore, a self-satisfied smile upon his lips, which deepened the moment their eyes met. No doubt, the other man had deduced that there was some sort of connection between Bradley and Harriet. Was it possible that Gillingham was responsible for Harry's disappearance?

"Your grace?"

At the sound of a soft, hesitant voice, Bradley turned to find none other than Miss Mortensen standing beside him. She wore a light blue gown, which made her skin seem even paler. Her eyes were wide, and Bradley could see at one glance that she was deeply agitated. "I apologize for approaching you in this manner," she said before casting a tense look over her shoulder at her parents, "but have you seen Harriet? Lady Harriet, I mean?" Her pale blue eyes looked up into his face. "She's not in her chamber and—"

Bradley's teeth ground together painfully. "I have not," he growled, inhaling a deep breath when she flinched at the mere sound of it. "I apologize. I didn't mean to frighten you. However, I have been searching everywhere, and I cannot find her either. Did she say anything to you?"

Miss Mortensen shook her head, fear paling her skin even further. "She said she would be here. She promised." Slowly, she shook her head. "She would not stay away without a word. It is most unlike her."

Bradley inhaled a deep breath, and his gaze moved back toward Gillingham. The man seemed even more self-satisfied than before, watching Bradley's conversation with Miss Mortensen with rapt attention. "Do you think...Do you think *he* could have anything to do with Harriet's disappearance?"

Reluctantly, Miss Mortensen glanced over her shoulder. The moment her eyes beheld Gillingham, her head snapped back around to

Bradley, a tremble shaking her delicate frame. "I hope not," she whispered, her lips trembling. "Oh, I truly, truly hope not."

Bradley had had enough. "If you'll excuse me, Miss Mortensen." He offered her a quick nod of the head and then strode past her, eyes fixed upon Gillingham.

Gillingham, in turn, responded with equal frankness. He did not even try to look surprised or confused as he found Bradley charging toward him from across the ballroom. Instead, the man's smile broadened in a way that sent an icy chill into Bradley's bones.

"Ah, Lord Clements," Miss Mortensen's father greeted him, a somewhat astonished look on his face. "I had heard you were in attendance. Is this not a spectacularly—?"

Bradley lifted a hand to cut off the man mid-sentence, not even bothering to mumble an excuse, his eyes fixed upon Gillingham. "A word in private," he growled, hard-pressed not to throw the man through a window right here and now.

Never in his life had Bradley known such fury! It was most unlike him; however, this was about Harriet!

His fiery-haired hellion!

Gillingham nodded his head courteously, as though Bradley had asked him most politely. "Of course." He smiled at Lord and Lady Hartmore. "If you will excuse me." Then he strode out of the ballroom, followed by Bradley, and sought out a drawing room only a few paces down the hall.

Stepping inside after him, Bradley pushed the door shut with a bang, unable to control the anger and fear coursing through his body every time he thought of Harriet. "Where is she?" he growled, not bothering to explain, certain that Gillingham knew precisely who he meant.

Gillingham chuckled darkly. "Oh, I've heard it whispered," he said with utter joy in his voice, but leaning forward as though sharing something confidential, "that she and Burnham ran off to Scotland together."

The blood in Bradley's veins turned to ice. "What do you mean?" The man could not be serious!

"Come now," Gillingham laughed as he strode toward the side table and poured himself a drink. "Even a man like yourself, always so far removed from society's most scandalous moments, must surely know why young couples, upon occasion, sneak away only to seek out a somewhat picturesque little village barely a stone's throw beyond the Scottish border." He fixed Bradley with a pointed stare, his brows rising meaningfully.

Bradley's hands balled into fists, and he had to suppress the urge to plant one in Gillingham's face. "You're lying," he snarled, wanting the other man's words to be a falsehood because if they were not...

Gillingham merely shrugged. "Truth or not, we both know that one wrong word will see her forever ruined." He grinned in that superior way of his.

"Don't you dare breathe a word of this to anyone," Bradley warned. "This was your doing, not hers. If what you say is true," he said with a deadly calm, "she did not go willingly. What did you do to her?"

Gillingham shrugged. "I admit, the lady needed some...let's say... persuasion to go along." He downed the contents of his glass in one swallow. "Women often do. However, Burnham will *compensate* her for any inconvenience suffered. He seems to be quite fond of her."

Losing all restraint, Bradley surged toward Gillingham and seized him by his lapels, shoving him back into the wall. "How dare you touch her? What kind of man are you?"

All humor left Gillingham's face, open hatred now blazing in his eyes. "Her sister ruined me," he spat, his voice dripping with venom. "This is nothing more than deserved payback."

Not bothering to dignify Gillingham's twisted view of the world with an answer, Bradley pulled back his right arm and then drove his fist into Gillingham's face. Instantly, the man's eyes rolled back, and he slumped to the floor like a ton of bricks.

Clenching and unclenching his throbbing hand, Bradley rushed from the room without looking back, knowing there was no time to lose. He did not know how much of a head-start Burnham had, but he was certain that every minute Harriet was with him, she was in severe danger.

"Was it him?"

Jarring to a halt at the sound of Miss Mortensen's faint voice, Bradley turned to look upon her pale face.

Taking a hesitant step toward him, she angled her head to look past his shoulder, her eyes widening as she spotted Gillingham on the floor. Her hands flew to her mouth, and she gasped. "Oh, heavens, no!" Her gaze snapped over to meet his. "Harriet!"

"I will find her," Bradley vowed. "I promise." Then he rushed past the softly sobbing woman and out into the night, his feet carrying him toward the stables as fast as they could.

Before he knew it, Bradley was thundering down a deserted road, heading north. He could barely see but did not care. He would make do with the faint glow of the crescent moon above, for he knew he could not stop. Every second mattered, and every second made him realize that Harriet had been right in her adamant refusal of marriage. Why had he never noticed that women were treated like chattel in this society? They were traded, bargained for, and even taken against their will with little to no consequence for the men involved. In short, they were owned by their fathers and husbands. If attacked, society's solution was to force them to wed their attacker or be ruined in the eyes of others. Was that justice?

Most certainly not!

Yes, Harriet had been right to refuse his marriage proposal, and for the first time, Bradley realized she had, in fact, never refused *him*.

CHAPTER FORTY-ONE

ON THE ROAD

Hearing herself groan, Harriet fought against the blackness that wrapped around her. Her head was pounding, and her body ached. She could not tell up from down or left from right. The world seemed to spin, and nausea rolled in waves through her stomach.

"All will be well," a male voice nearby whispered. "I promise. You shall feel better soon."

Harriet wanted to flinch when she felt a hand brush over her head, tugging loose strands back behind her ear. Her body, though, felt heavy. She could not even open her eyes, and her mind continued to lose hold of the world around her.

Everything seemed to sway but not softly like waves rolling onto a beach. No, the surface under her head felt hard, though mildly cushioned. It felt like fabric but rough and worn as it scratched against her skin.

The movement reminded Harriet of a carriage going fast across country roads. She felt as though her body would be flung from the seat at any moment, but the hands upon her held her in place.

Who was with her? Her drowsy mind wondered as the blackness receded once more. She dimly remembered walking through the garden at Atwood Park. The world had grown dark, and the sky had been lit with beautiful colors.

Cold gripped her heart then as she recalled rough hands seizing her from behind.

Gillingham!

Another groan tore from Harriet's lips. Where was he taking her? What did he want? Was this his way of getting revenge upon her family, upon Leonora for daring to refuse him? He had tried to bully her into marrying him, and she had not lain down quietly and played the victim.

"Hush, now! All shall be well," came the voice again, followed by another almost tender brush over her head.

Harriet stilled, for the voice did not sound like Gillingham's. Yet she was certain it had been he who had attacked her in the garden. Could she have been mistaken? No, she recalled his face clearly.

Then who was the man in the carriage with her? And where were they going? If only she could move!

As darkness tugged upon her mind yet again, Harriet dimly recalled a piece of cloth being pressed to her face. She had feared that Gillingham wanted to smother her, but now she recalled that an odd scent had emanated from the piece of cloth. She had felt lightheaded, her eyelids growing heavy and her limbs weak. Had he drugged her? Was that why she felt so far removed from everything?

Terror surged through Harriet's heart at the thought of what Gillingham and his accomplice had in store for her. Never had she felt so helpless and vulnerable...and alone. As capable as she had always thought herself, Harriet knew that this was something she could not get herself out of, and for the first time in her life, Harriet felt truly afraid...and more than willing to accept help. If only her family were here! If only Jack were here!

"We shall be there shortly," the man interrupted her thoughts, and this time, something about his voice struck Harriet as familiar. She had heard it before, and her mind tried to grasp that bit of memory, desperate to hold on.

Moments later, blackness returned, and it slipped away.

Adrenaline pumped through Bradley's veins like never before as he pushed his mount beyond its limits. Only once had he stopped at an inn to change horses and then resume his journey without delay. He had also asked after Burnham and Harriet, but no one remembered seeing a young lady. He could only hope that Gillingham had not lied to him about their whereabouts.

Riding hard, Bradley covered ground swiftly but not swiftly enough for his liking, for his mind continued to picture Harriet in Burnham's clutches. How had the cad forced her into his carriage? At gunpoint? By means of a threat?

All manner of images rose in Bradley's mind, tormenting him with the worst possible scenarios. He knew Harriet was brave and strong-willed, but even she could not hold terror and fear at bay under these circumstances.

Bradley could only hope that whatever Burnham had planned would be delayed by their journey. In all likelihood, he intended to force Harriet into marriage; why else head to Scotland?

The smell of rain lingered in the air as Bradley pressed onward. His eyes moved to the far horizon where dark clouds seemed to collect, a threat overshadowing his journey. Still, Bradley knew nothing would detain him. Come hell or high water, he would reach her in time. He would prevent her from marrying Burnham, for he did not for a second believe that it had been her honest choice to leave with him.

I will never marry. Harriet's words echoed in his head. Indeed, Gillingham had chosen the wrong sister, the wrong Whickerton, to make such a plan believable. After all, Bradley doubted that he was the only one who knew of Harriet's opinion of marriage. Yet perhaps the man did not care, thinking that so long as he ensured Harriet's ruination, she would have no choice.

Bradley gritted his teeth, thinking that he ought to have sent word to Lord Whickerton, informing the man of what had happened to his youngest daughter. Yet everything had happened so quickly that he had not even thought of it. Bradley wondered how Lord Whickerton would react if he learned of what had befallen Harriet.

Admittedly, Bradley had met Lord Whickerton a grand total of once. Yet he felt reasonably certain—especially after what Harriet had told him about her parents—that the man would not force his daughter's hand. Even if it became widely known that she had left with Burnham for Gretna Green, which Bradley did not doubt for one second would happen, considering that it was Lord Gillingham's dearest wish to see her and her family ruined, he could not imagine that Lord Whickerton would insist upon Harriet marrying the man.

No, it was not Harriet's reputation that he worried about, nor even her future. The Whickertons would always see to her, for they protected their own. Still, Bradley remembered well how Harriet had spoken to him of her sister, of how she had been attacked by Gillingham and had not been herself for a long time.

Urging his horse to greater speed, Bradley leaned forward in the saddle, praying that he would reach her in time to prevent any attack upon her person, Burnham might feel compelled to undertake should she prove uncooperative.

And Harriet *would* prove uncooperative.

She would not yield.

Not now.

Not ever.

CHAPTER FORTY-TWO
UPON ARRIVING IN GRETNA GREEN

Harriet drifted in and out of consciousness; yet the world remained far away. She heard distant voices now and then and dimly noticed that the air smelled of rain. Her body still felt heavy, and it took considerable effort to even breathe in deeply.

At one point, the sound of someone snoring nearby drifted to her ears as the carriage continued to sway roughly from side to side, now and then lurching forward. Harriet wished she could hold on to something, to open her eyes and make sense of her surroundings; yet her body would not move and her mind quickly drifted off again.

The next time Harriet came to, the carriage had stopped. The world no longer swayed, no longer moved from side to side, jostling her at every bump in the road. No, the world had stilled, and even though her eyes were closed, she pinched them shut tightly the moment bright sunlight fell onto her face. Again, voices spoke nearby, and this time, she could make out Burnham's voice clearly. It sounded drowsy, and she could hear him clear his throat a couple of times. "Here, take the purse," he said to someone as he stood not far away, perhaps outside the carriage door. "Procure us a room and then see to the horses. I shall be inside shortly."

"Yes, my lord," Burnham's coachman replied; after all, who else could he be?

Harriet groaned as she tensed her muscles to lift her head. They ached, and she sank back down. Yet she managed to crack open her eyes a little; unfortunately, the bright sunlight sent a jolt of pain through her head and she immediately pinched them shut again.

The carriage swayed slightly as someone stepped inside. "Ah, you're coming to. Good." Burnham!

Harriet wanted to lash out at him, claw his eyes out, or better yet cut his throat. Unfortunately, it still took considerable effort for her mind to hold on to reality. She felt exhausted, and sleep beckoned her closer, tugging her toward the promise of slumber.

Hands reached for her, and Harriet felt herself being lifted into his arms. Her head rolled back, and she felt a pinch in her neck before Burnham adjusted his hold on her. With one arm around her back and the other under her knees, her hand now resting against his shoulder, he carried her from the carriage. She could hear his boots crunching up on the gravel beneath. Voices drifted closer, and then she heard a door creak open. Instantly, the volume of the voices increased. She could hear people arguing as well as laughing. Where were they? Was this a tavern of some sort? Yet Burnham had instructed his coachman to procure them a room, had he not? Then this had to be an inn. Why would he take her to an inn?

An icy shiver crawled down Harriet's back, and once more, she fought to open her eyes. They fluttered slightly, and she could make out wooden beams running along the ceiling before her gaze fell on a group of men sitting in the far corner, drinks in their hands and their voices slurred.

"Did you get a room?" Burnham asked, his voice drilling into Harriet's mind like a sharp nail.

"Yes, my lord," his coachman replied. "Up the stairs, the third one on the right."

"Lead the way," Burnham instructed as he shifted Harriet in his arms. Was she growing too heavy for him to carry?

Harriet wished he would simply drop her right here and now because she did not want to find out what would happen once they reached the room. Still, he held on, and she could hear the soft creaking of the stairs underneath his boots. And then they reached the upper floor, and he carried her along the corridor. She saw faded wall coverings and doors lining each side of the corridor.

After a few paces, they stopped and the sound of a key turning in a lock reached her ears. Harriet blinked, and her gaze fell upon the tense-looking face of Burnham's coachman. The man swallowed hard as he stepped aside to allow them through, and Harriet could not help but think that he was no willing participant in this madness. Yet Burnham was his employer and a lord; what could his coachman do?

The moment Harriet felt Burnham settle her upon the bed, she stopped fighting the blackness that still pulled on her from all sides. Yes, perhaps it was preferable to being awake. If only she had her strength back. If only she had her dagger.

But she had lost it, had she not?

All hope was truly lost then.

Upon arriving in Gretna Green late in the evening, Bradley immediately guided his horse to the town's inn. It was a comparatively large building that no doubt had housed many a young couple after their vows had been spoken. Bradley could only hope that Harriet was not one of them.

Tossing his reins to a stable boy, Bradley crossed the yard in large strides, eyes fixed upon the door. He burst inside, eyes taking in the taproom where a few customers sat and drank quietly. A fire burned in the hearth as the air had cooled after last night's downpour. Bradley was soaked to the skin; yet he barely noticed.

All he could think about was Harriet. How long ago had she and Burnham arrived? While they had traveled by carriage, Bradley had made the journey on horseback, allowing him to cover ground faster. But had it been enough? How long ago had they arrived? And were they here now?

More importantly, what had happened to Harriet between arriving in Gretna Green...and now?

Bradley's gaze snapped around to find the inn's proprietor standing behind a large counter, eyeing Bradley suspiciously as he dragged mud all over his clean floors. Bradley could not have cared less. Ignoring the eyes that followed him from the taproom, he strode up to the front desk and fixed the middle-aged proprietor with a pointed look. "I am looking for a young couple who ought to have arrived within the last few hours." He swallowed hard. "The woman has fiery-red hair." *And the man is a spineless cad*, he added quietly to himself, feeling his insides tense as he awaited the proprietor's reply.

Scratching his thinning hairline, the man frowned. "I see lots of people coming and going. Canna say I've seen a red-haired lass. Married?"

Bradley shrugged. "I cannot say," he gritted out. "What does it matter?" Of course it did! "Are they here now?"

The man's face darkened at Bradley's sharp tone. "I could check the register if I had a name," he said with raised brows, making no movement to consult the ledger in front of him.

With an impatient grunt, Bradley placed a few coins on the counter. "Lord Burnham and Lady Harriet Beaumont," he growled after banging his fist upon the smooth wood. Indeed, Bradley barely recognized himself. Never had he felt such inner turmoil, not even when he had come from his father's deathbed.

With mind-wrecking patience, the proprietor reached for the ledger, then slowly opened it and began flicking through the pages. Bradley wanted to strangle him!

"Pardon me?" came a deep, heavily accented voice a second before a large shadow fell over the counter. "Did ye say Beaumont?"

Bradley turned to find a tall, broad-shouldered man beside him. He was dressed casually, yet more appropriately considering the sudden rain that had soaked the earth the day before. He had an angular face and dark brown hair that was pulled back from the top of his head to his ears and tied with a ribbon, while the rest hung loosely down to his shoulders. It gave him a bit of an uncivilized look. Still, unlike the proprietor, the look upon his face was friendly.

"Yes," Bradley said carefully and with no small measure of impatience. "Keep looking," he hissed at the proprietor, who had paused in his efforts and was looking back and forth between the two men. "Why?"

The tall Scot gave the proprietor a pointed look, who immediately turned his attention back to the ledger. "I've grown up hearing tall tales of a family by that name," he told Bradley with a grin. "The father is an earl, is he not? Whickerton is the name." His brows rose in question.

Bradley nodded. "Lady Harriet is his daughter," he offered carefully, then frowned. "How do you know the family?"

Not answering Bradley's question, the Scot instead asked one of his own. "Ye expect the lass to be here? Did she run off?" Again, he grinned, humor in his eyes.

Bradley shook his head. "No, she was taken." His teeth ground together. "Against her will."

Instantly, the Scot's grin vanished, replaced by something that made Bradley think the man was almost as outraged as he was himself. "Angus," he snapped at the proprietor. "Are they here?" His gaze was sharp as he leaned over the counter, peering down at the middle-aged man.

Angus, the proprietor, suddenly nodded his head vehemently. "They arrived an hour or two ago. The lass couldna even walk. He had to carry her up the stairs."

Bradley's blood ran cold.

"Which room?" the Scot demanded, grabbing Angus by the front of his shirt and hauling him toward him. "Which room?"

"Th-Third one on the right," the man stammered, one hand pointing toward the stairs leading to the upper floor.

The Scot simply dropped Angus, who fell to the floor in a heap of limbs. By that time, however, Bradley was already halfway up the stairs, taking them two at a time.

An hour or two ago. The words echoed in his mind, tormenting him, as he charged down the corridor.

CHAPTER FORTY-THREE
RECKLESS BEHAVIOR

Yet again, Harriet felt the fog retreat from her mind. Only this time, it did not linger upon its fringes. She still felt weak, her arms and legs heavy as lead; however, her eyes blinked open with ease and she was able to turn her head and allow her gaze to sweep over her surroundings.

Dimly, Harriet remembered arriving in this room, its sounds and smells dimly familiar to her. Two windows allowed in a sliver of gray light, and a warm fire burned in the grate. Still, a chill lingered upon Harriet's bones, which had nothing to do with the drop in temperature.

Noting that she was alone, Harriet breathed in deeply when the door suddenly flew open and in walked none other than her captor, Lord Burnham.

"Ah, you're awake," he said approvingly, greeting her with a joyful smile that seemed oddly inappropriate under the circumstances. "How do you feel?" He closed the door behind him and approached the bed.

Harriet tensed. "Where am I? What did you do to me?" she snapped, thinking it wiser to tap into her anger instead of dwelling upon the tight ball of fear that lingered deep inside.

Burnham paused in his step, a confused frown coming to his brows.

Then he took the last two steps toward the bed and sat down upon its edge.

Harriet pushed herself back, needing more distance between them. Still, her arms were far from strong. "Why do I feel like this? Did you drug me?"

A sickeningly indulgent smile came to Burnham's face as he lifted his hands to calm her. "I understand that you're a bit confused, my dear. It's the side effects of the remedy. Gillingham assured me it will pass quickly."

"Gillingham," Harriet mumbled, trying her best to piece together the fragmented memories that kept coming back to her rather out of order.

"Yes," Burnham said in a tone as though he were speaking to a child. "Do you not recall? You asked for his help so we could elope. He—"

"Elope?" Harriet shrieked or would have if her voice had been anywhere near strong enough to do so. Shock chased itself up and down her limbs as her gaze snapped to the window. "Where are we?"

Burnham frowned. "Gretna Green, of course. Where else?"

Harriet stared at the man seated upon the edge of the bed, no more than an arm's length from her. "What hap—? Did we—? Are we —?" She was uncertain if she wanted to know the answers to any of those questions.

"Not yet," Burnham replied with a smile that might have been endearing under different circumstances. "However, now that you're awake, I shall see that everything is arranged." He sighed longingly. "We shall be married shortly."

"We shall not!" Harriet hissed, working to push herself up to lean against the headboard. "I don't know what Gillingham told you," she heaved, feeling out of breath from the effort of moving her uncooperative body, "but I never intended to elope. Never!"

Burnham's brows drew down as he watched her, a dark look coming to his face. "Whatever do you mean? He said that—"

"Did it not strike you as odd that I was unconscious?" Harriet demanded. "He attacked me in the maze at Atwood Park. He drugged me and then—" Honestly, she did not know what had happened then. A thought that frightened her more than she liked to admit.

Though still frowning, Burnham tried to smile at her. "You're still confused. It's the remedy. Once it wears off, you—"

"What remedy? What did you give me?"

Burnham shrugged. "I don't quite know what I gave you. Gillingham procured it for your travel sickness. Do you not recall? You asked him to."

Staring at the man seated next to her, Harriet slowly shook her head. "I did no such thing as I am not afflicted by any sort of *travel sickness*," she growled, her voice rising in pitch with each word to leave her lips. This was outrageous!

Inhaling a slow breath, Harriet tried to stay calm. She fixed Burnham with a pointed look and spoke as unemotionally as she could under the present circumstances. "Gillingham is a man without honor or decency. Under no circumstances would I have gone to him for help in any kind of matter. Do you understand? He lied to you. I never wished to elope with you. Never!"

Burnham's eyes darkened, and his lips thinned. Harriet was dimly aware of a warning bell going off in her head, urging her not to antagonize him; yet she found herself unable to remain silent.

"What made you think I wanted to marry you? To elope with you?" she demanded, shaking her head at him. "It's lunacy!"

A muscle in his jaw twitched. "Why you now pretend that there is nothing between us, I cannot fathom. Perhaps it is the aftereffects of the remedy." He tried to pat her hand, but she pulled it away. "You've sought my presence repeatedly over the past week, do you not recall?"

Harriet felt sick. "Yes, for Sarah's benefit!" Oh, how wrong she had been!

"Sarah?"

"Miss Mortensen," Harriet retorted when he looked completely lost. "I was trying to help her win your...affections." Oh, what a mistake she had made!

Burnham scoffed. "I'm sorry to have to say this, but considering her family's circumstances, you cannot truly expect me to—"

"Careful!" Harriet warned, glaring at him. "I suggest you watch your tongue."

For a long moment, Burnham simply stared at her, the look in his eyes going back and forth between anger and disbelief. "Whether you wished to elope, no longer matters," he finally said, his lips set in a firm line. "We are here now, and someone will have noticed our absence or even seen us leaving together." He breathed in deeply. "We have no choice but to marry."

Slowly, Harriet shook her head. "I will not marry, not you or anyone else." *Jack*, her heart whispered in that moment, and a deep longing rolled through her, bringing tears to her eyes.

"You'll be ruined," Burnham snapped, tugging his right hand through his hair in an exasperated gesture. "No, we shall marry. There is no other way. I will not allow my reputation to be tarnished by your reckless behavior."

"My reckless behavior?" Harriet demanded, gawking at him open-mouthed. "Was *I* the one to drug you and drag you halfway across the country into Scotland? Perhaps before kidnapping a woman, you ought to have made certain she wished to be kidnapped!"

He glared at her. "Gillingham said—"

"That only shows that the man cannot be trusted! He lied to you, and you were dumb enough to believe him!" Her heart thundered in her chest. "He hates my family because my sister refused to be bullied by him. He attacked her, and now he is outraged that she didn't play the dutiful victim."

Burnham's face paled, and yet the look upon his face did not speak of outrage over the atrocity Gillingham had committed against Leonora. No, it was a selfish emotion that sparked in his eyes.

Fear quickly overruled Harriet's own outrage, and she moved to push her legs over the side of the bed. She needed to leave! Now!

The world blurred briefly before her eyes as she pushed herself toward the edge; her legs dangling rather uselessly in the air. *Focus*, she chided herself. *You can do this!*

The moment Harriet pushed to her feet, though, a heavy hand descended upon her shoulder, pushing her back down. In her weakened state, Harriet had no strength to hold against it, and she sank back down onto the mattress. "Let me go!" she demanded in a faint voice, her hands trying to push Burnham away as he leaned over her.

Instantly, he caught her wrists, pushing them down onto the mattress. "Whether or not you like it, we will be married," he growled into her face. "Think of your family! What would your father say if he knew—?"

"My father would never force me to marry," Harriet protested, "especially not a man like you. You're as despicable as Gillingham!"

Burnham's jaw tensed before he lowered his head closer to hers, his eyes hard and uncaring. "He might once you carry my child," he hissed, a sneer curling up the corners of his mouth that made him look like Gillingham.

Panic clawed at Harriet's heart as he tried to kiss her. She turned her head away, knowing it was all she could do. She was alone and weak and without her dagger. There was nothing she could do. Nothing but close her eyes and—

The door burst open in that moment, and briefly, Harriet thought she was hallucinating, for right there, storming toward her with a grim expression she had never seen upon his face, was Jack.

Her Jack.

Harriet wanted to sob with relief.

CHAPTER FORTY-FOUR

IN THE NICK OF TIME

The moment the door flew open and his eyes fell upon Burnham as he pushed Harriet down onto the bed, Bradley felt as though someone had taken a powerful swing to his midsection. He nearly keeled over in shock. Then outrage ignited once more, pushing all else aside and propelling him across the room.

Without conscious thought, Bradley grabbed Burnham and yanked him off Harriet. The man's face paled instantly, and he stammered something under his breath, but in that moment, words held no meaning for Bradley. He drew back his right fist and then drove it into Burnham's face, sending the man flying across the room.

Bradley dimly noticed the Scot step across the threshold after him, his jaw set and his eyes narrowed, before he spun back toward the bed...

...and Harriet.

"Jack." His name was only a sob that fell from her lips as she looked up at him with tear-filled eyes. Her face was pale and her wild curls in terrible disarray. She looked weak, barely able to hold up her own head, and Bradley's heart twisted painfully at the sight of her.

"See to the lass," the Scot said from where he stood by the door, his voice tense and the look upon his face far from smiling. "I'll handle...

him." He kneeled down and threw an unconscious Burnham over his right shoulder as though the man were only a rag doll. Then he stepped out into the corridor, closing the door behind him.

Without another thought, Bradley pulled Harriet into his arms. Her fingers curled into his rain-soaked coat as he cradled her on his lap, his arms holding her tightly against his chest. Sobs tore from her throat as she snuggled into his embrace, and he could hear her whispering his name over and over again.

"Hush now," Bradley murmured against the top of her head as he ran his hands over her back in a soothing gesture. "You're safe, Harry. You're safe."

Harriet clung to him as though she were in danger of drowning, and the shivers that shook her became almost violent. She seemed to fall apart right there in his arms, and Bradley could do nothing else but hold her.

He had never felt so powerless, so utterly helpless in his life.

Slowly, the room began to darken as the sun set, the only light coming from the slowly dying fire in the grate. Its soft orange flames cast a warm glow over the room, and yet Harriet's shivers would not cease.

"Are you hurt?" Bradley asked reluctantly, uncertain what to say.

Her shivers quietened, and she drew in a deep breath. "I'm...fine." Her voice was so weak that Bradley barely heard her. "I will...be...fine." She swallowed and drew in another deep breath. "He...gave me...something." Slowly, she shifted her head until her green eyes were looking up into his. "It's...It's wearing off." Her eyes closed, then opened again, but not without effort. "It'll...pass."

Bradley wanted to punch that miscreant senseless again and again.

"What can I do?" he asked instead. "Shall I fetch a doctor? Or—?"

"Water."

Nodding, Bradley eased her out of his arms, reluctant to let her go, and settled her against the pillows. Then he marched across the room to pour her a cup of water from a pitcher on the small table by the window.

Harriet drank slowly, her fingers trembling as they held the cup. When it was empty, her head fell back against the pillow, and she closed her eyes, heaving a deep sigh before opening them again. Her lashes fluttered as though she were trying to clear her vision, her mind working to put everything to rights.

Bradley seated himself on the edge of the bed, one hand reaching out to take the cup from hers while the other came to rest upon her arm, giving it a gentle squeeze. "Is it any better?"

Swallowing, Harriet nodded, her eyes slowly focusing on him. "I still feel tired," she said in a breathless voice, "but my mind feels... steadier now. It'll wear off. Whatever he gave me, it'll wear off." Her jaw tensed, and for a moment, Bradley saw anger spark in her green eyes.

"What happened? How—?" Bradley did not know how to phrase the question. Harriet seemed tense and on edge, which, of course, was no surprise. Still, he was worried that one wrong word might send her over the edge.

"How did I end up here? With Burnham?" Her lips curled into a sneer as his name dropped from her tongue. She heaved a deep sigh and then told him how she had walked in the gardens, how she had heard footsteps approaching her in the maze, how Gillingham had attacked her...

With each word, Bradley felt his hands ball into fists, the need to see Gillingham join Burnham on the ground overwhelming. Never in his life had Bradley been a violent person. Never had he entertained thoughts such as these. However, never in his life had he had to stand by and watch someone he loved be treated in such a way.

Yes, he supposed love changed everything.

"Where is he?" came Harriet's tense voice. She still spoke quietly, but Bradley could not help but think that a bit more strength now vibrated in her voice. "Burnham, where is he? And who was that man? The one who came in after you."

Wrapping her hands in his, Bradley met her gaze. "Honestly, I'm not quite certain who he is. From his accent, he's clearly a Scot, but—"

Harriet frowned. "Then why was he with you if you don't know who he is?"

"I was downstairs inquiring after you...and Burnham—the proprietor was less than forthcoming, by the way—when the Scot approached. From what I can gather, he heard me say your last name and recognized it from tales he had heard."

"Tales?"

Bradley shrugged. "That is all he said. When I told him you had been taken against your will," he swallowed hard, and felt her soft hands squeeze his with surprising strength, "he immediately turned toward the proprietor, insisting he tell us your whereabouts. Once the man did, all I could think about was to get to you."

A heartbreakingly sweet smile came to Harriet's face, and her right hand rose to cup his cheek. "Oh, my sweet Jack. Once again you surprise me...and in the most wonderful way." Tears misted in her eyes. "Thank you. Thank you so much for coming. I don't know what I—"

Reaching out, Bradley pulled her into his arms, cradling her head against his shoulder as tears flowed from her eyes. Never had he seen her so vulnerable. He would not have thought it possible; yet for all her bravado, a tender heart beat in Harriet's chest as well. "Why did you walk outside in the gardens by yourself?" Bradley heard himself say before he could bite his tongue. He did not mean to accuse her of anything, but the fear he had felt for her still lived in his chest, strong and terrifying.

At his words, Harriet stilled before she slowly lifted her head off his shoulder. Her eyes were blurred with tears as she looked up at him. "To clear my head," she replied, wiping the tears off her cheeks. "To breathe and think." There was an odd edge to her voice, and Bradley understood it for what it was: a challenge.

Breathing in deeply, Bradley battled down the fear that still gripped his heart. "I did not mean to say that—"

"Yes, you did!" Harriet exclaimed, yet her voice was far from strong. She blinked, then inhaled deeply, the look in her eyes clearly telling him that she was furious at herself for this weakness she felt. "You think because I'm a woman, I should've taken better care. You think that because you're a man, you don't need to. But let me tell you, even you can be taken unawares. Or do you truly believe that you're ready to defend yourself at every moment in your life? This could have happened to you as well. You're not stronger than me. You're not—"

Her voice broke off as she began to tremble; her eyes, however, remained upon his, bold and unyielding.

Slowly, Bradley reached for her again, gently cupping her face. "I did not mean to say any of those things. What I said I said because I was so very afraid for you." Tears rose in his eyes. "The thought of what happened to you, of what could have happened to you...is killing me." He gripped her shoulders harshly and stared into her eyes. "Don't you ever put me through that again!"

A soft smile teased Harriet's lips. "Do you truly mean it? What you said? You were afraid for me?"

"More than I have ever been in my life."

She regarded him curiously. "You don't think I acted foolishly?"

"No more than anyone else at any given time."

A tentative sparkle came to her eyes. "You don't think me...weak?"

Bradley smiled at her. "No weaker than I am myself." He pulled her closer. "Do you remember that day in the meadow when you caught me off guard and I found myself lying on my back in the grass with your blade pressed against my throat?"

Harriet nodded. "How could I forget? It was the first moment I realized I truly wanted to kiss you."

Surprised, Bradley momentarily stared at her before slowly shaking his head, clearing his thoughts. "Well, what I meant to say was that if you had meant to do me harm, you could have." He grasped her chin and looked deep into her eyes. "We are all weak and strong at different points in our lives. Sometimes we stand tall, and sometimes we fall. But, Harriet, asking for help does not make you weak. Do you understand that? You're the strongest woman I've ever met, even now, here, in this moment."

Harriet heaved a deep sigh. "I think I'm beginning to understand that. Frankly, before I walked out into the garden, I had decided to send word to my grandmother to ask for her help regarding Sarah. It is hard for me to do, to admit that there is something I cannot solve, but, yes, I think I'm beginning to see that we all have our weak moments. We wouldn't be human without them, would we?"

Bradley shook his head. "No, we would not. As much as we thrive in the sun, we need the night; otherwise, we would never see the moon."

Harriet grinned at him. "How poetic of you, Jack." Her teeth clicked together as a shiver gripped her.

"You need rest," Bradley told her. "It is late. Lie down and close your eyes. I'll watch over you. I promise." He made to rise from the bed, but Harriet held him back.

"And you need warmth," she told him before her hands swept over his soaked coat. "You'll catch cold if you stay in these clothes." A somewhat shy, but all the more teasing grin slowly spread over her face. "Hang them up in front of the fire...and then come to bed..."

Bradley's brows rose heavenward as he stared at her.

"...and hold me," she finished. "Will you do that?" Again, her teeth chattered and he could see her shoulders tremble.

After another moment of hesitation, Bradley nodded. "Very well." He inhaled a deep breath, then he strode over to stoke the fire back to life. He added another log or two, then began disrobing, very much aware that Harriet was watching him.

"You're blushing," Harriet remarked with a chuckle.

Bradley laughed, more than ever grateful for her direct words. "As are you," he told her before he pulled his shirt over his head.

Her eyes grew rounder as they swept over his bare chest. Then she swallowed. "Very well." Her eyes rose to meet his. "We'll both keep our backs turned. How is that?" Her nimble fingers moved to the laces of her gown.

Bradley frowned.

"I have no intention of sleeping laced-up. You do not know how uncomfortable this is." She snorted. "Another upside for men."

Bradley smiled at her. "Then why do you do it?"

Harriet paused. "Because..." She broke off, and a contemplative look came to her eyes. "Perhaps I shouldn't. Perhaps I truly should forgo corsets. Perhaps I should forgo even dresses. Perhaps I should wear what you wear. It does look far more comfortable." Her eyes glowed, and yet Bradley saw a glimmer of a challenge in them.

Smiling, Bradley nodded. "Perhaps you should."

Instantly, Harriet seemed to relax. "Perhaps I should." Then she pointed her right forefinger at him before spinning it in a small circle. "Now, turn around." A teasing grin rested upon her lips, and suddenly, she seemed far from weak. Nevertheless, her eyes were still guarded, seeking to hide the horrors of the past two days from him.

Perhaps even from herself.

Turning their backs to one another, they both undressed. Bradley could hear the rustle of her gown gliding to the floor. "Do you need any help?" he asked impulsively, a teasing note in his voice.

Harriet chuckled. "Nice try."

Fortunately, Bradley's undergarments were merely damp and not wet, so he left them on. "Can I turn around?"

"Yes."

As Bradley did so, he saw Harriet slip under the covers. Fortunately, she had only removed her gown and stays, her white chemise glowing almost ethereally in the light from the fire. Meeting his eyes, she held out her hand to him.

Swallowing, Bradley approached the bed, then he tentatively joined her beneath the covers. Every shred of decency he possessed urged him to rethink this decision; however, the deep need for comfort he saw in Harriet's eyes overruled every argument. Although she put on a brave face, Bradley could see that she was far from well.

Her teeth dug into her lower lip to keep them from chattering while her fingers were all but curled around the blanket in an iron grip, the tendons standing out white.

Lying down, Bradley held out an arm to her. "Come. Let me hold you."

With a shiver, Harriet sank into his embrace, her head coming to rest upon his shoulder as she curled her body around his. "You're so warm," she gasped, and her breath brushed over his skin, sending an answering shiver down his spine.

Indeed, even though he was the one who had gotten soaked almost to his skin, she was the one now shivering violently with cold. Her skin felt almost icy, and Bradley rubbed his hands up and down her back, trying his best to warm her. "Do you...want to talk about it?" he asked tentatively, not knowing what else to say.

Not knowing what she might need.

Her breathing stilled for a heartbeat or two. "No," she said, and then her chilled fingers moved across his bare chest, her body snuggling closer, seeking his warmth.

Bradley swallowed, aware of the tension that lingered in her body. "Did he...?"

Every muscle in Harriet's body tensed...before the strain slowly eased. "When you came in," she whispered, not lifting her head to look at him, "you saw the full extent of what he did...or tried to do." She swallowed hard. "If you hadn't come..." This time, she lifted her head and her green eyes looked up into his. "Thank you for coming after me."

"Always," Bradley whispered, hugging her closer. "Always." He felt her inhale a deep breath. "Sleep now."

Harriet nodded as her eyes closed, and with each heartbeat, her breathing evened.

"You know," Bradley whispered into the dim stillness of the chamber, "I think I understand."

Her chest rose and fell with even breaths, her eyes closed and her body slowly warming as she drifted off. Still, a small sound drifted from her lips. "Mmmh?"

"What you said about marriage," Bradley clarified. "About women in our society." He heaved a deep breath. "You're not wrong. In fact, you're right. You're very right. I see that now."

In answer, Harriet hugged him tighter and a soft sigh left her lips before slumber finally claimed her whole.

For a long while, Bradley lay awake, holding the woman he loved in his arms and wondering how life had become so complicated. He ought to be beyond happy, and yet the very woman he wished to marry was perhaps the only one determined to refuse him.

No, not him.

Marriage.

Bradley frowned. Perhaps not marriage in general, simply the way it had come to be shaped.

In its essence, marriage was nothing more or less than a union between two people who loved one another, stating their intention to continue on through life side by side. Only somehow it had become twisted, shaped by those seeking power, seeking control over others. Marriage had become no more than a contract, detailing who would gain what.

For a moment, Bradley's hand running up and down Harriet's arm stilled. "A contract," he whispered to himself before a slow smile came to this face. "Why ever not?"

CHAPTER FORTY-FIVE

THE WAYS OF THE WORLD

The next morning, Harriet woke with a smile upon her face. The shivers had left in the night, and her body felt warm all over...thanks to the large, half-naked Englishman currently holding her in his arms. His chest rose and fell with even breaths, his eyes still closed in slumber.

For a second, Harriet wondered if she ought to wake him. Then, however, a more appealing thought entered her mind.

With her head still upon his shoulder, her eyes sweeping over his profile, she slowly moved her left hand from his shoulder. Bit by bit, she trailed it downward, tracing the line of his collarbone and feeling his warm skin. The pulse in his neck beat calmly below her fingertips, and Harriet felt a new shiver dance across her skin, only this one felt devastatingly wonderful.

"What are you doing?" came Jack's voice, still heavy with sleep, but alert.

Harriet flinched, and her head flew up. "You're awake?"

A slow grin spread over his face as he turned to look at her, his eyes sparkling with mischief. "Yes," was all he said.

Harriet regarded him cautiously, then she shrugged. "A girl has every right to be curious, does she not?"

His grin deepened as he pushed himself up onto his elbow, bringing them face to face. "Would you grant me that same right?" His brows rose in challenge.

Harriet chuckled. "Definitely." Her gaze dropped to his lips. "But do you dare act on it?"

His deep brown eyes held hers, asking. Then Jack slowly leaned toward her, his warm breath tickling her skin before he brushed his lips gently against hers.

Harriet could have wept at the care and consideration he showed. She could feel in the tentative way he touched her that he was afraid to overstep, especially after what she had gone through so recently. And so, it was Harriet who deepened the kiss, pulling him down to her as she settled back into the pillows.

His weight upon her did not frighten Harriet, and she wrapped her arms around his shoulders, delighting in the movement of his muscles beneath her fingertips. His hands cradled her head, and she felt the pads of his fingers brush along her temples, tugging her wild curls back behind her ears.

It was an achingly sweet gesture, and Harriet smiled as he lifted his head to look down upon her. "Are you all right?" Jack asked, his brown eyes trailing over her face as though looking for an answer to his question.

Harriet had no words to express how she felt. Instead, she pulled him back down to her, her lips straining to reclaim his. Unfortunately, a sharp knock sounded on their door in that moment, and Harriet felt a growl of frustration rise from her throat.

Jack chuckled before his face grew tense, and Harriet could see the memory of all that had happened return. "Stay here," he whispered, then he rose from the bed and quickly donned his shirt and breeches.

Opening the door no more than a crack, Jack spoke to someone out in the hallway. Harriet could not make out what he was saying, but his shoulders remained relaxed. After a few moments, he closed the door once more and turned back to look at her.

"Who was that?" Harriet asked as she slipped her legs out of bed. She paused, a frown coming to her face. "What...What happened to Burnham? I completely forgot after..."

Jack stepped toward her, pulled her to her feet, and wrapped his hands around hers. "Do not worry, Harry. You don't have to see him again."

Harriet felt the frown upon her face deepen. "What does that mean? Where is Burnham?" She searched his face. "You never left the room… What…? I…" Indeed, her mind felt a little fuzzy, unfocused regarding what had happened the day before. "Who was that out in the hall?"

Jack inhaled a deep breath. "As I just learned, his name is Mr. Kier MacKinnear. He was the one who took Burnham away last night and tied him up in the stables."

"Kier MacKinnear." Harriet frowned anew, for the name sounded oddly familiar. "I think I know him," she whispered, raking her mind. "But I don't know…how." She shook her head, frustrated with the lingering effects of the drug. How dare Burnham! Anger surged through her veins, and Harriet vowed she would make him pay.

Jack continued to watch her most carefully. "We should dress and then eat something," he finally said, "before we head back home."

Harriet nodded. "Will you give me a hand?" she asked with a grin. "As much as I would like to change into something more comfortable, I'm afraid all I have is my dress."

"Of course," Jack replied with a smile. "Go ahead and dress as far as you can, and I will do the same. Let me know if you need help."

Harry chuckled. "Does that mean you will also require my help?"

Pulling on his boots, Jack looked up at her and grinned. "Don't tempt me, Harry, or we shall never make it out of this room!"

Although every moment was still overshadowed by a dark cloud, the memory of what had brought them here, Harriet could not deny that Jack's mere presence made her feel safe. She felt better than she ought to under the circumstances, for she remembered the devastating effect Gillingham's attack upon Leonora had had upon her sister's state of mind. Of course, Jack had burst into the room before Burnham had had a chance to…

Harriet swallowed hard as she reached for her clothes. She tried to remind herself that *nothing* had happened, and yet whenever she thought about it, the shivers gripped her anew. "Will you help me tie my laces," she mumbled rather absentmindedly, her thoughts still drawn to the past.

Harriet heard Jack draw closer until he came to stand behind her, his fingers moving swiftly, yet tentatively, without touching her. "Are you all right?" he asked, no humor in his voice any longer. "Harry."

Inhaling a slow breath, Harriet waited until he had finished tying her laces. Then she turned around and looked up at him. "No, I am not all right," she told him in a harsh voice, allowing all her emotions to rise to the surface. "In fact, I am furious. He had no right to do what he did. And yet no matter what I do, this," she gestured wildly, her movements meant to encompass everything that had happened, "will have no consequences for him." She scoffed. "Just like my sister, it is I who will be deemed ruined. Not that I care, mind you, but..." Her fingers tensed and then curled into fists. "This is beyond unfair. This is wrong."

Jack nodded. "You're right. Of course, you're right." He watched her carefully, and she could see that he truly agreed with her. He, too, was angry. She could see it in his eyes; yet she also saw resignation. He, too, knew that there was nothing they could do. It was the way of the world.

Closing her eyes, Harriet drew in a deep breath. "I will think of something," she mumbled, more to herself than to him. "This is not the end of it." She turned and reached for her dress, quickly slipping it over her head. Then she turned her back to Jack once more, and a moment later, she felt his fingers accidentally brush against her skin as he tied her laces.

"Let's go eat something," Jack said as he stepped back. He held out his hand to her, and Harriet grasped it, holding it tightly within her own. Together, they stepped from the chamber and made their way downstairs to the taproom.

Crowded with newlyweds and villagers alike, the noise that drifted to their ears was momentarily stunning. Harriet swept her eyes over the many merry faces, feeling their excitement, wishing it were her own. The aroma of fresh bread drifted to her nostrils, and Harriet's stomach rumbled loudly.

To her surprise, a tall, dark-haired man rose to his feet and waved them over. He had been seated at a table in the corner, its surface laden with food. The man's face looked utterly unfamiliar to Harriet, and yet he looked at her as though they had met before.

Jack pulled out a chair for Harriet, and for once she did not argue, seating herself as the stranger—presumably Mr. Keir MacKinnear—turned toward her. "Ye must be Lady Harriet," the Scotsman declared with a wide smile. "Ye look exactly as I'd always pictured ye."

Jack briefly paused as he pulled out a chair for himself. "Pictured her?" he asked, a bit of a hard edge coming to his voice.

Mr. MacKinnear seemed not to notice. "Aye, my grandmother spoke of ye often. She said ye were the wild one of the Whickerton clan." He chuckled, his blue eyes glowing with deep affection. "I think the first story she ever told me was how ye climbed a tree, trying to return a baby bird to its nest, and promptly fell off, breaking yer arm." He slapped his knee, laughing loudly. "Aye, ye've got the look of an untamed spirit about ye. With yer red hair, ye might as well be a Scot."

Out of the corner of her eye, Harry could see Jack observing the other man rather tensely. Still, he did not say a word but merely waited and observed.

"Your grandmother?" Harriet asked, her attention moving back and forth between Mr. MacKinnear and the piece of bread she was buttering. "I must admit your name sounds familiar, but I do not believe I have seen your face before. Pray tell, who is your grandmother."

"Her name is Adele MacKinnear; however, before she was married, she was Lady Adele, daughter to the Earl of Blackthorne."

Harriet closed her eyes on a sigh when suddenly the last puzzle piece fell into place and the picture she was seeing finally made sense. "Of course!" she exclaimed, dimly noting a look of surprise coming to Jack's face. "You're Keir MacKinnear. Yes, my grandmother spoke to us of you as well."

Beside her, Jack leaned forward, his eyes going back and forth between the other two. Although he did not say a word, Harriet knew that he still did not understand. How could he?

Smiling at him, Harriet said, "Our grandmothers used to be the best of friends, both equally meddlesome, it would seem." She glanced at Mr. MacKinnear, who nodded enthusiastically. "During their second season, they attended a Christmas house party somewhere in the north of England...I don't quite recall where. However, they both fell in love during those days and both managed to procure a proposal before the year was out." She chuckled at the memory of the mischievous gleam that had always been in her grandmother's eyes whenever she had spoken of that Christmas season.

Mr. MacKinnear nodded. "Aye, my grandmother always said the only bad thing to come from those proposals was that they suddenly found themselves separated from one another by a great distance; my grandmother in the Highlands and yours near London." He smiled at Jack. "Yet they always stayed in contact, exchanging letters. I think at one point they even kept carrier pigeons." He chuckled. "Over the years, I have heard many tall tales about the Whickertons."

Swallowing her last bite of bread, Harriet looked at Mr. MacKinnear curiously. "What brings you here? Now?" With a frown, she looked from him to Jack. "This cannot possibly be a coincidence."

The man shrugged, that wide, cheerful smile once more upon his face. "I dunna know about that. However, the fact of the matter is, that I'm here because I'm on my way to Whickerton Grove."

Harriet almost choked on her tea. "Pardon me?"

"Aye, your grandmother invited me," he said with a shrug, no small measure of amusement in his eyes.

"Why?" Jack asked, a slight frown drawing down his brows as he looked back and forth between Harriet and Mr. MacKinnear.

Again, the man shrugged. "That I canna say. My grandmother refused to give me any details. She can be very secretive when she wants to be."

Harriet heaved a deep sigh. "Honestly, she sounds exactly like someone else I know." She shook her head, then grinned at Jack. "So, you're saying that my grandmother invited you to Whickerton Grove and you were told about it by your grandmother and neither one of them offered you an explanation?"

Grinning, Mr. MacKinnear nodded. "Aye."

In all honesty, Harry could not say that she was surprised. After all, her grandmother was well known for her meddlesome tendencies and secretive ways. What was she planning now? Why had she invited Mr.

MacKinnear to visit them at Whickerton Grove? Harriet did not know; however, what she did know was that she would find out no sooner than her grandmother wanted her to.

"Well, then," she said, clearing her throat, "where is Lord Burnham?" She looked from Mr. MacKinnear to Jack. "I believe we have unfinished business."

CHAPTER FORTY-SIX

SWORDS OR PISTOLS

Bradley was well aware of the tightness that lingered in Harriet's shoulders, yet she held her head high as they stepped out into the cool morning air and walked toward the stables.

"When he came to," Mr. MacKinnear explained, "he made quite the racket, demanding to be released and threatening me with all kinds of colorful consequences." He chuckled, yet his jaw remained set, his lips tight as he spoke. "I spoke with Angus, the inn's proprietor, and he decided in exchange for a few coins he did not much care who lay tied up in his stables. Eventually, *Lord Burnham* quieted down."

Harriet nodded in acknowledgment of his words. Then she stopped in front of the closed door and inhaled a deep breath.

"Ye dunna have to see him," Mr. MacKinnear counseled before his gaze moved to Jack. "We'll ensure he'll never come near ye again."

Bradley nodded in agreement; however, he knew it would not be enough for Harriet. How could it be?

As expected, Harriet shook her head. "I know you mean well, and I thank you. However, there is nothing you can do to keep that promise. Nothing I would want you to do." She straightened and then pushed open the doors and stepped inside.

Following on her heels, Bradley exchanged a look with Mr. MacKinnear. He could see that the man did not quite understand, but he was equally glad to realize that he was not the kind of man to stand in Harriet's way. Perhaps his own unusual grandmother had ensured that.

Measured steps carried them down the aisle, stalls lining it on each side. Most were occupied, curious eyes looking at them, and a soft neigh reached their ears every once in a while. Toward the back, they found what looked to be an empty stall. However, as they stepped closer and looked over the door, their eyes fell on the *dignified* person of Lord Burnham as he lay curled up like a babe in the straw.

For a long moment, Harriet simply stared down at him, the look upon her face not betraying any thoughts that might be going through her head. Then, however, her lips thinned and she pushed the door open with a loud *bang*.

The sound startled Lord Burnham awake, and he shot to his feet, rubbing his eyes with his bound hands. Squinting, he peered at them, a frown coming to his face as he slowly began to recognize who had come to see him. "Release me," he demanded in a feeble voice, his gaze moving from Mr. MacKinnear to Bradley and then to Harriet. "I apologize for the misunderstanding between us, but this," he lifted his tied hands, "is beyond acceptable. How dare you detain me like this? I'm a peer of the realm. I deserve to be treated with respect."

For a long moment, silence lingered between them before Harriet took a step toward him, her eyes hard in a way that made Lord Burnham struggle to hold her gaze. "And I do not?" she asked in a voice that was almost soft. "Is that what you're saying? That you deserve respect while I do not?"

Bradley could not help but be proud of her. In fact, he was in awe to see her standing so tall this morning, to see her face the man who had kidnapped and drugged her with such unflinching bravery. She was indeed a force to be reckoned with, and he vowed to himself that whatever she intended to do, he would not stand in her way. Society's rules be damned!

Lord Burnham's eyes widened as Harriet turned his words around on him. "Of course," he stammered, trying to step forward, but finding himself restrained by the rope that kept him in place. "Of course, you deserve respect. I never meant to see any harm come to you. I assure you. You must believe me." Deep unease was etched into his face, and he looked past Harriet, his gaze moving from Mr. MacKinnear back to Bradley as though asking for assistance.

Bradley almost laughed at the ludicrous thought.

Scoffing, Harriet shook her head. "I would be a fool to do so, and whatever you might believe of me, I am no fool." Fixing him with a pointed stare, she stepped toward Burnham, who cringed standing tall. "You attacked me, and now I have every right to defend my honor."

At her words, Bradley felt a lump of ice settle in his stomach while a look of incomprehension came to Burnham's face.

Ever so slowly, Harriet unfolded her clenched hands, revealing an old, tattered glove.

Entranced, Bradley watched her, remembering that he had not seen the glove during breakfast. Where had it come from? Had she procured it from the innkeeper's wife perhaps? But why? Bradley was afraid he knew.

Holding the glove in her hand, Harriet stepped toward Burnham and then slapped it across his face.

Bradley almost groaned, feeling Mr. MacKinnear's eyes shift to him in question and concern.

Burnham's face paled, a deep frown drawing down his brows. "Why...? What...What is the meaning of this?"

Harriet regarded him with cold eyes. "Are you not familiar with common practices? I thought you were a peer of the realm." Disdain lingered in her voice, and she straightened her shoulders, lifting her chin another fraction. "I am challenging you to a duel, Lord Burnham."

At her words, the man blinked, his eyes moving from her face down to the glove in her hands. "A duel?" He shook his head in disbelief before his gaze rose to stare at her again. "What...? But you're a woman."

"How highly observant of you, my lord," Harriet remarked sarcastically. "As I am the challenger, you may choose between swords and pistols."

Bradley wanted to interfere. He wanted to grasp her by the shoulders and shake her. He wanted to stop this. But he knew he could not. Only moments earlier, he had promised he would not stand in her way.

As dangerous as this was, Harriet needed this; more than that, she had a right to it.

And he could not take that from her.

Burnham continued to stare at her with unblinking eyes. "You... You cannot challenge me. You're... You're a woman."

Harriet rolled her eyes at him and sighed in a fairly exasperated fashion. "Yes, we've already established that. Nevertheless, I am challenging you."

Burnham shook his head. "I do not accept. I cannot. It would be wrong. After all, you're a—" He clamped his lips shut.

Harriet scoffed. "Oh, that would be wrong? But drugging me, kidnapping me and forcing me into marriage, that is completely honorable behavior?" She inhaled audibly, then she took a slow step toward Burnham, her hands balled into fists at her side. "Listen carefully," she hissed under her breath. "You will face me tomorrow morning at dawn or I swear I will do everything in my power to ruin you."

Burnham's face paled as he continued to stare. "You... You couldn't." He shook his head as though hoping the movement would undo everything that had happened.

Harry chuckled, but it was a dark sound. "You are acquainted with Lord Gillingham, are you not?"

After a moment of hesitation, Burnham nodded.

"I assume you're aware that he finds the task of procuring himself a wife to be quite challenging at present." The corners of her mouth tugged upward into a superior-looking smile. "Should you fail to appear tomorrow morning, I will make certain, by whatever means necessary, that no woman will ever consent to be your wife, that you shall remain without an heir until your days are finally numbered, ensuring that your line ends...with you."

Even Bradley felt an icy shiver crawl down his spine at the dark tone in her voice, the menace and threat that were almost palpable.

"I cannot fight you," Burnham said again, disbelief echoing in his voice before he once more looked up at Bradley, no doubt hoping for support. "I cannot fight her. She's a woman."

Harriet scoffed, drawing his attention back to her. "Oh, dear, did you never learn? Has no one ever instructed you?" A challenging smile came to her face. "I assure you *I* did learn. However, out of respect for your sensibilities, I will agree to first blood drawn. If it sets your mind at ease, I promise I shall not kill you."

For the first time, Bradley saw anger spark in Burnham's eyes. His shoulders drew back, and he stared at Harriet with ill-concealed resentment. "As you wish, my lady."

"Which is it then? Swords or pistols?"

Burnham's lips thinned. "Swords," he finally said, and Bradley wondered why. Was he truly concerned for his own well-being?

Harriet stepped back and looked at Mr. MacKinnear. "Would you untie him?"

Keir MacKinnear's eyes lingered upon her face for a moment longer. Then he nodded and strode forward to do as she had asked.

"If you fail to appear in the meadow beyond that hill tomorrow morning at dawn," Harriet warned Burnham with a pointed look, "you will regret it."

Burnham rubbed his wrists once the rope fell away. He did not say another word but stalked from the stables with hunched shoulders.

"I assume ye truly do have some skill with the sword?" Mr. MacKinnear inquired with an odd tone in his voice. It held a whisper of disbelief, yet his tone showed he was also applauding her courage.

Harriet nodded, glancing up at Bradley. "I do. My father and brother taught me." She chuckled. "Somewhat reluctantly at first, but once they saw I had some skill with the blade, they never doubted me again."

Mr. MacKinnear nodded. "Very well. I shall arrange everything." He smiled at her. "Good luck, lass." Then he turned and walked out of the stables, humming a cheerful tune under his breath.

Harriet smiled. "I like him."

Bradley inhaled a deep breath, then reached out to her, urging her to look at him. "I know you do not want to hear this," he said, holding her gaze. "Do you truly believe this to be wise?"

As expected, her eyes narrowed into slits.

CHAPTER FORTY-SEVEN
A PERFECT MOMENT

Deep down, Harriet knew that Jack's objections came from a good place. She could see concern for her blazing in his eyes. Still, it took great effort to not lash out at him.

It was like an instinct. Something Harriet had honed all her life. She was quite accustomed to people outside of her family doubting her, and she had never once backed down from a challenge, determined to prove to them how capable she was.

To them as well as herself!

Thinking of it now, Harriet suddenly realized that most of the things she had done in her life she had done for one very simple reason: to prove herself, to prove others wrong when they believed her incapable. Although she had always enjoyed her fencing lessons with her father and brother, those, too, had initially started because she had overheard someone remarking that women were not capable of wielding a weapon.

Right here, right now, Harriet wondered perhaps for the first time what she truly wanted. Not out of spite. Not because she was not supposed to. But because she truly longed for it.

In an instant, Harriet's anger vanished, and she felt a warm smile curl up the corners of her mouth. She looked at Jack and knew in that moment that she wanted him.

Of course, wanting him went against every rule she had ever set for herself. Yet it was the truth. Undoubtedly, society would approve, would congratulate her on snaring a duke. The mere thought alone turned Harriet's stomach and made her stand tall, determined to defy them, determined to say no. Yet if she was honest with herself, Jack was what she wanted.

What a mess! What was she supposed to do now? Remain true to her principles, no matter how she had come by them or what they would cost her? Or give in to the desires of her heart?

"Harry," Jack addressed her, his hands tightening upon her shoulders. "Harry, did you hear me?" Concern narrowed his eyes. "Are you feeling all right?"

Shaking off those confusing thoughts, Harriet smiled up at him. "Yes, I'm all right." She glanced at the corner of the stall where Burnham had been, his hands bound. "Today's truly an odd day, is it not?"

Jack nodded. "And you are determined to go through with it?"

She eyed him teasingly. "Do you not believe me capable?"

"You know I said no such thing, nor did I mean it like that," Jack replied, the look in his eyes stating that he knew her very well. "The sole reason why I say this is because the outcome of a duel is not solely determined by skill. You know that, do you not?"

Harriet nodded. "Of course, I do. However, I need to do this. I need to do this for myself." A shiver of apprehension snaked down her back, and yet the determination in her heart never wavered. "This is who I am. Can you accept that? Can you accept me the way I am?"

"Yes," he said without hesitation, yet the look upon Jack's face was torn. Harriet could see that while he wanted to support her, he also wanted to stop her from risking her life. Not long ago, Harriet would have misinterpreted his reaction, certain he did not believe her capable. Now, however, she understood what he meant and how he felt.

And she was grateful for it. She was utterly grateful that he did not offer to take her place, that he did not forbid her from going forward with this, that he did not interfere...

...even though he clearly wanted to.

With a smile, Harriet sank into Jack's arms. He held her tightly, made her feel safe and free at the same time. Never had Harriet felt quite so at ease with someone who was not family. Though only a few short weeks had passed since their first encounter, it felt as though she had known him all her life.

"What now?" Jack asked, moving back slightly so he could look down into her face. "How do you feel?"

Harriet could not help but roll her eyes. "Please stop asking me that!" she chuckled. "I feel perfectly fine again." She paused. "Although come to think of it, I could do with some more food."

Jack laughed. "Very well. First, some food, and then back to bed."

Harriet grinned at him mischievously. "Aren't we being forward!"

Although he was still smiling, Jack's eyes narrowed. "I was referring to sleep. You still have dark circles under your eyes."

Harriet let her jaw drop in mock outrage. "Is this a way to speak to a lady?"

Jack pulled her back into his arms. "If the lady is you, yes, most definitely." Then his head swooped down, and he captured her mouth with his.

Harriet welcomed his kiss and felt most eager to continue when he pulled back far too soon for her liking.

"Food, remember?" Jack whispered against her lips, then he gently removed her hands from around his neck before steering her back toward the inn.

After wolfing down a warm, savory stew with slice after slice of thickly buttered bread, Harriet finally allowed Jack to guide her back upstairs. She delighted in the way he insisted he leave for propriety's sake and reminded him they had already spent the previous night in each other's arms. Eventually, he relented as she knew he would.

"You rode through the night...to get to me," Harriet whispered, her insides still tingling with warmth at the mere thought of it. "You need sleep as well." She nodded her head toward the bed.

Jack regarded her cautiously, as though he feared she might attack him once his back was turned. "We are only talking about sleep, are we not?"

Harriet laughed. "The way you look at me makes me think you loathe having me near you. Is that so?" Her brows quirked. "Admit it! You like me!" She stepped closer, having to crane her neck to hold his gaze. "Admit it!"

Grinning, Jack pinched her chin. "How can you still doubt that I do? Of course, I do." He lowered his head, his eyes drilling into hers. "I like you, Harry. I like everything about you. I like your brave heart, your stubborn mind and your daring spirit."

All thoughts of teasing left Harriet's mind as Jack's dark brown gaze held hers.

"I like how you infuriate me, how you kiss me." Ever so gently, he brushed his lips against hers. "I like that you can be vulnerable and strong at the same time. I like how you speak your mind. I like the way you go after what you want. I like how dauntless you appear even though you're terrified." He heaved a deep sigh, and his breath teased her lips. "I like the way you look at me, the way you make me feel. I like you, Harry. In fact, I think I'm in love with you."

Tears brimmed in Harriet's eyes. "I love you, too, Jack," she whispered, then pushed herself up onto her toes and kissed him. Her hands snaked upward and linked behind his neck, holding on, unwilling to ever let him go again.

In the deep recesses of her mind, a quiet, little voice urged her to consider what she was doing. But Harriet ignored it. Whatever would happen was tomorrow's problem.

"You need sleep, Harry," Jack murmured, trying to free himself from her embrace. "Remember?"

"Later," Harriet replied with a grin before kissing him once more. Her hands wandered over his shoulders, then slid down to his chest. His heart thundered wildly below her palm, and she could feel him tense the moment her nimble fingers began undoing the buttons of his shirt.

"Harry." A warning lay in his voice.

"Jack," Harriet mimicked him; still, she could not help the grin that came to her face as his eyes looked into hers.

For a dozen heartbeats at least, they merely breathed together, unspoken words passing between them. It reminded Harriet of her parents, the way they seemed to know each other's minds without a single word spoken. Never had Harriet expected to find anything even remotely like that for herself.

And now, here she was.

In a perfect moment.

With Jack.

Her Jack.

"Help me with my laces," she whispered as excitement coursed through her veins.

Jack's eyes lingered on hers for a moment longer before she felt his hands move to her back. Again, he said nothing, but she knew he understood her.

And then Harriet was kissing him again, abandoning all thoughts about what she was doing, what this could mean, where they would go from here. It did not matter.

Not here.

Not now.

Tomorrow would sort itself out.

Hopefully.

CHAPTER FORTY-EIGHT
ON THE FIELD OF HONOR

Mist lingered in the early morning air as they made their way down the small slope into the meadow. Bradley could not help but think of *their* meadow back home, and his eyes were drawn to the woman by his side.

As though feeling his gaze, Harriet looked up at him and a deeply enchanting smile came to her lips. Her cheeks shone rosy and her green eyes sparkled with excitement. Although Bradley could feel a slight tremble go through her, he could not deny that she did not look the least bit concerned. No, she looked eager and daring, like...an untamed spirit. Was that not what Mr. MacKinnear had called her?

The Scotsman walked silently beside them as they strode onward. He had procured appropriate swords and instructed Lord Burnham's coachman to meet them here this morning and act as the man's second. Even a doctor was present. Bradley was uncertain whether that fact calmed or distressed him.

Across the meadow, they spotted Burnham and his coachman. Burnham himself looked dreadful, as though he had not slept a wink. His hair was in terrible disarray, as though it had been picked apart by a bird, and his face looked so haggard that Bradley felt the urge to send him back to the village for a hearty meal. Above all else, though, Burnham looked terribly uncomfortable.

Bradley could not help but enjoy that fact. He could only hope that Harriet was not overestimating her own abilities. While she had been able to trip him, Bradley, with ease when he had not expected an attack, he could not be certain how things would go with a...somewhat alert opponent.

While Mr. MacKinnear greeted all parties present, quickly going over the formalities, Bradley turned to Harriet. "Is there anything I can do?"

"You could kiss me," she whispered as her hands snaked up his chest.

Bradley chuckled. "You're impossible."

"I'll take that as a compliment."

"You should," he murmured against her lips, then kissed her with all the passion and devotion he felt.

"I love how you can make me forget where I am," she chuckled, her bright green eyes looking up into his. "One more for luck." She grasped his face and pressed her lips to his, the tips of her fingers lingering upon the rapidly beating pulse in his neck.

Mr. MacKinnear chuckled, and they drew apart. "I've never seen anyone less concerned with a duel," he remarked with yet another chuckle. "Good luck, lass."

Harriet smiled at Mr. MacKinnear, then she squeezed Bradley's hand one last time before releasing it and stepped forward to receive her sword. The way she grasped the handle and then swung it in lazy circles, familiarizing herself with its weight, was deeply reassuring.

"Dunna worry," Mr. MacKinnear said beside him as they watched Harriet and Lord Burnham take up their positions. "She'll do fine."

Bradley nodded, not daring to allow his eyes to stray from her for even a second. "I thank you for your help in this matter, Mr. MacKinnear."

The other man chuckled. "'Tis been my pleasure." Affection swung in his voice, and Bradley wondered why the dowager countess had invited the Scotsman to Whickerton Grove.

Then the duel began, and all thoughts vanished from Bradley's mind. He stared across the meadow at Harriet and her opponent, who looked even more ill at ease than he had before. He looked hesitant and would not attack but took a step backward.

Bradley doubted it was cowardice. Although Burnham had not revealed himself to be the bravest of men, what held him back was no doubt the fear to dishonor himself should anyone learn he had dueled with a woman.

Harriet, however, refused to let Burnham ruin this moment for her. Her eyes glowed as she charged toward him, swinging her sword in a practiced fashion that proved her words true. Ultimately, Burnham had no choice but to react and defend himself if he wished to keep his head upon his shoulders.

"She's fierce," Mr. MacKinnear remarked beside Bradley, admiration in his voice.

Bradley nodded absentmindedly, his whole body tense as he watched the match.

Bit by bit, Burnham lost his restraint and Bradley saw his movements become more pronounced. He now acted with purpose and intention, strength driving the blade forward as he charged toward Harriet.

Fortunately, Harriet seemed to be well aware of her disadvantage when it came to strength. She did not even try to block hard thrusts from above but spun out of the way. Her speed and agility were her greatest assets, and she used them well.

Back and forth, they moved across the meadow, the sound of metal on metal echoing through the morning air as the sun slowly crawled up the horizon.

While Harriet's face shone red from the joy of the moment and the exertion alike, Burnham's had turned into a grotesque mask. His lips were pressed into a thin line and his jaw was set in a way that revealed his surprise and irritation with Harriet's skill. Indeed, he had not expected to find himself quite as challenged.

And then Harriet tripped.

Bradley's breath lodged in his throat as he watched her go down, ice freezing the blood in his veins.

As though locked in a frenzy fueled by anger and humiliation, Burnham charged, his sword cutting through the air with a soft hum.

Harriet's eyes widened, but she managed to roll out of the blade's path in the last moment. Within seconds, she was back up on her feet, her dress stained with grass and dirt. She sidestepped another attack and then whirled around, ducked and…

…tossed her sword to her left hand.

Bradley blinked in surprise, as did Burnham.

Harriet used that moment to step around him and then bring her sword down on his left cheek, leaving a trail of blood in its wake as it broke the skin.

Burnham howled in pain, his sword dropping from his hand as he clutched his hands to his bleeding face.

Bradley almost sagged to the ground in relief. It was over! Harriet had won! Most importantly, she was unharmed!

Charging across the meadow, Bradley swept her into his arms, delighted with the triumphant smile upon her face. "You were wonderful," he congratulated her as the doctor tended to Burnham's wound.

Harriet did not even glance at the man. "Oh, Jack, it *felt* wonderful."

"You're not planning on doing this again, are you?" Bradley could not help but ask, thinking of Gillingham. Indeed, something had to be done about the man. Who knew what else he might conspire to do in order to avenge his bruised pride?

The look upon Harriet's face sobered. "We need to head back and do something about Sarah. She cannot marry Gillingham."

Bradley nodded. "Then let's go."

Urgency lingered in the air as they returned to the inn for a hearty breakfast before setting out on their return trip. Harriet, in particular, seemed driven to make their way back to England as soon as possible. Her cheeks shone in a rosy color and her jaw was set in determination as she pulled herself into the saddle. All the effects of the drug had evaporated, her limbs strong and capable once more. "I can only hope nothing has happened in our absence," she said, looking at Bradley as he urged his gelding to her side. "What if they are already betrothed?"

Anger lingered in her voice, but Bradley had no trouble seeing a hint of fear.

He reached out and grasped her hand, giving it an encouraging squeeze. "Then we shall find a way to break that betrothal."

Harriet smiled at him. "My dear, sweet Jack," she whispered, leaning closer, "no day goes by that you don't surprise me." A mischievous sparkle lit up her eyes before her hand settled on the back of his neck, pulling him closer for a kiss. "Let's go." The moment the words left her lips, she spurred her horse on and charged down the path.

A low chuckle made Bradley look over his shoulder at the Scotsman, who was to accompany them back to England. "Are all the Whickertons so fierce?" the man asked as they rode out of the village side by side.

"I must admit," Bradley replied, his gaze remaining fixed upon Harriet as she charged ahead of them, "that Harriet is the only Whickerton I know well. However, from what I've glimpsed of them, I would say so, yes. While they are all unique in their own ways, I believe they're all fierce when it comes to family and friends."

"'Tis a rare quality," Mr. MacKinnear remarked. "I canna wait to meet them all." He chuckled. "My grandmother instructed me to pay close attention." He turned his head to Bradley and grinned. "To tell ye the truth, I think she was tempted to accompany me."

Bradley returned the man's smile, remembering the dowager countess, Harriet's grandmother. She, too, had struck him as far more capable than he would have supposed, judging from her age alone. "And you truly do not know why you were invited to Whickerton Grove?"

"I havena got a clue," the Scot replied with a chuckle. "But the day will come that we shall find out."

CHAPTER FORTY-NINE
TOGETHER

After a day in the saddle, the three weary travelers stopped at an inn for the night. Fortunately, the weather had remained fair, not a dark cloud in sight, as though Fate meant to speed their journey.

Yet Harriet's mind remained in an uproar. She knew she would never forget that triumphant sneer upon Gillingham's face, nor the frightened expression in Sarah's eyes when she had spoken of her parents' plans for her. Harriet prayed nothing had happened yet, that nothing had been agreed upon yet. Of course, a betrothal could be broken; however, the repercussions could be severe. Whispers already surrounded Sarah's family and Sarah herself. After all, she had been on the brink of matrimony before, and it had always ended in ways that had tainted her. If it were to happen again...

"Good morning, lass," Mr. MacKinnear greeted her with a grin as they sat down for a quick breakfast in the inn's taproom. "Did ye sleep well?" His grin seemed to widen as his gaze moved from her to Jack standing behind her shoulder.

Harriet well understood the suggestion behind his words, and yet she detected no hint of condescension or disapproval. Mr. MacKinnear knew that she and Jack were neither married nor betrothed, and yet they had spent the previous night in the same room. Harriet could not care less about whispers and gossip, about her reputation or any consequences that might arise from her actions. Yet she was accustomed to people disapproving, openly stating that she was acting wrongly. Mr. MacKinnear, however, seemed to be a different sort of man altogether.

"Are you teasing me, Mr. MacKinnear?" Harriet demanded openly, feeling no qualms about a direct approach, certain that he would not disapprove.

He laughed. "Aye, lass, I am, and I'm glad to see ye know how to take it." He reached for a piece of bread. "And call me Keir, will ye? Blood or no, we're family." He leaned in conspiratorially. "At least, that's what my grandmother says."

"Keir," Harriet acknowledged with a nod. "But then you must call me Harry." Her eyebrows rose challengingly before she cast a look in Jack's direction. Smiling, he shook his head at her and then turned his attention to his own breakfast, no doubt remembering the earlier days of their acquaintance.

"Harry," Keir exclaimed as though testing the name on his tongue. "Aye, it suits ye, lass."

After breakfast, they set out once more, relieved to see that the weather was holding. They made good time and were just coming over a small slope when Harriet's eyes fell on two riders in the distance. At first, she felt her insides tense; however, the moment they were close enough for her to make out their faces, Harriet felt her heart speed up, joy warming her insides as she spurred on her horse.

"Harriet!" her father called, his face tense and his eyes sweeping over her in apprehension, as he jumped out of his saddle and hurried toward her. "Are you all right?"

Harriet all but flung herself out of the saddle and into her father's arms, hugging him tightly. "I'm well," she assured him, wrapping her arms around his shoulders. "I'm well."

Still locked in her father's embrace, Harriet met her brother's eyes over her father's shoulder. Troy's face held the same concern, the same fear as he dismounted and stepped toward her. Clinging to her father, Harriet held out her hand to him and he grasped it. "Harry, what happened? What did you do this time?" Even though a hint of disapproval swung in his voice, his eyes shone with relief at seeing her unharmed. Then his gaze swept past her, and his eyes narrowed as they moved from one of her two companions to the other.

Finally releasing her, her father looked deep into her eyes. "What happened, Harry? Sarah sent us a letter informing us that..." His voice trailed off; however, the look upon his face spoke loud and clear.

Not knowing how many details Sarah had given in her letter, Harriet asked, "Do you know about Gillingham? And Burnham? That it was them?"

Her father's lips thinned before he gave a quick nod. "It's true then?"

Harriet nodded, and the moment she did, Troy spun around on his heels, stalking back the way he had come as he raked an agitated hand through his hair. His face looked tense, and his movements revealed how outraged he was.

"But you're all right?" her father inquired before his gaze moved past her shoulder to the two men who had come to her aid.

In a few quick words, Harriet explained what had happened, how Jack had gone after her and how he had met Keir by sheer coincidence...or had he not?

Nevertheless, whatever plan their two grandmothers were currently executing needed to wait until later. There were more important things to take care of now. "We need to return to Atwood Park as quickly as possible."

Frowning, Troy stalked back toward her. "Why?" He shook his head. "You need to go home. *We* will go to Atwood Park, and *I* will call out Gillingham." His eyes burned into hers. "The man needs to be dealt with after what he's done...to Leonora and now to you."

Harriet held her brother's furious gaze. "If anyone calls him out, it will be me."

"What of Burnham?" her father interjected, his voice calmer than the look in his eyes.

"She challenged him," came Jack's voice as he stepped forward to stand beside her.

"She did what?" Troy exclaimed, shock weighing upon his words, while her father exhaled a slow breath, his gaze still lingering upon hers.

Jack nodded as his eyes moved from her to her father. "She challenged him to a duel, and she won."

Her father's gaze narrowed. "Is he dead?"

Harriet shook her head. "No, we agreed on first blood drawn." She could not help the grin that came to her face. "But he'll have a nasty scar that shall forever remind him to treat women with respect."

A small smile teased her father's lips. "I'm glad you're all right, Harry." He shook his head at her the way he often did whenever she imagined her choices threatened to stop his heart. "Truly glad." He reached out a hand and brushed a loose strand of hair from her face.

"You shouldn't have," Troy growled, his hands balled into fists as he glared at her. "You should have left this matter to us. There was no need for you to—"

"To you?" Harriet snapped, pushing past her father to glare back at her brother. "As I recall, it was not you who was drugged, kidnapped and almost forced into marriage, was it, dear brother?"

Troy's jaw clenched, guilt shone in his eyes over what had happened, over what *he* had allowed to happen. Harriet knew her brother felt responsible for them all and no doubt saw this as a personal failure. "Yet, you needn't have done this."

Harriet inhaled a deep breath, placing her hands upon her brother's shoulders and looking him square in the eyes. "But I wanted to." She offered him a small smile. "You taught me well, big brother. It was your trick of switching sword hands that gained me the upper hand."

A tentative grin teased Troy's lips as he looked at her.

"He didn't see it coming," Harriet continued with a triumphant grin, once more feeling the exhilaration of the moment she had done Burnham one better. "It confused him, and I took my chance."

Grasping her arms, Troy pulled her closer, then leaned his forehead against hers. "I'm proud of you, little sister," he whispered, anguish tingeing his voice, "but, please, never do this again."

Harriet chuckled. "You know I cannot promise that." She lifted her head to look at him. "Someone has to look out for Sarah as you've always looked out for us."

Swallowing, Troy nodded. "Then we shall do it together." He lifted his brows, demanding an answer.

Harriet nodded. "Together."

"I thank you for your help, Clements," Harriet's father said as they rode side by side, following close behind Harriet, her brother and Mr. MacKinnear. "I know she would never admit it, but I can see how frightened she was." Lord Whickerton's brown eyes were calm as he spoke, yet Bradley could see the fears the man had lived through since receiving Miss Mortensen's letter.

Bradley merely nodded in acknowledgment, uncertain what to say. A lot had happened between him and Harriet, and he could not help but wonder how much Lord Whickerton suspected.

Long moments passed as they rode on, listening to the three up ahead of them toss around theories of why the dowager had invited Mr. MacKinnear to Whickerton Grove.

Then out of nowhere, Lord Whickerton said, "You know that any other father would, under these circumstances, expect you to marry his daughter?"

Bradley looked at the other man, seeing neither disapproval nor expectation in his face. "I know."

Lord Whickerton heaved a deep sigh before the hint of a smile played over his features. "And you are willing, are you not?"

Bradley closed his eyes, then nodded.

"She refused you?"

He nodded again.

"Even though she loves you." This time, it was not a question.

Bradley met Lord Whickerton's gaze. "She has her reasons."

Harriet's father nodded. "She does, and they are valid reasons; yet..." He paused, considering his words. "Harriet always knew what she did *not* want, that independent streak of hers pushing her to challenge each and every convention, not necessarily because she believed it to be wrong, but to prove to herself that she would not bow her head, that she was not weak, that she would not yield."

Bradley chuckled softly. "Yes, I've noticed that as well."

"I only hope that by the time she realizes what it is she *does* want; it will not be too late." Lord Whickerton's gaze moved to meet Bradley's.

"If..." Bradley swallowed, feeling suddenly nervous. "If she were to agree to marry me," he began quietly, casting a cautious look up ahead, "would you give us your blessing?"

Lord Whickerton smiled at him. "I would never stand in the way of Harriet's happiness, and I can see that she loves you." He nodded. "You're a good man, Clements, and I do hope that you'll succeed for her sake as well as yours."

"Thank you. I truly appreciate it." Bradley loved the feeling of warmth that spread through his middle at Lord Whickerton's words. It made him wonder what having a present and caring father in his life would have felt like. Now, it was too late to find out. However, perhaps, he would one day have a father-in-law. Bradley liked that thought very much.

"You look like a man with a plan," Lord Whickerton remarked with a chuckle.

Bradley felt the corners of his mouth stretch into a grin. "I cannot fault you for drawing that conclusion." He could only hope his plan would work, that it would be enough to convince Harriet.

He wanted her to be his wife, now more than ever, and he believed she wanted it, too, if only she would dare admit it to herself.

The rest of their journey passed quickly, and before long, they rode up the drive to Atwood Park. Dismounting, they handed their reins to the stable hands before approaching the entrance doors. "Do not act without thought," Lord Whickerton warned his children, his gaze moving from Harriet to his son. "Let us speak to Lord and Lady Hartmore. Perhaps we can dissuade them from a union between Sarah and...that man." His voice darkened on the last two words, revealing the anger that lingered in Lord Whickerton's veins despite his outward calm.

Bradley moved to Harriet's side, the look in her eyes ablaze with outrage. "Your father is right," he whispered as they stepped into the hall and were welcomed by Lady Atwood. "Speak to your friend first."

Inhaling a deep breath, Harriet nodded. "Unfortunately, her

parents have never been the most cooperative people. If a union with Gillingham serves them, they will not hesitate to sacrifice Sarah."

Bradley swallowed, wondering about how different parents could be. While some parents would walk through hell and back to ensure their child's wellbeing, others could not be bothered to even consider it. Poor Miss Mortensen!

"Oh, how wonderful to see you all here!" Lady Atwood exclaimed as her gaze swept over their little assembly with curiosity. "Frankly, we've heard the most unsettling rumors. People have been whispering that Lady Harriet eloped with Lord Burnham." Her gaze swept over the hall, noting no doubt that Lord Burnham was nowhere to be seen.

Lord Whickerton returned her smile. "Fortunately, only the feeble-minded believe rumors based on nothing but conjecture. Is that not so, Lady Atwood?"

"Of course, you're right, Lord Whickerton!" their hostess exclaimed, a hint of disappointment in her voice. Clearly, she had hoped to be the first to learn more of Harriet's adventures.

"I'll find Sarah," Harriet whispered as she leaned closer, her green eyes full of concern and impatience.

Bradley nodded. "I'll go with you."

"You don't have t—"

He pulled her closer. "Gillingham is still here," he told her, his voice harsh and not brooking an argument. "I will not let you out of my sight. Understood?"

Although Harriet's eyes narrowed for a split second, Bradley could see that she was not truly upset. Indeed, they had both come a long way since the day they had met.

It seemed like an eternity ago.

CHAPTER FIFTY

WORTHY OF ANOTHER

After knocking on Sarah's door, Harriet was surprised and relieved to hear her friend's voice asking through the closed door, "Who is it?"

"It's me, Harry," Harriet replied quietly as her gaze moved up and down the corridor, hoping that Sarah's parents were still downstairs in the drawing room. "Quick! Let me in!"

"I'll wait here," Jack told her, the look in his eyes insistent, as she listened to Sarah's footsteps hurrying toward the door.

Harriet smiled at him. "If you insist."

"I do." The way he was looking at her made Harriet feel... Honestly, she didn't quite know how she felt. Never had she expected to long for another the way she now longed for Jack...even when he was standing right beside her. She could not imagine spending a single day without him, knowing that she would miss him terribly if he ever were to leave. Indeed, the thought was unthinkable!

The door flew open, and Sarah's wide eyes looked into Harriet's. "You're back!" her friend exclaimed, her wide eyes searching Harriet's face. "Are you all right? What happened?"

Casting Jack a smile, Harriet ushered Sarah back inside and then quickly closed the door. "It's a bit of a long story," Harriet replied quickly as she grasped Sarah's hands. "What about you? Are you…betrothed?"

A jolt went through Sarah before she exhaled a deep breath, then slowly shook her head. "I'm glad to say that I am not." Relief shone in her eyes. "I don't know what happened. My parents told me they were on the verge of…procuring me a husband when…" Shrugging, she shook her head, incomprehension marking her features.

"When what?" Harriet pressed, feeling her own hands tremble with the need to know.

"He disappeared!"

Harriet felt her jaw drop. "Who? Lord Gillingham?"

Sarah nodded her head vigorously. "He was suddenly gone. My father had arranged to speak to him early this morning in the library when he failed to appear. No one has seen him since. As far as I have heard, his belongings are still in his chamber. However, no one saw him leave, and no one knows where he went."

Relief and disappointment battled in Harriet's chest. A part of her had hoped to confront Gillingham about what he had done; yet his disappearance had certainly come at a most convenient time for Sarah. Only where had he gone, and why? And when would he return? Once he did, would he still be determined to marry Sarah?

"I'm glad," Harriet replied, squeezing Sarah's hands for reassurance. "However, we both know that something must be done."

Sarah nodded; fear once more lurking in her blue eyes.

"I will do my best to find out what happened to Lord Gillingham," Harriet replied, struggling to maintain a calm tone so as not to alarm her friend. "We must find out what his intentions are. If we're fortunate, he no longer wishes to marry you."

Sarah heaved a deep sigh, a sad smile coming to her features. "I never thought I'd ever say this, but, yes, I do hope he does not."

"Do not worry," Harriet told her friend, as her thoughts were drawn back to Jack. She never would have thought it were possible for her to love another in such a way; and yet it had happened. What else was possible that had seemed impossible only days earlier? "Somewhere out there is a man who is your perfect match. I promise you! All you need to do is find him."

Sarah stilled, and an odd expression came to her face as she looked at Harriet.

"What? Why are you looking at me like that?"

Chuckling, Sarah shook her head, disbelief shining in her eyes. "Who are you? And what have you done with our Harry?"

Harriet rolled her eyes at her friend. "Yes, I admit I've...changed...a bit...perhaps."

Sarah sighed. "You're in love, are you not?" Her hands tightened on Harriet's. "Tell me everything. I know the duke went after you. But what happened?"

Settling onto the bed, Harriet told Sarah everything that had transpired in the past few days. With every word, Sarah's eyes grew rounder; yet the longing smile on her face remained, and Harriet wished she could one day see her friend free of her burden, free to choose as she wished.

As she deserved.

Perhaps there truly was a man out there who would be worthy of Sarah. Harriet could only hope that it was so!

The very moment Bradley stepped across the threshold of Clements Park, his aunt came flying toward him as though she had been waiting just around the corner, ready to pounce at a moment's notice. "Where in heaven's sake have you been, Clements?" she demanded, hands on her hips as she all but glared at him. "You leave with barely a word of explanation, and then a fortnight passes and I do not hear from you." Shaking her head, she threw up her hands. "The ball is in three days!"

Escorting his aunt into the drawing room, Bradley offered her a drink. Of course, he felt guilty for leaving her without a word after asking for her assistance in selecting a wife. She had worked most diligently on this event, hoping it would help him choose a suitable bride, and she deserved better than to be left standing without a word of explanation. He ought to have thought of that.

"I apologize, my lady," Bradley finally said as he seated himself across from her. "I had no intention of staying away this long; however, events transpired that made it impossible for me to return to Clements Park sooner than I did."

His aunt watched him with slightly narrowed eyes. He could see that she had questions, yet she did not ask them. "I am glad you returned in time," she finally said, heaving a deep breath. A small smile appeared upon her face, and Bradley could see that she would not hold his transgression against him. "There is much to discuss with the ball only three days away. I assume you have no intention of traveling elsewhere?"

Bradley shook his head. "I have not," he replied, carefully choosing his words. "However, there is something I need you to know." He could not help the smile that came to his face as he thought of Harriet. "While I am most grateful for your assistance, I no longer require it."

For a long moment, his aunt simply looked at him, her eyes unblinking as she tried to make sense of his words. "Are you...Are you saying you've already found a bride?"

Bradley did not quite know how to reply. Harriet had yet to accept his proposal; however, no matter her answer, he would choose no one else for his duchess. "I have already chosen the woman I wish to marry, yes."

His aunt blinked, a brief look of disbelief showing in her eyes before she clapped her hands together in a joyful gesture. "That is wonderful, Clements. I suppose congratulations are in order. Oh, we can announce your betrothal at the ball! This is perfect."

Bradley held up a hand. "I'm afraid congratulations are premature."

His aunt stilled, her eyes widening as she looked at him for an explanation.

Clearing his throat, Bradley held her gaze, wondering what she would think of his choice. "Truthfully, the young lady has yet to accept my proposal."

With a smile upon her face, his aunt scoffed. "Oh, Clements, what lady would refuse you? You're a duke! No, believe me. Any young woman would be happy to become your duchess."

Once upon a time, Bradley had thought the same thing, and then Harriet had come into his life. "Frankly, the lady in question has no wish to become a duchess."

His answer caused his aunt to drop her jaw, and she stared at him in a most unbecoming way. "She does not wish to—?" Blinking rapidly, she shook her head. "Being a duchess is not good enough for her? What otherworldly aspirations does she have?"

Bradley chuckled. "Yes, I suppose to most people her aspirations would seem otherworldly."

His aunt frowned at him.

Bradley inhaled deeply, remembering all the things Harriet had told him. "She wants to be herself," he said to his aunt, "free and unencumbered. She does not want to be a duchess, nor does she want a duke. She wants a man who sees her as his equal, who respects her as much as she respects him. She wants to be free in her choices and find happiness in her days." He smiled at his aunt, seeing a most thoughtful expression come to her face. "She does not care for titles or fortunes. Those things mean nothing to her. She is a fierce lady, and I'll have to prove myself to her because she would never marry the Duke of Clements, but perhaps, just perhaps, she will marry Bradley Jackson."

For a long time, the two of them simply sat there, and Bradley could feel his aunt's gaze sweep over his face. She looked thoughtful, no doubt taking in every word he had spoken. A part of him had expected her to voice her disapproval, or outrage even, but she did not. As much as his aunt had always cherished their family's reputation, always watchful to act appropriately and uphold society's unwritten rules, there was now a look upon her face that whispered of a deeper understanding than he had expected.

"You are in love, are you not?" she asked with a deeply compassionate smile upon her face.

Bradley bowed his head, trying and failing to hide his own. "I believe there is no use in denying it." He looked up at her once more.

Still smiling, she shook her head. "May I ask who this unique creature is?"

Bradley considered her question. "I'd rather not say just yet, for I admit I am still worried that no matter what I do, she will not have me."

Warmth shone in his aunt's eyes, as he had never seen before. "Oh, she will have you, Bradley. Do not worry."

Momentarily shocked at hearing his aunt address him by his given name, Bradley stared at her. "How can you possibly know?"

"Because she loves you as well."

Bradley felt his brows draw down into a deep frown. How could his aunt possibly know how Harriet felt about him? They had never even met! His aunt didn't even know who he was speaking of!

A rather unrestrained laugh drifted from his aunt's lips. "Isn't it obvious? Any woman who does not jump at the chance to marry a duke clearly—as you said—does not care for titles and fortunes. However, if that is the case, she would also have no qualms in refusing a man she does not care for. If she has not made it unmistakably clear that she does not want you, then I believe it is only a matter of time before she realizes she cannot deny her heart. Be patient...and steadfast."

With a sense of disbelief still lingering in his heart, Bradley smiled at his aunt. "Thank you. I'm truly grateful for your counsel."

His aunt nodded, a hint of incredulity in her eyes. "I wish we had spoken like this before." She reached out and placed her hand on his. "Perhaps this can be a new beginning for all of us."

"I would like that," Bradley told her, glad to see that he had family after all. "I would like that very much."

CHAPTER FIFTY-ONE

HANG THE LAW

"You challenged him to a duel?" Juliet gasped, her face paling considerably as she stared at Harriet.

Enjoying herself immensely, Harriet nodded, her eyes sweeping over her assembled family as they sat in the large drawing room of Pinewood Manor. Although her father had wanted to return home to Whickerton Grove, Harriet had insisted they head to Pinewood Manor instead. After all, Jack had invited them all to the first ball that was to take place at Clements Park in over two decades.

"Ye shoulda seen her!" Keir exclaimed as he stood by the fireplace, one arm leisurely draped upon the mantel. "She stepped right up to meet him without a twitch of nerves." He laughed, his blue eyes lighting up with mirth. "He, on the other hand, looked as though he wished the earth would open up and swallow him whole."

"Well done, little sister," Louisa cheered, her blue eyes twinkling with utter excitement and perhaps a hint of envy. "I wish I could have been there. Next time, please—"

"There will be no next time!" Troy insisted as he stepped forward, his eyes hard as they moved from Louisa to Harriet.

Harriet laughed. "Do not worry, big brother. You taught me well!" He opened his mouth to interject something. "But be assured," Harriet hastened to add, "that I have no immediate plans of issuing another challenge. There? Happy now?"

The dark glower upon Troy's face lessened a little. "Happier," he finally relented, tension still visible in the way he held himself.

Harriet sighed. Her brother was a worrier, always had been.

"What about Lord Gillingham?" Christina asked carefully as she looked from Harriet to Leonora and back. "Something needs to be done. Who knows what he'll plan next?" Thorne stepped forward and placed his hands upon his wife's shoulders. "We cannot allow him to marry Sarah. Something needs to be done!" Agitation swung in her voice, and Harriet nodded in agreement.

"You need not worry about Lord Gillingham any longer," Leonora said in a quiet voice. Her eyes were downcast, but she lifted them the moment the last word left her lips.

Everyone in the room turned to look at her. "What do you mean?" their mother asked gently before she crossed to the settee and sat down beside her daughter.

With a strange paleness upon her cheeks, Leonora inhaled a deep breath as she looked around at all of them. "He is dead."

Shock dropped more than one jaw, and Harriet stared at her sister in utter disbelief. "Dead? How?" And then it hit her! "Drake," she mumbled in a quiet voice, only now realizing that Leonora's husband was the only one absent from their little impromptu family meeting.

Leonora nodded. "When we received Sarah's letter about what had happened," she looked from her mother to her father and Troy, "Drake was…" She shook her head, words failing her. "He simply could not stand by."

Harriet nodded in understanding, as did the others. Although only Leonora knew the whole story, they were all aware that something tragic had occurred in Drake's past, something he still blamed himself for. "He called him out?"

Leonora nodded. "He did."

Harriet knew Drake was an excellent marksman and had fought several duels on behest of others who had had no one to stand up for them. "Is he all right?"

Her sister's face still looked pale as she nodded.

"He is." Phineas stepped forward, his voice strong and reassuring. "It is only a flesh wound. I assure you the man has survived worse." He chuckled. "He will be up and about in no time. I promise." He nodded to Leonora.

"You knew?" Louisa exclaimed as she surged to her feet.

"He's my friend," Phineas replied in a placating voice. "I could not let him go alone."

"I'm your wife!" Louisa retorted. "You could have told me."

Phineas smiled at her as he reached out to wrap her hands in his. "I did not wish to worry you, especially in your condition."

Louisa scoffed. "Oh, is this how it's going to be now? I'm with child, and that gives you the right to keep things from me?"

Daring as he was, Phineas replied with a single word, "Yes."

Harriet could see that Louisa was close to flying into a rage—now that she was with child, she truly had even more of a temper than under ordinary circumstances—when Phineas winked at his wife. It was a simple gesture that completely took the air out of her sails. "You'll pay for this," she hissed under her breath, her eyes sparkling with something that might be classified as delight.

"I'm counting on it," Phineas replied in a hushed tone as he pulled her into his arms, a wide smile upon his face.

Harriet chuckled. Indeed, her sister and her husband had their very own way of communicating. It was most intriguing to watch.

"Then Sarah is safe," Christina concluded as she looked around the room, seeking confirmation. "At least for now."

Everyone nodded.

"Her parents must be furious." Christina's gaze moved to Harriet. "Did you see them?"

Harriet shook her head. "We didn't stay long after returning from Scotland. However, I spoke to Sarah, and although she was clearly relieved, I could see that her parents' reaction to Lord Gillingham's disappearance was deeply upsetting for her." Harriet shrugged. "You know her. She always feels responsible."

Christina nodded. "Somehow, we need to find her a good match. It's the only way to see her safe."

"I agree," Harriet stated, no matter how much she loathed to do so. "But who?"

From the armchair in the corner by the fireplace, a familiar chuckle could be heard, and all heads turned to Grandma Edie.

Harriet glimpsed her father close his eyes and inhale a deep breath before he met his mother's gaze. "What did you do, Mother?"

A smile came to Harriet's face as she saw a rather innocent look take up residence upon her grandmother's. "Me? Nothing. Why?"

Their father rolled his eyes in a rather exasperated gesture but did not press the matter. Nor did anyone else. Although they were all looking at Grandma Edie with expectant eyes, not one of them demanded an answer, for they all knew it would be a futile attempt.

No one knew how to keep secrets like Grandma Edie, only ever revealing what she knew when she so chose.

And not a moment earlier.

As frustrating as that could be, Harriet could not deny that she rather liked that about her grandmother. She was a strong woman who lived by her own rules. Yet, she, too, had married...a man she had loved with all her heart.

Harriet barely remembered her late grandfather, but he had to have been an incredible man to have gained her grandmother's hand in marriage.

"What is on your mind, child?" Grandma Edie asked after the drawing room had emptied and only Harriet remained behind.

Heaving a deep sigh, Harriet met her grandmother's gaze. "Are you saying you don't already know?" she asked with a chuckle.

Her grandmother laughed. "Contrary to popular opinion, I am not all-knowing." She looked at Harriet, her head slightly cocked to the side, the look in her eyes contemplative. "Is it *Jack*?"

Harriet threw up her hands. "See? You know!"

"Only because it is written all over your face," her grandmother replied with an indulgent smile. "I can see that you love him."

Harriet's eyes snapped up.

"It is true, is it not?"

Swallowing, Harriet nodded. "What am I to do?"

"What do you want to do?"

Harriet sighed. "If only I knew." She regarded her grandmother for a long moment. "Were you not worried when you got married? I cannot imagine you ever having been the kind of woman who would bow her head to her husband's demands."

With a wide grin upon her face, Grandma Edie shook her head. "You're quite right, child. However, neither was your grandfather the kind of man to make such a demand."

"But how could you know he never would?" Harriet demanded as she began to pace. "How could you know that one day he would not change his mind and exert the power he had?"

"Of course, I could not be certain," her grandmother replied in a calm voice. "We cannot control the world nor those in it. All we can determine is how we handle what comes our way."

Harriet paused, eyes fixed upon her grandmother. "So, if he had, what would you have done?"

Her grandmother scoffed, as though the answer should have been obvious. "I would never have bowed my head. If it had come down to it, I would have left him. It would have broken my heart, but I would have never allowed him to stand taller than me."

Harriet gaped at her grandmother. "But the law would not have been on your side! What if—?"

"Hang the law!" her grandmother exclaimed as she pushed herself out of her armchair, her right hand curled tightly around the curved top of her cane. "Harriet, you're a strong woman and you're not alone in this world." Despite the cane, the way her grandmother stood before Harriet spoke of strength and determination. "Do not let fear of the future keep you from being happy now."

"But what if—?"

"If what you fear proves true, then you will do what needs to be done." Her pale eyes shone with pride. "You are not one to cower. You faced Burnham with your head held high. Now, do so again when it comes to the fear that lives in your heart."

Staring at her grandmother, Harriet felt a tentative smile sneak onto her face.

"Should you ever feel the need to go against your husband because he keeps you from being who you are," Grandma Edie reached out a gnarled hand and placed it upon Harriet's shoulder, "then you will not stand alone. We will all stand with you as we always have and always shall. Do not doubt that."

"Thank you, Grandma," Harriet whispered, with tears in her eyes. "You always know just what to say." Then she embraced her grandmother, grateful to have such a strong woman in her life. "Thank you for everything."

"But don't forget," Grandma Edie murmured as she rubbed a hand up and down Harriet's back, "your husband deserves to stand tall as well. Compromises are part of marriage, of family, but they do not mean that one bows their head to the other."

Pulling back, Harriet looked at her grandmother. "Will you tell Mother and Father not to worry?" she asked as her heart sped up, excitement coursing through her veins.

Grandma Edie grinned. "Do I dare ask?" Then she shook her head, chuckling. "Go and speak to him. You'll not catch a wink of sleep anyhow."

After kissing her grandmother on the cheek, Harriet ran from the room, her eyes drawn to the sun already hanging low in the sky. Fortunately, she encountered not a soul on her way to the stables, and before long, she clung to Moon's back as the mare galloped across the wide fields.

Westward.

To Jack.

CHAPTER FIFTY-TWO

LIKE FATHER, LIKE SON

Even an hour after his solicitor had left, Bradley was still standing by the tall window in his study, his gaze directed outward, his eyes sweeping over the expansive grounds of Clements Park. The sight was slowly becoming dear to him, and he could not deny that the garden held some beauty. Still, deep in his chest, Bradley felt a distant ache for a time long gone. What he longed for were not the beautifully tended gardens of Clements Park but the untamed wilderness—as his mother had called it long ago—of Laurelwood Manor.

A lifetime seemed to have passed since he had last visited. It had been too long. Bradley wished to return; more than that, he wished to return with Harriet by his side.

Glancing over his shoulder, his gaze touched upon the document resting upon his desk. Would it be enough? He wondered for the thousandth time.

The sky was slowly dimming, the bright blue disappearing, changing into shades of violet and orange. It seemed to glow, casting warmth across the world, closely followed by long shadows wrapping everything into a quiet stillness.

Always had Bradley enjoyed the quiet setting of the sun. It made him feel peaceful and centered, balanced and at ease, even after a trying day. It had the power to—

He paused, feeling the little hairs on the back of his neck slowly rise. An odd awareness swept over him, whispering of a presence besides his own.

With his back still to the door, Bradley felt himself tense, wishing he had eyes on the back of his head. Someone was nearby; yet he had not heard footsteps approach. Who could it be? Certainly, his butler would make his presence known. As would his aunt. What were the odds of an intruder making his way into Clements Park?

"Hello, Jack."

Closing his eyes, Bradley almost groaned before a small smile tugged on the corners of his mouth as he drew in a deep breath. Of course, he should have known.

Slowly, he turned from the window. The moment his gaze fell upon Harriet, he felt an excited shiver dance down his spine. Only two days had passed since they had bid each other farewell at Atwood Park, since they had last seen one another, and yet a part of him felt as though years had gone by. Not until this very moment did he realize how much he had missed her.

As always, her hair was in a bit of disarray, her wild curls straying every which way like a flame with a life of its own. Her cheeks shone from exertion, and her breath was coming fast as though she had urged Moon into a gallop the whole way here. Her green eyes shone with longing as she looked at him, the expression upon her face everything he had hoped for.

Bradley chuckled. "Once again, you are here without a chaperone," he remarked because he ought to, not because he wanted to. Yet it had become some kind of game between them. It felt familiar and strengthened the connection between them.

Harriet's face brightened at his words, and she took a step toward him. "And once again, you disapprove." Her brows rose questioningly. "Or do you only *seem* to disapprove?" Another step brought her closer still. "Admit it; you're happy to see me." She lifted her chin a fraction, green eyes holding onto his.

Bradley inhaled a shuddering breath, completely thrown off balance by her mere presence. Months ago, he would have thought such an effect to be impossible. Now, however, he realized he had come to cherish these light tingles that shot through him whenever Harriet was near, that sense of awareness, that slight tremble that reached out from the center of his being.

It was for her.

Because of her.

Her alone.

"Very well," he relented with a smile. "I admit I am happy to see you. There? Is that why you came for?" His gaze swept over her, once again taking in her slightly disheveled appearance. Indeed, she had not even bothered to change into a riding habit. His eyes narrowed with concern. "Is something wrong? Has something happened?" He took an alarmed step toward her.

Harriet chuckled. "Is that what you think? That the only reason for me to come here is to seek your help? Can you not imagine there to be another reason that might bring me here?" Something challenging sparked in her eyes.

Bradley felt himself relax and tense at the same time. Clearly, no emergency had occurred, and yet the fact that she was here to see him brought every muscle in his body to full alert. "Why then?" he dared her, seeking to reclaim the intimacy that had existed between them in Scotland. They had spoken openly, holding nothing back, knowing that the other would understand with heart and mind alike.

"Do you truly have to ask?" The smile vanished, and she inhaled a shaky breath, a nervous expression flitting across her face. "I am here to see you," she said, the words rushed, spoken quickly as though she feared she might not be able to say it if she hesitated.

Bradley paused. Never had he seen Harriet so uncertain of herself. Had he been wrong? Had something happened after all?

"You asked me to marry you," Harriet said, surprising him. "You also said that you asked your aunt to arrange this ball tomorrow night so that you might find a bride." She swallowed hard, and Bradley could not help but think that speaking those words had taken a lot of effort. What was she trying to say? He could not deny that he longed to find out, hoping that he was not mistaken.

Bradley nodded. "You refused me," he reminded her, watching her most carefully. "You said you would never marry." He remembered his shock at first hearing her express those thoughts. "You said you would never give up your freedom. You said you would never dare to trust another to such an extent." He held her gaze and nodded his head. "I might not have understood then, but I do now." He stepped forward and gently grasped her hands. "You were right to refuse me. You were right to demand what you did. You deserve all that and more."

Her eyes looked up into his, disbelief shining in their green depths. He could see that his words surprised her, pleased her, and the smile that came to her face made his heart almost beat out of his chest. "Truly?" was all she said, for once in her life seemingly at a loss for words.

Bradley nodded. "I would never ask you to marry me if it meant giving up who you are."

A shadow fell over Harriet's face, and he could see the breath still in her chest. "You no longer wish to marry me." It was not a question, but a statement instead, and the shock of that realization slowly spread over her face, chasing away the rosy bloom her chase across the fields had brought on.

Bradley smiled at her, gently squeezing her hands. "That is not what I said, Harry." He pulled her closer, holding her gaze as her eyes searched his. "But I cannot deny that your reaction pleases me. I want you in my life. Always." He reached out a hand and brushed a wild curl behind her ear. "Come. There's something I want to show you." Holding her hand in his, Bradley pulled her along as he stepped toward his desk, then he picked up the parchment that had been lying there since his solicitor had left.

Turning to Harriet, Bradley inhaled a deep breath, his gaze briefly dropping to the words on the page. "This," he began slowly, even hesitantly, his pulse beating more rapidly than it ever had in his life, "is a marriage contract."

Harriet's jaw dropped ever so slightly before her gaze followed suit, touching upon the document in his hands before rising once more to look into his eyes. "A marriage contract? Are you saying you…?"

"I want to marry you," Bradley said loud and clear, not wanting her to have any doubts as to his intentions. "I want you as my wife, and I want to be your husband. I understand your reservations; however, this is meant to put your mind at ease."

A slight frown came to Harriet's face. "It is not…an ordinary marriage contract," she concluded, a most endearing spark coming to her eyes. "Am I correct?"

Again, Bradley nodded, belatedly realizing how tense his fingers were upon the parchment. "It is not. In addition to the usual contract, I added specifics that will grant you equal standing in this marriage… should you agree to it." Trying to swallow the lump in his throat, Bradley held the document out to her. "Here. Read it. Of course, you have every right to make changes."

Slowly, Harriet's hands rose and then, almost tenderly, touched the sheet of parchment as though it were a delicate flower, easily crumpled and destroyed.

Bradley felt the breath lodge in his throat as he watched her step away to the window, her gaze dropping to the parchment as she began to read. He closed his eyes, praying that she would not refuse him again.

Bradley was certain he would not recover from that, and he did not want to end like his father.

CHAPTER FIFTY-THREE

A MARRIAGE CONTRACT

Countless times had Harriet heard young women gush about romantic gestures bestowed upon them, making them the envy of all those who could only hope and dream. Be it a bouquet of the lady's favorite flowers, a poem dedicated to her or any other thoughtful—or less thoughtful—gesture that was intended to further a gentleman's suit. Always had Harriet shaken her head at these foolish creatures, going into raptures about a worthless trinket or a meaningless turn of phrase. In the end, they held no sway over the future, ensured nothing but the woman's acquiescence to the man's demands.

This, however, this document was a truly meaningful gesture. While there were those who would certainly dispute its romantic nature, Harriet had never received anything more precious.

More thoughtful.

Tears pricked at the backs of her eyes as she read, each word evidence of how well Jack knew her, how deeply he cared, how much he longed for a future with her.

The essence of why Harriet had always known she could never marry was that, upon marriage, a woman all but ceased to exist legally.

She became one with her husband, and no longer even possessed the rights an unmarried or widowed woman was granted. A husband could not even transfer funds or property to his wife because she was one with him and he already owned everything she had ever possessed.

The mere thought turned Harriet's stomach and raised her hackles.

While a marriage contract generally settled matters like pin money, provisions for future children and a wife's situation once she became a widow, Jack's contract included so much more.

It clearly stated that Harriet would have equal say in all matters; be it with regard to their future children—their education, their living arrangements, their health—as well as the purchase and sale of property and the use of their fortune. The contract did not refer to pin money at all, for it granted Harriet the same right to spend their fortune without her husband's consent as he was free to do without hers. In matters that concerned them both—such as their future children—an agreement needed to be reached; indeed, if they were one, then they needed to be of one mind to act.

Harriet smiled...then paused as her eyes fell on the last paragraph. She swallowed, then blinked before raising her eyes off the page. She turned to look at Jack. "Do you mean this?" she asked, noting the tension that lingered in his shoulders. "Would you truly grant me a divorce without dispute should I ever ask for it?"

His jaw clenched as his teeth ground together. Still, he nodded. "I would," he confirmed, although she could see how deeply the thought alone pained him. "You're not an unreasonable woman nor one to torment others with the power you may have over them." He swallowed hard. "Should you ever feel the need to leave this marriage, I will no doubt have given you reason to do so. While I cannot imagine it now and will do my utmost to ensure that it will never happen, neither one of us can say what the future will hold." He took a step toward her. "I understand the risk you take if you agree to this marriage." He glanced down at the marriage contract in her hands. "This is the one I'm giving you. I'm asking for your trust, and I'm giving you mine." A deep breath rushed from his lungs. "It is all I have, and I pray it is enough."

Harriet could not bring herself to say a single word, for the lump in her throat made it all but impossible. Tears lingered in her eyes as she looked up at Jack, and one by one, she felt them spill over and run down her cheeks.

Whether this contract would truly be binding by English law, Harriet did not know; she could not help but doubt it, for it was in her nature to always prepare herself for the worst. Yet should the worst indeed come to the worst, she would still make do. After all, Grandma Edie was right. Harriet had a family who would stand with her no matter what. They would fight at her side against any injustice the law might see fit to let rain down upon her.

In the end no one could predict the future. Would she come to regret marrying Jack? Or would she come to regret *not* marrying Jack? Both were, of course, possible. However, Harriet could not help but think that the latter possibility was more likely. It might be wishful thinking, her gullible heart overruling her mind because she simply *wanted* to marry Jack. Never would she have thought it possible, but every fiber of her being longed for him and the future they might share.

"I cannot tell," Jack began carefully, his voice sounding choked, "if these are tears of joy," he swallowed hard, "or of farewell." His dark brown eyes held hers as he reached out a gentle hand and brushed it over her left cheek in an utterly tender way.

"Oh, sweet Jack!" Harriet exclaimed as the contract fell from her hands and she flung herself into his arms. "My dear, sweet Jack!" Her hands reached up to touch his face. "I never would have thought this possible. I never would have thought I could ever feel like this." Shaking her head, Harriet stared up at him, reveling in the look of utter relief and joy that washed over his face. "I thought I knew what I wanted, and although I was not mistaken, you showed me it was not *all* I wanted." She laughed, feeling suddenly reminded of her grandmother. "Sometimes the world seems impossible, the road ahead so twisted and overshadowed that we do not dare take a single step. But there is always a way." She smiled up at him.

"Does this mean you'll marry me, Harry?" Jack asked, a hint of unease still visible upon his face.

Grinning—unable not to—Harriet nodded. "Yes, I'll marry you." And before the smile that came to Jack's face had any chance of making itself at home, Harriet pushed herself onto her toes and claimed his lips in a kiss that said more than words ever could.

His arms immediately came around her, holding her clutched to his chest in a deeply possessive way, yet Harriet knew that this intense need for her had been fueled by his fear of losing her, nothing more. They clung to one another, both equally relieved that their respective fears had not come true. They would not be forced to walk separate ways but instead face life side by side.

It was an unexpectedly reassuring thought!

"We need to settle this tonight," Jack rasped as he pulled back, his dark gaze staring down at her.

Harriet grinned. "Do we? How forward of you, your grace!" Oh, how she loved to tease him...and would continue to do so until the end of her days!

Shaking his head, Jack laughed. "I meant that we need to speak to your parents."

Harriet's brows rose teasingly. "I'm of legal age, you know."

"Not because I need your father to sign this document," Jack replied with a chuckle, "but because...I need them to know."

"Are you afraid I'll change my mind?"

He shook his head. "No, I'm not. I simply...wish to share this with them." His mouth opened and closed a few more times, and yet it seemed words would not come.

It was all right; Harriet did not need them. She understood his desire to be a part of her family, to be looked at with affection and understanding, to be welcomed after feeling separated from his own parents all his life.

"Honestly," Harriet replied, "I had hoped we could delay until morning." She wiggled her brows meaningfully.

Jack laughed. "As tempted as I am," he whispered, brushing a quick kiss onto her lips, "I would never want your parents to worry about y—"

"Grandma Edie knows where I am and why I'm here."

Again, Jack laughed. "Of course, she does. I must say I'm looking forward to getting to know her better. She sounds like a most intriguing woman."

Shaking her head, Harriet chuckled. "Hold on to that thought because it will not last. Before long, she will drive you mad with her meddling."

"You adore her, admit it!" Jack challenged, giving her chin a slight pinch. "However much you like to complain about her, you would not want her to be any different."

Slowly, Harriet nodded. "Is that how you feel about me?" She lifted a finger to stop him as he started to object. "Don't pretend you don't find me exasperating or even infuriating now and then!"

The smile upon Jack's face spoke of someone completely at peace with himself and the world. "I have no intention of doing so," he assured her with a grin. "All I'm saying is that I don't want you to be any different than you are. That infuriating side of you also makes you brave and loyal and daring. It is a part of who you are as a whole. Even if I could, I would never dream of changing any side of you because..." He sighed, shaking his head. "You would no longer be who you are, and that is the most awful thought there is."

Harriet blinked up at him, once again feeling close to tears. Indeed, she had cried more times since meeting Jack than in all the years before. He made her feel! He made her feel weak and vulnerable but also strong and almost invincible at the same time. Never would she have thought that possible!

"Well," she said, pulling his head down to place a quick kiss upon his lips, "let us go and speak to my parents."

Lacing his fingers through hers, Jack urged her to fall into step beside him as they headed out of his study and down the corridor. Harriet's eyes swept over the immaculate garden as they stepped outside. "You know, I think this place would look almost magical if you'd let some of these bushes grow wild." She glanced up at him.

Jack turned to her with a grin. "I know it would. I think..." He inhaled a deep breath. "I think that's why Laurelwood Manor means so much to me. My mother was like you in one particular way." His grin widened. "She was a free spirit, and the estate reflected that in every way."

"I'd love to see it," Harriet replied with a sigh, regretting that she would never know his mother.

"You will," Jack assured her as they walked toward the stables.

CHAPTER FIFTY-FOUR

THE ESSENCE OF FAMILY

The sun had almost disappeared by the time they reached Pinewood Manor, and Bradley could not help but worry how they would be received. Any ordinary father would no doubt object to his daughter returning home in this fashion; however, Lord Whickerton was far from an ordinary father.

Lights shone in many windows, and the moment their mounts were led away by eager stable hands, Harriet and Bradley climbed the few stairs toward the front door, then stepped into the foyer...

...full of anxiously waiting family members.

"Where have you been?" Lady Pemberton demanded, her face slightly pale as she rushed toward Harriet.

Her elder sister, Lady Barrington, chuckled, brushing a blond curl behind her right ear. "Where do you think she was?" Bradley felt the lady's gaze linger upon him in a most curious fashion.

"Welcome, Lord Clements," Lord Whickerton greeted him with a suppressed smile upon his lips before his gaze moved to his daughter. "Harry, how good of you to grace us with your presence." His brows arched up meaningfully, then dropped back down.

Beside Bradley, Harriet chuckled. "Don't pretend you didn't know precisely where I was!" She slowly looked around room until her gaze fell on her grandmother.

A slow grin came over the old woman's face. "Well, are you betrothed?" she inquired with a frankness that stole Bradley's breath.

"I am," Harriet replied with a grin, as well as a most fetching and unexpected blush.

"Well done, Clements," the dowager exclaimed, then took a step toward him and patted his arm. "I always knew you could do it."

Bradley was thunderstruck. As much as he had learned from Harriet about her most unconventional family, he had not expected this.

Cheers of joy erupted around him as congratulations flowed from more than one tongue. Hands grasped his or gave him a companionable slap on the shoulder while Harriet embraced her siblings and parents.

"Thorne," Lord Whickerton said, turning to his newest son-in-law, "would you grant us the use of your library?"

Pulling his wife closer into his embrace, Mr. Sharpe—Thorne—nodded. "Of course."

"Thank you." Then Lord Whickerton offered his wife his arm, and together, they moved down the corridor.

"Well, into the lion's den," Harriet chuckled quietly beside Bradley as they followed. "Are you certain you do not wish to reconsider?"

Bradley grinned at her. "Not a chance in the world."

The joy that lit up her eyes at his answer surpassed any emotion Bradley had ever felt, ever cherished. This was it! She was the one! Bradley was absolutely certain of it.

Following Lord and Lady Whickerton into the library, Bradley wondered how this conversation would go. After all, ordinary expectations could be tossed out the window where the Whickertons were concerned.

"Oh, you do look happy, my dear," Lady Whickerton remarked with a joyful face as she stepped toward her daughter and reached out to grasp her hands. "I'm not certain I've ever seen quite such a luminous smile upon your face." She glanced at Bradley.

Lord Whickerton chuckled, then he stepped forward to stand beside his wife, his own gaze equally curious as it moved from his daughter to Bradley and back. "Honestly, I never thought I'd ever see this day."

Harriet's brows drew down in mock outrage. "Why? Only a married daughter is a good daughter?" Brows rose in challenge, and yet Bradley could tell that she was merely jesting, teasing her father as she often teased him.

Understanding her equally well, Lord Whickerton laughed loudly. "Only a happy daughter is a good daughter," he corrected her before he stepped around his wife and toward Bradley. "Clements, however did you do it?" Over his shoulder, Lord Whickerton cast a smirk at Harriet. "I've always known my daughter to be quite stubborn, and I am utterly dumbfounded that you managed to change her mind, especially about marriage. Frankly, I never thought it possible."

Although the frankness with which the Whickertons conversed with one another still felt unfamiliar to Bradley, he was slowly beginning to expect it. It would take some time for him to feel truly at ease with speaking his mind so openly and having others do the same in his presence; however, even now, here, in this moment, he saw the benefits of it.

Retrieving the marriage contract from his inner coat pocket, Bradley held it out to Lord Whickerton. "Truthfully," he began slowly, holding the other man's gaze, "I am not here to ask for her hand in marriage. I am here to ask for your blessing." While another might have been confused by the specific distinction between the two, Bradley could see that Lord Whickerton understood.

Always had Harriet been free to choose her own path, and when it came to marriage, she was as well. She did not need her father's approval, for he did not believe it his right to deny her, to stand in her way. Still, both of them wanted her family's blessing, their support and goodwill. They wanted them to share in their happiness and be a part of their lives henceforth.

A knowing smile came to Lord Whickerton's face before he stepped back, back to his wife's side, and unfolded the parchment. Both of them slowly started to read, and Bradley could see on both of their faces no small measure of surprise as they began to understand what this document truly was.

With a smile, Harriet moved to Bradley's side, slipping her arm through his. "You truly know me," she whispered, a spark of surprise in her eyes. "I had never dared hope..." Her voice trailed off, and yet Bradley understood precisely what she meant to say.

Bradley nodded. "Neither did I." Shaking his head, he brushed the tips of his fingers over her cheek, a sense of awe rushing through his body as though he suddenly stood in front of a being that could not truly exist. "I never thought it possible, and then I met you."

"Are you serious about this contract?" Lord Whickerton asked, the look in his eyes matching that of his wife. Both of them regarded Bradley curiously, hope and goodwill restrained only by the mild caution visible upon their faces.

Exchanging a look with Harriet, Bradley nodded. "Does it truly surprise you?" He looked from Lord Whickerton to his wife. "Is it not the essence of every good marriage, including yours?"

Lady Whickerton nodded knowingly. "It never occurred to me to write it down," she mumbled as though to herself. Then her eyes once more turned to her daughter, and a joyous smile came to her face. "Perhaps it should be. Perhaps this is a first step." She held her daughter's gaze and nodded slowly.

Bradley understood the silent conversation between Harriet and her mother. Indeed, they were right. Change was needed in more ways than one. He remembered how Harriet had spoken to him of her brother-in-law's ambitions to change laws pertaining to working conditions and compensation for the lower classes. In fact, Mr. Sharpe had initially come to London to seek aid in this endeavor after having seen too many atrocities committed against people who were in no position to protect themselves. Unfortunately, the women of English society had to be counted amongst them. They had no voice, but they deserved one.

Looking down at his future wife, Bradley knew that no matter how long it might take, he would do everything within his power to see that day of change come sooner than later.

CHAPTER FIFTY-FIVE

A BALL AT CLEMENTS PARK

Harriet was happy. It was a simple truth, and yet it echoed within her being as it never had before. She had *felt* happy before, but she had never *been* happy in this way.

After receiving her parents' blessing, the Whickertons had celebrated Harriet's and Jack's betrothal long into the night. She had delighted in seeing him with her family. At first, he had stumbled upon words here and there, only slowly growing accustomed to her grandmother's frankness or her sisters' inquisitiveness. However, as the night had progressed, he had grown more relaxed, speaking animatedly to Troy and her father as well as Phineas and Keir.

Somehow, even after only such a brief acquaintance, Keir felt like family. They still did not know why Grandma Edie had invited him to Whickerton Grove, but Harriet was willing to allow the old woman her secrets. One day, she knew, they would find out.

After spending the night in a guest chamber, Bradley had returned to Clements Park the next morning. Harriet had been loath to see him leave, but she knew it would only be for a short time. After all, the ball at Clements Park was tonight.

Indeed, the hours passed quickly in preparation for the grand event. Harriet felt as though she was locked in a henhouse from all these fluttering hands tugging upon her gown and her hair. Excitement lingered in the air, and Harriet turned toward the clock on the mantle more than once.

Countless times, to be precise!

When the time finally came to leave, Harriet's hands were trembling; a fact that, unfortunately, did not escape her family's notice. "You look nervous," Louisa remarked with a trained eye, "and you're even blushing a little." Absolute delight at seeing Harriet so ill at ease drew up the corners of Louisa's mouth.

"Do not tease her," Juliet chided in a kind voice as she smoothed a wrinkle upon Harriet's gown. "Tonight is a big night for her." A rather maternal smile came to her eldest sister's face as she brushed a red curl from Harriet's forehead.

"Yes, precisely," Louisa exclaimed as they stepped outside and moved toward the waiting carriages. "A night we never thought we'd ever see. Can you truly blame me for being surprised?"

Harriet shook her head at her sister, well aware that Louisa was not teasing to make her feel bad but to make her realize how fortunate she was to have found someone to love. After all, it was a rare enough occurrence. Few could claim such a joy for themselves.

Upon arriving at Clements Park, they were greeted by Jack and his aunt, a tall, proud woman who looked at Harriet with carefully concealed curiosity. Still, Harriet did not detect even a hint of disapproval, rather a certain apprehension that spoke to her affections for Jack.

"I will make him happy," Harriet promised Lady Easton in a quiet moment when she was certain no one would overhear. "I promise."

For a moment, Lady Easton looked quite taken aback, and Harriet wondered if her bold statement might have lost her the woman's good opinion. Then, however, after a contemplative moment, a slow smile came to her face. "I know you will."

Harriet returned Lady Easton's smile and then squeezed her hand reassuringly. "Family."

The other woman nodded. "Family."

Harriet knew well that this was not the way things were usually done. However, she did not care. It was her way. Her family's way, and it was a good one. Eloquent words meant nothing if the meaning behind them was lacking. In her experience, it was better to be bold, to get everything out into the open and find a way to compromise, to get along, to find common ground. It was her way, and it always would be.

Fortunately, not only Jack but also his aunt could see the benefits of it.

Before long, a long line of carriages snaked its way up to the front door. More and more guests arrived, their curious eyes sweeping over the grounds and the house itself. The orchestra played a lively tune, its vibrant notes drifting from room to room, echoing to the vaulted ceiling. People conversed animatedly, casting curious glances at their host and the woman that continued to linger by his side.

Harriet could not help herself when she offered a grin to an old tattletale who stared a bit too boldly, too inquisitively. She loved to see a look of shock come to their faces, equally delighting in the fact that Jack joined in her laughter even if it was considered poor manners by some.

Indeed, it was a glorious night, and Harriet was surprised at how at home she already felt in Clements Park. Of course, it was not the building that made her feel thus but the presence of those she loved. She watched her parents and her siblings dance with their spouses, joy lighting up their eyes and wide smiles decorating their faces as they all enjoyed the night. Only Grandma Edie and Juliet stood off to the side, her eldest sister as always faithfully doting upon their elderly grandmother. Still, as she had countless times before, Harriet once again wondered if perhaps at least a small part of Juliet longed to join them, longed for the same joy Harriet had only so recently discovered for herself.

"Are you happy?" Jack asked beside her, his warm brown eyes looking into hers in a way that made her feel lightheaded and warm at the same time.

Harriet nodded, moving closer. "I am." She sighed deeply, looking up into his eyes. "I'm glad I went westward that day. I'm glad I found you." If she had not... Harriet shook her head, chasing away that awful thought. "I don't believe in Fate or providence or whatever you want to call it. I never have. But," she felt her pulse once more quicken with that intoxicating feeling that seemed inexplicably connected to Jack, "I believe I was meant to find you."

His hands drew her closer, his eyes on her alone, the look upon his face telling her he was all but oblivious to the many guests casting curious glances in their direction. "I feel the same," he simply whispered, never having been a man of many words. "Are you ready?" A grin teased the corners of his mouth. "There will be no turning back." He spoke as though his words were a threat.

To Harriet, however, they were a promise she longed to hear. "Good," was all she said, slipping her hand into his.

Then Jack drew her forward and into the ballroom, nodding to the orchestra in the corner, which immediately stopped playing. The music faded away, and silence fell over the large room and the countless guests within. Expectant eyes turned toward them, and Jack cleared his throat, his hand upon hers tensing not with nerves but with certainty. "Welcome to Clements Park," Jack greeted the crowd with a confidence that surprised Harriet. "For too long, these halls were absent of music and laughter, and so I knew the time had come to turn over a new leaf." He turned to smile at her. "I am proud to announce that I have found my duchess, Lady Harriet Beaumont," he said with a voice so loud and clear that it echoed through the vaulted chamber.

Gasps and murmurs of surprise erupted around them. Gossips flew into a frenzy, and Harriet heard faint whispers of *Burnham* and *Scotland* fall from lips here and there. Yet Harriet hardly noticed. Her eyes remained locked on Jack; after all, she had never cared for the opinions of others. Neither had she ever wanted to be a duchess. She still did not. What she wanted—or rather, who!—was Jack.

Everything else did not matter and never would.

Without another word of explanation, Jack nodded to the orchestra once more. The melody that drifted through the air as he led her onto the dance floor was hauntingly beautiful, almost devastatingly sweet, like the man himself.

And then Harriet was back in his arms, and he was in hers, precisely where they belonged. Life might not always agree with them, but together, they would weather the storm. Harry had no doubt.

"Happy?" Jack asked again as he guided them around the room.

Harriet kept her eyes fixed upon Jack's. "I'd be happier if all these people weren't staring at us."

Jack chuckled. "Shall we kick them out?"

"I like your thinking," Harriet said teasingly.

"I invited them, though," Jack replied with a slightly furrowed brow. "It might be bad manners."

"Then let's make a pact," Harriet suggested, "that starting tomorrow, we'll only invite those we like, those we truly wish to see, those—"

"Those we consider family or friends," Jack finished for her.

"I do like how you think," Harriet replied once more, knowing how rare it was to feel at ease in such a way with a room full of people watching her every move, some even leaning in, hoping to catch a word.

"Likewise," Jack murmured as he pulled her closer. "Would you like to take a walk in the gardens?"

Harriet grinned at him. "Would your guests not be disappointed?"

"I'm certain they would be," he laughed. "However, I don't even want to pretend to care."

Harriet heaved a deep sigh as the last tense knot of nerves came loose. Indeed, she had made the right choice. This felt good.

It felt right.

It felt free.

What more could she ask for?

EPILOGUE

Laurelwood Manor
Three Weeks Later

"What is so urgent?" Harriet inquired with a frown as she followed Grandma Edie down the hallway. "You remember that it is my wedding day, do you not?"

The old woman chuckled, smirking at Harriet from over her shoulder. Her steps were quick for someone who *required* a cane. "Far be it from me to stand in your way, Harry." Still, she kept on walking, passing door after door until she reached the one leading to her own bedchamber.

Although Laurelwood Manor was nowhere near as grand and expansive as Clements Park, it easily housed the Whickerton clan and a few choice guests. Harriet loved its unique charm, its old bricks weathered by the elements year after year and covered in ivy of all shades of green. It made Harriet think of an enchanted dwelling, and she half-expected to see trolls and goblins when turning a corner. Still, the inside was cozy and warm, portraits lining the walls. Not portraits that impressed but those that sought to capture precious family moments.

Every room seemed to echo with the loving spirit of Bradley's mother, and although Harriet had never met her, she was certain that the late Duchess of Clements was relieved to see her son happy once more.

"What is this about?" Harriet asked as her grandmother pushed open the door to her chamber and beckoned her inside. "Does it have something to do with me...or Jack? Our wedding or—?" Her voice broke off as she found herself not alone with Grandma Edie. Indeed, three of her sisters—Louisa, Leonora and Christina—were assembled in their grandmother's bedchamber, the expression upon their faces revealing that they had no notion why they were there, either.

"Will you finally tell us what this is about?" Louisa demanded, the look upon her face slightly exasperated as she lowered herself into an armchair. Her face was pale as her hand fluttered to her belly. Over the last few weeks, her pregnancy had caused her some *mild discomfort* as Louisa called it, for she hated to be treated like an *invalid*—as she said.

Settling into the only other armchair in the room, Grandma Edie sighed, granting them a somewhat conspiratorial smile. "I've asked you here," she began, her eyes moving from Louisa to Leonora before darting across the room to Christina and Harriet, "because I need your help."

Harriet all but gawked at her grandmother...as did her sisters. "I'm sorry. Did I hear that correctly? *You* need *our* help." She looked at Christina. "That's a first."

Grandma Edie chuckled. "I could do this on my own, but with your help, success is all but ensured."

"Success?" Leonora asked, frowning. "What do you mean?"

Louisa cleared her throat. "If this—whatever it is—is so important, where is Juliet? Should she not be here? And Troy? Or is this a ladies-only conspiracy?" She wiggled her brows meaningfully.

Looking at her granddaughter, Grandma Edie nodded approvingly. "Very observant of you, Lou. Indeed, Juliet and Troy are not here because what I have to say concerns them."

"Should they not be here *because* it concerns them?" Christina inquired, her eyes narrowing as she looked at their grandmother with calculation.

Inhaling a deep breath, Grandma Edie set aside her cane, her gaze momentarily distant and contemplative. Then her pale eyes cleared once more, and she smiled at them. "It brings such joy to my heart to see you all so happily married."

"Well, almost," Harriet grumbled under her breath, wondering how much longer this would take. She was up for a bit of conspiratorial scheming any day; however, today was her wedding day. Frankly, she had other things on her mind.

"Oh!" exclaimed Louisa, her eyes suddenly wide and luminous as a slow grin curled up the corners of her mouth. "I sense a matchmaking scheme afoot!"

As all eyes snapped to her, Grandma Edie chuckled like a child that had stolen biscuits from the kitchen and gotten away with it.

"I knew it!" Harriet exclaimed, all thoughts of her wedding momentarily suspended. "There is a reason you've always kept Juliet from mingling, from dancing, from...everything! Is there not?"

"We thought you wanted her as your companion," Louisa remarked, her cheeks no longer pale but rosy with enthusiasm.

A somewhat indulgent look came to Grandma Edie's face. "Whatever you might think, ladies, I am not that selfish." She chuckled wickedly. "I merely sought to prevent her from marrying the wrong man."

"Do you have someone in mind for her?" Leonora asked, now equally excited. "But why now? Why not before? And what does that have to do with Troy?" She shook her head in confusion.

Christina frowned. "Yes, Troy has never shown even the least bit of interest in a woman. At least not so far. Men marry later in life, do they not?"

"Oh," Grandma Edie mused, "he was in love once."

The sisters' jaws dropped collectively. "He was?" Louisa exclaimed, her eyes going wide.

Grandma Edie nodded knowingly. "He still is."

Their jaws dropped even farther.

"Who is it? And why didn't he ask for her hand if he...?" Leonora inquired, her voice trailing off as she exchanged a confused look with Louisa.

"Something interfered," Grandma Edie replied cryptically, a sorrowful look in her usually so cheerful eyes. "Troy as well as Juliet have been in love for many years, but the time was simply not right."

"And…is it now?" Harriet asked carefully, wishing her grandmother would simply get to the point.

Grandma Edie nodded. "I believe so."

"Because…," Harriet pressed, giving her an exasperated look.

Her grandmother chuckled. "Because I just received word that Lord Hayward was killed in an altercation."

Silence fell over the room as four sets of eyes stared at Grandma Edie in confusion. "Grandma, you need to make a lot more sense!" Louisa stressed, now sitting at the edge of her seat. "What does Lord Hayward have to do with…anything?" A confused frown drew down her brows as she looked around the room at them. "Who is Lord Hayward again?"

"Nora," Leonora gasped, her eyes going wide and her hands clasping over her mouth as she stared at their grandmother. "She's the one, is she not? The one Troy loves?"

Smiling approvingly, Grandma Edie nodded.

Harriet frowned, trying to place the names she had heard. Indeed, Lady Leonora—Nora, for short!—had married Lord Hayward years ago. Harriet had been only a girl then and barely remembered her. Although Nora had come to visit them at Whickerton Grove only the previous year for a few short days, it had been her only visit since her wedding years earlier.

Lady Hayward—or Nora!—had struck Harriet as a quiet, somewhat sad, young woman, who tended to keep to herself, favoring quiet walks and hours spent in the library with a good book. Their paths had never crossed much.

"How did Lord Hayward die?" Christina inquired, eagerness and a multitude of questions visible upon her face.

"That is of no importance," Grandma Edie replied, dismissing the question with a wave of her hand. "What matters is that now they'll receive a second chance."

"But she is a widow now," Leonora threw in with a quizzical look. "She has a year of mourning ahead of her before..." Her voice trailed off meaningfully as she looked around their small circle.

Grandma Edie grinned wickedly. "That is why we should focus on Juliet first," she pushed to her feet, "after we see Harry happily married. Shall we go, ladies?"

All four of them cried out in objection as their grandmother hobbled toward the door. "You need to tell us who he is!" Louisa insisted as she moved to block the door with a quickness neither one of them would have expected.

"Yes, what does Lord Hayward passing away have to do with Juliet?" Christina inquired before Harriet added, "Who is the man you've been saving her for?"

"All in due time," Grandma Edie chuckled as she waved her hand at Louisa, urging her to give up her position at the door.

"Do we know him?" Harriet asked quickly, well-aware that secrets their grandmother did not wish to share rarely made it past her lips.

The old woman grinned at them. "Of course, you do." Her gaze moved from Christina to Harriet. "The two of you might have been a bit young, but..."

"Who is he?" Louisa pressed once more as Grandma Edie opened the door.

"You tell me," their grandmother challenged with a wicked look in her eyes.

Harriet felt her jaw drop. "He is here today? At my wedding?"

Their grandmother nodded, and within moments, all of them cleared out of the room, eager to learn who the mystery man was. How was it that they had not noticed him before? How on earth had Juliet managed to keep her love a secret for so long?

Harriet smiled as she rushed after her sisters. Indeed, her wedding day was turning out to be highly unusual. Then again, they were a highly unusual family to begin with, so this suited Harriet well. She could not wait to find Jack and share this bit of news with him. Perhaps he could help her figure it out.

A full day had passed since they had last seen each other, and she missed him.

Well, from today onward, he would be hers.
The thought made her smile...
...rather wickedly.

THE END

Thank you for reading *Once Upon a Devastatingly Sweet Kiss*!

Four sisters married. One still unkissed. And then, he returns - with a little help from grandma Edie, of course! Read Juliet's story in *Once Upon an Achingly Beautiful Kiss*.

ALSO BY BREE WOLF

THE WHICKERTONS IN LOVE

LOVE'S SECOND CHANCE SERIES: TALES OF LORDS & LADIES

LOVE'S SECOND CHANCE SERIES: TALES OF DAMSELS & KNIGHTS

ALSO BY BREE WOLF

LOVE'S SECOND CHANCE SERIES: HIGHLAND TALES

FORBIDDEN LOVE NOVELLA SERIES

HAPPY EVER REGENCY SERIES

For more information visit www.breewolf.com

ABOUT BREE

USA Today bestselling and award-winning author, Bree Wolf has always been a language enthusiast (though not a grammarian!) and is rarely found without a book in her hand or her fingers glued to a keyboard. Trying to find her way, she has taught English as a second language, traveled abroad and worked at a translation agency as well as a law firm in Ireland. She also spent loooong years obtaining a BA in English and Education and an MA in Specialized Translation while wishing she could simply be a writer. Although there is nothing simple about being a writer, her dreams have finally come true.

"A big thanks to my fairy godmother!"

Currently, Bree has found her new home in the historical romance genre, writing Regency novels and novellas. Enjoying the mix of fact and fiction, she occasionally feels like a puppet master (or mistress? Although that sounds weird!), forcing her characters into ever-new situations that will put their strength, their beliefs, their love to the test, hoping that in the end they will triumph and get the happily-ever-after we are all looking for.

If you're an avid reader, sign up for Bree's newsletter on www.breewolf.com as she has the tendency to simply give books away. Find out about freebies, giveaways as well as occasional advance reader copies and read before the book is even on the shelves!

Connect with Bree and stay up-to-date on new releases:

facebook.com/breewolf.novels
twitter.com/breewolf_author
instagram.com/breewolf_author
amazon.com/Bree-Wolf/e/B00FJX27Z4
bookbub.com/authors/bree-wolf

ACKNOWLEDGEMENT

A great big thank-you to all those who aided me in finishing this book and made it the wonderful story it has become. First and foremost, of course, there is my family, who inspires me on a daily basis, giving me the enthusiasm and encouragement, I need to type away at my computer day after day. Thank you so much!

Then there are my proofreaders, beta readers and readers who write to me out of the blue with wonderful ideas and thoughts. Thank you for your honest words! Jodi and Dara comb through my manuscripts in an utterly diligent way that allows me to smooth off the rough edges and make it shine. Thank you so much for your dedication to my stories! Brie, Carol, Zan-Mari, Kim, Martha and Mary are my hawks, their eyes sweeping over the words to spot those pesky errors I seem to be absolutely blind to. Thank you so much for aiding me with your keen eyesight!

Printed in Great Britain
by Amazon

25162692R10192